ISLAND OF
CLOUDS

THE GREAT 1972 VENUS FLYBY

GERALD
BRENNAN

Other titles in the series:

ISLAND OF CLOUDS

THE GREAT 1972 VENUS FLYBY

PART OF THE ALTERED SPACE SERIES

GERALD BRENNAN

TORTOISE BOOKS
CHICAGO, IL

"Then I reflected that all things happen to *oneself*, and happen precisely, precisely *now*."

> — Jorge Luis Borges, "Garden of the Forking Paths"

"Before I went to the moon, I was a rotten S.O.B. Now I'm just an S.O.B."

> — Alan Shepard

"He is such a curious mixture of magnificent confidence bordering on conceit and humility, this man I married."

> — Joan Aldrin

"If we truly saw the universe, perhaps we would understand it."

> — Jorge Luis Borges, "There Are More Things"

Venus Mission
Part I: Departure

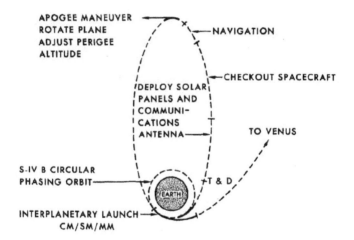

APOGEE MANEUVER
ROTATE PLANE
ADJUST PERIGEE
ALTITUDE

NAVIGATION

CHECKOUT SPACECRAFT

DEPLOY SOLAR
PANELS AND
COMMUNI-
CATIONS
ANTENNA

TO VENUS

S-IV B CIRCULAR
PHASING ORBIT

EARTH

T & D

INTERPLANETARY LAUNCH
CM/SM/MM

I'm thinking of my last cup of coffee.

It's my first breakfast in space in three years; I'm floating in an Apollo command module, sunlight blasting through the windows on the first full day of what looks to be the greatest voyage in human history, one that will shatter all records for time in space and distance travelled, while bringing three humans face-to-face with another planet for the first time ever.

And yet here I am injecting hot water into a foil pouch of freeze-dried coffee, thinking back to that last breakfast at the Cape, the traditional steak and eggs. It occurs to me that it will be a year before I can do something everyone takes for granted: to simply take an open-topped ceramic mug and put it under a metal coffee urn, turn on the spigot so gravity can do its work, and add cream and sugar as needed.

My mind tends to float off when I don't stay busy. It's been a life lesson of sorts: passive moments breed useless thoughts. So I hurry up with my breakfast. I do not want to wallow in the past. There's no time for it, and much work to be done.

We've folded up the center of the spacecraft's three couches to make it feel a little roomier, and to let Joe sleep behind them, in the area that's somewhat grandly called the lower equipment bay. In front of us is the console, the old familiar Apollo panel with all the backlit gauges and buttons. And behind the center of that is the tunnel, the connection path out through the snout of the cone-shaped command module and into our home for the next year, the manned module. It launched with us yesterday on a Saturn V, tucked away where the lunar lander would have been if this were a moon mission. This module holds the experiment suite that will give our days meaning and purpose; it has the solar panels that will provide power to keep the spacecraft running; it contains the bulk of the consumables necessary to keep us alive.

"Solar panels are still nominal," Shepard says, floating back in from the manned module. He's polishing off the last item of his breakfast, a chunk of freeze-dried peaches the size and shape of a floor tile. "The voltmeter was steady as a rock. I think this sonafabitch is really going to happen."

"How about that," I say, maybe too flatly.

We have been monitoring every instrument with particular care ever since yesterday's launch. The mission profile had us entering low Earth orbit, then reigniting the third stage to go into a high-energy elliptical orbit with a very long period, a full 24 hours from perigee to apogee. During that climb to the orbital high point, I turned the command and service module around so we could dock with the manned module, and we spent the rest of the day deploying its solar panels, checking out its systems, and in general making absolutely certain it will be able to sustain us for a full year. This morning, at apogee, we'll fire the service module's engine to test it out, and continue to double- and triple-check the manned module. After all, tomorrow's the big decision-point, the GO-NO GO day. If there's any doubt as to the condition and safety of the manned module, we will simply jettison it and ride the command module home through a normal reentry and splashdown. (It says something about this trip that a highly elliptical orbit ending with a fiery reentry, something that was beyond man's capabilities a mere decade-and-a-half ago, is now the safe option.) But assuming everything continues to check out, we'll be swinging back towards Earth, picking up speed as we approach perigee, and then igniting the service module's engine for the final burn, the one that will give us that last extra kick of energy that will send us on our merry way. TVI: Trans-Venus Injection.

"You sound...less than enthused," Joe observes, happily floating up between us.

"Come on. Why would I be disappointed to spend a year in a tin can, going to and from a planet where we won't ever be able to land?" I smile: forced, perhaps, but it's there. "Why would anyone be disappointed? Hypothetically speaking, I mean."

"Why on earth?" Joe asks.

"Indeed." I chuckle, late.

"Need I remind you gentlemen, we're all volunteers here." Shepard flashes a grin: bug eyes and a big smile, but lots of teeth, so it also looks sharklike. "If you're mad at the sonafabitch that put you here, go stare at him in the mirror next time you're shaving."

"Oh, I will," I assure him.

"He always stares back," Joe says. "That's the problem. The man in the mirror. You get angry, he gets angry right back. He's relentless. Try going easy on him."

"He's got a tough job," Shepard says. "He's gotta look at you every day."

"Ouch," Joe observes.

Here I chuckle for real. "There is a lot to be said for being up here. Get away from the paparazzi for a bit, take a vacation from the sauce so my liver can rest..."

"There is that," Shepard says.

"How about...uhh, discovery, the thrill of exploration, the chance to seek out new life?" Kerwin asks.

"But not new civilizations," I smile. "The prospects for Mars are a lot better. But Venus...aerosolized life in the upper atmosphere, *if* we're lucky."

"Still. The chance to boldly go where no man has gone before!"

"Yeah, yeah, yeah." I smile.

"Explorer, Houston." The radio reminds us there's a roomful of people waiting on us. Today's voice: Ron Evans, pulling CAPCOM duty. "Breakfast almost done?"

"Going back to VOX, gentlemen," Shepard says for our benefit: no more swearing or petty complaints. And then, to our bosses below: "Just finishing up, Houston. Ready to get to work."

Joe's been distracted by something; he's turned his body and his attention to the large hatch window. "We might want to get a picture of this first," he says.

He backs away from the window and I take a look. We're close to 70,000 nautical miles from the earth, about a third as far as the moon, but our orbit's taken us in the opposite direction, so Earth and moon appear as fat crescents, the earth blue and glorious, and the moon hovering above and beyond it, smaller than anyone's ever seen it, a drab little chip of rock that looks all the more depressing by comparison with our beautiful bright planet.

It's a breathtaking sight; the hair on my neck bristles. This is why I do what I do, this is why I'm up here: to see things nobody's seen. Shepard hands me the Hasselblad, and I snap several pictures before leaving the window to give him a look.

I float to one of the smaller windows. Our destination is, of course, on the opposite side of the craft, the sunward side, difficult to pick up in the glare but distant enough that it looks like it does from Earth, like little more than a bright star. And it occurs to me that, once we're there, this scene we've just seen, this planet we've just left, will look every bit as small and insignificant.

"Neat," Shepard says.

And that's that. We start stowing our trash, and Joe folds the center couch back into place as we get ready to test the engine that will kick us away from all of this.

•••

I've never been much of a writer. I suppose there's a ghostwriter out there who can pick up my thoughts and make them eloquent, squeeze feeling into my words. This mission will be long enough that I do at least want to keep some sort of diary, though. So before settling down, I set down my recollections from the day:

> *3 APR 1972*
>
> *First full mission day. Smooth checkout of the manned module in high elliptical orbit. Amazing view of Earth and moon from 70k miles out. Trying to get some rest before TVI tomorrow.*

When all the lights are out, I peer into the darkness and wait to see the flicker-flashes.

•••

Why am I up here?

Obviously Shepard's right. We are all volunteers.

But I do blame Lyndon Johnson.

I should be grateful for Johnson, because we wouldn't have made it to the moon without him. The moon was Kennedy's dream, of course, his speech echoing in newsreels and television coverage and our memories. But Johnson made it happen. He's a typical Texan, uncouth, wearing his brashness like a badge, but I suppose you need someone like that in charge when you're trying to actually get something done, as opposed to talking about it.

Because that's the thing: everyone wanted to go to the moon, but the will of the people can be fickle when a task gets too costly or time-consuming or hard. (I've been going back through Scripture recently, a little each night. And in Exodus you can see this with the Israelites: they were oppressed, and they wanted a leader to bring them out of Egypt, but during their empty desert wanderings they mourned for what they'd lost—they wanted to go backwards, rather than forwards.) You need democracy, but you also need a leader to tell the people: this is what we started, this is what you wanted, now let's finish it.

Johnson being Johnson, though, he wasn't content to just do the things Kennedy talked about. He wanted destinations and goals of his own. The moon was not enough.

Some planning group started talking about planetary flybys in 1967, when they were first starting to think of alternate uses for the Saturn V. When you've designed something with so much capability, it's natural to start thinking of what else it can do, additional tasks like orbiting a manned laboratory, or flying past Venus or Mars. For if you build a rocket mighty enough to fling not only three men, but a command module, a service module, a lunar lander, and an empty S-IVB stage all the way to the moon, you can also throw that same mass anywhere in the Solar System: a big stack of metal, and three people on board, just to keep it interesting. The only trick is picking the right path to bring them back home, and giving them enough consumables to survive the trip.

So the idea came up, and one of Johnson's people caught wind of it, and the next thing you knew, he had a goal of his own, before we'd even fulfilled Kennedy's. A new goal, the morning star: Venus. And plans beyond that for other flights, flybys of Mars in preparation for a manned landing.

But for a while it seemed like the man who'd gotten us moving towards the planets wouldn't even be in office to see us reach the moon. There was the fire in '67, that flash fire in the Apollo 1 capsule during the pressurization test. And although the crew wasn't on board, we had to extensively redesign the capsule, and that of course set us back. And the country went through a rough summer after that. Even with all the training and work we were doing, all the cross-country T-38 flights and long workweeks in Bethpage or Downey or wherever, it was hard to ignore the screaming headlines on hotel lobby newspapers, all the riots, Detroit and Newark burning along with so many others. A year of fire.

And when the Tet Offensive came in early '68, it seemed impossible that Johnson could ever win re-election. There were rumors that he wouldn't even run, that he'd sit it out and pass the torch to Humphrey and go back to the ranch so he could waste away his days drinking and playing dominos. But then there were rumors that Bobby Kennedy would run, and I think Johnson didn't have the stomach to even contemplate the possibility that a Kennedy might succeed him. And so he campaigned on, miserable poll numbers be damned; he campaigned on in the face of King's assassination, and another round of rioting, and all the difficulties in starting the peace process. And of course Bobby stayed out, and Nixon and Wallace were both licking their chops to defeat Johnson, and the country itself seemed angry as hell at the leader they'd elected so triumphantly just four years before, but at the end of it, things were looking slightly better in Vietnam, and we were almost on the moon, and Nixon and Wallace split the angry vote, and still Nixon of course won the popular vote, but as we all learned that year, it's the Electoral College that matters, and that's how Landslide Lyndon squeaked back into the presidency with something around forty percent of the vote.

And so we've had moon landings and now a Venus mission under Johnson, but also more protests, multiple failed attempts at peace. For better or worse, he's an obstinate man, and some of his critics are inclined to look at, say, Vietnam, as evidence that such obstinacy can get you in trouble as often as it saves you. I say there is some value to it, as long as you're pointed towards a worthwhile goal.

•••

Now another day has passed. We are all strapped back in, side-by-side, waiting to be propelled into the void.

Earth is large again in the windows; when we looked yesterday it had been a mottled blue-and-white golf ball, but now once more it occupies a large arc of our view, and I can see details in the landscape. (The thought pops up that, should something happen on the mission, this will be the last time I ever see it up close. But of course there's nothing to be gained by dwelling on this.) I steal a glance here and there, but not too often.

"We're good on the tanks?" Shepard asks coolly.

"Houston, Explorer. Tank pressures are looking fine," I say.

We are creeping up on the most eventful few minutes of my life, at least in the pure physics sense. (Even on my trip to the moon, most of the burns committed us to trajectories that were pretty short-term, compared to this.) For whatever intermittent qualms I've had, I've worked like hell to make it happen. I refuse to be the person who causes a failure.

"Explorer, Houston, everything is good and you are a GO for TVI. Under a minute to go."

"I'll know when it starts?" Joe asks.

I say: "You'll feel it."

There is a quick pulse of the thrusters to settle the fuel in the tanks. Ullage: a term stolen from the brewery industry.

"And the light is out," Shepard observes, as the couches press against our backs.

"There it is," Joe says.

"We have ignition," Shepard says.

"Tank pressures are looking good," I add. "H-dot as expected, less than one degree of pitch."

There is no noise and only a very slight vibration to even let us know we're accelerating, and Shepard calmly observes: "Very nice, very smooth."

"Explorer, Houston, we copy a smooth ignition. Godspeed." Up until now it's been all business, but there's a quiet reverence in this transmission, a certain awe for what we've undertaken.

"Roger, Houston," I acknowledge.

We are monitoring the burn intently, of course. The numbers are climbing and there is not much to say, other than to read them off and watch the cue cards and keep comparing predicted values to actual ones.

"Very good. Beautiful," I say. "0.7 gs."

"Feels heavier," Joe says.

"Imagine what it'll be like when we get back."

And at last, cutoff.

"EMS function off." I flip the last switch.

"Beautiful burn, baby," Shepard crows. (With him, when things go well, it's always "baby.") "Very impressive production, Buzz."

"Buzz B. de Mille, at your service." I flip my binder to a graph showing abort parameters. "20 minutes remaining in the two-impulse abort window." If something has gone wrong, we have a very limited amount of time to fire our engine in the direction opposite travel and return ourselves to an elliptical orbit. And the amount of velocity change required increases steadily during that time. After six minutes, for instance, two burns of just over 3400 fps would cause us to fall back into an elliptical orbit with a two-day period. But after 19 minutes, that same change would leave us in a 10-day orbit.

"Explorer, Houston, everything is looking fine. We're right where we want to be. Congratulations to our first interplanetary voyagers."

"Thank you, Houston," I transmit.

"Do you have a projected time for LOS Goldstone?" Shepard asks. (As the globe turns, our tracking station in California will dip below the horizon, and we'll lose their signal. Further out it will not be an issue, but for now we have to pay attention to these things.)

"Shouldn't be for another four minutes," they say. "ARIA is standing by after that."

And just like that, we're back to routines. The normal back-and-forth of regular mission discussion.

•••

"How was your week in the barrel?" Deke asks.

It is the summer of 1969. The moon mission took a week; the "week in the barrel" has been much longer, an exhausting grind of state dinners and speaking engagements and press conferences and photography sessions in country after country, England and Sweden and India and so many others. (The barrel reference comes from a crude joke, not worth repeating in polite company—an ungracious reference, but one I can relate to.) We've been selling the world on something we've already done. And being back at the office doesn't feel much better; I still have massive stacks of mail, overflowing piles of letters from all around the globe.

"A week would have been tolerable," I tell him.

"Everything's tolerable with the right attitude, Buzz. The public put you up there. It stands to reason you'd have to do publicity."

"The American taxpayer put us on the moon. Not the people of...Colombia, or Japan."

"These things generate goodwill. Winning hearts and minds. You know this."

"Next time, we need to spend six months in space and a week talking about it." There's a heaviness in my chest, either at the memory, or the thought of more to come: the fear I'll spend the second half of my life talking about a single day in the middle of it.

Deke half-smiles. "It wasn't all bad, was it?"

"I suppose there were some good things. It deprogrammed me a bit, got me to stop talking in acronyms."

"How so?"

"Telling a story at some noisy party to foreign dignitaries who barely speak English, every time you say 'The LM,' the other person says 'The what?' So it's like 'The LM,' 'The what?' 'The LM,' 'The what?' 'The...lunar lander.'"

This earns a chuckle.

Now I get serious again. "I want to get back on flight status."

"For the moon?"

"Well, I'd love to get back up there. But it'd be selfish to get back in line when so many other guys are still waiting their turn. The Original Nineteen, that group that came after..."

"They're calling themselves 'The Excess Eleven,'" Deke says. "They write it out like it's a...designator for an experimental aircraft or something. XS-11. Helps to have a sense of humor, I guess."

"I guess."

Deke purses his lips. One of those gestures that can mean many things. "Well, we are crewing up the Venus mission. We're gonna need some people with some heavy experience."

"A year in space."

"362 days," Deke corrects me with a wry smile. "Far enough away that conversation with Earth won't be possible."

"Sounds dangerous."

"Yep. Of course, we still have to fly the test mission. Three men in the manned module, in a high elliptical orbit with maybe a five-day period, so we'll be able to bring them home relatively soon if anything goes wrong. Keep them up there for three months or so, monitor the systems, make sure it's all feasible. It'll be a useful, necessary mission. Set some temporary endurance records. But I won't insult you by offering that."

"Thank you," I nod. "What about Mars?"

"That's not on the table."

This isn't what I'd been hoping to hear. But I feel like I can't back out.

"Venus comes first," Deke continues. "And we're gonna need some people who've been around the block a few times already. So to speak. You want six months up there? I'll give you double."

I'm assuming, of course, that I'll be in command. It only stands to reason.

•••

"Are you excited?" Kerwin asks.

He's upside-down relative to me as I float in from the command module with the last of my personal effects: a Bible and some books.

"Excited?"

"First night in the new digs."

It is one of the more noteworthy mission events; we're putting the command module to sleep for the bulk of the trip, to conserve its fuel cells and energy. We're only planning to power it up for a course correction on the outward trip, for the Venus encounter itself, and for two course corrections on the way home. For the vast bulk of the 360-odd days remaining, the can-shaped manned module will be our home, a tin mini-planet blazing its own lonely trail through the solar system.

"It is a pretty neat place," I admit.

Floating in from the command module tunnel, there's a main deck with the bulk of the equipment necessary for us to live and work in space. From "above," it's shaped like a mushroom; the "stem" is a narrow corridor with the latrine area at its base, and the "cap" is a larger semi-circular area where Kerwin's now floating suspended. (There's a bit of what I'd call a gravity bias to its layout, by which I mean it was definitely built with everything right-side-up relative to the "floor," which is opposite the command module tunnel, like it was on the lunar lander.)

"No nausea?" I ask.

"Nope. Feeling fine." He tucks into a somersault, pushes off against the mess table, and spins like a pinwheel.

I reorient myself so I'm right-side up relative to the so-called floor, facing out of the corridor and into the larger room. There's all the familiar stuff from training: a mess table and food reheating station on the right, telescope console on the left. On the curved outside wall there's a decent-sized window, with the radio equipment and solar panel controls and circuit breakers arranged around it. It's a good bit roomier than the command module, which doesn't mean it's large, per se, but it is large by space standards. (In zero-g every volume feels a little bigger; the area above your head is no longer wasted dead space, but rather a usable part of your physical environment, a place you can reach with as little thought and effort as you'd put into grabbing something right next to you.) Everything looks strange, though. Or maybe it's me.

"Where's Shepard?" I ask.

He nods behind me, towards the latrine.

"Gotta get in there myself," I add.

"Gonna have to wait in line," he says.

"Cripes."

"We all shut down?" he nods up towards the command module.

"Still gotta run the last two pages of the checklist. We were behind on the schedule, and I wasn't up on the manned module comms yet, so they said to go eat. Finish after dinner."

"OK," Kerwin says.

We float and wait.

"Christ, whatd'ja bring a newspaper in there, or what?" I mutter towards the toilet.

No response.

"I know you didn't fall in. Nothing falls up here."

Joe chuckles. Still no sounds from the toilet.

I suddenly imagine Shepard dead in there, maybe from a heart attack. What would that be like? Us floating up here for a year with a corpse? Old man Shepard, a decade older than us, and already a grandfather: it is a plausible outcome. And I would be in command... (An ugly thought. I smirk and shake my head.)

At long last, he opens the latches and pulls down the curtain.

"There he is! You didn't hear us?"

"Hear you?"

"We were talking about you."

"I don't think the sounds carry well in 5 psi. Plus, with the curtain…"

His answer's reasonable. To make things simple and easy for the environmental control systems, our spacecraft and module have been pressurized at a lower pressure than we're used to on Earth. Rather than the 14.7 psi one gets at Earth's surface, it's only 5; you get the same partial pressure of oxygen, but much less nitrogen. And one consequence is that you have to be right next to someone for them to hear you.

Still, it bugs me. "Your whole crew's lined up for the john," I observe.

"Rank has its privileges," he grins as he floats our way, and gives me a look, like he's daring me to defy him.

This strikes me as a prime example of Naval Academy bullshit, the product of a dysfunctional ethos built on exaggerated respect for hierarchy and technology; it's a culture where things are more important than people. (For all my time in the Air Force, graduating from West Point at least got me to value the Army's take on leadership. In the Navy, officers eat in separate wardrooms, waited on by enlisted men; in the Army, officers follow their troops through the chow line at the mess hall, only eating whatever's left after all the enlisted men are fed.) I know my place, but I still feel the need to keep him in his.

At last I take a deep breath and give a little twisted smile. "Lotta pressure in other parts of the system. We don't want to have an explosion."

"Ew. Oh. OK, you can go ahead," Kerwin says.

"Thanks," I eagerly move past Shepard and float on in.

"Are we shut down upstairs?" Shepard asks before I can close the curtain. "I wanted to have that done before dinner."

"I can't hear you." I mouth the words and point to my ears for comic effect. "5 psi!"

The toilet/hygiene area is pretty crude, a circular curtain with a shitter and a shower all in one space. (I shouldn't knock it, for it is in fact a tremendous improvement over what we had on the moon missions. We had to piss into a tricky condom/tube contraption, which pinched a bit but wasn't as awful as taking a crap; on the moon we were supposed to do that in our undergarments, whereas in the command module we had to do the deed in plastic bags which had a blue chemical pellet that you had to knead into your fecal matter, supposedly deactivating it and rendering everything safe and sanitary, but in reality only doing a partial job at best, leaving the most advanced machine in human history smelling like an open-pit latrine by the end of every mission.) We have an airflow device that pulls all the waste in the right direction, ensuring that your urine and feces don't go floating off towards your fellow crewmembers. And unlike past space toilets, this one does at least give you the truly essential attributes of any good crapper: not just cleanliness, but time for silent contemplation.

I spend my time in there replaying our recent dialogue in my head. I have to say, I don't entirely buy Shepard's explanation. As plausible as it is, the guy can be an ass, and I wouldn't put it past him to just take his sweet time and not even acknowledge that we were waiting. (Is that what it takes to be a leader? To just not care what everyone thinks of you? Sometimes it seems that way.)

I put my head in my hands, although of course it doesn't feel anything like it does on Earth. I will myself to be still, and try to calm my mind.

•••

Soon after Deke first talks to me about the mission, I'm back in New Jersey, on a quick visit home to see my father.

We're in the study, where he usually holds court: a stately dark room with books all precisely arranged on dust-free shelves, waiting for a white-glove inspection that will never come. He's poured us both whiskeys from a crystal decanter. You might see this scene and think we're relaxing over drinks, but one never relaxes around my father.

"Is he offering you command?" my father asks.

"I interpreted it that way."

"He should be offering you command, right?"

"Believe it or not, I want to have it even more than you want me to have it."

"He needs to offer you command, Edwin." As usual, he feels the need to repeat himself a little more insistently. And he stares at me.

I look away. You have to look away eventually; it's like being in the same room as the sun. (Back at the Academy, our mil art classes talked about the forts of Vauban and Louis XIV, the Sun King; I remember hearing that name and immediately thinking of my father. And here I am again, with the Sun King holding court. And it still feels the same. My father's the sun. I am the son of the sun.)

"I'll be sure to discuss it with him."

"You will."

I scan the room. He keeps rare titles, wonderful books on aeronautics and rocketry, signed originals from Goddard and others with personalized inscriptions, the type of stuff that would be immensely valuable if he ever had a notion to sell. It's like a temple to the past. But there is at last, something of me in there: a picture of me on the moon. (Obviously that, too, is a picture of the past. But at least it's my past.)

Again he speaks: "I'm proud of you, Edwin. You know that. But they need to give you the respect you're due, and they won't give it to you unless you demand it. Like that business with the stamp. First man on the moon. Man, singular, and a picture of Ed White. You did it together, as a team."

"We've talked about this already."

"I know, it just...gets to me. You've done a lot for them. You made it happen, more than anybody else. You're capable of command. They need to put you in command."

I look back at him. There are vague thoughts I cannot understand, let alone speak: thoughts about father and mother, and life and death, and the sun and the moon.

I clench the crystal tumbler of whiskey. There are many things I can do with it, but I set it down in a measured and deliberate fashion, with an excess of control.

I think: the center of gravity has shifted in this relationship. You will be remembered as my father, not I as your son.

But of course I do not say it. I need to keep things under control.

I pour another whiskey and drink. I turn to face him, and stare, and speak: "I will discuss it with him."

Only later, in the room with Joan, do I finally let myself go.

"I don't know what he wants!" All that pent-up emotion now tears at the edges of my voice and makes it sound ragged and weak, far weaker than I want. "I just don't know what he wants. How can you please a man like that?"

"You can't," Joan says.

"How? I mean, what is 'enough?' How can you please him?"

"You can't, just..." Her voice spikes and breaks. She takes a deep breath and puts the pieces back together. "You can't. Stop trying."

•••

After dinner, I end up back in the command module, alone.

"Houston, Explorer. Standing by to complete power-down."

There is a slight delay. The distance between us and Earth is ever growing, a yawning chasm. (We had that on the moon trips, too, but there was a limit to it. Here it will get inexorably larger until we can't even converse.)

"Explorer, Houston. Confirm we are on page 11-2 of the power-down checklist."

"Confirmed, Houston. I'm up on the manned module comms." I'm no longer transmitting via the service module's high-gain antenna, so we can keep talking once I cut the power.

Another delay.

"Go ahead."

"OK, pulling Circuit Breaker 2, 6, 7, 8, 11. Master Alarm." The light on the panel is flashing red, accompanied by an insistent tone.

I pause, then hear: "Expected. Proceed."

I clear the alarm. Silence returns. "Main Bus A and Main Bus B are zero. DSKY in standby mode. Pulling breakers 13, 15, 16 and 17. All console lights are off."

It feels wrong, turning off a spaceship in flight. I know it has to happen; they've calculated every margin for fuel and power, and this is actually the safe responsible option. And they already did it on the test mission. But still it feels wrong.

I float over to the alignment platform. "Telescope retracted. Cover in place."

"Explorer, Houston. We copy telescope stowed."

I flick off the cabin lights. "And we are dark."

"Very good. That about covers it. We will need a dosimeter reading from everyone when you can get to it."

"Copy that." Now that we're in deep space, they are more closely monitoring the amount of radiation we get, just as they did on the moon mission. "CMP dosimeter reads 12472. Others coming shortly."

I float back through the tunnel into the manned module to find the others. Our command module, the part where we do the actual active flying, launch and orbital insertion and course correction and reentry, is an inert mass of unpowered circuitry and dead metal. We are all passengers now.

• • •

Back in Houston, I stroll by Deke's office. He's in there alone, but still I walk to the bathroom and check myself off in the mirror one last time. I think of those old cadet routines: dress-offs and gig lines and shoeshines.

When I stroll back, he's still there alone.

I take a deep breath. (I have no problem speaking up for myself. Some have accused me of being blunt. But if I don't do it, who will?)

"Got a minute, Deke?"

"Sure thing, Buzz."

I step in and close the door. "I wanted to clarify something from our conversation the other week. This Venus mission…" (Somehow everything feels all awkward and wrong.) "…what I'm saying is, I think I should be in command."

"I'm not offering you command, Buzz." Deke speaks flatly. "I had someone else in mind that'd be better for the job."

"Someone else?"

"Shepard."

"He just got back from the moon."

Deke shrugs. "He wants this. I think he's the best man for the job."

The best friend for the job. (I think this, but I know enough not to say it.) Instead: "Well, I think I should have a shot. You're not worried about the ear thing flaring back up?"

Deke purses his lips. "I'm well familiar with how skittish doctors can get when it comes to medical issues."

I nod.

"Anyway," Deke continues, "he hasn't had any problems since the surgery. None. We threw him on the centrifuges before that, he did fine. And Apollo 13? Nothing. He'll be fine."

"But I…" I protest meekly, even as I know what he'll say next.

"If you don't like it, I'd be happy to switch places with you."

This is his trump card; he plays it every time anyone drags out a conversation about assignments. (When you're an astronaut and you're getting to fly, you don't have grounds to complain to one who's been grounded without a flight.) So I keep my mouth shut.

"Besides, I've got something better for you," he continues. "Man's first deep-space EVA."

Now he has my attention. Now I'm not thinking about command.

"We have something similar planned for the J-missions. A little excursion by the command module pilot, to retrieve film, and so forth. But that's still within earshot of Earth. This…you'll be on your own. If things don't go according to plan, the conversation lag won't let you ask us for advice and wait for an answer. You'll need to figure it out on your own."

"Sign me up," I smile.

•••

"Pretty active observation day on the telescope tomorrow," Kerwin observes.

"Uh-huh," I say.

We're in the mess area, eating dinner at last around a tiny triangular table. Or rather, the other two are eating while I pick at my tray.

"You're probably more excited for the main event, huh?" Kerwin says.

"Can you blame me?" I grin. "Getting out of this thing and getting a look around when we've just flown past another planet? Looking down and seeing the Venerean atmosphere, right there?" I glance over at Shepard.

"Venusian is the preferred nomenclature on this mission," he says, as usual, then adds: "Venerean sounds like...something you'd pick up from a hooker in Titusville."

I laugh, despite myself. Then I feel bad, something far down in me. "Yeah, I caught the Venerean disease. That's why I'm up here."

"Wife put you out, huh?" Shepard chuckles.

Again, a twinge in my bowels. I'm usually stopped up in space. But not tonight. "Excuse me, gentlemen. I think I need to hit the latrine."

"You mean the head." Shepard grins: Navy lingo, as usual, but I don't correct him; I'm already half-gone, floating down the hallway.

I make it just in time. There's some unpleasantness, but nothing I can't handle with a little bit of cleaning and the suction hose. I stay in there for a few minutes, alone with my thoughts about Joan and the kids, and all the angst and brittleness of the past three years. It doesn't make me feel better, thinking of all that.

I force myself to stop. Shut it all down. They never explained it at the Academy, not in so many words, but that was the point of it all, bracing with chin tucked in and eyes straight forward while upperclassmen yelled in your face so close their nose would brush against your cheek, doing left- and right- and about-faces towards whomever was lighting you up at that particular moment, reciting passages memorized from your *Bugle Notes*, "Scott's Fixed Opinion" or "The Definition of Leather," or maybe handling table duties at the mess hall, cutting the pie when three of the upperclassmen insisted they didn't want any and you didn't have a nice evenly divisible number but instead had seven slices, calculating the exact angle for each ($51.42857°$) with the precision of a draftsman even while your classmates at nearby tables were being yelled at to within an inch of their life, then slicing into it with every ounce of concentration you could muster even despite the absurdity of it all, like you were a surgeon and the butter knife was your scalpel. They never explained the purpose of it all, not in so many words, or maybe they yelled it in one or two words. "Do something!" or even just "Function!" Because that was it. You had to function. You had to do something, regardless of how you felt at that particular moment. You had to ignore everything that wasn't essential to the task at hand, and shut down your feelings, and just DO.

Soon I feel better. Not good, but better.

I undo the latches and float back.

"All right?" Shepard asks.

"I'll manage."

•••

In the middle of the large part of the main deck, there's a curtained circular passage leading down into the sleeping chambers.

In a rare example of governmental willingness to admit that we have private lives, the mission planners have scheduled private communications windows throughout the mission for each of us to talk to our wives and families. Now that the big early stuff's over and we're settling into our routine, we're having the first one. By a vote of two-to-one, it's been allocated to Joe Kerwin, so Shepard and I pull ourselves down into the sleep area to give him some privacy. It's a much narrower space; it almost feels like an afterthought, or maybe a cellar or a crawlspace; there are lights, but no windows.

"He probably can't hear us, huh?" I ask as we rearrange ourselves.

"Probably not," Shepard says. Then: "Joe? Joe?"

The curtain stays closed.

"It's funny," I observe. "The guy with the best marriage gets the first chance to work on his. Gotta reinforce success, I guess."

Shepard gives me a look. "Don't knock Kerwin. He's probably the only truly decent guy on this mission. And I do include myself in that assessment."

I'm sure I give him a look right back, one that says: I include you, too.

•••

4 APR 1972

TVI today. There is no going back.

We have shut down the CSM as planned. For better or worse it felt like a spacecraft, a mode of transport, something to take you from one place to another. Something with controls that you could at least fly. But the manned module feels like something else. A house or a prison.

Some unpleasantness tonight. Not sure why I'm not feeling quite right.

•••

"Feeling better?" Joe asks as we peel open our breakfast trays.

"Not bad."

"Nausea?"

"I've never had nausea in space. Even on the Vomit Comet, I only had it once, and that was from one too many martinis the night before. No, it was...I dunno. Something in my bowels."

"Well, hope it's done."

"You're a cheerful one today, huh? Morning Joe."

He shrugs.

"Good talk last night? Everything OK on the home front?"

"Can't complain," he says. "It was really nice to hear them. You can hear the pauses getting a little longer, but it was still a nice conversation. You've got yours tonight, right?"

"Yep. Looking forward to it."

But first, of course, the workday: there is far more to our mission than talking to our families as we wait to fly past Venus.

Our voyage is officially the Inner Solar System Exploration Mission, colloquially shortened to "ISSEM" on planning documents and "ISM" in conversations. Everything, every window and bulkhead and packet of food and gyroscope and instrument, has been carefully designed to keep the total mass of the system reasonably low, just as was the case on the moon missions. Back then, our objectives were simple: getting as much equipment as possible onto the surface of the moon (laser reflectors, seismometers, etc.) and then taking as much of the moon as possible (dust, rocks, hand-drilled core samples, etc.) home to Earth. But here, we have a couple priorities. Obviously, we're looking to vastly expand our knowledge about Venus; we'll be releasing a mix of orbital and descent probes once we're close to the planet. But we'd also like to have full and productive workdays on the long journey. So after all the heavy engineering work, the mass reduction, the paring of bulkheads and the shrinking of windows, we're carrying an observation package that includes a telescope for visible and hydrogen-alpha observation, an x-ray telescope, a coronagraph, and an extreme ultraviolet spectroheliograph. The scientists hope we'll revolutionize man's understanding of the sun every bit as much as the lunar landings did for the moon.

Soon, Kerwin's behind the console and Shepard is at the computer, and Houston is on the radio, guiding us through the checklists to open up the telescopes and start observation. I follow along mechanically.

"...and H-alpha AUTO to OFF, DOOR to OPEN," they say at last.

Kerwin reaches up to the console to flip the last switches.

"H-alpha AUTO switch to OFF. H-alpha DOOR switch to OPEN. Talkback is white...and now gray."

The six-inch CRT screen comes to life, a small TV image of a grainy red sun.

"And we're in business," Shepard says. "Wow. That is really neat!"

I look over to see Joe's reaction. Shepard sometimes acts like a dumb pilot who doesn't really care about the science stuff but memorizes just enough to get by; even after months of training, I can't tell if it's the truth, or just a role he plays to get Joe going.

"We've seen this in training already," Kerwin smiles. "The 656-nanometer wavelength, the light from the chromosphere, this stuff all makes it through the atmosphere."

"Oh, yeah, of course. This is all from electrons falling from the third to second orbit, right?"

"Well, they're not really in orbit," Kerwin says. "They use the word 'orbitals,' but it's really a probability cloud at each level. All that weird modern physics stuff where you don't know exactly where something is. Particles tunneling through classically forbidden regions, starting out in one spot, ending up somewhere else where they're not supposed to be…" He trails off, enchanted by the telescope, motions on the surface of the sun.

As the science pilot, Kerwin has the bulk of the telescope time, but for the next few hours we help him out, recording observations, making calculations and counting camera frames. (Kerwin's a doctor by training; he's up here, in part, to help keep us healthy, and deal with any medical emergencies. Still, by now we've all been through enough astronomy instruction that we'd probably be eligible for advanced degrees.) It makes for a long workday: not physically tiring, of course, but the mental effort is taxing.

Then before dinner, medical experiments. First we take tape measurements, baseline marks for muscle mass. There's also a spring contraption that allows us to get some semblance of a workout, stretching and pulling and curling until each of us is coated in a glistening film of sweat that of course refuses to drip off or go anywhere but must instead be wiped off with a washcloth.

At the appointed hour, I'm up on the main deck in my communications headset, alone.

In theory it's the early evening, but the sameness of the sky makes it easy to forget all of that. (On Earth, there's an unspoken agreement of sorts between you and the sun: you work a full day, and at the end of it, win or lose, the world resets itself and the heavens get dark. But on this mission, nothing changes; the sun's still up, like it's expecting you to keep working, too. It's like a breach of contract.)

"Houston, Explorer here. This is the Command Module Pilot, checking in for my personal communications window." I take a deep breath. I am actually looking forward to talking to Joan. I do need to vent a little about Shepard, and it'll be nice to talk with the kids...

"Explorer, Houston." Ken Mattingly's on the other end. "We're...ahhh...just stand by for a minute." Normally Ken's all clipped and professional, but here there's uncertainty and lost words.

I float over to the window and rotate so my feet are near the so-called ceiling; I place my forehead on the glass and try to look back. I can just barely see two of the receiver dishes on the high-gain sticking out from the side of our dormant service module. Earth and moon are somewhere back there; we'll soon be farther away than any humans have ever been. But despite my best efforts, I can't see what we're leaving behind.

"Houston, Explorer. CMP standing by."

I pull down the shade. There's no real point to having it up, anyhow. The scenery's stopped changing. We're never in shadow, so we can't even see that many stars.

"Explorer, Houston. I apologize, Buzz. We are trying to determine your wife's whereabouts."

There is a twinge in my gut and I force myself to take a deep breath. The walls of the manned module are mute witnesses to my frustration, sterile and metal and gray. "Houston, Explorer. Is she in the building, at least?"

The pause feels interminable.

"We are trying to figure that out, Buzz."

"Roger, Ken. Maybe call the gate, see if she's cleared that at least."

Then: "We tried that, Buzz. They haven't seen her yet."

Again I breathe. I have to remind myself there is no point getting worked up. There is nothing I can do. Or maybe... "Call my house, Ken."

I wait for his reaction.

"Buzz, I don't know if..."

"I'll give you the number if you need it, but I know you guys have it down there in a binder somewhere. Find it and give Joan a call."

I wait.

"OK, Buzz. Stand by."

I wait. I wait. I wait. I wait some more.

I want to climb the walls. I want to do something. This is the frustrating thing about zero gravity: you can't even pace back and forth. I'm reduced to rubbing my headset, frustrated.

"Explorer, Houston. I'm sorry, Buzz. There's no answer."

"OK, maybe she's left already." The words sound hollow as I speak them; I know they're untrue, the false hopes that burn like lies.

"Roger, Explorer. How long do you want to wait?"

I'm reluctant to give a number. "We'll give it a few, Houston."

"Explorer, Houston, understood."

I float. Now I cannot blame the conversational pause on transmission delays, or on anything but my own awkwardness. How to fill the void? The eternal question. Small talk: always a big deal for me. "How's the weather down there, Ken?"

"Starting to get warm. I had to turn the air conditioner on last night for the first time."

I chuckle. "We've been running ours nonstop up here."

I breathe.

"I bet," he says.

"Well, the sun is relentless."

I wait, and at last: "Worse than a Houston summer, I'm sure. At least it's not as humid. And you've got someone else paying the bills."

"Yeah, there is that…" I trail off.

Again, silence. Awkwardness.

"I'm sure something came up, Buzz. We'll get a message to you as soon as we know something."

"Houston, Explorer. Understood. We can close the window."

I open the curtain to the sleeping chamber. Kerwin floats up.

"Everything OK?" he asks. He knows it's early.

"Yeah, fine," I say.

•••

5 APR 1972

Long workday on the telescope. Unknown communications issue with home.

In the night I see the flicker-flashes.

I do not tell the others.

•••

"...and the XUV monitor is on downlink. You should be able to get it on your TV feed."

It's morning of our second day of observations. We're sending the imagery from our ultraviolet instruments down to Houston so we can coordinate with earthbound astronomers.

"Explorer, Houston, we are picking it up." Then: "Before I forget, we do have a quick message from your wife. She apologized for missing the window last night. Everything's fine, and she'll fill you in during your next PCW."

"Understood, Houston." I don't want to think about it. In some strange way, I was hoping for an emergency. Maybe a car accident where it was the other driver's fault and nobody was injured but the car was totaled and they couldn't make it to Mission Control. Nothing too too serious, but something understandable, at least. Given our trajectory and the growing distances, it'll soon be impossible to have a real conversation. "Thank you."

Kerwin floats up behind me, returning from the bathroom. "All right, ready to take over, Buzz."

"Actually...I think I'll take the first block. Get a little telescope time."

"Sure thing."

We get started on the day's observation program, and soon my worry dissolves in a frenzy of work.

Now that I'm truly paying attention, the sun is actually quite fascinating. Under the hydrogen-alpha, it's no longer a bland white disk, but a mottled red orb; we can see a tremendous amount of detail: not just sunspots, but huge granules of hydrogen plasma a thousand kilometers wide that bubble to the surface and then disappear in a matter of minutes, and larger supergranules that linger long enough for us to track their slow movement across its face. Through the extreme ultraviolet and x-ray instruments, it becomes even more compelling: a churning and boiling cauldron of plasma. And because Earth's atmosphere blocks those wavelengths, we can study the sun like it's never been studied in all of human history.

"Look at the edges of those granules on the limb," Kerwin points to the detail screen.

"Yeah, they're not perpendicular to the surface. Angled. And the edges of the active regions, those loops...it does look like a lot of magnetic activity."

On the other screen, I see a promising bright spot, and I steer the telescopes towards it.

"It looks like we've got a subflare in active region 37." We're hoping to photograph a solar flare in multiple wavelengths throughout its lifecycle, from the early stages of eruption, through its full ascent and then its fall back to normalcy. We don't know when the opportunity will present itself, but this could be our chance. "I'll start the JOP."

"Explorer, Houston, we copy. We'll keep our fingers crossed."

Nobody on the training mission was able to capture one; I'm hoping to be the first. I work through the checklist: point H-alpha telescope at bright point, roll slit for uniform emission, maximize Detector 1, repeat the process for a second bright spot. I use the console to take hopeful pictures through the H-alpha telescope, then turn the dial so I can take still more with the x-ray one, and then the extreme ultraviolet device.

"Keep an eye on the frame count, Buzz," Shepard says as the digital counter ticks down.

"Flare's still rising."

But the spot peters out.

"Waste of film," I mutter.

"And now back to our regularly scheduled programming," Kerwin adds.

We return to the routines. For a while, I'm kicking myself about the flare failure, but I work a little harder and those thoughts fade away. The scheduled tasks are still simple ones today, meant to get us used to working on the telescope and coordinating with the observation teams back on Earth. So we're mostly verifying the work of past astrophysicists: tracking supergranules as they appear and disappear, writing down numbers in observation logbooks, estimating rotation times for the chromosphere at various solar latitudes.

The next thing I know, we're floating around the dinner table. (We have no need for chairs, and no desire; our bodies tend to float in a default space posture, arms a little forward, hips and knees slightly bent, so forcing yourself into a chair position feels completely unnecessary.)

"Quite a day on the telescope," Joe says.

"It is interesting," I admit. "You tend to take the sun for granted, but there's a lot to it."

"If you say so," Shepard says.

"No, really," I tell him. "It's funny, you take a good long curious look at anything, and really pay attention, it becomes...fascinating. Like how the sun rotates. You could probably ask most people about that, and they wouldn't have a clue."

"The sun rotates?" Shepard smirks. "Sonofabitch. This changes everything."

Now he's got me wondering. "Weren't you paying attention in training?"

Shepard just grins.

"It *does* change everything," Kerwin says. "Everyone treats the sun as a constant, but when you start to see it as a dynamic, changing thing, with variable weather patterns and cycles..."

"I'm just here for the ride," Shepard says. "See the sights, fly to places nobody's flown before."

"This is crucial to that," Kerwin says. "Outside the magnetosphere, obviously we're absorbing a lot more solar radiation than we'd get on Earth. We all know we're taking some unknown risk. But if we can understand the patterns and cycles, we can start planning and forecasting, and mitigate that risk."

"Just like you'd forecast the weather on Earth," I chime in.

"Exactly! Before these things were known..." (He looks at Shepard, who's turned himself upside-down relative to us and is eating with his feet on the ceiling, just because he can.) "...well, you're a Navy man, you know how it is. Ships used to get...stuck in the doldrums crossing the Equator, or locked in ice trying to navigate the Northwest Passage. But now we can plan. It's the difference between hazardous exploration and reliable travel. Tourism and commerce and what-not. We need to know this stuff if we're ever going to make travel around the Solar System a routine, regular thing."

"I'll leave all that for you guys," Shepard says. "I plan when I have to, but I prefer to fly by the seat of my pants."

"Always a good way to lose your ass," I smirk. Somehow when it comes out, it's not as funny as I thought.

Shepard shrugs. We eat for a minute in silence.

"Talking to Louise tonight, huh?" Kerwin asks.

"Yeah. Looking forward to it," Shepard says.

A thought pops up: Speaking of losing your ass. "How's everything holding up with her?" (I'm half-expecting some tale of woe, a disastrous epic of imminent divorce that will at least put everything in perspective for me.)

But he just says: "Great."

•••

After everything's stowed away, Kerwin and I pull ourselves down into the sleeping chamber so Shepard can have his comms window.

"Can you believe him?" I ask when the curtain's closed.

"How do you mean?"

"All that he-man macho superpilot thing. Fly-by-the-seat-of-your-pants bullshit..."

Kerwin shrugs.

"None of this..." (I gesture around, meaning the ship, space travel, everything.) "...none of this will ever be reliable and routine with men like him around."

"It will be eventually, though."

"Still, it seems like it...bugs him that anyone would ever want to...plan and actually make things safer."

"And this bothers you?"

"Well, yeah," I sputter. "It's like...there are two kinds of astronauts. The ones who want everyone else to have the experience too, someday, and the ones who are just...riding on pure ego, determined to be unique. And I think we all know where he fits."

"I don't think he cares who comes after him, so long as he's first. Do you think Christopher Columbus would mind that people are crossing the Atlantic every day now?"

"So Shepard's Columbus?" I smirk. "I coulda been Columbus."

"They're not gonna forget your name, Buzz! There'll be room in the books for all of us!"

This stops me short. "I'm not worked up about that...it's just...that guy...I just..." Somehow I'm getting more irritable, just talking about it. "And now...calling home like he's some...model husband. The way he chases tail..."

Kerwin shrugs. "This job is tough on marriages."

Once more, it takes me a while to formulate a response: "Yeah. You can say that again."

"How are you guys holding up, by the way?"

"Great."

Kerwin looks at me like: What's your real answer?

"I mean, I'll admit, we have our issues." (There is a certain...resistance in the astronaut corps to having marital problems. These things can have a detrimental impact on one's career and flight status.) "We're working on it, though."

"I'm sure they are too," he says.

"It does seem...easier being up here, sometimes," I admit. "There's...manuals and procedures for everything." (I consider telling him about the missed communication window. "Consider" being the operative word.) "You know what buttons you're pushing."

"It is nice, having some control," Kerwin says.

"Down there you're just a...cog in the...family machine. Here you get to fly a machine, at least. Although that feels a little lacking up here, too," I allow. "But I guess I'm getting used to it. Getting into the swing of things."

"I have to admit, I was a little worried about you the other day."

"How so?"

"It just seemed like you were having second thoughts about the mission."

"And you were like, 'Uh-oh, I don't wanna hear this guy complaining for a year...'"

He laughs. "The thought did cross my mind."

And somehow now a few things cross my mind. There was a strange spell after Gemini XII where I couldn't seem to get myself out of bed. And then after coming back from the moon, I felt...slack. Of course, I told Deke and everyone else how much I hated the publicity tour, the grind, the constant strain of overscheduled appearances, the need to always be "on." But once we were "off," I felt slow again, lethargic and heavy. "Sometimes I..." I stop.

"Sometimes you...what?" he asks.

"Do you still consider yourself a doctor?"

He laughs. "You have some medical issues you want to talk about, Buzz?"

"Well, I..." Something in me says it's OK, I can talk, Kerwin isn't the type of guy to repeat something he heard in confidence. And he's one of us, anyway, as good of a pilot as anyone in the astronaut corps. But still...

He continues: "I know everyone's reluctant to talk to doctors. You know. That whole macho he-man pilot thing..."

"Well, you know how it is. There's only two ways a pilot can come out of the doctor's office. 'Fine' and 'Grounded.'"

"I've got news for you, Buzz," he says with a grin. "Even if this were a doctor's office, it's not in anyone's power to ground you right now. I don't think the laws of physics will allow it. At least not for the next year."

But I think of the rest of the mission. I think of the EVA. Even now they could change their minds, give it to Shepard. "It's all right. I'm fine."

Shepard pulls back the curtain. "All done," he says brightly.

"Finally!" I float back up to the main deck. "Man's gotta take a leak. Everything OK?"

He grins: "Yeah, fine!"

I have the sense that the sonafabitch actually means it; still, I give him a skeptical look.

"Louise's really glad I'm up here," Shepard adds.

"Really?"

That toothy grin: "I think this is my first trip in a long time where she doesn't have to worry that I'm up to no good."

Against my better judgment, I laugh.

Joe asks: "What about Apollo 13?"

Shepard's grin gets wider still. "Well, there is something you don't know about Ed Mitchell and I..."

Again I laugh. He can, after all, be a charming sonofabitch when he wants to.

• • •

6 APR 1972

Plenty of discoveries today on the telescope. The sun is even more complicated than I realized. I'm learning I've been taking many things for granted.

• • •

"...we have a new active region 39 at 260 degrees, 0.3 solar radii. We would like you to keep an eye on it. Over."

"Will do, Houston." Kerwin's back on the telescope today. It wasn't my decision.

There is still a lot to do backing him up, so I'm trying to keep on top of that. We're starting to understand more about the magnetic activity on the sun, how the active regions interact with each other. We learned a lot in training about flares and prominences and magnetic field lines, but now that we're doing it here, it's starting to make sense on a fundamental level. These magnetic field lines sometimes cross and throw material off the sun, giant looping prominences of charged particles; we're tracking these so we can correlate them with auroras back on Earth, and see how fast it takes material from the sun to make the trip.

"All right, we're getting a high PMEC count," Kerwin says. "I'm going to start the JOP."

He turns the dial and presses the button; the frame counter counts down.

"Wow. A lot brighter than what we saw yesterday. By about a factor of ten."

For the next 20 minutes or so, he works the console like a maestro.

"Houston, Explorer," he says at last. "I'm very pleased to inform you that we are the proud parents of our very first full flare. Pictures to come."

Everyone congratulates him. My mind keeps wandering elsewhere.

●●●

At the end of it all, Joan is on the line, right on time this time.

"What happened the other night?" I anxiously await her response.

After the five-plus seconds of round-trip light-speed communications time, plus the pause in the middle for her to choose her words, at last I hear: "So that's how it's gonna be, huh? No 'Hello, how are you?' Can't you just say you're glad to talk to me?"

"I am glad to talk to you. I wanted to talk to you the other night. What the hell happened?"

I hold my breath waiting for the answer, which takes even longer than physics makes necessary.

"We had to take Andy to the hospital."

My blood flashes to boiling, and the lid's about to come off the pot. "Jesus Christ, your message said everything was fine!"

The long pause.

"Would you rather it was because we just ignored you?"

I say nothing.

"It is fine, Buzz. It's being taken care of. It's not like you could have done anything about it. There was no point telling you."

"Put him on, would you?"

I await the end of the delay.

"He's not here."

Clenched fists. I wish I could stop this. "What do you mean he's not there?!?"

Five seconds, plus a few more.

"Mike had a play at school. They wanted to show up for him. It's not like you talk to them when you *are* home..."

I don't even wait for her to finish; her words of course have already been spoken and there's no way for me to stop or interrupt them, but I don't want to hear any more. "Jesus Christ, is this necessary? Right now, is this necessary?"

Silence. It occurs to me that we'll have to go to normal radio communications protocol soon, even with our wives, saying "Over" after every transmission, and so forth. So much distance...

"I'm sorry. It's been a stressful week."

"Still, I'm...I'm up here. I can't fix what's down there."

Pause.

"I'm sorry. I know. I should be used to all of this by now."

A long, deep breath. "All right. What happened?"

I have time for another long breath before the answer.

Then: "He fell off his bike, heading home before we went to go talk to you. There was a gash on his hand. We had to take him to the emergency room to get stitched up."

"You couldn't let the control room know what was going on?" As usual, I have a few brief moments to wonder whether this was the best thing to say, but only after I've said it.

Then: "Buzz, I was rounding the kids up and going to the hospital! By the time things settled down, we'd missed your window! And I didn't have the number to call and tell them anyway because I was at the hospital! You have a room full of people watching you all the time, taking care of you. I'm on my own down here!"

I look around at the empty main deck of the spacecraft, silent and sterile and forbidding. Compose myself. "Well I guess it figures. If somebody's gonna have an accident, it's gonna be him."

After the long pause, a chuckle. "God, Buzz, I knew you'd say that. You are so predictable sometimes. I love it and I hate it, but you are so predictable."

"It's true though!"

I wait. Then: "It is true."

"Broken bone, Andy. Eye surgery, Andy. Everything, Andy."

Again, I wait. "It's true," she says. "You're right."

"Yep. Keep that in mind. I'm right."

Surely this one will get a reaction.

At last: "You're pushing my buttons."

"That's what I do. That's why I'm up here. It's what I'm good at."

I take a breath.

Finally: "Don't I know it. My predictable, reliable button-pusher." At last there is something like love in her tone, at least.

"That's how it has to be. There's no point spending hundreds of millions of dollars on a spacecraft and making all the parts work perfectly if you're not gonna hire reliable people to push the buttons."

There's a pause. Then: a sigh, perhaps? "I know, Buzz."

•••

7 APR 1972

It sometimes seems like all I do is try to avoid catastrophes.

I wake in the middle of the night. The others slumber in the dimmed light. I float upstairs and relieve myself, but when I return, I find I'm feeling more awake than I should be. Restless.

I try to make out the dim corners of the little chamber. I listen to the whir of pumps, water and air and coolant cycling through the system.

I see them again, like light that registers deep in your brain, deeper than your eyes somehow: flicker flashes. I still haven't heard the others mention them, so I, too, have kept quiet.

I am wondering if there's something wrong with the machinery.

•••

Besides the telescope work, we're keeping eyes on ourselves; there's a full program of medical experimentation and observation. The main goal's to see how well we're surviving up here, if we're staying strong or slowly wasting away.

Rather than weighing ourselves, we have to calculate our mass. (It's a distinction most people don't get. On Earth, when I was suited up in the moon suit, I weighed 360 pounds; on the moon, it would have been about 60. Here, suited or not, I'm weightless. But we still have the same amount of matter in us, the same mass.) But how to measure it here? You can't simply step on a bathroom scale.

One of the many clever people at NASA, a former doctor named Bill Thornton, came up with the answer. It required a piece of spring steel with a known spring constant and damping ratio. He designed a weight measurement device around it, with the spring attached to a fixed point at one end, and the other end floating free, like a platform on top of a pogo stick. We tuck ourselves in on the platform, set ourselves in motion (what would be up and down on Earth), and measure the period of the oscillations. Given this information and some calculus skills, it's a simple matter to run some differential equations and calculate mass. And by measuring it on successive days, we can track how the body adapts to extended periods in space.

The device is stowed away under the floor when not in use. While the other two are unfolding it, I have to break away so I can add water to the meals and get them in the heating compartment so they'll have time to warm up before we eat. The trays are stored in the lockers in spring-loaded stacks, like bullets in a magazine; we pull out one and the next one pops up. By virtue of our cramped confines, the lockers are pretty close to the latrine. I'm over there, caught up in my routine, when I notice a taped card in Shepard's handwriting that says HEAD. I float back to the mess area, add the water and load up the heater, and I see another one that says WARDROOM.

"So everything's gotta be nautical, Al?"

"I put 'em up two days ago. You're just noticing now?"

I give him a look.

"Gotta keep everything ship-shape," he says. "Ready with the timer?"

Kerwin is attached to the mass measurement device, crouched forward holding the handlebars, and Shepard's standing by to get him going. I reset my stopwatch. "Ready."

Shepard pushes Kerwin what looks like down, making sure the measurement pedestal is all the way against the stops.

"Go."

Shepard releases him. Kerwin's body moves up and down through the air, suddenly reduced to...well, a body in motion, an object having mass, immobile and impersonal.

I count three cycles and then click the watch. "Mark. 12.3 seconds."

Shepard writes it down so we can do our calculations later.

"It doesn't feel like a ship," I point out. "It doesn't even feel like we're moving."

"I'm pretty sure we're moving, Buzz," Shepard says, more condescendingly than I care for.

"Well, obviously. It just doesn't feel like it."

Again we get Kerwin ready. Again, release, and the smooth oscillation.

"12.3 seconds," I say. "How's that for consistency?"

"We'll see after number three," Shepard replies.

"Do you need to feel like you're moving?" Kerwin asks.

"I don't know if I like moving or I just dislike standing still. The last weekend at home, I was trying to get some errands done. A trip to the hardware store for a new toilet seat, and Joan had dry cleaning to pick up. But she got upset. 'You're not here even when you're here,' she said. And I was...well, I was confused. I told her I just wanted to take care of some stuff so she wouldn't have to do it on her own when I was gone. But she said 'Be here when you're here.' And I must've given her a look like I didn't even know what she was talking about, because she had to explain herself. 'Sit in the living room. Talk with the kids. Pet the dogs. Just...be still.' And I did. But it was..." I don't even know how to articulate what it was. I'm not good with feelings.

Again we get Kerwin going, but after two oscillations, he says, "Wait, stop. I lost my grip, I don't think that'll be accurate."

"All right." I reset the watch.

"Pilots do make horrible passengers, by the way," Kerwin observes as he repositions.

"We do, don't we? We really, really do! Horrible passengers."

"That's the most excited I've heard you all mission, Buzz," Shepard says.

"Well it's true!" I don't know that I've put it into words, but that must be what it is, what I've been feeling these past few days. It's nice to have someone else recognize it. "I had a hard time on the tour. That must've been it."

"That's how I felt the last time I flew as a civilian," Kerwin says. "You get used to looking at the world through the canopy. All those...expansive panoramas. Then all of the sudden you're in a seat with a...sad little window next to you. No way to see what's in front of you, even..."

We repeat the process. It occurs to me that I could fudge the results and tell Shepard it came out the same. But I've never been that type of man. "12.2 seconds."

"I am starting to miss the views a bit," Shepard says. "Flying over the mountains in California..."

"I like that," I chime in. "The way it all looks rumpled. Like a...like a brown blanket on a woman's body in the morning sunlight."

"That's...very poetic, Buzz."

"Or over the Midwest, even," Kerwin adds. "It's funny, it's some boring driving, but from the air, I really like it. There's that...patchwork, but it's not like a quilt, because there are so many shapes."

"Yes," I chime in. "Trapezoids, rectangles, triangles, squares. Maybe a raggedy quilt. Or some...abstract modern art collage. Personally, I really like getting above a good layer of cumulus clouds, though. You get up there, and sometimes they're so...thick that they seem real."

Shepard smirks.

"Well, you know what I mean. Not just real, but...solid. Like you could just get out and explore. And it's like some alien landscape. And there's nobody else anywhere."

After their turns, I turn back to the workbook and do the calculations. We've all lost mass. Shepard less than the rest of us, but he's down two pounds.

They'd done these measurements on the three-month test mission as well. The data seems to suggest that we'll lose mass for a couple weeks, then level off as we reach a lower plateau. I have no reason to believe we'll be any different than the test crew, although it does occur to me that the size of the sample is statistically insignificant.

Before long, we're floating lazily around the dinner table.

"I was reading one of those articles about how we'll be able to float huge structures in Venus someday, in the upper atmosphere," Kerwin says.

"Yeah, I saw that, too," Shepard chimes in. "All that CO_2, you could keep something up there with plain old oxygen."

"Obviously we'll have to gather the data to find out, but like they said in training, it might be the closest thing to an earthlike environment in the whole rest of the Solar System."

"Do you think that could ever work?" I ask.

"Sure, why not? I mean, it would take a while to get started, but it's bound to happen eventually. Also, one of the planetary scientists, that Sagan guy, was talking to me about terraforming, and that might be a way to do it. I mean, I'm hopeful we'll find something already there, floating aerosolized life forms, or whatever. But if there aren't any, why not introduce our own? You could set up floating labs, introduce various forms of plant life, start monitoring to see what grows. Algae, even. Reverse the greenhouse effect from the CO_2 and transform the planet. These probes we're launching could start laying the groundwork for that. Obviously it'll take some time, but who knows...maybe we *will* be remembered like Columbus."

"Personally, I'm excited for the EVA," I tell him. "The probes are interesting, but I'm most excited to just...do something out there. That's what I'm missing about flying. Not just the views. Being in control."

"Yes," Shepard says, his voice suddenly warm. "Grabbing the stick, zooming down over some beach to flat-hat the civilians...when you get so low that you can see faces and tans, you can spot the women in bikinis..."

"They let you do that in the Navy?" I half-smile. "I got an official reprimand for that once. That's gotta be against regs even for you guys."

"Well, officially, I've never done it," Shepard grins. "And if I have, it must've just been a...momentary error in judgment, a grave mistake I'll never repeat. But...you know. Sure beats being a passenger."

"Amen to that," I add. "I remember when we were flying back from Tokyo at the end of our tour. Late in the year, short days. And I knew, with the route we were flying, that we were somewhere over the Aleutians. But damned if I could see anything. Like Joe said, just a sad little window. A...useless black rounded rectangle. And feeling like whatever was out there, dark ice, angry ocean, whatever, we were just stuck in a tin can hurtling over it for the next few hours."

"I hate that. No control," Shepard says.

"Well, some," I tell him. "I figured I could at least get drunk. Speed up the trip."

"Time travel!" Shepard says. "I like it."

"Yes!" I chuckle. "Time travel. But I just got dried out. Slept for a bit, then woke up with that awful...dislocated feeling."

"No fun," Shepard says.

"No fun," I echo. "Kinda wouldn't mind a little now, though."

Shepard gives a strange look that I cannot quite interpret. "Yeah, it might be nice."

After we eat, he gets on the radio.

"Houston, Explorer, we're ready to provide a status, over."

The uncomfortable pause.

"Explorer, this is Houston, go ahead."

"Houston, we've all eaten, and we're ready to start our evening rest period. Frame count for the 35 millimeter mag is 9787. Dosimeters are as follows: Commander, 16874, Pilot, 14382, Science Pilot, 12838." (The dosimeters measure cumulative radiation exposure; they started each one at different levels so as to make it easier to keep them separate for the course of the flight.) "We've taken no medication. Everyone is in good spirits and good health."

Now that things have settled down, we have time to read a little at night and wind down. I get out a book: *Kon Tiki*. Sometimes I think Shepard isn't so bad after all. But these things he says, these little snide remarks...I realize I need to make two signs: LATRINE and MESS HALL. But when to put them up? Probably during a nighttime bathroom break. Or maybe my next communications window...

I look back at the book. It occurs to me that my eyes have been skimming over the words, absorbing nothing. Sometimes it seems like that's all a book is: something you can hold in your hands so you don't look stupid daydreaming. I force myself to pay attention for half an hour.

Shepard is sometimes a decent guy, and he can be genuinely entertaining. But he's also far too seat-of-the-pants for a mission like this. The flying isn't even flying, per se. We've calculated the direction we needed to travel and flung ourselves into space. Course corrections aside, we're just along for the ride.

Before heading to the sleeping chamber, I press my head against the large window, as if I'll be able to see something. I remember doing this over the Pacific, peering out into the blackness in forlorn hope, with something else in my chest, some tight restlessness.

And this is how I feel now. In a can with two other men, headed to Venus. Very few windows, and little to see out them anyway. (Jim Lovell complained about two weeks on Gemini VII, but he and Frank at least had a planet to look at!) I should be glad for the time off every night. Instead, I'm eager for the morning. Our days are filled with work. At night, there is nothing to do now but wait.

> *8 APR 1972*
>
> *The excitement of launch is fading, and we are settling in to our routines. We are no longer in control, no longer pilots. We are passengers of physics.*

•••

Our mission continues.

The days drift by, one by one, seemingly endless, numbered but otherwise indistinguishable. We fill them with groundbreaking science, unprecedented in human history, but soon it feels routine. Granted, routine can be comforting: when you float over to the pantry and pull out three trays, you want to look through the little metal slot and see more trays springing up into place, with no end in sight. But it doesn't make for a good story, because the whole point is repetition, and knowledge of what will happen next: what makes a mission successful also turns a story stale.

Through it all, our spacecraft home flies smoothly onwards, alone in the great emptiness.

Interlude:
Cocoa Beach

It's late 1977, a couple weeks before launch, and we're at the Cape, at the Holiday Inn: me, Shepard, and Owen Garriott.

It's all orange and aqua outside, all bright and presentable, but the inside's dark. It's another one of those places where everyone looks good, and everything sounds like a good idea, like there's a dimmer switch for your conscience. Shepard's been going here for a decade and a half, back since the Mercury days.

We order drinks at the bar. I don't know if we're here to celebrate the mission, or because we want to cram in as many nights at the bar as possible before we have to go into quarantine. Our wives are back in Houston for a few more days. And I'm not sure how much that matters to some of us, because nothing outside the bar feels real.

There's a table of young women close by, two brunettes and a blonde. They're making eyes at us and talking in whispers. Women: the giant conspiracy.

"Come on, let's go," Shepard says to me.

"Me?"

"Yeah, I need a wingman. You Air Force pukes don't believe in wingmen?"

I snort. "You Navy pukes don't believe in matrimony?"

He laughs. "How many of us are saints here? None of us. Not a one."

I have to admit, he has a point.

"Speak for yourself," Owen laughs.

Shepard gives him a look. "I'm talking to Buzz here." And to me: "And I'm not talking matrimony, I'm talking air support. It's not always about racking up kills, sometimes it's about flying cover."

"I didn't know you needed that."

"Everybody needs protection from something."

"Be it hostile bar girls or angry wives." I polish off my whiskey.

"I don't know that they're hostile," Owen says. "Why else would they be here? And you never know, they might be obliterated soon anyway."

"Right. Easy mission," Shepard says. "Should be a milk run. Let's go."

"Well..." I think it over. "There is always a certain allure, for a certain kind of female..."

Shepard snaps. "I'm talking to Owen now!"

I lower my tone. "You're about to say goodbye to Louise for over a year, and you're gonna go try and get laid?"

"Who said anything about getting laid?" Shepard grins. "Maybe I just want to hang out and enjoy their company. Maybe I want to tell them some stories. I don't know."

"Some leader. You want a wingman and you won't even tell us what the mission is," I smirk. "I'll stay here. This sounds like a disaster."

"Nothing wrong with a little conversation," Owen says.

They summon the bar girl, order up a preparatory bombardment of beer to soften up the defenses a little more, and take off soon afterwards.

I linger a while. I do not want to think about Joan, but I think about Joan. I polish off my drink and try to sit still for a minute. After a while, curiosity gets the better of me and I wander over.

Shepard's mid-story, showing off, as usual: "...were trying to decide what to feed us before the mission. I mean, all these unknowns, going into space. They tried to launch a few chimps up there, but it wasn't like they could *explain* how they felt during the thing."

"Ohh! Ohh! Eeeeh! Eeeeh!" Owen says, in a passable imitation of our primate cousins, and some of the girls laugh.

"Kinda hard to decipher," Shepard says. "And of course, you don't want anyone vomiting in the craft, which wasn't so much an issue with us, being highly experienced aviators and all. But of course...and, well, you can try and discuss it delicately, but there's no getting around it, everything's gotta come out the other end eventually."

The blonde (who's, truthfully, pretty fantastic looking) turns to one of her companions and mumbles something. As I lean close to listen, Shepard looks over his shoulder at me, annoyed.

"Look at this guy, buzzing around…" Everyone laughs.

"Real original, Al," I observe. "Never heard that before."

"Nothing wrong with catching a little buzz." The blonde smiles and hands me a Schlitz; I realize it's untouched, from the round Al had ordered.

"Nothing wrong at all," I reply, and take a long pull.

"ANYWAY," Shepard continues. "This was a problem, because it was a small spacecraft, and they hadn't made provisions for that, especially on the short flights. So they were trying to decide what to feed us, and it was hard, because they didn't want to overfeed us, but also they didn't want to leave us with nothing in our stomachs, all hungry and anxious. So at last, one of these Germans was all 'Vee have decided to feed you ze steak und eggs. It ees a very high protein diet, so zere vill be very little residue.' And…" (Here Shepard chuckles…he's always had a hard time keeping a straight face for a punchline.) "…and I said 'No shit.' And he said 'Exactly.'"

Shepard laughs. One of the brunettes says: "Eww."

"Great story, Al," I observe.

"Stop buzzing around. You're killing my buzz, Buzz!"

Again the ladies laugh.

"You know, rather than telling old war stories, you could actually...engage these ladies in conversation. See who they are and what they're all about," I point out. "That might liven things up a bit."

"Yeah, there's a thought," the blonde smiles.

"Ehhh, we just need to get our buzz back. Our other buzz." Shepard summons the waitress. "Let's do some shots. Shots? Shots?" He makes a show of asking the girls, but doesn't actually wait for a response. "Cutty, all around."

The waitress disappears.

"So you're launching soon, then?" the friendliest of the brunettes asks.

"Yes. Venus, Mars, Venus," Owen says.

"Shouldn't you be...working late, or training, or something?" the blonde asks. "Centrifuges and simulators and such?"

"Oh, we've done all that," Shepard replies. "It is dangerous and demanding work, don't get me wrong. Requiring nerves of steel. But rocketry and gravity, that's all taken care of." The waitress comes back with shots. "My biggest concern is, we've got some long and lonely nights ahead of us..." He passes out the shotglasses. "So I would like to offer a toast: To no more lonely nights."

We slam our drinks, but a couple of girls leave theirs on the table.

"That actually is a big concern," Owen says. "Have we given any thought to...I don't know, policies for getting our needs met up there?"

"Well I'm not gonna take care of you, if that's what you're asking," Shepard replies. "Maybe Buzz here..."

"Jesus! Oh my God!" the less friendly brunette exclaims.

"Christ," I say.

"I'm not asking for my own benefit!" Owen clarifies. "And if I was, no offense to Buzz, but I would want to keep it all self-service. Still, we might want to think about privacy considerations, time schedules, things of that sort."

I can't believe we're talking about this. "Whatever your needs, however you want to deal with them, I just don't want to know about it."

"Easy there, Buzz," Shepard laughs. "Man's got needs, he's just trying to make sure his needs are met. Reminds me of the story about the barrel."

"Good Lord." We've all heard the one about the barrel too many times to count.

"It is something to discuss," Owen says.

I shake my head. "I had to deal with a roommate doing that crap when I was a cadet. No shame at all. Christ, we're not...zoo animals."

The women snicker. "Are you sure?" the blonde asks. "Manners-wise, you seem to be aping the apes."

"You didn't take your shot," Shepard suddenly notices.

"I don't remember asking to be on the receiving end of your shots," she says saucily. "Here, you take it. If you're man enough."

"Don't mind if I do." He hoists it. "Raise a glass, whatever it is you're drinking."

She lifts what looks like a gin and tonic.

"I'm sorry if I was rude, my lady," he says. "To what shall we drink?"

"To primates."

"To our primacy among the primates," Shepard says, and she gives him a look. "OK, to primates." They clink glasses; he knocks his drink back while she sips hers. "You'll never make a monkey out of me," he adds.

She mumbles something under her breath. Then one of the brunettes whispers in the blonde's ear, and she grins. She leans back and smiles like she's heard a big and beautiful and terrible secret.

"There you go," Shepard says. "See? We can all be friends."

"You're right, Captain Shepard..."

"Admiral."

"You're right, Admiral Shepard. We can be friends," she smiles. "And we should at least send you some friendly shots as well."

"Actually...please, call me Al!" he grins.

Again the waitress is summoned. The more attractive brunette speaks: "We'd like some…Sambuca, maybe?"

"Sambuca?" Shepard makes a face.

"Aren't you man enough?" she smirks. Then, to the waitress: "White Sambuca. Six shots."

She excuses herself to go to the bathroom. And Shepard and Garriott don't notice, but she circles around and says something to the waitress, and slips the other woman some money. As the waitress returns to our group, I am watching her with the tray, and it looks like there's something off with some of the shots, some variation in the viscosity of the liquor, in the way they slosh when she sets the tray down.

She hands out the shotglasses somewhat more deliberately and carefully than seems normal, and meanwhile the blonde leaves, and the brunette returns, and we all do our shots, and the brunette even grabs the extra one and pounds it, and I keep my eye on the server's tray as she brings it back to the bar.

And here I get up to go to the bathroom, and when I pass the bar, I notice on the server's tray that she's spilled a little from the shots, and where the spillage had mixed, it looks milky and white.

On the way to the bathroom, I see the blonde coming back.

I stop her: "Your friends weren't doing shots of Sambuca there. The brunette was drinking…"

"We have names, you know. I'm Heather. She's Anne."

"Well…Heather. Your friend Anne was drinking water."

She gives a little look, then a laugh. "Guilty as charged. I try not to be dishonest these days, but I don't drink anymore, and my friends aren't really looking to get plastered. So...a white lie."

"A white Sambuca lie," I smile.

She chuckles: a blessed, beautiful chuckle.

"If it mixes with water, there's this effect where the mixture turns a little milky. I noticed it on the tray. If you want to keep it up, maybe switch to vodka."

Here she laughs. "Wait, you're trying to help me out here? You and your boss..."

"We have a complicated relationship."

Another brunette walks up, one that hadn't been in our group; she looks familiar, but I don't recognize her at first. Heather grins and says, "Hello! I didn't know you were here already, too!"

"Yes, we..."

As soon as I hear the accent, I know. "Wait, you're..."

"Orianna Falacci," the new brunette says. "Good to see you again, Buzz."

And to Heather: "So you're all..."

"Journalists," she smiles. "Modern liberated women."

I'm truly flabbergasted. "I thought you were..."

"...horny astronaut groupies?" she grins.

Here I have nothing to say.

Back at the table, Shepard's still holding court, though somewhat more inebriatedly; he's explaining how close he'd been to beating Gagarin, how very close, only they'd launched the monkey one last time, just to be safe.

"How goes the war, Admiral?" I ask.

"These are some tough customers we're up against here, Buzz," he opines.

"I bet they can drink you under the table."

"Never. We need to get some more shots in them."

"We're standing right here," Anne reminds him.

"If you get any more shots in *you*, you'll get shot down," the other one chuckles.

"Never!" Shepard says defiantly. "Another round!"

"How about vodka?" I suggest.

"Yes!" the other brunette echoes. "We'd like some shots of vodka."

"Yes! In honor of our vanquished Russian adversaries!" Shepard exclaims.

The other brunette gets up as if to talk to the waitress again; I stop her, whisper in her ear: "It's OK. I know what's up. I'm on your side."

The waitress heads off for the drinks. For the benefit of the group, I say, "Oh, wait. I was gonna get a chaser." Then I dart after her and speak in her ear: "Five shots of water, one shot

84

of vodka, which goes to Admiral Shepard. I'll pay you for six shots. And a Schlitz."

The waitress grins and nods at the women: "You've defected?"

"Just for tonight."

She goes on her way, and returns with a tray and a beer and six shots.

I whisper in Owen's ear: "It's water. Just play along."

"To the Russkies," Shepard says. "If they hadn't beaten us to space, we might not have beaten them to the moon." And everyone tosses back their shots, Owen and the girls exaggerating their effect, except Heather spills hers and runs off to the restroom instead.

I follow her, as discreetly as I can manage. "You OK?" I ask.

"Yeah, sorry. I really shouldn't be doing this. I can't afford to go back to that life. That seemed a little too much like Russian roulette."

"Except with a tray instead of a revolver chamber." I chuckle. "You're funny."

"You're married," she observes.

"What does that have to do with anything?"

"Well, it's just...the sense I get from you..."

"It's been tough," I sigh. "My marriage. I don't know where it's going. I'm..." Against my will I start to spill my guts. I haven't defected; I've been captured. "Joan wants to see a shrink, but my dad says...with my career, I mean...but I have been...things have been stressful at home. I was drinking too much, after the moon. I've been cutting back."

"Cutting back?" She raises an eyebrow.

"Well, special occasions excepted. I really should quit. I got back on flight status to go on this Venus-Mars thing. I figured I just needed something new to do. A reason to get out of bed in the morning. I was depressed."

"It doesn't help with that," she says, with a nod down at my beer. "At least in my experience. It seems like it does, but it doesn't. But there's no point talking about it now."

She pulls out a notepad.

"Oh, Jesus, are you gonna write about this?"

She laughs. "No, no, no! This is all off the record. And this is more important than work." She writes down a telephone number. "Here. If you still want to quit tomorrow, when you're sober, call."

"This is your number?"

She gives a little smile/smirk. "I can't help you, Buzz. One of us might have mixed motives. This is a guy I know. A really good man. He'd be glad to talk to you."

She turns and heads for the door.

I wander back to the table. Shepard's pretty lit.

"You were saying about a barrel?" Anne asks.

I've heard the one about the barrel too many times to count, but I don't stop him. (I don't know if I want to hear it, or if I just want to see him fuck it up. Half the fun of watching Shepard tell a joke is seeing him bust a gut laughing before he even gets the punchline out.)

"Of course." Shepard clears his throat. "So, this guy. Goes to work in Alaska, in a mining camp, back in the gold rush days. Camp's so small, actually, there's only…" (Shepard chuckles, then chokes it down.) "…there's only three other guys. No women for miles around. And this guy…" (A longer chuckle escapes.) "…this guy, he's a regular guy, he figures he just wants to earn some money, maybe spend it on whores or whatever, but he's…" (Shepard snickers, and recomposes himself.) "…he realizes this camp is way the hell out there, you know? Way out in the back country. So at the end of the first workday, he goes to the old-timer there, and he's like, 'There's no whores or nothin' up here?' And the old-timer's like…" (After more chuckles, Shepard takes a break, then gets back to it.) "…the old-timer's like, 'Nope.' So the young guy's like, 'Well, what do you do for…you know…' And, I mean, he doesn't want to whack off, he's been swinging a pickaxe all day, his hands are all cramped up and blistered, last thing he wants to do is use his hands for THAT. And the old-timer's like, 'Well, for the next few weeks, you can just fuck this wooden barrel.'" (Shepard chuckles; the brunettes give a look like: *Who is this guy?*) "And he points to this barrel in the middle of the camp. Regular wooden barrel, with a hole, dick-high. And the young guy's like, 'A barrel? That sounds like, I mean…I don't think that'd feel that good, I mean…you could get splinters…'" (Shepard loses it, and starts laughing uncontrollably.)

"Jesus," I interject. "Do I have to finish this?"

"No, I can, I just…" Again, Shepard melts down laughing.

I'm not nuts about this joke, but the notion of leaving things half-done appalls me, so I pick up where he left off. "OK. So the old man, he's like, 'No, no, no. This thing feels better than you can imagine.' And the young guy tries it, and it's just…amazing. Best thing he's ever felt." (The brunettes look at each other with some odd combination of curiosity and disgust. But I'm drunk, and it's too late to stop, and I think the fact that they don't want me to keep going makes me want to keep going.) "Next thing you know, he's going over to the barrel first thing in the morning, he's sneaking back to camp on lunch, he's getting in a quick one before dinner, he's going over there when he wakes up in the middle of the night…"

"…with a woodie…" Shepard interrupts, then bursts out laughing again.

"That's not the point of the joke," I respond, then continue. "He goes to the barrel when he wakes up in the middle of the night…with a woodie." (I nod to Shepard.) "Until one Sunday, he's headed over there just…ready to go. And the old timer stops him and says, 'Not today.' And the…'"

"IT'S YOUR WEEK IN THE BARREL," Shepard blurts out, half a sentence too soon. He doubles over laughing, red in the face.

"This guy clearly needs to get a little more drunk," I say, and to the waitress: "Another round!" The waitress gives a look;

I say in her ear, drunk but too loud: "Three shots of water, two shots of vodka. And a beer chaser for me."

I look over at the brunettes for approval; they talk amongst themselves, then announce they're headed to the bathroom. They never come back.

The waitress deposits all the shots; I motion for her to take the waters back, but Al catches it. He grabs one of the waters, tastes it. "The hell is going on here, Buzz?"

"I can explain," I say, which I do. And I decide to get him drunk enough that it won't matter.

•••

I start seeing snapshots.

I know there is racing in the night: Corvettes, long stretches of flat asphalt, ripping through forests of palmetto and pine, watching the headlights vacuum up the yellow dotted roadway line, finishing cans of beer and throwing the empties straight up so they get whisked away in the slipstream.

•••

Of course, we have work to do the next day. Reviewing pad procedures, talking to techs: a day in the Florida sun. We park our personal vehicles in the lot, where the duty van will be picking us up to take us out to 39A. Owen and I actually get there a few minutes early, and stand there waiting for our fearless commander.

Al shows up on time, wearing sunglasses.

I smile. "Good morning, sunshine!"

He glowers.

"Partly sunny, partly cloudy?" Owen says hopefully.

He removes his sunglasses, glares at us with bloodshot eyes, walks past us without saying a word, gets in the van, and slams the front door so hard I'm worried he'll get written up for damaging government property.

"Stormy," I observe.

Venus Mission

Part II: Flyby

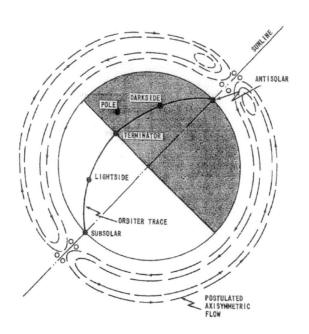

"Good morning, Explorer. It's Thursday, July 13ᵗʰ, 1972, and by the time our words reach you, it'll be 8:00 a.m. Houston time." Bob Crippen's Texas-tinted voice sounds surprisingly clear over the great cold distance. "And here's the news from planet Earth."

Over the past few months, the capcom's radio newscast has become a valued part of our morning, a welcome connection to home and normalcy. Barring any minor emergencies in the night, it's the first thing we hear from them each day. Today, as usual, it reaches us mid-breakfast; we arrange ourselves around the radio as if it were a fire on the hearth at home, as if those few feet of subtracted space make any kind of difference compared to the thousands we're adding every second.

"Robert Kennedy formally secured the Democratic nomination for president yesterday at the party's convention in Miami, capping a long and hard-fought battle with Vice President Hubert Humphrey. Observers credit Kennedy's win to the Johnson administration's inability to address the economic issues facing the country, and to the continuing instability in Vietnam. Kennedy promised to fight hard into November and beyond, to fulfill what he calls 'The Great American Promise' for all citizens. President Johnson, who skipped the convention and has been largely absent from the campaign trail thanks to his own abysmal polling numbers, had no official statement, while Humphrey urged rank-and-file Democrats to unite around the party's nominee as he gets ready to face off against his likely Republican adversary, California Governor Ronald Reagan."

"Son of a bitch, he pulled it off," Shepard muses as the broadcast continues.

"Meanwhile, fighting erupted yesterday in South Vietnam between Republic of Vietnam forces and what appear to be North Vietnamese Army regulars. The clashes in the country's central highlands mark the first large-scale violence since the latest cease-fire went into effect in early June. Should the cease-fire collapse, it will mark the third failed truce since the Johnson Administration started peace negotiations in 1968, and the second since the final withdrawal of American combat units in 1971."

"Shit." I shake my head.

"And in Northern Ireland, a cease-fire between British forces and the Irish Republican Army also apparently came to an end, as six civilians were shot by British troops. This phase of the ongoing conflict is now in its third year, and hopes for a settlement are..."

"Well I'm ready for sports already," Shepard mutters over the broadcast.

"...and in baseball," the capcom continues, "the Royals beat the Orioles 11 to 4, the Reds topped the Pirates, 6 to 3, the Padres edged out the Expos 6 to 5, the Mets shut out the Giants 4 to 0, the Dodgers beat the Phillies 9 to 5, the Cardinals shut out the Braves 7 to nothing, Boston held on against Oakland 7 to 6, the Twins pounded the Brewers 7 to 1, the Tigers beat the Rangers 3 to 1, the Yankees defeated the Angels 5 to nothing, the White Sox topped the Indians 5 to 4..." (Crippen pauses, saving the best for last) "...and the Astros shellacked the Cubs, 10 to 6."

Shepard and I burst into a chorus of jeering laughter, to which Kerwin says, "I wouldn't call that a shellacking."

"...nding by for crew status and any updates," Crippen is continuing, oblivious to our mirth. "Over."

"Houston, Explorer. We are nearly done with breakfast. Everyone is well-rested and ready to start the day." (It sounds like a conversation, but only for the moment. Given our trajectory, we're almost 180 light-seconds from Earth now. So it took three minutes for the newscast to reach us, and it will take that long again for our words to slog their way through the vastness of space to get back to them. In other words, the normal back-and-forth has become a back-

----

----and-forth.)   "Dosimeter   readings   as follows...Commander, 19379, CMP 18912, Science Pilot 19010. We've taken no medication."

Kerwin chimes in, perhaps to fill the silence. "As for the news, Venus is sounding better and better. When you get a chance, work up a PAD so we can do an orbital insertion burn when we get there. We might want to stick around for a bit."

Shepard and I chuckle. There's no way to know if Houston finds the joke funny, though. I feel suddenly awkward, like when you say the wrong thing at a party and the whole room falls silent.

"You can hold off on that PAD, Houston," I feel the need to add; it kills whatever was left of the mood.

Shepard talks again, all business now: "FYI, Houston, once we're all cleaned up here, we'll be ready for command module power-up. Standing by for timeline adjustments. Over."

We finish cleaning up, getting ready for the day. I steal a glimpse of myself in the mirror by the toilet: there is a dark spot on my skin, near the neckline. I don't remember seeing it before. Also, my beard has grown in thickly. Nobody seems to care.

••••

It is a moderately exciting day, actually, a bright oasis in the desert of routine: we're firing up the command module for a checkout and possible course correction.

Shortly after breakfast, we strap ourselves in up there, in front of the old familiar console, which now looks strange and new. We work methodically through the checklist, pressing circuit breakers and flipping switches, providing Houston with a running commentary all the while.

For all of the testing they did on the earlier mission, all of the work on shutdown and restart procedures, you always feel a flicker of emotion in your chest when doing these things yourself. There's always the simple knowledge that the more extreme the situation, the less the margin for error. So there are moments of blessed relief when the systems come back on line, needles on ammeters and voltmeters springing into position, and all the indicator lights as bright as they've ever been.

But relief is a pale substitute for excitement.

It turns out there's no real need for a course correction burn, other than as a test of the main engine. So they hold us to five seconds at ten percent thrust, just enough to make sure the engine is gimbaling correctly.

We radio back for permission to give the attitude control thrusters a quick workout.

We've all been pushing for this; it's a chance for a fresh look at our destination, visual proof that these seemingly infinite days are, in fact, taking us somewhere.

The delay in their response feels especially ponderous. (We've trained for this, of course, but it's still annoying. Waiting all the while would fill your days with dead empty time, so you tend to transmit with one eye on your wristwatch, so as to work for a few minutes while the signals make their slow round trip. Then when the time is up, you stop what you're doing and float there, pen and pad in hand, patiently anticipating the voices in your headset, the chance to snatch the transmission and scribble it down. You can, of course, set up the magnetic reel-to-reel machine to record the conversations and play them back, but chances are if you can't understand the transmission live, you won't be able to get it when the Data Storage Equipment plays it back, either, and you'll waste a lot of time trying. So you pay attention to the transmissions, and you try to catch them the first time around. Because if you don't...well, it's annoying enough in normal conversation to ask someone to repeat themselves, but here, it's excruciating.)

"Explorer, Houston. You can go ahead and enable the quads," they say at last. "Instructions as follows..."

To conserve fuel, they radio up the exact set of controller movements that will put Venus in the center of the large window. Given the orientation of the spacecraft stack, it hasn't been easy to see it during our normal operations, and I've been making it a point not to look for it. So I've been eager about this: not my first glimpse of Venus, of course, but the chance to see that it's different from every other point of light in the firmament: an island of clouds in a sea of stars.

When I rotate the spacecraft stack, I see: a white BB pellet, mostly in shadow, with only a small crescent sliver showing on the sunward side. It still looks incredibly far away.

"We are going somewhere, right?" I ask.

"Shit, I hope so," Shepard replies.

•••

13 JUL 1972

A day of unpleasant news from home. A glimpse of another world. We're ten days out but still three million miles away. It does not look like much.

• • •

On Friday, it's time for some public relations work. We've used up most of the telescope film, and we want to save the rest of the magazine for the Venus approach; we won't be able to replace it until my spacewalk. So we've decided to cancel a few days of solar observation and make science films for the kids back home.

Shepard fiddles with the television camera and curses, while Kerwin floats near the telescope console and reviews his handwritten script. This little film we're about to make was his idea, but it was one I enthusiastically supported, which means two-thirds of the crew is on board, so to speak. We're going to explain to our children, and all children, why we're up here.

I float over to check on our leader. "Doing all right there, Al?"

"Fucking connector doesn't want to go in," Shepard says. "Bullshit P.R. I thought I didn't have to spend any time in the barrel until AFTER we get back."

"On this trip, we're all in the barrel," I point out.

"Be glad you're behind the camera," Kerwin adds.

"Rank has its privileges," he replies. And to me: "And you're the only one that's gonna get OUT of the barrel for the next eight months."

"I am, aren't I?" I grin; the EVA is getting closer.

"Bite me," Shepard says.

"Come on, Al! Turn that frown upside-down!" Joe says.

He glares. "All right. I think it's up. Let's just fucking do this. Back to VOX."

I flip the switch. "Houston, Explorer, we are starting the transmission on the S-band antenna." They'll be picking it all up and editing it together later.

"Hello to the schoolchildren of America," Kerwin starts. "We're here to..."

Right then I sneeze violently, cutting him off. I try to get my hand in place to cover it; the body movement sets me tumbling, and I bump into the bulkhead.

"Jesus," Shepard looks over his shoulder, suddenly amused. "You're gonna throw us off course!"

Kerwin chuckles. "When asked why the spacecraft crashed into Venus, NASA had no answers, but acknowledged they were investigating a violent burst of sound heard on its last transmission..."

"Come on, I was trying to save us all from...dodging floating sneeze droplets for the rest of the day!" I smile a little at last. The bad mood has lifted.

"All right." Shepard raises the camera. "Let's try this again."

"Hello to the schoolchildren of America," Kerwin intones. "We're…"

It seems like I'm about to sneeze again; I "ah" but catch myself before "choo."

"Come on," Shepard says. "Didn't they teach you any military discipline at that school of yours?"

"All right. Military discipline. No sneezing. Let's go."

Again Shepard raises the camera.

"Hello to the schoolchildren of America. We're sending you greetings from a classroom of our own, over 33 million miles away. Here on the longest voyage in human history, we're taking a few minutes of our time to remind you that learning is a lifelong process, a journey that never ends. It's also a trip you cannot take alone. The passing of knowledge from teacher to student, the sharing of knowledge with one another as you grow and perhaps become teachers yourselves one day: these things remind us that learning isn't something we do for ourselves, but for the good of all mankind. With that in mind, we're here to share some knowledge about the sun, which we've been studying in detail for the past few months, and Venus, which we'll be seeing more of soon.

"Astronomers have known for some time that the sun is far more than a simple bright ball of fire in the sky. Long ago, they identified and named three distinct visible layers. The outermost of these is the corona, the 'crown of the sun.' It does look like a crown, but it's usually only visible during solar eclipses. Next comes the chromosphere, or 'color sphere.' This layer actually sends out red light; like the corona, it's usually only visible during eclipses, and even then, just the edge of it. Because underneath that is the photosphere, or 'light sphere,' which is far brighter."

I'm waiting for Kerwin to flub a line or make a mistake, but he plows on, impressively erudite.

"But even this seemingly bland bright ball is more complicated than it seems. Oriental astronomers sometimes saw dark spots when the sun was setting or rising. Still, it wasn't until Galileo and his contemporaries, and the invention of the telescope, that we were able to really study these sunspots. By watching them, we learned that the sun rotates. And soon astronomers were drawing them in great detail. But we still didn't understand them. We thought they were clouds. Sir William Herschel, the man who discovered Uranus..." (He carefully pronounces it YOUR-a-niss, so as not to send the kids into fits of giggling.) "...was one of the first to speculate that they were actually holes through which we were observing a darker layer below. But he thought there were aliens walking around down there, strange creatures we couldn't imagine. Why didn't astronomers know any more? Because they hadn't yet learned to combine astronomical observation with a real understanding of physics. And this shows us why the sharing of knowledge is important. Physics, astronomy, chemistry: all the sciences need to talk to one another to make sense of our sun, and our universe.

"Long before Herschel, Sir Isaac Newton understood that light was made up of a spectrum of many colors. Then an Englishman named William Wollaston, working around the same time as Herschel, realized that when you looked carefully at sunlight that had been split with a prism, there were lines in the spectrum. Not long afterwards, a German named Joseph von Fraunhofer invented the spectroscope, which allowed us to split the light more carefully and see the lines more clearly. Two other German scientists, Bunsen and Kirchoff, realized that these lines were caused by different chemicals and the way they released light when heated to certain temperatures. You may have heard one of those names before, for one of these men invented a device that may have found its way into a few of your classrooms: the Bunsen burner.

"All of this sharing of knowledge helped scientists learn still more about the sun. An American astronomer, Charles Young, determined that the photosphere gave off light across the spectrum, except for those dark absorption lines, but the chromosphere ONLY gave off light in those parts of the spectrum. So by using telescopes with filters that blocked out those other frequencies, we were able to see the entire chromosphere, even when there wasn't an eclipse. And we realized that sunspots were cooler than the rest of the sun's surface; another American, George Hale, discovered that they were caused by giant arcing magnetic fields; these fields pushed material out of the way and caused it to arrange itself in a way that resembled magnetic field lines. In fact, magnetic fields are a major driving force for solar activity.

"We've done our part to build on this knowledge. Our spacecraft carries telescopes and instruments that can see in wavelengths that are blocked by the earth's atmosphere, so we've learned still more about activity on the surface of the sun. We've photographed huge storms, loops of gas that are large enough that you could roll all of planet Earth through them, with room to spare. We've seen enormous flares, and learned a great deal. But now it's time to turn our attention towards a new target: Venus."

Here I'm sure Kerwin's going to take a break, but he plows ahead.

"Even in ancient times, man knew there was something special about this brilliant spot in the sky. When our ancestors began studying the heavens, they realized most of the points of light were fixed in place in relation to one another, but some of them were brighter and moved around in the night sky. These restless roamers got their own name: planet, which means 'wandering star.'

"And one planet was brighter than the others, brighter than anything else besides the sun and the moon. But it didn't get one name, because we didn't know it was one object. It appeared in the sky at two distinct times: close to dusk, and close to dawn. So for centuries, it was both 'evening star' and 'morning star.' For the Greeks, 'Hesperus' and 'Phosphorous,' for the Romans, 'Vesper' and 'Lucifer.' This name sounds evil to us, of course, but for them, it just meant 'Bringer of Light' or 'Bringer of the Dawn.'

"At some point, the ancients realized these were both one object. And the Romans eventually named it, and all the other planets, after their deities. But unlike all the others, which were named after gods, they named this one after a goddess. Venus, the goddess of love and beauty.

"Even before Galileo, astronomers had observed Venus in transit across the face of the sun, and hypothesized that it was between Earth and the sun, which explained why it was only visible in the morning and the evening. But it took us a long time to learn much more about Venus. In the late 1700s, astronomers realized it had an atmosphere, and that it was shrouded in clouds. But the atmosphere made it difficult for us to realize other things, like the planet's rate of rotation. We were only able to get a rough measurement in the 1950s, and even on this mission, we're working to refine those observations.

"In the absence of information, imaginations run wild. Especially the collective imagination. Back then, writers imagined a lush jungle world, with vast oceans and giant trees, and creatures of all shapes and sizes. And given the advances in rocketry that were going on at the time, it seemed only a matter of time before man would land on Venus. But these science fiction dreams were long on the fiction and short on the science. Sooner or later, the facts had to catch up.

"In 1962, we launched Mariner 2. We discovered some things we don't like about Venus. The surface is around 800 degrees Fahrenheit, for instance, which is one of the reasons we won't be able to land any time soon. This happens in part because the atmosphere is full of thick carbon dioxide, which creates a greenhouse effect, trapping heat from the sun's rays.

"But there is still room for hope. One of our scientists, a man named Carl Sagan, thinks we might be able to introduce genetically modified bacteria that would reverse this effect, removing carbon from the atmosphere and creating oxygen, much the way plants do for us on Earth. Also, since the atmosphere is so thick, we could potentially float massive balloons using ordinary oxygen. Humanity's never attempted anything remotely like this, and it may be beyond our abilities for some years to come. But we owe it to ourselves not just to dream big dreams, but to put in the work it takes to make them real. Centuries from now, some of our ancestors might be living in the Venusian atmosphere, floating under massive blimps, or even creating cities in the clouds."

Shepard puts down the camera; I can tell he's impressed.

"There we go," Kerwin says.

"Some of our descendants," I point out.

He doesn't understand the correction. "Descendants?"

"You said 'Centuries from now, some of our ancestors...' I think you mean 'some of our descendants.' Our ancestors are never gonna make it to Venus unless we dig them up."

Kerwin shakes his head. "Man, it's always the little things."

"We'll fix it in post-production," Shepard says.

"I can rerecord that that last little bit," Kerwin offers. "Maybe they can splice together the audio, put some visuals over it."

"We don't have a lot of visuals," I point out.

"He has given 'em enough to fantasize, at least," Shepard says.

"Well, you do have a walk outside coming up." Kerwin gives me a little smile. "You can provide the visuals."

•••

"Spacecraft's getting gross," I observe as I pass out the food trays.

"A little," Shepard replies, which seems to me to be a quintessential bit of New England understatement.

We've been keeping up with the housework as best we can. After every meal, our trash goes in the vacuum airlock, which we've been rigorously maintaining so it won't get jammed up; on the other side of that, our debris ends up in an expandable net, exposed to the vacuum of space, sterile and hygienic. And we wipe everything down in the mess area as best we can. But there's a good amount of food spatter inside the grating for the intake vent; every little fleck of mashed potatoes or pureed carrots that misses our mouths ends up circulating up there eventually. And while the lack of gravity means the toilet doesn't have quite the same spatter issues one might expect from three men living on their own, there have been...accumulations in the tubing.

"We should really remove that kitchen grating eventually," I suggest.

"I'm afraid to remove that grating. We might have an unknown lifeform lurking in there."

I give him a look.

"We'll do it, we'll do it. The rest of the ship's still gonna smell like a locker room, though."

"Probably," I concede.

We haven't been using the shower much. Obviously it was designed with zero-g in mind, and we have decent reserves of stored liquid hydrogen and oxygen to generate water as needed, but cleaning yourself with water clinging to your body, and then vacuuming it off of you, makes for an annoying and time-consuming process. So we've generally stuck to wiping ourselves down with washcloths every few days. As for clothing, we have limited-use garments, but they don't go in the airlock, so the odors have definitely accumulated.

"I'm starting to smell us. That's bad," Kerwin chimes in.

"Jim Lovell said when he and Frank were up there for two weeks, he didn't notice how bad they smelled until after splashdown, when the recovery crews cracked open the spacecraft and...recoiled in horror."

"We must be even worse than that," he replies. "I think we're shedding a lot."

"I lost my calluses a few weeks in," Shepard says. "They just fell right off my feet."

"Me too," Kerwin says. "I guess without the regular friction..."

"What did you do with them?" I ask Shepard.

He gives me a funny look. "I saved them in my personal preference kit."

I have no idea whether or not he's joking.

"Shedding, though," Kerwin says. "I am slightly concerned about the air filters. I think we're gonna be tight on those by end-of-mission. Every time I change them, they're...caked with dead skin cells."

"All right. This is getting gross. Trying to eat here," I point out.

"I'm not worried about those. We have backup systems," Shepard says.

"Backup systems?" Kerwin asks. Spacecraft mass is always at a premium; we might have a single backup for some things, but never systems, plural.

"Our lungs," Shepard grins.

"Jesus," I shake my head.

"Even those can't do anything about the...methane smell, though," Kerwin continues.

"No, they can't," Shepard acknowledges.

"We might want to do something about that, too," I add. (One other side-effect of the 5-psi environment, one most astronauts don't talk about in front of kids, unless the kids are in a really goofy mood and you're looking to get their attention, is this: when your digestive tract is used to operating at a certain pressure, and it's placed in a larger system that's running at a lower pressure, the former system tends to reduce its own pressure through the most convenient orifice available. And once that flatulence is out there, it has no place to go.)

"What can we do?" Shepard asks.

"Full-system air purge?" I ask hopefully. "Maybe during the EVA?"

Shepard smirks. "I'm not sure that's the wisest course of action, Buzz." Again with the understatement.

It is, indeed, unwise. Doing an EVA so far from Earth is risky enough as it is; we'll be getting back in the command module and depressurizing it, opening the hatch and allowing me to venture forth, retrieving film and instrumentation packages and doing a little television, giving the people on Earth a closer look at Venus. But we're sealing off the manned module and keeping it pressurized all the while. We have another EVA planned for very late in the mission, so I'm sure we have enough O2 on hand to dump the rest of the atmosphere if absolutely necessary, but it's one of those only-do-this-in-case-of-emergency things.

"That experiment...those spiders might explode in the vacuum," he deadpans. "I don't think the kids would like that."

I laugh.

"I don't think they'd explode," Kerwin says. "We wouldn't even explode. Pulmonary embolisms after a few minutes. And with the spiders, the exoskeleton would keep them..."

Shepard gives him a look like: I know.

"You know what we could do," Kerwin continues. "Rather than using the CSM tanks to repress the command module, we could vent the manned module *in*, and then let the manned module systems bring the pressure back up. That'd cut down on the smell, at least."

"That's not a terrible idea, actually," Shepard says.

So: rather than venting all the methane-laced air into space, we'd at least be drawing some of it into the command module and sealing it off. I laugh. "Jesus. The most advanced scientific mission in human history, and we're...using all our brainpower trying to figure out how to keep from smelling our own farts. I guess we've all got a reason to look forward to the EVA now."

"Yeah, we'll be plugged in that whole time," Kerwin observes. "Clean air for everyone!"

"You are really looking forward to this, huh?" (Our commander's mood can be very gruff: borderline asshole, or maybe south of the border. But there are times like this, too, when he's downright solicitous, more of an Al than a Shepard. It always catches me off guard.)

"Well...yeah. When I'm out there, I get that feeling like: 'This is it. This is exactly what I'm supposed to be doing in life.' I don't always have that feeling."

"Why is that, do you think? Why EVA and not something else?"

"I dunno." I'm not one for analyzing my feelings, and I haven't really thought about this. "It does remind me of scuba diving. And that's been a helpful hobby. Doing all the pool training before Gemini XII...I really think that was one of the things that allowed us to pull that off, to prove we could work out there." (I can see the others' eyes rolling, and I know I'm repeating myself, plunging into one of my old standard monologues. But it *was* an important thing for us, to learn how to get out of the spacecraft and actually work in a weightless environment. You could only do so much in thirty-second increments on the parabolic aircraft flights. And some of the early spacewalks nearly came to a bad end because the training hadn't been thorough enough. But I was the first to do my training underwater. And sure enough, we had a successful mission.)

"You get a lot of dives in, usually?" Kerwin asks.

"Yeah, a few times a year."

"Not this year," Shepard smirks. Back to being a dick.

Kerwin, at least, is dependably decent: "Acapulco usually, right?"

"Usually."

"You really enjoy it, huh?"

I find myself unexpectedly antsy. "Yeah. It's nice," is all I say.

And with that, the conversation flickers and dies.

I'd prepared the meal, so the others get busy cleaning up. And I find myself floating over to the window, thinking about diving.

Even getting ready, there's something wonderful about the whole process: checking and rechecking your equipment, preparing your weight belts and buoyancy compensators and air regulators and masks. It's like a mechanical ritual, a ceremony with purpose. And then you get out on the boat and the water's all blue and shimmering...turquoise in the Caribbean, but in Acapulco you see that deep Pacific blue, and the hills all hazy in the distance. And the boat goes for a while, until you get to some idyllic tropical cove or sun-baked limestone island. And you waddle and shuffle over to the edge of the boat like some sort of rubberized penguin before it's finally time to step off into the water. There's always that last-minute regrouping on the surface, the clumsy floundering, still discombobulated with all that equipment. But then you deflate your compensator and slip beneath the surface.

When that final hiss of air gives way to the first gurgle of water, all the awkwardness slips away, and you're somewhere else. It's another world, a world hiding in plain sight of our own, concealing much that is strange and wonderful beneath its boring and familiar façade. There may be a few moments of peaceful passage first, down through nothingness, alone with only the sound of your breathing. But if you've picked your dive site well, you make it down to a reef or a wreck, and the same waters that had seemed dull on the surface now reveal themselves to be teeming with life—alien life, in a sense. Darting schools of silvery fish, or preening colorful ones, or maybe an ugly green eel emerging from its cave all crass and grumpy like some old geezer yelling at you from his front porch.

You putter around with your dive partner, and all you can hear are breathing sounds and bubbles, very relaxing. Everyone communicates with simple hand signals, and there's only a few of them, so there's not much need to figure out what to talk about. "Look at that." And "Swim." And "Are you OK?" And "I'm OK." And you spend forty-five minutes down there, maybe, just long enough for it to start to feel normal, just enough time that you don't get bored.

Eventually, of course, it's: "Time to go up."

You ascend slowly. Every once in a while you'll be down there with some dive group with some new idiot who forgets his training and inflates his compensator on the bottom and goes rocketing up like a champagne cork. But the idea is to take your time and swim up. Even if you're not diving deep enough that the bends are an issue, you want to stay in control. So you scissor your legs lazily, gently paddling upwards with your fins while the dive leader winds up the rope that leads to the float that tells the dive boat where you are. And above, there's a patch in the blue-green water, a silvery shimmering patch that gets steadily bigger.

When you're back on the surface, you climb on board the boat and stow your gear. And you grab a sandwich and a beer from the cooler, and you notice every crumb on the bread, every bead of sweat on the bottle. And maybe then you look around again. And somehow this familiar world suddenly seems different, beautiful and sunlit and sharp, with greener greens and bluer blues than you'd remembered from a mere forty-five minutes before. Every time you emerge from the water, it's like a baptism; the old familiar earth becomes fresh and new.

•••

It's my communications day. At the appointed hour, I'm floating alone on the main deck.

"Hey, Dad, it's Andy." The voice comes fairly clearly through the headset; I'm amused and slightly put off by the fact that he felt the need to identify himself. Then again, his voice has been changing; he probably thinks he sounds like Mike now.

"I hope you guys are having a wonderful trip and learning a lot. I'm enjoying the last month of summer vacation and spending a lot of time with my friends. Obviously in our neighborhood..." (Crackle.) "...n't get to brag too much, because it's hard running into someone whose dad hasn't been in space at least. But I'm very proud of you. I've been listening in on the squawk box, and I'm looking forward to the flyby. It'll be neat to see you out there, next to a planet. But I'm hoping you guys do some more TV stuff inside, so we can actually see your face, too. I think you said last time that you had a beard going. I'm curious how that looks. Also, I know football season's still a couple months off, but I..." (Hiss.) "...ad when I realized we're gonna miss the whole season."

I don't much like it either; the Oilers games have been my go-to with him, one of the few reliable pastimes during these long years of training and planning. (You often have to fly off on Monday morning in a T-38 to Downey or Bethpage or the Cape, and you don't get back until Friday, and on Saturday you need to pop in to the office for a couple hours to catch up on the paperwork. So it's usually Sunday before you can catch up on parenting.)

He continues: "I know you and mom got me the tickets, and I'm grateful for that. It's just going to be strange going with her. But everything else is going well. Oh, yeah...no new accidents."

Then Mike comes on: "Dad, I hope you're doing well and not too sick of all the astronaut food yet. Slodey and I have been going out for walks at night after it cools off. He still hasn't been very well-behaved; I brought that girl Mary over for dinner the other night, and she bent over to take her shoes off, and Slodey goosed her. And it all went downhill from there. I do kinda wish you'd been here for it, though." Here I get a little lump in my throat. Mike's been a bit sullen and uncommunicative of late, especially in the months leading up to this flight, so I don't expect much from him; it's a strange relief to hear him say he wants to spend time with me.

Then, Jan: "Dad, we've been going..." (Crackle.) "...morning and evening like you said to see Venus. It still looks like another star to me, but I've gotten good at picking it out. I can't believe how far away it looks! Mom got the binoculars down, and I was kinda hoping we'd be able to see you guys out there somehow, even though I know it's impossible." (More static.) "...you bring back lots of pictures from the flyby."

Joan speaks: "OK, kids, say goodbye so I can get a minute." And there's a chorus of "Bye, Dad" and "We love you."

At last, Joan takes over. "Buzz, I sent the kids out of the room so I can talk to you alone. It's been a rough few weeks. You know how it goes: we are all proud, happy and thrilled. But it's scary, too. I'm terrified, this trip especially; it just seems so long that something's bound to go wrong. And I'm afraid, especially for the kids' sake. I hope you can see how much they miss you, how much they need to have a father in their lives when you get home. Andy especially. You're missing a whole round of birthdays with this trip. And as for us...we are going to have to take a look at some things. Everything that's happened..." Her voice catches; even across the distance, I can tell she's on the verge of tears, and my chest tightens, hearing it. "I'm sorry…I know we can't change any of this right now, I should just…" There's a long pause. "It's hard keeping up appearances. I know you're used to it. I guess I should be. But it's not just another role, it's not like I can go backstage…I…"

For a couple seconds, nothing: I wonder what else she has to say. I imagine many awful things. I wish we weren't talking about this. Then again, I never heard "over." I wonder if she forgot, if it's my turn to talk, what kind of response she expects. My mouth opens, ready to say words that don't exist.

Then she continues, and it's like a new conversation: "Well, we'll have to save all that for later. Speaking of birthdays, Jan and Mike are coming up, of course. For Mike, I would say get him a car, but since you won't be using yours for a while…I was thinking we could get another dog for the two of them. I know, I know, you're probably gonna say we're fine with the animals we already have, you don't want to come home to a menagerie, but I do think they'll both be very happy. Anyway, I guess it doesn't matter. I'm just gonna go ahead and get it. I just wanted to let you know so you can act like you know what you're getting them."

And here something comes over me, some great and confusing feeling I don't want to feel, along with a tightness in my chest.

"It's strange. They rigged up that squawk box in the kitchen. When it's on, we can hear every transmission. We hear you talk more now than when you're here. But it's still not actual conversation. I…" Her voice breaks. "…I know it's not fair to bring all this up now. But I feel like when you are here, I can't..." (A static-y noise that could have been caused by her.) "...ry, I told myself I wasn't going to do this. I need to stop now. I should let you say your piece, at least. Transmission over."

This, of all things, sets me off: I've told her a million times that you don't have to say "Transmission over," that it's redundant, that "over" is enough. Maybe she's just trying to rile me up...

I breathe, and try to force some cheer into my voice.

"Joan, it's good to hear from you..." I start, then stop. It's strange, talking at these distances. Somehow it's more like writing letters than conversing; you say more words at a time, and you think more about getting them right, rather than getting them out of your mouth right away. Under the assumption Joan's still alone, I give the paternal stamp of approval to the dog, but obliquely enough that the secret will still be safe in case she messes up and lets the kids back in while my words are still in transit. But in case they are still out in the hallway, I tell her to bring them back in so I can talk directly to them; I give her a minute to do that, three minutes from now. And I start talking again. I speak of discoveries, observations of the sun, other stars, galaxies, and the universe, all across the electromagnetic spectrum: gamma and x-ray and ultraviolet and visible, infrared and microwave and radio, the unseen rainbow beyond the rainbow, so much more expansive than any of us can comprehend. I tell about the filmstrips we're filming, all those explanations that will make it all make sense. I talk about how much I miss pizza, and order them to make their mom order one so they can eat vicariously for me. I tell them of my love, and hint at wonderful birthday surprises to come.

When that's over, I float over to the food vent and remove the grating to do some cleaning. Hopefully in six minutes there will be another message, thanks and goodbyes, some warmth transmitted across the void. Until then, I've got time to kill.

•••

14 JUL 1972

Conversation with home. Birthdays remembered and arranged. The illusion of normality.

Some flicker-flashes last night. The others have seen them now, at least. I'm not losing my mind. At least not about that.

If it's radiation, though, that's cause for concern. Do you lose brainpower over time up here? Or does it change your personality? How much of you is you, and how much is the machine, the circuitry? Strange pathways with no schematics…if only you could let someone take a look. Maybe they could tell you: all you need is a resistor here, a capacitor there, some shielding here, and you'll be all set.

•••

The flyby's drawing closer.

"You ready, Buzz?" Kerwin asks. He and I are both in front of the camera this time.

I scan my script one last time, stroking my beard. "Ready as I'll ever be." Kerwin's jotted down some general notes, but I've printed out every word I want to say precisely, on index cards I've taped to a clipboard.

"I can do this one solo if you want."

"No, it's all right." I place the clipboard in front of me, just below the camera's field of view.

"All right," Shepard says. "Lights, camera, action."

The red light comes on and I start talking.

"Hi, kids. Today we're going to talk about physics, about the laws that set our spacecraft in motion and determine how long it'll take for us to get home. These same laws apply to the exciting things in life, the rockets and spaceships, and to the boring and mundane events as well. You may not always stop to think about it, but every time you drop a pencil off a desk, or release a balloon to go shooting around the room, you're seeing physics in action. These laws govern our lives. It's been that way since the dawn of time, but many of them were only set down by Sir Isaac Newton."

"One of his laws states that a body set in motion will stay in motion, unless acted on by another force. This is the law of inertia. Now on Earth, this can be hard to see, because we're used to other forces getting in the way. If you throw a ball, gravity will pull it down, and friction will make it roll to a halt. But if you throw it in space..." I've been holding a small rubber ball; I turn towards our little hallway and give it a toss. It flies straight and true, not slowing down or arcing to the ground but heading straight to the curtain around the toilet.

Shepard doesn't film it.

"I thought you were gonna get that," I say, annoyed.

"This isn't live, Buzz. They're gonna edit it together."

"All right, I guess we'll do it again." While Shepard repositions himself, I float down the hallway. The ball has ricocheted off the curtain and a locker handle; energy dissipated, it's floating lazily back towards us. I pluck it from the air and float back. "Act One, Scene One. Buzz throws the ball. Take Two."

From right in front of the camera lens, I toss the ball gently. This time Shepard pushes himself off the bulkhead and follows the ball with the camera.

"Ohh, tracking shot. Getting fancy there, Stanley Kubrick," Kerwin observes.

We head back to the mess area. "We are not immune to gravity here in space. When we were orbiting Earth back on my Gemini mission, the force of gravity was still 87% as strong as it is at ground level. But we could still observe this same weightless behavior. Why is that? Well, on Earth, if you're standing on something solid, it is pushing against you, and you feel that force. In orbit, gravity pulls you and you're falling, but the spacecraft is falling, too, so there's nothing to push against you. To stay in low-earth orbit, the spacecraft has to travel so fast that, by the time it falls, the surface of the planet has fallen away, too. Here we…"

"Here we," Joe is talking over me.

Shepard stops filming.

"I thought I was going to take this part," Kerwin says.

"I was on a roll."

"But I feel dumb just floating there while you talk."

"The silent partner," Shepard says.

"I can pick up from there, talk about the trajectory."

"There's gonna be a discontinuity..."

"They're gonna edit it together," Shepard points out.

"What are you, the cameraman *and* the director?" I force a strangled smile. "There'll be a discontinuity. If I'm talking, and there's a cut, and it's still looking at us, and you're talking..."

"They're gonna edit it together," Shepard points out.

"Yeah, they do stuff like that all the time," Kerwin adds. "All those artsy movies. Whatsit, French New Wave? I think that's a jump cut."

"What are you, the cinematographer? This isn't...French New whatever," I point out. "This is a classroom documentary."

"They're gonna edit it together," Shepard points out. "Probably put in some graphics. Drawings or something. Man's gonna be on camera, he should get to talk. What are you, the star?"

"Yes." I laugh, at last. "And I...can't...work under these conditions!" I throw my hands in the air, a mock tantrum.

Fortunately the others chuckle, too. "Hey, if you stay too long in space, I guess you get to act like a star," Shepard says.

"You want the part?" I ask Kerwin. "All right. Al's right, we should switch off more."

Kerwin runs through the lines about falling around the Earth. Then: "We've escaped from Earth's orbit, but we haven't escaped gravity. Essentially now we are in solar orbit, on a lopsided trajectory that will speed up as our planetary flyby draws near, in what we call a gravitational slingshot. So we're falling around the sun, and falling towards Venus."

•••

I end up sitting in on Al's communication window that night. He has business to transact, real-estate wheeling and dealing, and I've become a partner of sorts for those discussions.

For a navy man, Shepard spends a lot of time thinking about the land. Not casually like the rest of us, but professionally, with a keen eye for what can be bought and sold, both above and below. When Mercury was winding down and NASA was moving to Houston, the astronauts found themselves getting invited to various social events by a host of local businessmen: car dealers and bank presidents and what-not, rich folks eager to meet the town's new elite. And it turned out Shepard was an ace at networking and socializing, all that stuff that makes me want to throw up in my mouth a little. When his ear condition developed and he went off flight status, he had time to burn on those side pursuits, and he did very well for himself indeed. Once he was back in the rotation, he had to dial it back a little, but by then he'd already established himself in a way most of us are waiting to do until *after* we leave NASA. Rumor has it he was a millionaire long before he went to the moon.

Given the length of our current voyage, one would think Shepard would've finally had to choose between being an astronaut and being a tycoon. But he's never been the type of man to be forced into anything. He gave his wife power of attorney to act as his proxy in his business dealings, and once we started getting far enough from Earth, he recruited me to sit in and listen during his consultations with her, to cut down on the back-and-forth.

"There were some hiccups with the strip mall on Westheimer," Louise says as we get down to business.

"Hiccups?" Shepard mouths the words and looks at me; he knows it would be counterproductive to say anything at all, and impossible to interrupt.

Indeed, even as he's doing that, Louise is continuing. "The Italian restaurant is having problems with their..." (Crackles.) "...ey have to do a lot of remodeling, and bring in a new pizza oven, but the order's been delayed, and they can't open the restaurant until that work's done, so they're not bringing in any revenue yet. They're asking for a rent reduction. They'd like three months at fifty percent. The other partners want to give it to them, because it would take a long time to get in a different tenant, so it'd be counterproductive to force these people out of business. They want your OK, though."

Shepard is jotting down notes, neat and legible: *1) Tenant rent reduction request – 3 mos. 50%. COUNTER. 2 MOS. 60%*

"The next item's about the horses. We've gotten an offer on Jupiter from a stud farm in Kentucky. Six thousand dollars, and they'll pay to transport him back there. Given his age and the stabling costs, I think it's a decent deal. I think we paid a thousand for him."

Shepard jots: *2) Jupiter - $6000. NO.*

"And finally," Louise continues. "Most importantly. The wells outside of Odessa. Between the two of them, we've spent $350,000 on equipment and drilling. One of the holes is at 8,100 feet, and the other's at 7,900. Frank says..." (Static.) "...ly normal for the Permian Basin, but Mark says with oil at three-and-a-half dollars a barrel, we may be facing a loss even if they do start producing. He thinks we should investigate other options..." (Indecipherable.) "...ompletion costs. Maybe just halt the drilling. Or sell them."

Shepard writes: *3) Odessa wells. HELL NO. Keep drilling.*

I'm watching him write, but he catches me, and gives a look I don't much care for.

"That's it for now," Louise continues. "I'll stand by for your direction. Over."

"She did say six thousand on the horse, right?" Shepard asks.

"Yes, that's what I heard, too."

"OK. And three months' rent reduction for the restaurant at 50%. And the wells, I won't even bother with that. Jesus

Christ, people think because I'm in space for a year I'm gonna be a pushover. All right, you're free to go."

"You're all set?"

"I'm all set. Thanks, Buzz."

He's been friendly, somewhat: the friendliness of a man who knows he's asking for a favor that falls outside the normal strictures of command and control, one where you have every right to say no. But the dismissal still feels abrupt: the curtness of a man who would prefer not to ask for any favors at all.

As he turns away, I remove my headset and move towards the passage to the sleeping chamber, but slowly, on the off chance I'll be able to catch a little of his side of the conversation. I do want to know how they talk to one another when no one's around.

Shepard's just about to start talking when he looks over his shoulder and catches me lingering: "Are you gonna to head down there, or what?"

The tone stings. I don't speak; I just pull myself down out of earshot. To do anything else would be to acknowledge I'd been curious about the rest of the conversation. But I know I should know better. Shepard's never been the type of guy to let you know more than he has to.

•••

On Sunday, we're filming again.

"Gyroscopes provide yet another way for Sir Isaac Newton's laws to govern our lives," Kerwin says, back alone in front of the camera. "Just as bodies in motion try to conserve their momentum, rotating objects try to maintain their angular momentum. You can see this with a child's top: the faster the spin, the less the wobble, the more quickly it steadies itself. Even in zero gravity, it wants to stay in place." He's brought one up here, a metal string-pull top with a large central disk; he pulls the string to set it spinning and it floats in the air in front of him, a miniature space station. After I zoom in for a close-up, he nudges one end with a pencil to set it moving. It stays upright and doesn't tumble.

"Our guidance system operates around this principle. We have a gyroscope not unlike this, a metal disk spinning at a tremendous rate. And the axle points are set in a metal ring, which connects with a different set of axle points to another ring, which connects with yet another set of axle points to still another ring. When you rotate the spacecraft, the disk tries to stay level. It's like it's invisibly glued to the heavenly firmament by physics."

"So the disk stays in place, and the rings rotate instead. The system measures the rotation in each axis, and sends these measurements to our control panel so we can see our orientation relative to three-dimensional space. We call this orientation 'attitude.' This is different than altitude, which is your height above something. There's a good way to remember the difference: when your teacher tells someone they have a bad attitude, that person sometimes rolls their eyes. And as our spacecraft moves, the attitude indicator, which we call an 'eight-ball,' rolls around, and it looks like when a kid rolls their eyes. Trust us, as parents, we've seen it a lot."

I suppress a little snicker.

"We use gyroscopes for more than guidance, though. We use another set to actually control the spacecraft's attitude. We call them 'control moment gyros.' With these, you actually *try* to move the gyros. When you apply power to them to push them in one direction, it causes the spacecraft to rotate in the opposite direction. It's a great system for long missions like this one. Rather than firing our thrusters all the time and worrying about running out of fuel, we can reorient the spacecraft using electricity, which we're always generating via..."

I put down the camera. All of it seems just...off.

"What's wrong?"

"You think that'll work?" I ask.

"Sure, why not?" he says.

I'm not sure, but I think I roll my eyes.

"Too wordy?" he asks.

I shrug, like: yeah, well, kinda. "I don't think we have enough for a good film lesson about the control moment gyros."

I half-expect him to make some lame joke about my attitude. Instead: a segment of a smile. "You know what? We could probably use some more visuals in this part."

"Yeah, like maybe pushing against something that's fixed, and rotating the other way."

"Or maybe...I could show *why* we need to control the spacecraft's attitude. How we have to keep the solar panels and sunshade towards the sun. Maybe…" (He rummages around in his pockets.) "…get a flashlight, put a sheet of paper like it's one of the panels." (He places the objects neatly in the airspace in front of him.) "Then we can show how the paper catches the most light when it's perpendicular to the flashlight." (He places the paper in front of the flashlight beam and angles it back and forth.) "And explain how we need to do that with the panels to keep a full charge. Whaddaya think?"

"I guess we can try."

We reshoot the scene, but it still doesn't seem like we've done enough. Shepard floats up to check on our progress.

"We got a little more footage," I tell him. "I'm trying to think of something else we can do."

"Maybe give the kids some shots of the spiderweb experiment," he suggests.

A couple schoolkids had suggested this experiment a year or so before, and NASA had given its blessing, the end result being that we now have a small metal box screwed to the wall, and a window through which we can observe two spiders and their webs. There had been some pre-launch speculation about whether or not they could work in space, but within a couple days of launch, the spiders had gotten the swing of things and started spinning their weightless webs every bit as effortlessly as if they'd been born up here.

Shepard takes over the camera and puts it up to the glass while Kerwin ad-libs some dialogue, something about how the spiders are adapting well and keeping a good attitude.

"That's still not a lot of footage," I point out when they're done.

"Well, do you have any suggestions, Mr. Attitude?" Shepard asks, a little more coldly than I care for.

"Actually, I've got another idea." Kerwin floats off and comes back with a drink container and the piece of string from the metal top we'd used for the gyro demo. Then he releases a giant globule of water that shimmers suspended in the air in front of his face. (How can there still be those crazies who believe we've never been in space? A minute of footage of a floating water blob is enough to prove them wrong. Nobody can do that on Earth, not even Kubrick.) "Here, get a shot of this."

"Sure thing." Shepard lines up to film.

"You can see tension at work here in the blob of water," Kerwin says. "Surface tension means the water molecules adhere to each other. They try to pull towards each other so there's as small a surface area as possible. Water has a stronger surface tension than many liquids. And without gravity, there are fewer forces to counteract it; it's almost like there's an elastic skin around the water." Kerwin moves a piece of string very slowly through the water; the surface tension keeps the blob from re-forming on the other side. Working carefully, he splits it in half, the way a man at a deli might cut a block of cheese with a piece of wire. "It can make it difficult for us when we spill something; if a blob of water hits the wall, there's no gravity to make it drip down, so it clings, and it's harder to clean up. But tension also keeps things interesting."

He breathes gently on one of the globules, blowing it back into the other until the two reassemble. Then we stab straws into the water and drink from it as Shepard films. When he's done, the remnant's about the size of my fist. For as long as we've been up here, this is still a mesmerizing sight, strangely relaxing; I watch the blob for a full minute as it hangs there, shivering and ghostly.

•••

Monday is a big day, perhaps the most important prelude to the great fly-by. We're shooting Venus in the side from a million and a half miles away.

The probes have been nestled for the past four months in a series of metal canisters at the bottom of the manned module. All told, we're carrying three thousand pounds' worth: an orbiter, two floaters, six dropsondes, two landers. (Or penetrators, depending on who you're talking to.) The landers are fat metal kamikazes on a fast one-way mission; after the initial fiery plunge into Venus's atmosphere, they'll be descending to the surface as rapidly as parachute technology will allow, taking pictures as they go, monitoring temperature and pressure, and surviving just long enough to snag a soil sample and transmit back some basic data. The dropsondes are smaller probes, similar to the ones weathermen launch from aircraft into hurricanes; like the landers, they're carrying heat shields to survive, but they'll deploy slower parachutes and take more thorough atmospheric readings during a more leisurely descent. And the floaters will also use heat shields to aerobrake; they'll stabilize themselves with a smaller parachute, then inflate a large Mylar balloon to stay aloft. They'll measure wind speed and weather conditions at altitude; more importantly, they'll capture atmospheric dust and analyze it for metabolic processes—signs of life.

(If all of this sounds complicated, that's because it is. The Venus probes are more than 10% of the module's mass budget, and their employment has been very elaborately choreographed, with everything sequenced and timed precisely. Because the landers and the dropsondes may not survive for long, they need to transmit data at a high bitrate via our spacecraft and its high-gain antennae. So they're equipped with solid rocket motors; a 1050 fps burn 132 hours before periapsis will allow them to reach Venus several hours ahead of us and transmit back to us during our approach, while we're still within line-of-sight. But the metabolic analyzers on the floaters will take several days to register their results, by which time our spacecraft will be long gone, so they'll be arriving at a more leisurely pace and transmitting data to the orbiter, which will send it all back to Earth.)

We need to deploy everything successfully, or else the mission will be a failure. We also need to keep from shooting ourselves in the face.

While Kerwin and Shepard have been readying the probes, I've been upstairs in the command module, turning it back on. I work methodically through the checklist, pushing circuit breakers, watching instruments and panel lights revive, scribbling calculations based on the manned module's guidance platform, plugging the results in to the command module's platform, rotating the spacecraft stack, keeping everyone appraised via headset. "And we're back up," I say at last. "Attitude program is complete. Still nominal on all propellants. Disabling all quads."

"Platform still looks good here," Shepard says. "Control moment gyros will be back up shortly."

I unstrap from the couch, execute a floating pivot, pull myself under the control panel and back through the tunnel, then swim into the manned module.

"All set here?" I ask.

Shepard says nothing, just finishes plugging numbers into the computer.

"We're looking good," Kerwin announces.

"And the gyros are back up," Shepard says. "Proceeding with the launch checklist."

"Cover latch disengaged," Kerwin replies, reading from our binder.

"Very well. Retract the cover."

"All right, I'll handle visuals." I float over to the window. It seems like they're ignoring me.

The probes are all spring-loaded in their canisters; Kerwin will eject each one in turn while I watch at the window to confirm a clean separation and proper antenna deployment. We've reoriented the spacecraft stack so they'll be launching in the direction of our flight path. This forward launch is essential to get them ahead of us and at a safe distance for the more dangerous part: firing the solid rocket motors. If one of them is facing the wrong way and its alignment systems fails, it'll come shooting back towards us. No one wants to know what'll happen if we're struck by one of our probes: it could be embarrassing, or merely fatal.

"Indicator is barber pole," Kerwin says. "And gray. Awaiting visual confirmation."

I angle myself around, my face close to the window. The system's been designed so we can get a visual on the canister cover once it's open; sure enough, I can see the sunlit metal edge of the door. "Visual confirmation."

"And I do believe we're ahead of schedule," Shepard responds.

I shouldn't be surprised. We're performing a script that was written for us months before launch, one we practiced offstage, with no real way to get a full dress rehearsal. It was written loosely, with plenty of time between lines to complete tasks and troubleshoot. Worse, our audience is far enough away that we won't be able to get their reaction for a while.

Still, I don't like the wait: hanging suspended, wondering if we'll get it right.

Shepard eyes the computer panel and watches the numbers count down. It seems nobody wants to speak. We just float there blankly for a good couple of minutes.

Then comes a quick static crackle, a belated acknowledgment from home. "Explorer, Houston. We copy you are beginning deployment sequence." We glance over at the radio, at each other, at nothing. "Attitude looks good.

Once the cover is retracted you are GO for deployment. Over."

But still there's time in the timeline. Shepard watches his watch for another minute, then finally speaks: "You may fire when ready, Gridley."

"Panel 2, Circuit Breaker 1." Kerwin reads his own list. "Activating breaker. Safety released. Lander 1 is ready. Counting down. Three...two...one...Launch."

From the main window, I can see the probe spring forth, a spindly spinning sputnik with three silvery arms, gleaming and metallic in the sunlight. "Clean separation. All arms deployed. Very good. Estimating separation rate at six feet per second. Clean rotation, not cone-shaped. Roughly two revs per minute." It's a relief. Then again, I wouldn't mind some minor drama. Nothing dangerous, mind you, just enough to quicken the pulse.

"We have barber pole on the indicator," Kerwin continues. "And now gray."

"Excellent," Shepard says brightly. I'm suddenly imagining him as Captain Ahab, eager to harpoon the Great White Planet.

We launch the second lander. It separates a little less cleanly.

"I think that might be a slow tumble," I say.

Shepard floats over. "I don't see it."

We keep watching as they fade into the starry distance.

"All clear on the penetrators?" Shepard asks.

Kerwin ignores the verbiage. "Lander tubes clear. Switches depressed."

"Poor guys. They've got nothing left to do," I comment. Shepard gives me a look, so I explain: "The switches. They're depressed."

"Jesus, Buzz," he shakes his head.

"Don't look at me. Doctor Kerwin's the one diagnosing them."

"Maybe they're sad 'cause their friends are going off to get lucky."

"Explorer, Houston." Ground cuts in, unexpected. "Goldstone is receiving telemetry from both landers. Estimating good separation all around. You are GO for the rest of the sequence. We'd like a two feet per second retrograde translation once..." (Crackle) "...plete. We'll start lighting them off..." (Static, but it sounds like "after that.") "...Over."

"They said 'after that,' right?" I ask. "We still don't want them firing them off for a while yet." The spring launcher should have given them a delta-v of about 10 fps, or 6.8 miles per hour, which means time is our friend; every bit of distance makes it statistically less likely that they'll hit us if something goes wrong. Unless, of course, the alignment sensors mistake us for Venus...

Shepard ignores me. "Houston, Explorer, we copy your transmission. We will proceed with the launch sequence for the remaining probes. Two feet per second retrograde afterwards..."

"Tell them about the tumble," I interject.

Shepard gives an annoyed look. "There might have been a tumble on one lander, but the maneuver should still give us enough separation. Please give us a few minutes' notice before you fire them off. We'd like to get a look, if we can. Over."

Next, Shepard's reading the checklist for the dropsondes, which are bundled on a single platform, like a ballistic missile with multiple warheads. I eye the window anxiously, as if my hopes can keep the vehicle aligned. It launches without a hitch.

"We'll see if reentry goes that smoothly," Shepard observes.

"Entry," I correct him. "They've never been here before."

After that, we eject both of the floaters. Again I'm keeping a watchful eye, intent that it will all go well. And at last it's time for the orbiter: again, the same script, indicators and confirmation, countdown and launch and separation. It sails smoothly into infinity.

"Explorer, Houston." Ground cuts in again. "We're..." A burst of static obliterates the next few words. "...firing off the probes. Over."

A momentary spasm of alarm seizes me: not panic, but deep concern. We haven't done our separation maneuver, and if they're saying they're about to ignite the solid rocket motors, maybe the words are just catching up to us and they've already issued the command...and the landers are the largest probes, five hundred pounds apiece, and if that one tumbled wrong-end first...

In a rush, I float back up towards the command module. Shepard gives me a look.

"The maneuver," I remind him. "I'll just do it solo."

"Oh. Carry on."

Alone up there, I reactivate the thrusters. "Attitude is correct. Two feet per second. Ready to proceed," I say, for the benefit of Houston and my crewmates.

"Wait a sec up there," Shepard says, and I'm wondering what the hell he wants to wait for. Then: "Go ahead."

I pulse the thrusters and feel a slight nudge of the spacecraft, and a touch of relief to go with it. "Posigrade maneuver completed. Over."

"Retrograde, you mean," Shepard says sharply. "You did do retrograde, correct?"

Jesus. A spasm of doubt: did I just make it worse? I scan the instruments, just to make sure. Then: "Yes, I misspoke. Retrograde."

Again, Houston cuts in. "Explorer, Houston. Waiting on confirmation you've executed the separation maneuver. We'll start lighting 'em off twenty minutes after that. Over."

I exhale. Something stabs at me...shame? Obviously there's been a disconnect. I was worked up over nothing: they were, in fact, waiting for us. They'll get their confirmation in a couple minutes, but they also felt the need to remind us they were waiting for it, and giving us some extra time on top of that. And I know Shepard's going to say something when I get back down there, and I'm not looking forward to it...

My eyes wander up to the hatch. There is so much emptiness outside our little metal bubble. Many thoughts you cannot help but think: not constant, but nagging, possibilities rather than desires.

My mind floats back to a man I met at a bar once, a mad mathematician who claimed every decision created alternate universes, one for what was done, and one for the not-done, an infinity of alternate universes constantly multiplying. Maybe in another one...

I find myself wanting to get back to the others after all. Wanting to not be alone, at least.

I float back through the tunnel, careful and precise. Over and above anything else, I do not want to fuck anything up. My chest tightens...

I float upside-down back into the manned module. Shepard glares but doesn't say anything.

When it's time, we crowd around the window, bodies facing every which way. At first I'm waiting to see that one lander coming back towards us, proving me painfully right. Then I'm looking for anything at all, trying to spot the light of a rocket motor between us and bright distant Venus, or moving amidst the scattered static stars. Shepard eyes his watch, again and again, until it's clear we missed seeing anything.

"At least we didn't shoot ourselves in the face," Kerwin says.

Shepard smirks. "I almost wouldn't mind the excitement."

"I met this guy in a bar once who said every decision point created a parallel universe," I say. "Like soap bubbles dividing. He said everything that was physically possible from your past actually happened somewhere else."

Shepard gives me a look. "That sounds crazy."

"Well, obviously," I concede. "Another universe? For every decision ever made, anywhere? Still..." (When I stop talking, there is a silence, an emptiness. As always, I feel the need to keep trying to fill it.) "I guess the reason I bring it up is, sometimes after big decisions, I think about that guy. Like maybe it did happen the other way, too, for another version of me."

The others give me a look like I am, in fact, crazy.

•••

17 JUL 1972

Decision points. Branching universes? Is there another universe where I'm back home on Earth? Another one where I made the burn incorrectly? Where we botched the probe launch and fucked it all up? There are so many decisions you have to get right...

Ordinarily it feels like a waste of time to dwell on these things. But if there's anything we have too much of up here, it's time.

It's time to turn off my mind. I reach into the fireproof bag and pull out a worn paperback, a collection of science fiction stories from Ray Bradbury, other visions of other worlds, most of which have been proven to be nothing like the fantasies. It does make for a pleasant diversion, at least, another way to burn the days...

• • •

"Hello, Explorer. It is July 18th, 1972, and here is the news from Earth."

We've finished eating, and again we gather around, going through the comfortable motions.

"Heavy fighting continues in South Vietnam between units of the Republic of Vietnam and North Vietnamese Army regulars. The State Department is calling the latest fighting a clear violation of the cease-fire agreements, but there are still no indications as to what further action the United States is willing to take."

Shepard shakes his head in disgust.

"In Northern Ireland, four people were shot amid ongoing clashes between Catholics and Protestants in Belfast. And in New York, police say the victim of a shooting late Sunday night was Thomas Eboli, head of the Genovese crime family..."

"Some planet we've left behind," I mutter, as the capcom moves on to sports.

•••

Meanwhile, Venus grows ever closer.

We've caught glimpses of it here and there over the past few days, but I'm curious how much larger it will appear now. I do want to be impressed by it at some point. Even unseen, its influence is ever more evident, not just in our changed workday schedule, but in the simple physical trajectory of our bodies through three-dimensional space. Its gravity is pulling us faster by the day, faster by the hour.

After lunch we have a photography session scheduled; it's time to get a better look at the object of our voyage. Kerwin plugs the commands into the manned module's computer, and the control moment gyros do their work. We'd put the spacecraft stack back in its normal attitude after the probe launches, and now once more we can see the stars moving across our field of view as we turn.

"There we go," Shepard says.

"Houston, Explorer," I transmit. "We are beginning the initial Venus photography time block." Like most of our transmissions now, this is more for informational purposes than anything; we're letting them know, not seeking their approval. "Rotating the ship into position."

"Ship?" Shepard grins.

I turn off the voice activation. "Fuck, you've got me calling it that, too. Spacecraft."

I ready the Hasselblad. A shot of sunlight hits me in the face as the window comes around; it's hard to tell in the glare, but the sun does seem noticeably different, maybe a third larger than it appears from Earth, and a notch brighter. And then there's Venus. It looks like a marble, distant still, with a crescent edge visible in the sunlight. Or less than a marble: a bright droplet of milk.

"I can't believe we came all this way for that." Shepard says.

There is not much to it, really. Much of it's still in shadow thanks to the angle of our approach. But even the sunlit part's pretty bland. Here and there, you get the barest suggestion of what might be streaks within the clouds, long wispy cirrus streaks. And that's it.

"We're still almost a million and a half miles away," Kerwin observes. "And it is getting a little bigger."

"Yeah. At least we know we're heading in the right direction." I float over to the other side of the window to get out of the sun; from here I can see Venus a little more clearly. It is interesting to actually see it as a three-dimensional object; it's maybe a quarter the size of the sun, relatively speaking, and I'm starting to appreciate it more. I start snapping pictures like a fevered man, like there's a running tally of all the pictures taken *of* me versus all the pictures taken *by* me, and I'm trying to balance it out.

"I like it," Kerwin replies.

"You like it?"

"Sure. Kind of a...hazy little mystery. A probability cloud. Nothing's for certain. Very...feminine."

"Ha," Shepard says. "So Mars *is* the masculine planet, then."

"Well, that's what the symbols say. A shield over a spear, versus a hand mirror."

"She's not a very good mirror," Shepard points out. "You can't see anything."

"Maybe you see yourself." Kerwin replies.

I wonder: Who wants that?

"And as far as the clouds go, yeah, Venus is opaque. With Mars, what you see is what you get."

Is that a masculine trait? I find myself wondering. One could argue the point.

Shepard, meanwhile, totally buys it. "I guess it does fit, doesn't it? She's keeping it all hidden. 'Venus, what's wrong?' 'Oh...nothing.' Meanwhile she's...hot enough to boil lead."

I dig out a zoom lens for the Hasselblad, hoping to get some more detail in the pictures. "I kinda wish there was a moon."

"No way she'd have a moon," Shepard replies. "She's a modern woman! Liberated. Independent. Unattached."

"Lonely," I chip in.

"A spinster?" Kerwin asks.

"Except she's not spinning all that much." Which is true: based on radar observations we took earlier in the day, we're estimating her rotation's terribly slow; her day's almost half as long as her year. "She might be depressed."

"I'm sure the probes'll tell us more," Shepard says.

"She might not like all this probing," Kerwin points out.

"She does look like a virgin."

Kerwin laughs. "Yeah. Very pristine. She's a good girl! Saving herself for marriage."

"Or just…waiting feverishly for some action," Shepard grins. "Sure, she looks respectable, but under the covers, she's hot and bothered."

"I thought you said she was a liberated woman!" Kerwin chuckles.

"Liberated women need action, too! More than the attached ones. And she's been missing out. Jesus, no wonder she's depressed."

I've been snapping away with the zoom lens, picture after picture, trying to carve the scene into interesting slices: the terminator dividing Venus night from day, the faintly visible cloud streaks, the sunward edge of the atmosphere.

"Jesus Christ, Buzz!" Shepard looks at me like I've gone a little nuts. "How many pictures are you gonna take?"

I say nothing.

Before returning to our normal attitude, we rotate back to face Earth. We are at last far enough away that it's just a bright point of light in the firmament. But even at this distance, it looks different from the others. Different, too, than Venus from Earth. For one, the moon is evident, a distinct pinprick of light right next to it. But also it's blueish. Special.

I steady the long lens in the window. I suspect it's hopeless, a task better suited to the telescope. I snap a couple desperate pictures, then lower the camera.

•••

I've made it a point to exercise well during our outbound voyage. The others have, too, but I have an extra incentive: I'm worried they'll find some last-minute excuse to give the spacewalk to Shepard. (I'm not worried about Kerwin; they gave him a non-EVA-capable suit, so he pretty much has to stay inside. But Shepard is my backup, and he is the type of person to hold you back if he has a chance to get ahead.)

Two days before the flyby, there's time for one more session with the spring contraption. They've radioed up a modification to our schedule, though: they want Kerwin to give me a checkout before and during the workout. We've already done one this week. So this could be it: an opportunity for them to come up with a medical excuse to keep me inside. Still, what choice do I have? I submit to the stethoscope and the inflatable arm cuff device.

"Resting heart rate...60," Kerwin floats next to me, fingers on my carotid. "And we'll do blood pressure..."

"What the hell is this thing called again? I can never remember." I ask as he puts the cuff around my arm and pumps it up.

"Just a sec." He puts on his stethoscope and lets the air out and listens. "122 over 85. This? The sphygmomanometer?"

"Sphyg-mo-man-o-met-er. That always sounds like too many syllabalales."

Kerwin doesn't quite laugh, which is cause for concern. "Sphygmos. Greek for 'pulse.' And of course, a manometer is a pressure gauge. It is a lot of 'm's," he concedes. "We covered this in training."

"I heard it once and forgot. I didn't want to ask again."

Now he chuckles a little, at least. "All the flight physicals you've done, you've only heard it once?"

"I'm like any other pilot at the doctor's. Get in, get out, say as little as possible, and pray they don't ground you."

Kerwin chuckles again.

"I guess I should pay more attention," I continue. "'Know your enemy,' huh?"

"Hmmmph." He takes a look in my ears.

"Everything OK?"

"Yeah, I think so." He gives me another look; I'm not sure what it means. "Quite the beard you've got now."

"Oh...yeah." I stroke my whiskered chin. "I figured it'd be a fun project for the outward voyage. Explorers have beards, right?"

"You're gonna shave it before Sunday?" Meaning before the EVA.

"Of course." I know I should take my advice and not say too much, but the silence and the sense of judgment are killing me. "They give a reason for this extra physical?"

"Oh, you know," he says. "The usual."

"Nothing about anything we're doing is usual, Joe."

"Well, exactly. They just want an extra validation. Some warm fuzzy feelings before they send you out into the cold. Obviously nobody's ever been up here this long. The physiological changes we're going through, nobody's done this before. And the psychological..."

"Psychological?" I'm worried about what they were thinking when Shepard and I had the little to-do about the retrograde burn. I've been feeling a little...off. I was wondering if they'd noticed, and apparently they have. Still, it's surprising to hear these things out loud.

"It's...well, nobody's able to work at 110% for four months straight. But they want to make sure everyone's staying fit, staying motivated..."

For a few seconds I say nothing. Then: "When we were heading to the moon, there were people who thought we were in danger, that the moon dust would be combustible. Like how they have explosions in grain silos, particles in the air and what-not. So after we got back in the lander, I put a little handful of moon dust out in the open, just to humor them, to see if it...caught fire or something when we repressurized. And sure enough, nothing. No smoke, no fire. But that's the thing. The naysayers are always looking for reasons why something won't work. Planning disasters in their head, waiting to say 'I told you so.'"

"So what are you saying?"

"Well, it seems like they're being...overly fussy."

He sighs. "I'm just the doctor, Buzz."

I work out for a good twenty minutes, doing butterfly arm spreads, leg extensions with my foot in the spring strap, and mountain climbers with a waist harness to hold me close to the floor. Maybe it's the conversation beforehand, the implied insult of the extra scrutiny, but my blood's up and I push myself hard.

Near the end, I feel a little off: heart pounding, vision dimming, a very slight sense of something that might be called dizziness. I don't particularly want to mention it.

But I think Kerwin's noticed. "You all right, Buzz?"

"Yeah. Fine." I pant the words.

"You look a little..." He puts fingers on my neck, counts. "Huh. Pulse is really up there. That was about 190."

"Huh." I take a deep breath.

"Let's have a listen." He puts stethoscope to chest.

"Everything's." Breath. "O.K." This is perplexing: I pride myself on my fitness; I was quite the gymnast at the Academy, and I've kept it up far more than most men my age.

He gives me a look. "Are you?" he asks, like he doesn't believe my answer's correct, and he's giving me a chance to fix it.

"Yeah." I breathe deeply. "I am." I feel normal again. Or my normal, at least.

He smiles: a partial, incredulous smile. "I'm not the enemy, Buzz."

It's Shepard's turn to prepare dinner, so I have a little time off. I spend it in the bathroom area, hacking away at my beard: first with scissors and the vacuum hose, trying to catch all the stray cuttings before they float off, and then with my razor, which I haven't used in months. At the end of it all, I'm late for dinner, and my face is speckled with blood.

"Jesus, Buzz, you look like a lunatic," Shepard says when I finally float in.

"Jesus Christ," I shake my head. I've been trying to bite my tongue and keep my frustrations in check, but enough's enough. "What the fuck is wrong with you?"

"You all right?" Kerwin asks again.

"It's...it's always the same with this guy." I force a smile. "He's always gotta take you down a notch, for no reason whatsoever. It's like the laws of thermodynamics. You can't win, you can't break even."

And now I feel I've said too much; I wonder if this little outburst will, at last, give them an excuse to keep me inside. It felt good to get it off my chest, but I can't say it was worth it. Maybe there's another universe with a version of me that hasn't fucked anything up.

We settle in to a stiff silence.

As we're finishing up, the radio cuts in. "Explorer, Houston. You should be just about done eating. Standing by for your daily report."

Shepard says: "Would you two mind heading downstairs for a bit?"

It's the absolute last thing I want to hear. I float down there, heart heavy, like a man heading to the gallows. Kerwin follows close behind. We don't say anything.

I root around in my sleeping area as if I've got tidying up to do. My mind's on the conversation upstairs, working as hard as my body did earlier; I can't hear anything, but I'm spinning through probability matrixes, all the permutations and combinations of phrases, forecasting horrible things.

Then the curtain opens. Shepard's face fills the hatchway: "Joe, I need you up here for a minute."

And with that I'm alone, imagining.

Distractedly I root around for my Bible, but I'm not feeling it, so I pull out the Bradbury collection. I start reading, or scanning my eyes over the pages at least: none of it's sinking in. I force myself to concentrate. The next story, "All Summer in a Day," opens with a group of schoolchildren on Venus. On this version of the planet, they endure relentless and non-stop rain, except for a one-hour break in the weather every seven years. Most of the kids can't remember seeing the sun, but there's one girl who's a more recent arrival, who grew up in Ohio before moving to the new planet. And they lock her in the closet right before the break in the weather; they lock her in, and she misses her chance to go outside...

When the curtain opens again, I wait for Shepard to summon me and give me the bad news. I wait, but he says nothing.

• • •

The next day, the last before the flyby, everything proceeds normally.

It's a little unsettling.

It's so easy to imagine them replacing me that I feel the need to bring it up obliquely.

"You know, come to think of it, I might have been a touch dehydrated yesterday," I tell Kerwin.

And he smiles: "That's what I thought, too. We'll stay on top of it during the EVA, it should be fine. Maybe swap out the drink bags, give you a larger one."

So it seems like I'm still on, but I find myself wondering if Shepard will have something else to say. And soon we're in the command module, working ourselves into our spacesuits. It's a dress rehearsal for the getting-dressed part of our upcoming one-day-only extravaganza.

I'm anxious to do well, and I analyze every action, making a point to do everything very deliberately and not make any stupid mistakes. On the descent to the moon, we had to wear a fecal containment garment, basically a grown-up diaper. I'd already made it through my three-day Gemini mission without having a bowel movement, so I knew that 30 hours on Apollo were doable as well; I made it a point not to take a dump on the moon. Here I'll only be outside for an hour, so I've considered going without it...then again, the consequences of error would be substantial. So I put it on, and then the liquid cooling garment: a coverall interwoven with water tubing to keep us from overheating while working, something that had been an issue for Gene Cernan on Gemini. Then, my spacesuit itself: a single-piece white monstrosity, headless and handless, that you have to enter through the back. And at last, the black-and-white snoopy cap headset.

We take turns: Kerwin, then Shepard, then myself. They have to go through the whole rigamarole too, of course, because the entire command module will be vented into space before we open the hatch. (Shepard will at least get his head and shoulders out and get a look around, but Kerwin has to endure the hassle without even a change of scenery.) The whole process has been carefully choreographed so as to keep the chaos to a minimum: we unstow everything in the proper sequence so we can either put it on immediately, or easily reach it later. But we're out of practice, and it takes the better part of a half hour.

"Houston, Explorer," Shepard transmits at last. "We're all suited up and ready to start connecting the rest of the hoses. No major hiccups. Switching to VOX to test the individual comm loops." He turns a switch on the panel. "Commander testing now. Here we are." He nods to me.

"CMP, testing one, two, three," I say, then look at Joe.

"Science Pilot here. Testing. Give us a reading when you get this. Over."

While we wait for their answer, we proceed with the remainder of the hose connectors. For Shepard and me, there's one with water that feeds the garment, and another for the oxygen/nitrogen mix. Shepard's and Kerwin's hoses connect directly to the environmental control system, while mine feed through a connector plate on my abdomen and into an umbilical cord on my left hip.

At last the ground gives their feedback on the voice test. "Explorer, Houston, we copy your com loop check. Try turning the sensitivity up a notch. Over."

Shepard stops connecting hoses and reaches up to the panel. One by one, we speak into the microphones, then get back to the checklist. Once the hoses are connected, each one needs to be locked into place so they won't come out and start spraying air into space; I do everything cautiously and double-check every connector.

"Pressure alarm. Repress valve is off," Shepard says; we need to turn off the flow of air until we have our gloves and helmets on.

"Explorer, Houston. We copy your second com loop check." Again we have to go back to where the ground was three-and-a-half minutes ago, which is where we were three-and-a-half minutes before *that*. It's like chasing your tail, but through time rather than space. "You guys are all five by five. Over."

"Houston, Explorer, we copy five by five on the comms. We are finishing with the hose connectors. Repress valve is off."

"Let me see about the umbilical," Joe says. Something happens below my field of vision, and the cord starts filling the space in front of me: a sterile white snake, unwieldy and chaotic.

"Whoops," Shepard says.

"Yeah, I may want to do this differently tomorrow," Kerwin says.

"Yeah, it's definitely in the way, this way," I reply, trying to gather the umbilical in my arms and pass it down to him.

"Maybe if I float kinda crossways, down by your feet. I can kinda keep it under control and feed it up."

"Yeah, let's do that," Shepard adds. "And I'll just stay up here, watching it at the hatch."

"OK," Kerwin says from down by my feet; bit by bit he's getting the cord under control. "How's that?"

Now I have a much clearer view of the control panel. "Wonderful."

"All connectors locked," Shepard says.

"Connectors locked," we echo.

Next, helmets, then gloves. There are neck locks and wrist locks on those, too, to keep them from shooting off once the suit's pressurized.

"Suit circuit return valve to closed," Shepard says.

"Yes, sir, turn it to closed," I reply. "Direct O2/N2 closed?"

"Direct O2/N2 is closed. I'm going to open up the equalization valve a little."

Now that we're all suited up, we are bleeding off a little cabin pressure. This way, when we do our integrity checks; we can make sure the suits are staying pressurized at a higher level, so we'll know there are no leaks anywhere.

"Flow is normal, suit pressure is fine," I say. "Moving on to suit circuit integrity check. Suit test valve to PRESS."

"OK, it's there," Shepard says after turning the control.

"All right. Direct O2/N2 flow is OPEN." I announce. "Suits are going to start pressurizing now."

"It's dropping a little. 0.2 delta-p," Shepard says.

"Yes, it will," I say, eager to show them I know. "They regulate to about 4.5 psi."

"Yeah, that's right. I should bleed off more from the cabin, then," Shepard says. "We'll drop it to about 4 psi." The suit pressure stays where it's supposed to be, and everything is looking good.

I take a few deep breaths. It's been a stressful couple of days. But I've been a good team player, and they don't have cause to keep me inside tomorrow.

"Explorer, Houston. Everything is looking good from our end. You've probably moved on to the suit integrity check now, so please give a status when that's done. Over."

"Houston, Explorer, we are good on the suit checks. O2/N2 flow is normal, pressure is steady," Shepard says, and I know they're going to respond with a GO when it's all said and done.

In the meantime, we read through our lines for tomorrow, the sequence of events for the spacewalk itself. We practiced it all back in the pool before the mission started, floating in neutral buoyancy alongside submerged mockups of the spacecraft, but that was months ago now. We need to refresh our memory, and mission control needs to pass along a few last-minute changes.

But it is all happening, at least. And that is a relief.

I glance above our heads, at the window in the center of the hatch, and the emptiness beyond.

• • •

We set up the telescope for automatic operation, so it can take pictures of Venus throughout our approach, storing up the film I'll be retrieving during the spacewalk. Then comes a late, tired dinner. And at last I'm up on the manned module main deck, alone for my last communications window before the big day.

But the time rolls around, and past, and: nothing.

"Houston, Explorer, CMP standing by for personal communications window. Over." I try to sound as nonchalant as possible, even though this is a big deal. Joan knows we're coming up on the high point of the mission, and if she's going to do this again, on this, of all days...

I watch my watch, and wish: hopefully it's nothing. It could be a simple comms issue, or a matter of timing: maybe they assembled a couple minutes late, but they're talking now, telling me all their happy little mundane news; their words are already in transit, and just about to get here.

But I hear nothing. And nothing. And nothing.

I grab a washcloth and putter around the module, cleaning things I've already cleaned. I try not to check my watch again. Passivity is not in my nature.

Still, I don't hear anything until seven minutes after my message, which means, of course, that everything *isn't* set, and they're just trying to tide me over. "Explorer, Houston, your kids are on their way and should be in shortly. We're estimating another five to ten minutes. Over."

My kids? No Joan? I'm perplexed. Maybe I shouldn't be: this is it, this is the way things have been going.

Then as I float past the hallway entrance, I glance over beneath the pantry cabinets and see a smudge of something white. It seems to be leaking out from inside. Is it...food?

My mind accelerates until suddenly the issue with Joan has been left far, far behind. We have enough meal packages for the mission, plus a few days: very little extra. Given the mass constraints on the manned module, everything has been calculated precisely, our trajectory and our caloric needs, with enough margin of error to be comfortable, but not sloppy. We have no refrigerator; everything's been freeze-dried or irradiated so as to be fine at room temperature for a year without spoiling. And the packets are stacked with metal dividers every ten meals or so; they're attached to the magazine spring mechanism so as to keep the meals separated, so they won't press against each other and rupture. But if something mechanical happened to the magazine, or if we've screwed up our temperature control regime for the spacecraft, or if there's a heating or a cooling leak down there, or if there was some defective sealing machine at the factory and the packets *are* all bursting somehow...

I imagine a mess of food down in the bowels of the pantry magazines, exploded food packets spoiling in the open air after exposure to whatever germs or microbes we're carrying with us. Maybe the air *has* been smelling different, and maybe this is why. How will it play out? Like some bad shipwreck movie, maybe, one of those ones where there are four or five people adrift on a lifeboat on the high seas with two chocolate bars and a jug of water and they have to eat one little square and drink a capful of water every day, so they start fishing and trying to gather rainwater...but of course for us this isn't the sea, it's emptiness...

There is no point panicking. I know this. I'm aware of all the possibilities. We all are. Being brave doesn't mean being unaware of danger, it means facing danger, which I'm doing, and taking action, which I'm not doing yet. And you need information to take action: speculation won't do.

I am waiting for the radio to come back on. Waiting for a distraction from all of this. And yet I also wish it *wasn't* communications time; I wish I had time to really investigate this. We need to do an inspection, figure out whether this is really happening...

"Explorer, Houston, everyone's assembled here at last, and you're all set." A cheerful voice, distant and oblivious, jarringly disconnected from my problems. "We're handing off the mike to...well, Mike."

I cock my head towards the radio, but I can't give it all my attention, not right now; I'm floating down towards the floor to inspect the smear of food...and it *is* food, mashed potatoes, and as I open the pantry door, I can see that it *is* coming from a burst packet, one I can just barely see at the bottom of the stack that's pushing up through the pantry magazine...

"Hey, Dad. I'm sorry we're late. I know how important it is to be on time for these windows. Mom is really sorry, too. She had a play rehearsal, and she had a flat tire heading home, so she had to walk to the gas station and use their pay phone to get ahold of me..."

"I..." I want to interject, but of course it's pointless; I bite my tongue and listen. Or try to listen: I imagine us inventorying the remainder of the food and rationing it carefully, realizing that we have enough food for one or two of us but not all three, but still of course trying to keep all three of us alive, wasting away for the next eight months, starving slowly, or drawing straws to decide...

"...over." I've missed the last of whatever Mike was saying; I'm wondering if I should tell them to postpone the rest of the conversation while I sort this out. But no, I don't want them to get everyone all worked up...

"Houston, Explorer. It's...uhh..." (I realize I sound distracted, unenthused.) "...it's great to hear from you guys! Mike, it's still hard for me to believe you're driving everyone now. I trust you're driving responsibly...setting a good example; it won't be long before your brother and your sister are behind the wheel..."

I'm thinking about how we're going to inventory the food: should we unload the magazine from the top? That would take a while. Then again, maybe there's a way to remove the panels from the hallway floor, a simple screw removal, although the screwdriver is in the tool kit in the equipment bay of the command module...

I talk distractedly with the kids, asking about reporters; I am a little curious to see if there's anyone staking out the house yet. But mostly I'm just waiting for the conversation to be over so I can let Shepard know what's going on. And as soon as I'm done talking, I stick my head down there and summon him.

"A burst food packet?" He looks up at me perplexedly through the hatchway.

"There could be a lot more. It's at the bottom of the stack, we don't even know what's going on beneath it."

"I'm sure it's fine. There's dividers in there, everything was fine on the test mission..."

I cut him off. "That was three months. We've been up here four. We need to pull up the panels, take a look down there. Maybe do an inventory."

"Jesus, Buzz."

"I know it's not something we *want* to do tonight, but..."

"No, it's not." His gaze freezes over. "We do not have time for this. Flyby is tomorrow. If there *is* a problem, it'll still be here after that."

He turns away, and I close the curtain to the sleeping chamber. According to my watch, my words are still racing to Earth, an invisible smattering of radio waves struggling through the darkness. So I've got a few minutes. I float up to the command module to try and find the toolkit, at least...

• • •

"Explorer, Houston! Good morning from planet Earth. It is Saturday, July 22rd, 1972, the day of the great Venus flyby, and here's the news from back home." Crippen's capcom again; his voice is smooth and comfortable and familiar. "Fighting is intensifying in the central highlands of South Vietnam between Republic of Vietnam forces and regular units of the North Vietnamese Army. The Johnson Administration is reportedly weighing a request from the South Vietnamese government for military assistance in beating back the attacks. Meanwhile, the North is threatening a full-scale offensive should the United States re-enter the war."

"Protests erupted in major American cities yesterday, inspired by rumors of renewed American involvement. In Washington, D.C, hundreds of thousands gathered on the Mall, while in Chicago, protestors clashed with police in scenes reminiscent of the 1968 Democratic convention."

"California Governor Ronald Reagan, the presumptive Republican nominee, strongly criticized the Johnson Administration's handling of the war, saying the withdrawal of U.S. forces during the peace process has effectively given the communists a free hand in Southeast Asia. Reagan said it is time for new and strong leadership, but did not say whether he favored reintroduction of U.S. ground forces should the fighting continue."

"A series of bombs ripped across Belfast yesterday, killing nine people and injuring over a hundred others. As many as twenty devices went off in the space of eighty minutes, plunging the city center into what one observer described as 'total chaos.' British authorities say the devices..." (Crackle.) "...r to have been planted by the Irish Republican Army in response to the breakdown of peace talks. July is now shaping up to be the most violent month in Northern Ireland since the current round of troubles began three years ago."

"And the crew of the Inner Solar System Exploration Mission is nearing the planet Venus after a four-month voyage, with a flyby and spacewalk scheduled for today and tomorrow." Crippen pauses, then deadpans. "Son of a gun. How about that."

"Glad to see we made the papers, at least," I observe, as Crippen rattles off the baseball scores.

Kerwin and I float up through the tunnel and into the command module so we can start the morning's checklist. The cameras attached to the telescope have been clicking away all night in automatic mode; we have to activate the additional flyby instrumentation in the equipment bay on the side of the service module, the mapping radar and the infrared cameras.

"Instrumentation panel, pushing Circuit Breaker 6, 7, 8 and 9," I read.

"Here we go. 6, 7, 8, 9," Kerwin replies.

The flyby itself won't be until the late evening, but given the tight timeline and the speed of our approach, we are eager to confirm everything's up and running. Also, at this point in our trajectory, we are still able to make observations on the dark side of the terminator.

"Indicators are all gray," Kerwin calls out.

"And we are transmitting data," I add.

When I float back into the manned module, Shepard is hovering right there in the pantry hallway, looking at the floor plates and scowling. He's topsy-turvy relative to me, of course.

"Hey, we've finally turned that frown upside-down," I joke.

"What happened to this panel?" he asks, poking near the base of the pantry stacks.

I don't say anything.

"Did you crack open the floor panel last night, Buzz?"

There's no point avoiding this. And none of us got to where we were by being dishonest in uncomfortable situations. So: "Yep."

He glares. "What did I say last night?"

"We don't have time for this right now. It's almost time for the flyby. If there is a problem, it'll still be there tomorrow."

I'm quoting him; there's a vague part of me that suspects this isn't the wisest or most professional thing to do.

Sure enough, he looks about as mad as I've seen him. His jaw clenches, and at last he says: "We do not have time for this right now."

"Great! I agree completely." I try to float past, to get back to the work. When he doesn't budge, I explain: "You said we don't have time for an inventory. So I didn't do an inventory. I pulled up the panel to take a look. I couldn't see too much."

Again he glares.

"Look, I..." I stop. There's obviously no point explaining this to him. "We don't have time for this now. We'll talk about it later."

"We most certainly will," he says.

Kerwin and I take up positions by the telescope console. "All right, let's focus here," he says with a little grin.

"Yes, focus," I echo. "Focus focus focus."

But first I look out the window, and I get chills. Venus is right there, 250,000 miles away but closing fast, as big as the Earth from the moon; it's taking up more than two degrees of sky now, very bright on the sunward side, close enough I can see at last that it is not pure white, more like a stained cue ball, with faint smudges stretching as far as we can see. And whatever issues I've had with the mission, no one has ever seen this like this, not in all of human history, and that at least counts for something.

"Switching to VOX," I say: time for the play-by-play. Then: "Houston, Explorer, we are beginning today's visual observations. From what we see of the sunward side, the planet is completely covered in cirrus clouds, with no breaks whatsoever. There's very little differentiation visible; the color ranges from a pure white to a tan off-white, almost like a coffee stain. There are a couple cloud bands parallel to the Equator that appear to encircle the planet completely. There's a whitish one near the planet's north pole, and a whiter one close to the south pole. That band of clouds is between about 60 and 65 degrees of latitude, and it stretches from the terminator all the way around the sunward side. And..." (I find myself at a loss for words; what else is there to say about it?) "...we're going to take some pictures with the Hasselblad."

We are moving fast now, almost three-and-a-half miles per second relative to Venus. But it doesn't feel like we're zooming towards it; it's more like watching the minute hand on your watch, how you only really notice the change when you look away. I raise the camera and snap a few shots.

"That should be good for now," Shepard says, even though I've barely started. "We're gonna go ahead and rotate the spacecraft to begin telescopic observations." Before either of us can agree, he punches commands into the computer, and Venus moves back out of sight.

"All right, then." I put the lens cap on and place the camera in the air over our heads.

"All right," Kerwin announces. "I have coordinates. Steering the telescope onto the terminator." As he moves the controller, we can see the picture changing on the console

TV monitors. "Picking up some cloud details through the telescope. It's hard to see much."

"Should we try the spectroheliograph? Might be better detail."

"Worth a shot." He turns the dial on the console, then throws the switches to change the TV inputs. The streaks in the clouds now look darker, more pronounced. "There we go. Much better in UV. Near the poles, the cloud streaks seem more or less continuous, and it looks like they are going around the entire circumference. I count maybe...seven or eight streaks between the south pole and, oh, we'll say 45 degrees latitude..."

I do the math. A circumference of 37,000 miles gives you about 103 miles per degree of latitude, and eight streaks in 45 degrees comes out to 5.65 degrees per streak, which means each streak is over 500 miles wide...

"That's gotta be pretty heavy winds at altitude, to make those patterns," Kerwin observes.

"Say goodbye to your floating cities," Shepard smirks.

I give him a look. "Let's wait and see what the probes have to say, at least."

• • •

Meanwhile the probes have been ranging on ahead of us. I've been tracking them on the VHF, listening to the lonely metallic beeps as the dropsondes peeled off from their delivery vehicle and began their staggered deployment sequence. Thanks to the solid rockets, the first one's now more than 100,000 miles ahead of us, and by the time we're done with lunch, it's getting ready to enter the Venusian atmosphere; per the mission plan, we have set up our S-Band to retransmit their data back to Earth. We don't have the means to decipher it ourselves, so we're stuck listening to Crippen narrating it all after the fact.

"Terminator probe...seeing some heavy deceleration." As he starts his delayed play-by-play, we divide our attention, ears perked up for the distant voices in our headsets as we continue our telescope observations. "9 gs. Communications blackout." I imagine the heat shield ablating in the flame of the alien atmosphere, ionized gasses blocking transmission. We continue to work. Then, a couple minutes later: "And we're back. 2 gs. Still slowing." And finally: "1 g. And we have parachute deployment. Everything holding steady. We're calling it a clean deployment."

"All right." I exhale. It's only one of six, but still, that's something. The others nod a little.

(Crackle.) "...re getting good telemetry. Estimating 2 degrees south Venusian latitude. Altitude a little over 92,000 feet."

"How about that," Shepard says.

We get back to work, observing the coffee-colored cirrus streaks of the high-altitude clouds, trying to cobble together a picture of the Venusian weather patterns. The floaters will tell us more, but I'm starting to realize just how windy it is down there.

Crippen's distant play-by-play cuts back in. "Atmospheric pressure 1.25 atmospheres. Temperature 175 degrees Fahrenheit and rising."

"Little balmy," Kerwin says.

"No kidding." I glance at the telescope screen. What it would be like in a floating city? Thick and hot. A desert city above the clouds where you'd need a mask just to go outside and feel the sun on your skin. A scuba dive in the sky, but unpleasantly warm. Would you bother having streets? Maybe balloons full of air with habitation modules beneath, and tunnels linking all the modules. But of course, if the wind speeds are too high, you couldn't hold together something that big; a little turbulence would tear it to shreds...

As if he's reading my mind, Crippen comes back on. "Wind speeds...based on the data, they're saying close to 200 miles per hour. 2 atmospheres now. 240 degrees Fahrenheit."

"Ouch."

Shepard chimes in: "That's, what? Tornado speeds."

"Severe tornado, extremely severe hurricane," Kerwin says. "Across the whole planet, I'd bet."

I don't want to say it out loud, but Shepard was right: no floating cities. A single balloon with a module might be a possibility. With a small enough structure, you could float along with the winds and they wouldn't be as noticeable...

"4.8 atmospheres, temperature 300 degrees."

Then again, you'd need something to power your instruments if you were staying up there for any length of time. Solar panels wouldn't work with winds like that; you'd also be at risk of drifting onto the nightward side of the planet, getting stuck in the doldrums like some eighteenth century frigate...you'd have to try to use radiothermal generators, like on the floaters...but you'd still have to get back up into orbit at some point...

"335 degrees, 5.6 atmospheres."

"And we're still pretty high up, right?" Kerwin asks.

(Crackle.) "...8 atmospheres now and 394 degrees."

"Yeah," I answer.

"9.4 atmospheres, 480 degrees. And we've lost signal. Altitude just below 60,000 feet. They are printing out and analyzing the atmospheric composition data. We should have some numbers for you shortly."

"Houston, Explorer, we copy. If it's like that at altitude, I hate to think what it's like on the surface," Shepard calls.

A couple minutes later, Crippen's back. "And we have some composition numbers for you: CO_2, 96.4%. N_2, 3.5%. Just over a hundredth of a percent of sulfur dioxide, possibly sulfuric acid, even less water vapor."

"Not much hydrogen," Kerwin observes, with a nod towards the radio.

I float around to face him. "What do you mean?"

"All that talk of terraforming, you'd need enough water for photosynthesis. You've got plenty of CO2, but if the water's that limited..." Kerwin trails off in a way that seems to say: it's hopeless. "We are looking at a very hot and dry and nasty planet."

It is depressing. Whatever notions we've entertained about our nearest neighbor now seem like foolish fantasies. We work on. I do not feel quite as energetic as I had in the morning. It's something else that keeps us going now: duty, rather than hope.

Over the course of the afternoon, the other probes follow in succession: a dark side one halfway between the terminator and the antisolar point, another on the light side, yet another at the antisolar point, one more at the subsolar, and one near the north pole. The temperature readings are remarkably consistent, even on the dark side. And everywhere, high winds.

"That was a fantastic delivery job, guys," Crippen says when they're all in. "This is a remarkable day for planetary science."

"And we can stop looking around for a landing site," I joke, and there is silence. I've been so caught up in the communal feeling of shared work that I've momentarily forgotten how far away they are.

By the time the lander deployments are starting, we've finished telescope observations, and rotated back to look at Venus through the main window. I take a few pictures but then stop. What's the point? I don't know what I'm feeling about this planet. Not longing, but maybe something else.

What could it be, if it could be something different? But it isn't, and it can't be. We know that no one will ever go.

"Hell of a scene," Shepard says at last.

"It is hell, maybe," Kerwin observes.

"The moon looked uninviting." I reply. "This looks...innocuous. But it's worse. Back there, you knew you could go everywhere. You can't go anywhere here."

"Explorer, Houston. Landers are entering the atmosphere," Crippen cuts in.

"Houston, Explorer. We copy. Looking forward to seeing some pictures from the surface," I say; the landers are probably my favorite probes, little mechanical tourists that are going where we can't, and taking pictures to show us what we're missing.

"Maybe it's for the best," Kerwin says. "You figure any kind of thick atmosphere, how would you be able to land and return?"

"How do you figure?"

"Well, it took all we had to land on the moon," he goes on. "All the weight they could shave off the LM, all the engineering they could manage, just to land on an airless place with one sixth the Earth's gravity. And since Venus is almost Earth's size, *and* it has an atmosphere, you'd practically need to land a Saturn V on the planet to get back home."

"We'd figure something out eventually." I do still want it to be true. "Balloons to get you off the surface, then launch from altitude. Or make it a one-way trip. Just drop in with everything you need. And Earth could send a supply drop every year or so."

"Jesus, Buzz. Now that would be a lonely life," Shepard concludes.

"Gentlemen, we've lost the landers." Crippen's voice is as flat as East Texas.

There is a pang in my chest, and we sing a chorus of damns and shits and fucks.

Crippen, meanwhile, is continuing, oblivious. "...malous wind readings suggesting chute failure, but the instruments started cutting out as well, somewhere above 30,000 feet for both."

"Houston, Explorer, we copy loss of the landers," Shepard says flatly. "Apologies if you caught some foul language. Hope you closed your ears before it got there."

It's quite a kick in the nuts. These would have been the first pictures from the surface of another planet. I try to put it out of my mind. We continue with the observations, determining wind direction at different latitudes, speculating about atmospheric thickness.

All the while, the planet looms larger and larger and larger.

We work with the anxious knowledge that it is all happening, Venus is rushing towards us; we see it full in glances out the window between bouts of science, a golf ball and a baseball before, and now a basketball, a beach ball, and we have only this one chance to get it all right, to justify our existence, all the millions spent to put us here for these few brief minutes.

And at last we get the call: "Explorer, Houston. Estimating periapsis in five minutes. Altitude: 660 miles. Velocity just shy of 15,000 miles per hour relative to the planet's surface, just over 40,000 miles per hour compared to us on planet Earth. Fastest men alive."

Kerwin doesn't say anything, but simply lifts his face from the eyepiece and floats over to the window. I take my eyes off the gauges and head over as well.

Outside, the planet's massive, an off-white wall of lightly-streaked clouds, so bright it's hard to really look at it, so close we can only see the horizons when we're pressed against the side of the cabin.

"Don't fog up the windows, guys," Shepard says as he joins us.

"Time to flat-hat the Venusians, huh?" Kerwin asks. "I don't think we'll see beaches or bikinis."

"You never know," Shepard smiles.

I'm about to say something, too, when I think better of it. What are words, compared to this? So I just float there, my forehead inches from the glass, from emptiness.

And here we are, arranged around the window as the planet stretches out beneath us. It's massive now, about 120 degrees of our entire field of view. We are fully over the sunward side, so we can no longer see the terminator, just pure brightness, and it hurts my eyes, like a snow-covered field when the sun's out and you've been inside all day. But despite the brightness we can see very slight bits of texture down there, some very small gradation between the darker streaks and the brighter areas. It doesn't look anything like when you're above the clouds on Earth, though; here the details are brownish, not silvery-gray; this enormous expanse of wispy cloudscape truly is an alien world. And for whatever issues I've had with my crewmates, I feel connected now, one with them, at peace in the face of this gigantic accomplishment. And I'd been afraid that it would be anticlimactic, but it is not that at all, it's something big and real and unique and amazing and inconceivable, and I'm feeling all of these things but also that sense that I need to remember it now, I need to burn this image into my retinas and etch it into my brain because it will never be there again, and the pictures won't be able to do it justice, the sheer massive scale of it all; they'll probably just look like solid white rectangles, and anyway, they always somehow fail to capture things that are this big. (You can't look at the pictures and feel exactly what you felt; you can only get echoes of the original feeling, fading with time. And more importantly, no one else can feel that same "Oh, wow!" They might say it anyway, but you know they can't feel it, because if they did, they wouldn't ask what it felt like, and you wouldn't need to find the words.)

Of course, none of us want to stay, but we want a few more minutes. Just a few more minutes, and the chance to leave at our leisure. But maybe it's better that we can't; maybe it's better to be left unsatisfied.

"Explorer, Houston, hope you guys have been getting a good look around. We're getting telemetry from the orbiter and floaters. The orbiter is in a stable orbit and we'll be starting its radar soon. In the meantime, we are all set up for downlink, so you can take care of the TV broadcast."

"Houston, Explorer, we copy you are ready for us to transmit."

"They're not going to be able to really see anything out the windows," I point out.

"Yeah, we might want to get the horizon in there, at least," Kerwin chimes in.

Shepard plugs in a few commands to rotate the spacecraft. Kerwin retrieves the camera, then takes position next to me, in front of the window. He looks a little surprised I'm up here.

"You got this?" he asks.

"Yeah."

Behind us, there's a white band of horizon, stark against the blackness. I can't imagine it'll look like much on TV. Shepard gives me the signal.

"Greetings, planet Earth! We're over 40 million miles away from you now, passing the planet Venus at over four miles per second. We can't stay and take our time observing it, unfortunately, so we have to cram in observations while we can. But we wanted to take a quick break from that so all of you could get a look at our nearest planetary neighbor." I feel the need to sell this planet, to convince people of its worth, even though I'm no longer convinced.

Shepard bobs weightlessly, the bore of the camera aimed at me like a gun.

"It's a harsh place, and we already know it has a fairly inhospitable environment, but perhaps your grandchildren or their grandchildren will be able to live there someday, either because we've terraformed the planet, or because we've built floating cities high in the atmosphere." And it hits me again how we now know this won't happen. Suddenly I feel self-conscious, like a used car salesman trying to sell something I wouldn't buy; I'm wishing I hadn't taken this mission, wishing I'd held out for Mars. "Uhh…Joe, did you have anything to say?"

This catches Kerwin off-guard. But he catches up quickly. "It isn't always easy to see the value in a place like Venus, a place we're not sure about. But it is in man's nature to explore, to see what's out there, to find out whether or not there's something better. And that's why we explore, because we don't know what we're going to find. Because we have questions and not answers. And it's better to know the answers than to spend a lifetime wondering."

Shepard puts the camera down. "Well done, Joe."

I look back at Venus, this coffee-stained ball now falling away from view, the shadowed side creeping our way again. We still haven't been able to touch it, not really. So it's a sad scene now, in a way: a massive empty world, a thick hot sulfuric acid atmosphere covering: what? Rock? Volcanoes? Craters? The orbiter and the floaters are still alive, and they'll tell us more, at least; there is still hope for some sort of single-celled life floating up there in the high atmosphere. But somehow now the overall reality of Venus is sinking in, in a way it never had before: it's a big hopeless void, a place that can never be home, with nothing manmade on the surface but the metal carcasses of a few dead machines.

•••

It's been a long and demanding day, but I cannot just turn off my mind. This is it; I've seen the greatest thing I'll see on the trip, and thanks to the godawful realities of orbital mechanics, I've seen it after less than four months of travel, with another eight to go before we get home.

"Early climax," I say as we finish up on the main deck. "I hate that."

"Look, Buzz, you should probably keep those problems between you and your wife," Shepard quips.

"It is odd," Kerwin says. "If this was a story, it'd break every rule of good storytelling. Rising action, a high point near the end...we're not even a third of the way through the trip."

"Maybe that's life," I reply. "All the excitement comes early, and then there's this...long dull slog for the last several decades."

"Jesus, Buzz," Shepard says, for what must be the millionth time. "Doctor Kerwin, for the sake of overall crew morale, I'm recommending that we keep him outside for the remainder of the voyage."

"All right, all right, I'll try to be less of a downer." I force a little brightness into my tone. "I guess it's not so bad. We can spend it in the hibernation chambers, right?"

"Hibernation chambers?"

"Yeah, Deke promised me we could put ourselves in suspended animation for the next eight months." I pause as if I really believe it. "Wait. That is the plan, right? Sleep for the rest of the mission?"

Kerwin laughs. "Sorry. They didn't get those installed in time. We're gonna have to tough it out. And hey, we've got the EVA tomorrow, Mercury observations after that, then the deep space stuff…"

It is true. There is at least more to do. There is always more to do.

"I am glad we're here," Kerwin continues. "It's better to know than to spend your life wondering."

"It is better to know," Shepard says. "It's like…when you see a hot woman from across the room. You can spend the rest of the night wondering what she's really like, or go talk to her. Sometimes it turns out she's…kinda plain."

This gets me smiling. "Yeah, Venus. She's hot, but she's not."

Shepard chuckles. "I prefer the phrase: 'Good from far, but far from good.'"

"And we're all married anyway," Kerwin muses, and that's the end of that.

I steal away to the bathroom and take a look at myself in the mirror. The dark spot on my neckline is still there. I wonder if it's cancer and, if so, if all this is worth it.

I tell myself to keep my spirits up. The next weeks will at least be interesting. We're going to be relatively close to Mercury, 0.59 AU now, and even less as the planet catches up to us. There's a whole program of telescopic observation scheduled; we should soon be close enough to see some surface details, at least.

Still...Venus...

Down in the sleeping area, I root around in my fireproof book bag for that Ray Bradbury collection, and turn again to "All Summer in a Day." Again I read about the schoolchildren on that unknown jungle planet version of Venus that's stuck in near-perpetual rain; I imagine their faces tight against the classroom windows, hoping to see the sun.

> It had been raining for seven years; thousands upon thousands of days compounded and filled from one end to the other with rain, with the drum and gush of water, with the sweet crystal fall of showers and the concussion of storms so heavy they were tidal waves come over the islands. A thousand forests had been crushed under the rain and grown up a thousand times to be crushed again. And this was the way life was forever on the planet Venus, and this was the schoolroom of the children of the rocket men and women who had come to a raining world to set up civilization and live out their lives.

The yellowed paper softly scrapes my fingers; the book smells vaguely dusty. And suddenly I'm overcome with this slackness, this heavy sense of the falseness and pointlessness of it all. I'm floating here in a hanging cocoon, with a fan stirring the air in front of my face so my own carbon dioxide doesn't accumulate around me and suffocate me in my sleep. The planet we're leaving behind is so different than the one I'm reading about that they only really share a name.

But even though I know the one on the pages doesn't exist, can never exist, I can't help but prefer it to the real one.

I burrow deeper into the book; my senses fall away and I'm enchanted by Bradbury's vision, a lush and gray and writhing jungle under the Venusian clouds. I read on, and spend a few blissful minutes lost in the beautiful lies.

•••

"Good morning, Explorer. Here are the top stories for today, July 23rd, 1972, straight from the AP wires. In space news, you flew past Venus, marking man's first encounter with a planet. So that was exciting for some of us."

"Hooray for us," I say to nobody in particular.

"...while, back on Earth, North Vietnamese Army units are advancing in the Central Highlands in what now appears to be a full-scale offensive meant to cut South Vietnam in half. Many refugees are attempting to flee Da Nang for the relative safety of Saigon; Pan Am and TWA are reporting flights clogged with passengers, and some even stowing away in aircraft wheel wells. There has been no official comment from the White House, but President Johnson is rumored to be contemplating U.S. airstrikes in support of the beleaguered South Vietnamese forces, despite Congress's vote earlier this year to rescind the Gulf of Tonkin Resolution. Protests across the countr..."

"Jesus Christ," Shepard mutters.

The transmission continues, an ongoing litany of troubles in Vietnam and Ireland and elsewhere.

•••

I still have the spacewalk, at least.

Within a few hours, we are back in the command module, suited up; we have run through all of the checklists, and we're ready for the final depressurization. Beyond my nose and the helmet glass, the central hatch window beckons, metal gleaming in the sunlight.

At last, the words arrive: "Explorer, Houston, you are GO for depress."

Shepard answers: "Roger, Houston, the side hatch dump valve is coming open."

"Pressure coming down," I narrate for their benefit as our atmosphere hisses away. "3.5. 3.3. 2.9..."

"Readying the camera," Shepard says.

"...1.8. 1.3..." The air sound is fading. "...0.7. 0.2. 0.0." Outside my helmet, everything still looks innocuous, but there is that nagging knowledge that it's hostile now, that one simple turn of a valve would be fatal. But it's best not to dwell on these things. "And we are ready to begin."

"Go ahead and unlatch," Shepard commands.

I depress the safety lock and squeeze the handle, then gently push the hatch. It opens wide, like a mouth trying to swallow the emptiness.

"And the hatch is open. Jettison the first bag…"

Kerwin hands me a Beta cloth sack full of odds and ends, broken equipment and debris that we hadn't wanted to put through the trash airlock. Holding on, I ease myself upwards and float a little out of the hatch and look around.

I'm surrounded by stillness, by this tremendous infinite space, and the bright distant sun off low to my right like a giant stage light. My chest tightens. Would Joan call it stage fright? This is opening night, in a sense, and I haven't rehearsed in months. But I stop and take a breath. Any tension must be in me, for there is none outside, for there is nothing.

The blackness surrounds: amazing, disorienting, and supreme. It takes a moment to find what I'm looking for. Venus is of course behind us, trajectory-wise, but given our orientation, it looks like it's far above, a swollen crescent. With the golden outer visor down, it's dimmer than normal, and I can't see as much, but then I flip that up for a second to see this little alien planet we've just flown past, a half-shadowed marble, a fat drop of milk with a little coffee swirled in.

Below, I feel hands on my toes. Past the white bag and the snaking umbilical, I can see the top of Kerwin's helmet, and his gloved fingers. "Just making sure you don't kick any switches," he says.

"Roger. Especially 'Manned Module Jettison.'"

"I think there's a cover on that one," he chuckles.

"I hope." Over and above everything, I do not want to fuck anything up. "All right, throwing out the bag."

With a stiff double-handed shove, I push the jettison bag up towards Venus. Not that it will get there, of course; orbital mechanics being what they are, it will follow us all the way around the sun and back to Earth, and burn up after we reenter. But this way we'll get some distance from it, and maybe make a quick posigrade maneuver to get a little more. Kerwin passes up a second bag, and I toss that one as well.

"All right. Coming the rest of the way out now." I pull myself out and turn to grab the handrail. (People usually imagine us floating away from the spacecraft, dangling free at the end of the umbilical cord. But it's hard to work that way, hard to move, even. We've planned this out meticulously; I'll be holding on to handrails the whole time.) With a gentle pull, I'm clear of the hatchway. Everything's easy and familiar, not all that different from Gemini XII all those years ago; with a pivot of the wrist, I can swing my whole body around.

"Coming out with the camera," Shepard says; I turn back and see his head and shoulders popping out, and the lens aimed upwards. "Buzz! You threw trash on Venus!"

I look up and sure enough, there it is, my second jettison bag just floating up there, blocking our view of the planet. "Whoops."

"All right, hopefully it'll drift off so we can get some video. Turn around and we'll get a shot of you."

"OK, just a sec." I float around to face the hatch; I force a smile for the cameras, although I know no one can see it.

I'm about to start talking when Shepard launches into his own narration: "We're half a day away from planet Venus, leaving the relative safety of the spacecraft to conduct the most distant spacewalk ever attempted by man. We are inspecting the craft, retrieving several experiments meant to measure solar wind and micrometeorites, and collecting film from our telescopic observations of the sun."

"Took the words right out of my mouth," I say, not entirely pleased.

Shepard pans the camera upwards; I'm hoping the jettison bag has drifted off a bit; I want everyone on Earth to see Venus as we can. I want them to see something, at least, although I know how impossible it is to really convey all of this vastness. (How can you reduce it to a magazine cover, or a rectangular television screen? You can't. It's like trying to capture the earth on a globe and then flatten the globe into a map and cut a piece of the map and put it in a book: the person who only sees the book can never understand. But even I cannot see it all; after all, I have the spacecraft in front of me, I have to work with the sun visor down, I have this spacesuit wrapped around me like a cloth cocoon.)

"We have quite the scene here," I say. "And it's clearer than ever just how small we are in all of this. As man ventures farther and farther from Earth, flying to Mars and beyond, it's a scene we'll have to get used to. But we can't pay too much attention. The work is too important to let yourself be distracted. It's OK to dream, but not to daydream." This comes out sounding wrong. Do I want to try and find the right words? My body floats easy but my tongue feels tied, the only part of me that's not free. I turn away from the camera. "All right, I'm going to move on down to the SIM bay."

Hand over hand I go, with the silvery spacecraft a foot from my helmeted face. It does call to mind scuba diving; I'm in a sea of blackness, alongside a gleaming metal beast. But the beast isn't moving. Or it's moving in fact, but not according to my senses.

Down the handrails I go, further down along the service module, every movement slow and deliberate. The spacecraft no longer looks fresh and new; it's still silvery and bright, but near the thruster quads, the paint is blistered and scorched. "Little wear and tear around the quads. The paint's bubbled up quite a bit more than I expected. There's maybe a four-inch section adjacent to each nozzle where it's chipping. I don't think we can do anything about it, but the engineers might want to take it into account. I'm moving over to the SIM bay."

With a few more moves I'm there. It's a recessed rectangular area with extra cameras, infrared and ultraviolet; they've been snapping pictures for the duration of the flyby, storing them up in metal canisters that I now have to bring back inside. There are foot restraints to keep me in place so I can use both hands as I work; I guide myself into them and get down to business.

"All camera covers have fully retracted. We should have a good set of prints." I sip from my drink bag, then press the first of the stiff metal latches holding the canisters in place. It takes a bit of effort, but we planned the work well, and simulated it regularly in the months before the mission, so soon the movements are coming back to me.

Soon I have the ultraviolet canister in hand, tethered to me for safety. I move myself one-armed back along the railing to Shepard so I can hand it off, then go back for the infrared. When my feet are back in the restraints, I take a sip from the drink bag. The second canister takes a bit more effort, but soon it yields.

I'm nearly back to Shepard when I feel something cold and wet near my neck.

For a moment I wonder if it's sweat, but no, it's colder. It's not a comfortable feeling, but I can still work, so I don't report it. I still have to collect the micrometeorite package and, most importantly, I have to get the telescope mount film, all the pictures we've taken of the sun, of the flares and loops and prominences and granules, the fruit of four months of hard work.

Again, we replace my tether clip with Shepard's; while he brings the infrared canister inside, I pull myself around the hatchway to the manned module, and then use the handrails on the roof to get my head and arms up over the side. A piece of exposed metal sheeting stretches out in front of me. This is the micrometeorite package, a simple way for engineers to determine how often we're striking miniscule debris in interplanetary space. After I loosen the clips, I turn and hand it to Shepard. He ducks inside with it, then comes back with a fresh film canister, the replacement for the telescope mount.

"Houston, Explorer," Shepard announces. "We've retrieved both flyby film canisters and the micrometeorite package. Buzz is moving on to manned module inspection and telescope film replacement."

I clip the new canister to my tether and grab its handle. With my free hand, I pull myself back up the handrail to the side of the manned module. Once up there, I survey all the metal and Mylar and the solar panels stretching wide like wings, the minus-z one right in front of me now, all this unknown territory that's been inches from us for months, unseen.

"Solar arrays are looking good," I report. "The sun shade is in decent shape. There's some evidence of micrometeorite impacts, but no major damage. Moving on to the solar t…"

Something down by the drink bag lets loose: a surge of water down there. With all of my willpower, I silently urge it to stay put so I can finish my job.

"Repeat your last, Buzz," Shepard says.

"Moving on to telescope film retrieval."

Our main telescopes are separate from the body of the manned module; because they need to rotate independently of the spacecraft, they're attached to a mount, which is why we need to go outside to get the film. We've rotated the mount so I can access the rear service panel. I slide my feet into the restraints, clip the new film canister to the handrail, retrieve my torqueless screwdriver, and remove the service panel. Then I start unlatching the canister, the massive white metal box containing every picture we've taken during all our solar science over the past four months. I pull it towards me.

The motion disrupts the water near my neck. A massive glob of it drifts into my field of view, too close to see clearly.

I take a breath.

There is no point panicking.

"I'm...uhh...getting some water in my helmet here," I say flatly. And the mass of water moves, and now there is still more, and I'm not sure how to stop it.

"Uhh, Explorer, Houston, we copy you have retrieved both canisters and are proceeding to manned module inspection and telescope film retrieval, over." They're distant and disconnected, lost in the peace of a few minutes ago. "Make sure you're providing us some detailed feedback on the sun shield's condition. The engineers are looking to..."

I am still holding the old film canister, the one with everything. I still haven't clipped it in. I try to, but with the water I can't look down, so I fail. I move it down by my side and grip it tight.

"Buzz, I copy you have water in your helmet." Shepard at least is here in the present, but the message from Houston is still coming, something about more inspection tasks, and it's disorienting and chaotic, the last thing we need. "Joe, turn that off! Put us internal," Shepard barks. "We'll need some quiet until this is resolved."

A click: the switching of comm channels. Now we're on our own.

"Buzz, I copy water in your helmet," Shepard repeats. "How much?"

"There's a few ounces right in front of my face, but I feel more down by my neck." I breathe in gently. My strategy now is to drink the bit in front of me, then return to the command module with the old canister, then come back to replace the new one. "I think the drink bag sprung a leak."

"Can you do anything about it?"

"I might be able to drink this bit." I draw in a little air, trying to suck it towards me, but something tickles my throat; I snort, and the globule shivers and makes contact with my forehead and eyebrows and nose, and now it's in my eyes. My hand come up to my face by reflex, although of course there's nothing it can do; from the mass near my neck I can feel still more water coming in to the helmet now, and all of it has no reason to go anywhere, no gravity to make it drip down, so it clings to my face, and there's more joining it now, still more in my eyes, and I can feel myself drifting away from the spacecraft now, and I can't see anything, just shapes.

Cautious and semi-blind, I grope until I feel the handrail. When I finally grasp it, I pause and think.

I am out here at the far limit of it all, and I can't see.

I try to blink away the water, but nothing happens. I feel the tickle of still more, down near my mouth and the bottom of my nose.

I breathe very carefully, through my mouth only now, but I can still feel the mass of water quivering with every breath, and now it's seeping into my nose.

It occurs to me that I still haven't clipped in the old film canister.

Then it occurs to me that I could drown out here.

But I stop and think. There is no point panicking.

An animal panics when it doesn't understand its situation; it thrashes blindly and makes the situation worse. In the lifesaving classes at summer camp, we learned that drowning victims don't always flail about; they grab whatever's in front of them and try to hold it down so they can float, and by doing so, they sometimes drown their rescuers as well. In a panic, people revert to their animal state, and throw away their greatest asset, their ability to think their way out of problems.

So I must think.

My feet are in the restraints, and I'm still holding the old canister, and I know I shouldn't move around wildly. I am still close to the minus-z solar array, and if I damage that, we'll all be in a lot of trouble even if I do make it back inside. Plus there are sharp edges on it, and the last thing I need is a suit puncture when I can't move around easily. So I stay there for a second. My eyes are uncomfortable and useless; I can only see silvery watery shapes. I close them and the blackness is complete.

It occurs to me that, as a last resort, I can try closing my mouth and opening the side valve on the helmet really quickly. I do not know what will happen. Or I do know, but not in what sequence: the water in my helmet will evaporate instantly once the pressure drops, or it will spray out through the valve and evaporate outside, or my eyeballs will freeze, or the nitrogen in my blood will un-dissolve and my blood will froth like a shaken-up soda and I'll get the bends...

"Buzz, what is your status?" Shepard asks.

I am not sure I can talk without making my situation worse. But I need to say something. He's too far away to come get me. Carefully I ease out the words. "There's...more water now."

And it seeps into my nose, my sinuses. My lungs are empty and I cannot just exhale it out. I try to inhale but can't. Every cell in my body is telling me I need to, soon. Thought's becoming impossible.

A distant voice. Shepard. "Buzz, you're going to need to move back along the handrail."

I slide my feet out of the restraints and back up, slowly and methodically, legs first through the blackness, one-armed, still clenching the film canister. My lungs are burning. Thanks to the snoopy headset over my ears, I can still hear everything, but I can feel the moisture starting to seep in...

Again the far-off voice: "Doing good, Buzz. I can see your feet now. You're almost there. All you have to do is..."

My headset shorts out.

Every cell is yelling now, screaming at me to breathe. I risk a shallow inhalation. I get a very small bit. Then water. Everything is water.

I try to swallow.

It is very hard to think.

My lungs are burning and I know I don't have much time.

Gently I bring my right leg forward.

My knee is against the side of the spacecraft, but my toes are unimpeded.

My lungs are ready to burst.

I push myself backwards.

Then things fade and I breathe and there is water.

It's the last thing I feel.

•••

When I open my eyes, my face is dry.

My lungs feel like lava.

I am still on the Venus mission. My helmet is off and the hatch is closed and the spacecraft is pressurized, and Shepard and Kerwin are floating on either side, eyeing me with looks of great concern that give way to grins, even as I start coughing violently, so hard my head hits the instrument panel.

"There he is," Shepard says. "Attaboy, tiger."

"Gave us quite a scare there, Buzz," Kerwin adds.

I blink. Everything feels thick and slow.

"That settles it," Shepard says. "This is a ship, that we're on. If you go overboard and you drown, it's a ship."

"What happened?" I croak.

"You drowned."

"Well..." Kerwin says.

He turns the radio back on. "..plorer, Houston, we have received no comms for several minutes. What is your status, over?" Another man on the capcom console. Henize.

"Houston, Explorer," Shepard says. "EVA is complete. We are closed and repressurized and everyone is safe. We retrieved the flyby film and the micrometeorite package but lost the telescope film. We had to turn off the comms momentarily. Stand by for a more detailed report. Over."

"You must've blacked out right after you made it off the manned module," Shepard says.

"There was...water. A lot of water. I think my drink bag sprung a leak somehow. My whole helmet was full."

"Explorer, Houston, we have received no comms for several minutes. What is your status, over?" Henize sounds as clipped and professional as possible. Our relief hasn't caught up with their uncertainty.

Everything feels slow. "What else happened?"

"Well..." Kerwin starts.

"What do you think happened? We got you in!" Shepard exults.

"I mean, how long did it take?"

"Faster than you ever would have thought possible," Kerwin chuckles.

"We had to cut a few corners," Shepard concedes.

"What did you do?"

"Explorer, Houston, we have received no comms for several minutes. What is your status, over?" Despite my foggy mind, I give a dead little chuckle: again the same message, without even a change in wording. It's like a phone call with my father. Or one of those jokes someone tells until it isn't funny, then keeps telling until it's funny again.

"Your whole goldfish bowl was full of water. We had to crack the valve and evaporate it all," Shepard says. "It just...flashed to cold steam before our eyes. Damndest thing I ever saw."

"Christ," I reply. "Really?"

"Well..." Kerwin says.

"I was thinking of doing that," I say. "Up there on the manned module. I wasn't sure I could make it back. But I was worried about the bends. And I wasn't sure I could close the valve after..." I shake my head and look back at Shepard. They say decompression sickness hits in your joints first; I move mine tentatively, trying to decide if they're hurting. "Christ. Really?"

"Actually, we had to close the hatch fast and repress," Shepard says. "We unlocked your visor when it was about 2 psi. And all that water…"

Now I'm envisioning it, them pulling off the helmet bowl, and the mass of water still not having a reason to fall to the floor, but instead shimmering there around my head like a crystal blob. "What did you do with the water?"

"Well, I had a couple straws." Shepard starts out serious, but as usual, he can't keep a straight face. "I figured, hell, let's drink it off!"

"Well…" Kerwin adds.

"This is kind of an awkward question, but…did you have to give me mouth-to-mouth?"

Both of them laugh, and Shepard shakes his head. "Don't ask questions you don't want the answers to, Buzz."

"Explorer, Houston, we have received no comms for several…uhh, stand by." Our words are reaching them at last. "Explorer, Houston, we copy your last. Understand you were unable to retrieve the telescope film. Standing by for a full update, over."

"The telescope film…" I echo.

Shepard: "We lost it."

Shame floods me. The bulk of the work of the mission so far, and we've pissed it away. I've pissed it away.

"We needed to get you back in," Kerwin says. "You're alive, that's what counts."

"What do you want to tell them, Buzz?" Shepard asks.

But I still don't know. "What happened?"

•••

We've scrapped most of the rest of the day's activities. There's nothing to do but report back to Houston, and clean up, and eat dinner.

From the window we can still see the film canister, a white box bright in the sunlight, tumbling lazily a few hundred feet away. We were supposed to power down the command module, but we don't. I am wondering if we'll get permission to maneuver over to it and pick it up. I can't imagine it would throw us off out trajectory that much: a quick translation with the thrusters, nothing that couldn't be corrected later. At worst we'd change our splashdown point by a couple hundred miles. So I am hoping. Still, there is the fear that it'll drift further away and they'll decide to cut their losses. So it is a desperate hope.

"Well, that was an...eventful day," Kerwin says as we float over to the meal trays.

"That's one way to put it," I reply. "Not exactly what I was hoping for."

"No. Not for any of us."

"Not at all," Shepard echoes.

There is a long and uncomfortable silence. I spoon food into my mouth half-heartedly.

"I guess that's the point of exploring," Kerwin says at last. "If you knew what was going to happen and what you were going to see, it'd be...tourism."

"Yeah," I echo. And again, the silence.

Before all of this, I'd wondered if we were going to get a phone call from the president, like we did when we were on the moon, although of course here it would be one-way, another Johnson monologue. After the near-disaster there were of course many other things to worry about. But it occurs to me now that it didn't happen, and I'm wondering what that says about all of this, about us, about me.

"I am still glad we're here, though," Kerwin says, repeating himself from yesterday. I'm wondering if he's trying to convince himself.

"It was neat to see everything," I concede. "But I don't know, I..." My words trail off. What else is there to say? I was already disappointed yesterday. And now this.

We still haven't heard from Houston about retrieving the canister. And the other one still isn't installed yet; it's floating tethered up there. We can't do much on the telescope until that's resolved, so they have to let us out again. They have to.

But they don't, not yet. They are deliberating.

Meanwhile the old canister floats, out of reach, mocking me. I can't tell, but it looks like it might be drifting off.

•••

There are legitimate medical concerns for people who've been in my situation, effects that may take many hours to manifest themselves. It's decided that Kerwin will stay up with me to keep an eye on things, and that if all goes well, Shepard will take a spacewalk tomorrow to set it all right.

Joe and I float lazily upstairs in the main deck, pretending to think about other things. But the silence exhausts me, and I imagine the question in his heart, the one he's too decent to ask.

"You want to know what it was like, don't you?" I say at last.

"Well…" He draws it out, as if embarrassed by his curiosity.

"You want to know what it was like."

Finally he says: "You are the odd man out, in a way."

Something about this phrasing catches me off-guard. "That's how I always feel. The odd man out."

"What I mean is…" He's apologetic now. "I mean, you've had this experience now. But we're all a little odd, in a way…"

I'm used to being the one awkwardly fumbling for words, so this amuses me. But only for a second. "No. Before this, too."

"Well, we are…selected officials. We're in a profession that emphasizes over and over again that we've been chosen. By the government, the taxpayers, the people…so essentially, by everyone we meet. So we're always different from them."

"I've always felt different," I tell him. "It doesn't always feel good."

"How does it usually feel?"

"Well I guess sometimes...yeah, like you said, selected." All this talk of feelings is foreign still. "I mean, West Point, flight training, Korea. But in all of those, you end up surrounded by people going through the same thing."

"So it's not such a big deal."

"Well, I guess..." How *do* I feel? "I guess in the end, you don't always feel particularly special, even though everyone on the outside thinks you are. You know how hard you've gotta work to keep it, and how much harder you've gotta work to stand out. And I mean, even becoming an astronaut, I thought that was..." So much of this has been wordless for so long, formless and dark. It's so much simpler dealing with things that can be measured and quantified, scientifically proven and forced into equations. "...I mean, I was thrilled to get the news, of course, but you realize pretty soon that an astronaut who hasn't been up here isn't really an astronaut. You have to explain to every school group and Rotary Club that, 'Well, I've been picked, but I haven't been in space yet,' and it's almost worse than never having been picked, because you know that everything's still just a hazy possibility, that one stroke of the pen by Deke or the doctor, and..."

Kerwin smirks, something I'm not used to from him. "Welcome to my life for the past few years."

"Yeah." I've forgotten who I'm talking to, apparently. "On Gemini XII...that at least felt like something. Up there with Lovell, the only two humans above the atmosphere at that moment. But even then, part of me felt...off..."

"Why?"

"Well, I'm...I'm not sure if I would have made a flight on Gemini if it wasn't for what happened to Charlie Bassett." It feels strange actually saying this, hearing the words come out; they've spent a long time sitting on my chest. "Obviously he and Elliot See were backing up Gemini IX when the crash happened. So of course they should have been prime crew on XII, instead of me and Lovell, because that was Deke's normal rotation. Lovell and I were backing up X, and there was no Gemini XIII, so he shouldn't have flown again on Gemini, and I shouldn't have flown at all. And I got the sense nobody was really going to push for me on Apollo. But when Charlie and Elliot died..."

"It worked out to your advantage."

I don't reply but just sit there and maybe give a little nod.

"And you feel guilty about that."

Something releases in me: tears welling, pooling in my eyes, no gravity to pull them anywhere. It is such a strange relief to have my feelings named and described.

"And you figure you wouldn't have gone to the moon, but for the fact that those guys had that awful thing happen to them."

I try to talk but can't. I'm mute. Overcome. And...it is just a flat recitation of the facts. There is nothing beyond that in his voice, no judgment or bitterness.

"You know it's not your fault, right?" he asks.

"I know that," I say, although I'm not sure I *have* known it, until just now. "It's just..."

"You feel like you don't deserve what you got."

"Is there a name for that?"

"Survivor's guilt. Impostor syndrome, maybe," he says. "You know, it's pretty normal in these situations."

"I did feel good in some ways after Gemini. In a lot of ways. The EVA went so well, and everyone knew how much I'd done to make it happen. That was a good feeling. But after the moon, you get that feeling of truly being set apart. You talk to people, and there are...questions on their faces, and no matter how many times you answer, you both know that they don't know, they don't *really* know. But you're still *you*, you're still looking at the same old you in the mirror, you're not sure what's the big deal. And now this, today...it's not good, feeling different this way."

"Buzz, you did a hell of a job today, just making it back to where we could pull you in," Kerwin says. "It could have ended very badly for all of us."

"I didn't do the job! Shepard's gonna think I..."

"Don't worry about Shepard. None of us could've done better than you did, with what happened. You didn't panic. You did what you needed to do."

"I…" There is a heaviness in my chest. But this needs to come out. "I felt a little water when I was coming back from the SIM bay. Based on the mission rules, I should have come right back in, rather than going up on the manned module."

He thinks for a second. I'm waiting for judgment. At last he says: "Buzz, there's not a human being alive who would make all the same decisions if they knew all the consequences. You dodged a bullet. Let's be grateful for that. This is a story we're going to be…laughing about when we're old men."

Now again things are quiet, but it's more comfortable. I am noticing the sounds, the fans and glycol pumps. "So you want to know what it was like?"

Nothing. A polite nothing.

"You want to know. It's OK. I'd want to know, too. It was…it was hell."

"I bet."

"Especially when the headphones cut out. I already had my eyes closed, because I couldn't see shit, but when the headphones shorted out…" I take a deep breath. It is done, after all, although it still feels real. "It was just this…alone feeling. My thoughts were getting narrower and narrower, until all I could think about was that breath I knew I wouldn't get. And it was hell. Hell is cold and wet and dark and quiet."

He gives a little friendly smile. "Nothing like the pictures, huh?"

I smile a little, at last. "No, not at all."

After all this, I'm feeling better, until I make the mistake of looking out the window. The canister has drifted off a ways; it's a distant star now, the only one twinkling. I make a pathetic wish.

•••

We set alarms and wake every hour so I can tell Kerwin how I feel.

It is a surreal night, a kaleidoscope of frantic dreams and tired examinations. And sooner or later in those situations, you wake from a sound sleep and need to go to the bathroom, and the mere act of moving leaves you irrevocably alert, the way you get when young kids are crying in the night and you're running around just a little too much to fall back asleep easily.

And tonight there's a lot to think about. That never helps.

Somewhere in there, I look out the window for the film, and I don't see it; I wonder if we've truly lost it at last.

I anxiously hover between sleep and wakefulness, trying not to bump into Kerwin as he floats lazily on the other side of the main cabin. He's in the default zero-gravity position, the one you fall into when you're not restrained in a sleeping bag: legs bent at the hips and knees, arms out in front, like a dead man floating face down on the surface of the ocean.

Eventually he's up again for the last checkup. Everything's fine. Which means we should have tried to retrieve the canister yesterday.

We blink and try to shake off our numb tiredness; we pull up the light shades and get started on our day. Soon Shepard joins us and we make breakfast in silence.

"Explorer, Houston," Crippen says when the morning broadcast comes on. "It looks like it is...uhh...not your normal news day. There's breaking news out of Washington that President Johnson was found unresponsive in his room. We've got a couple TVs on down here, and they're saying there'll be a press conference shortly. We will keep you advised, over."

"Jesus," Shepard says.

"I wonder if they can patch that in for us. The broadcast." I'm eager to hear it, even though I think I know what they're going to say; for all my profoundly mixed feelings about Johnson, it'll be another one of those days where everyone remembers where they were and what they were doing. I imagine the scenes across the country, all the morning routines: men shaving in their bathrooms with one ear tuned to the transistor radio next to the sink, hand on the faucet but not turning it, just so they can catch the bulletin; others heading to work already, walking past the TVs in the department store displays, slowing down as they see the screens; women back at home pouring cereal for the kids, then stopping, forgetting the milk so they can smoke a cigarette and listen. It feels odd to not be a part of it.

Shepard flips a switch. "Houston, Explorer, we copy about the president. If there's any way we can listen in, please make it happen, over."

We wait.

"Jesus. Johnson."

"Wow," Kerwin chimes in. "This is…"

"We don't know anything yet," Shepard points out.

We wait.

"Well, I guess our little…event won't even make the news," I say. The words feel wrong coming out, and I immediately want to take them back. "I do have a bad feeling."

We wait.

And then at last: "Explorer, we copy your request. Stand by."

We wait again. Then static, and: "…suffered a severe myocardial infarction sometime between 5:00 and 6:30 a.m. Upon discovering him unresponsive at 6:30 a.m., Secret Service personnel attempted to resuscitate him, without success. He was rushed via ambulance to George Washington University Hospital, where he was pronounced dead on arrival. Vice President…excuse me. President Humphrey has taken the oath of office. We have no further statements at this time." And with that, and a brief eruption of unacknowledged questions, it was over.

I float numbly. "Jesus. Johnson."

"Wow," Kerwin says. "He's one of those people, it almost doesn't matter whether you love him or hate him, you just…somehow assume he's always gonna be around."

I think back on my conversations with him: the moon, the White House, back at the LBJ Ranch. "I doubt we'd be here without him."

"Probably not," Shepard says. "There's something about all this that really...struck his fancy. I was in a motorcade with him, not long after my first flight, when he was still veep. Just one of those...ridiculous, overwhelming motorcades, heading into this arena in Houston, and it was hot as hell, and still the people had turned out in droves. Cheering, cheering. And I said to him, 'Is this what it's like being a politician?' And he said, 'It's never like this. My God, these people love you!' Like that was all that mattered."

"You know what De Gaulle said at Kennedy's funeral," Kerwin chimes in. "'This man Kennedy, he's the mask America wears. But this man Johnson, he's the face behind the mask.'"

"I wonder what they'll say now." I give up on my meal and start readying the remainder for the trash airlock.

"They won't say much. Not at a time like this. People respect death, even if they've stopped respecting the man."

Shepard looks around at the spacecraft, as if appreciating it anew. "I will say this. Johnson was the type of asshole to do something like this just because people said it couldn't be done. I can respect an asshole like that."

"Well that's a...hell of a eulogy." I chuckle. "If Houston asks us for our response, we should pass that along. Comments from our fearless leader."

Shepard gives me a dirty look.

•••

Eventually we get the go-ahead for the second EVA. Since the old film canister's drifted off, it is decided that we'll just complete the installation of the new one.

Because we haven't entirely determined the cause of my water malfunction, it's decided that I'll suit up without my undergarment and play the role Kerwin had played yesterday. Meanwhile Kerwin gets to keep an eye out while Shepard performs the spacewalk. I don't even get to stick my head out the hatch this time.

We perform the same sad routines, somewhat tiredly this time.

And soon we're depressurizing again, and Shepard's heading out, and I'm just floating there mutely in the command module, staring through my helmet at the brightly-lit vacuum, trying not to mope. Shepard's doing the work, but everybody's anxious about me.

Everything goes perfectly this time. I'm happy, to a point.

•••

"Buzz, can I talk to you for a moment?" Shepard asks once everything's done and the command module's finally powered down.

"What's up?" I look around and realize Kerwin's off in the bathroom. This feels like a setup of some sort.

"The issue with the food inventory the other day. We do have to deal with that." Now that he's talking about it, I can tell he's upset: the coldness and sharpness of tone are both at levels I would call historically high.

Was I insubordinate? I'm trying to be a good crewmember, to have some teeny tiny bit of say in what we do and how we do it, and there's no need to apologize for that...is there? I take a deep breath. "It was something we needed to look at. If something's happened down there..."

"Exactly," he says. "And I think the only fair way to deal with this situation is to have you do a complete inventory. Solo. Top to bottom. Inspect every food tray, every packet. Write down the numbers and compare them to where we're supposed to be. If this is such an important issue for you, I figure it'll benefit from your close personal attention."

"That's gonna be quite a job..." I imagine it: a mess, very difficult, trying to unload all the stacks and corral the trays and put them all somewhere *else* in a way that doesn't screw everything up.

He smirks. "I'm sure you'll manage."

•••

For the rest of the day, I'm unloading the stacks, one at a time, counting every meal. It's the part *after* the counting that's the headache; you can't just stack things in neat piles, so I'm forced to go section by section, ten at a time, putting the trays in a loose floating cloud, an airborne constellation. When each section is done, I scoop up the group in a clean Beta cloth bag and bring it up to the vacant command module; when each stack is done, I reload it. It's mindless and repetitive, and although I can appreciate Shepard's artful matching of punishment and crime, it still rankles me, a bit.

There are two burst packets in the entire inventory. That's it. We're in no danger of running out of food. I should feel relieved, but I don't.

I report the results to Shepard. He doesn't say anything.

•••

After dinner, we are winding down. I'm still waiting for Shepard to make some comment about the incident, all of it, my unwanted efforts at independent thinking.

But his mind is elsewhere. Here and there, I try to make eye contact, but his are distant and calm now, as if he's hiding a pleasant secret.

Once the day's trash is in the airlock, he floats down to the sleeping chambers and comes back with something wrapped in plastic and tape, something lumpy and misshapen, but just about the right size to be...a bottle. "Gentlemen, it's celebration time," he says.

"What's that?" I ask, even though I already know; my mind's twisting into strange knots of apprehension and excitement.

"What do you think it is? Scotch."

"On a flight?" I'm absolutely incredulous. Nothing like this has ever happened before.

Shepard laughs. "This from the man who flew communion wine to the moon."

"That was a very small vial in my personal preference kit. Not nearly enough to cause anybody any...headaches."

Shepard looks from the wrapped bundle to me. "So you're saying you don't want any, then."

"Well, I wouldn't say *that*." I float on over.

"Joe?"

"I'm good. Somebody's gotta keep an eye on things."

"This is one bottle!" I'm amused and annoyed by his reluctance. There's that odd combination of calculations: a momentary suspicion that I'm being judged by someone who's abstaining, trumped by an awareness that I don't mind, because I'll get more. "Right, Al? One bottle? Don't tell me you've stocked the cellar."

He laughs. "No such luck. One bottle. Even I have my limits."

"As do I." To Kerwin I nod: "And one bottle should keep us pretty far from them." Then, back to Shepard, curious and admirous: "Should I ask how you described this little package on the sheet for your Personal Preference Kit?"

"You should not."

"I guess I shouldn't be surprised," Kerwin says. "All you service academy grads seem to have a keen appreciation for rules and policies, and how to...artfully dance around them, should the need arise."

Shepard and I float together, huddling over the bundle; he unwraps it as delicately as if it were the core of a booby-trapped nuclear weapon. I'm impressed by the engineering of his packaging: a thick outer plastic bag, a sensible amount of tightly-wadded newspaper taped together to prevent settling, another inner plastic bag, and a thick cardboard tube with the bottle snugly inside, and still more wadded paper in the empty space between the inner wall and the bottle neck.

I help with the final extraction. "Cutty Sark."

"There's a ship on the label," he deadpans. "Is that OK?"

"I guess we'll allow it, in the interest of…interservice cooperation." There's even an impromptu handmade wax seal over the bottle cap. "Taking no chances, huh? You didn't want Maker's Mark?"

Kerwin: "The bottle geometry might've been…"

"All right, enough critique," Shepard interrupts him. Then, to me: "Make yourself useful and get some glasses," although obviously it'll be plastic containers with straws.

"Coming right up." I turn to the kitchen area.

"No arguments today, huh, Buzz?"

I chuckle. For once, I don't mind the imperial attitude: I hadn't thought anything like this would be a possibility for quite some time, and it does seem like the right way to clear the air between us and start fresh. And Lord knows I've earned it…

In short order we have our two containers at the ready. I leave one floating and unscrew the top of the other. Shepard loosens the wax, holding it up near the air filter intake so as to not have any loose shavings floating around. Then, ever so carefully, he unscrews the cap. With a magician's flair, he releases a small globule of glistening amber liquid. It looks delightfully alive; it shivers and shudders and quivers like…well, like a man who's taken a shot of it. I trap it cleanly in the first container. Once that's done, we repeat the process.

"All right." Shepard caps the bottle tightly, then plucks his container from the air and raises it to offer a toast. "We've…"

"Shouldn't we drink to the president?" I ask.

He gives me a dirty look. "We've gone where no man has gone before. We've stared Death in the eye sockets and pissed all over his bony face. We've pissed each other off, too, but more importantly, we've done something that's never been done. And now it's time to kick back for a bit."

"Indeed." We touch containers and I drink gratefully; I expect the usual, a wonderful comet of fire shooting down my throat, but there's a laziness to it up here, a slower burn, no gravity or urgency. I'm not complaining.

We drink in silence.

"This is good," I say at last. "This was a good idea."

Shepard doesn't say anything.

"It's been a busy few months," I continue on. "A lot of pressure, for all of us. Nice to release a little of it."

"Let's just relax and enjoy our drinks, Buzz."

"Yeah."

More silence. I take long sips at short intervals. The cabin smells wonderful and smoky now. Kerwin floats downstairs, leaving us to our devices. Outside the windows: infinity. And inside there is warmth.

"We should drink to the president," I repeat.

"All right. To the president," Shepard toasts. "Sometimes you have to be an S.O.B. to get the job done."

Again, silence. There are so many ways to interpret this sentence; my mind spins through all of them.

"I was a little worried," I say at last. "The other day, with the food. I mean, I want to do a good job, you know that. I want a successful mission. That's all I want, to come home and be able to hold my head up high."

"That's all any of us wants, Buzz."

"I know. You didn't say anything earlier, so..."

"Leadership isn't a conversation, Buzz. It's not a negotiation. You should know this. You can't get your panties in a twist about whether or not people like you. So I don't. You should know this by now."

I nod, contemplating.

"If someone's done what they need to do, fine, if not, once you've made it clear what needs to happen, they need to do it. At that point, talk doesn't matter. If a subordinate is...making you justify yourself, you're not in charge any more. In fact, you only really know you're in charge when you shut up. In that silence. That's when it either happens or doesn't happen."

Kerwin emerges from the sleeping chamber passage; his eyes dart warily. Somehow it reminds me of a soldier emerging from a foxhole, ready to duck for cover at the first sound of shelling.

"Come on up, Joe! Hang out for a bit. I was just about to hit the head." Shepard floats off.

Kerwin watches him go and waits until he's behind the curtain; we know the sounds don't travel well, but even so, he lowers his voice a register. "Everything good with you two?"

"I guess." I shrug.

"Just out of curiosity, have you...thanked him for saving your life?"

It occurs to me only just now that perhaps I haven't, and I let out a nervous chuckle. "Well, I thought it would go without saying."

"You have to say these things, Buzz."

I shrug. Maybe he's right.

When Shepard comes back, Kerwin takes his turn in the latrine.

"I don't think I said this yesterday, but thank you. You did a hell of a job. Thank you for saving my life."

He says nothing.

I wait for the click. I wait for it to kick in.

I drink more: longer sips at shorter intervals.

Time passes faster, and somewhere in there it starts to skip around. It is hard to tell if I'm getting drunk; it's not an outrageous amount of booze, but this is the end of the longest dry spell I've had in...a while. I don't even remember. And floating changes everything, too.

The next thing I know I'm heading to the toilet, an awful feeling in my stomach, heading there on pure instinct, because nothing goes *down* the toilet here, not without help, but I figure if I can get the fans on in time...

I'm not quite there when I convulse and heave and spew awful foulness into the air. Somewhere behind me I hear Shepard say, "Jesus, Buzz."

"I'm sorry. I didn't think..." I can't even finish the sentence before I'm vomiting again.

I've never had nausea on a spaceflight before. I've never even had any odd feelings until the beginning of this flight, and that still came out the other end. I've always looked down a little on those like Rusty Schweickart whose stomachs just couldn't handle it. And now here I am. At least I can blame the booze. But then again, I can't, really, or at least not to anyone outside this spacecraft: another thing you learn at the Academy is that there are certain things you will never ever ever repeat to another human being who isn't equally culpable, certain events you all must keep your mouth shut about, for the sake of all concerned. Because if someone asks about it, you have to tell the truth, but if nobody knows, nobody can ask. And...well, I've already said too much.

•••

Morning.

Morning is awful.

I am back floating suspended in the sleeping chamber. I don't want to go into details about my physical condition. But there is that awful shudder, that morning panic when it all comes flooding back.

I hang there, full of hate.

I want to be mad at the others, but I am the one who put myself in this condition. Shepard's words from later last night now echo in my head in a repeating loop: What the hell is wrong with you?

I wish I knew.

Nature is calling, so I know I must at least head upstairs and take care of that, even though I don't really want to, don't really want to do a damn thing except maybe skip ahead in time, twenty-four hours or eight months or forever.

Upstairs, I bump into Kerwin. He gives me a look. Shepard does, too, but it's the one from Kerwin that hurts.

I remember things, from after I threw up. I do not remember everything. The others might. I know better than to ask.

In the bathroom, I catch my eyes in the mirror and shake my head in disgust. Again the voice: What the hell is wrong with you? I have got to stop doing this.

Back on the main deck, they've already started heating up the morning meal trays. The news is a welcome distraction: they're discussing the first day of the Humphrey administration, and the plans for Johnson's funeral. He'll be the second president in a row to get one while in office. I have a hard time really concentrating, though.

It feels like they're avoiding me, like they'd leave the room if they could.

It's only when the Mercury observation program starts that they say anything to me, and it's strictly professional, the normal clipped banter of telescope operations.

We're not actually much closer to Mercury than Earth is when it's at its closest; the only reason it makes sense to even do these observations is because we have a better angle, and we're not staring directly into the sun. (And, frankly, we need something to do...although I suppose we'll have plenty of makeup work on the telescope now that we've lost everything from the first four months of the mission.) So we can't see much: dim and distant outlines of surface features. We already know it's a lot like the moon, but somehow more depressing. For the moon is visible to everyone. No leader needs to explain it; it's a place that already captures the imagination of the lowliest human. Meanwhile Mercury's hard to even see from Earth. And what's worse, the energy budget required to get there and into orbit and back means it will never be a great candidate for human exploration. Because its orbit is inside ours, we'll be getting closer over the next few weeks, but at the closest, we'll be about .4 au away, still. So our observations feel pointless: sterile glimpses of another dead world.

The other two film a short movie to beam back to Earth, something about Mercury, for the kids. Shepard stays behind the camera while Kerwin prattles on. I remain uninvolved, absent from the credits. They don't ask for my help, and I don't offer.

•••

Meanwhile, back in the Venusian atmosphere, the floaters have been gathering information. Hanging suspended under hydrogen balloons, drawing power from radiothermal generators for a growth and metabolism experiment that's using spectroscopes and a gas chromatograph to try and determine if there's anything in the atmosphere, anything at all, that's turning light and CO_2 and water into chemical energy. Aerosolized plantlike cells, bacteria, protozoa: we don't care. We're curious to see something. Anything.

"Explorer, Houston." Crippen's distant voice comes over the radio later, breaking the silence of an unpleasant afternoon. "We're analyzing the preliminary data from the floaters. It's a little early, but we're not seeing any evidence of metabolic processes. We're not seeing any organic chemicals, even."

No signs of life.

•••

When the alarm goes off the next morning and the others start stirring, I close my eyes and fall back asleep.

I wake to Kerwin tapping on my shoulder. "Come on, Buzz. Up and at 'em."

"I'm not feeling well." And indeed there is a heaviness in my heart that seems entirely out of place in space. I can't think of a single thing I'm looking forward to in the next eight months. And even then...

"Come on. There's a lot to do today. More Mercury observations, mass measurements…"

"You can make do without me. I'm really not feeling well."

I hang there, floating loosely in my sleeping bag, a warm cocoon. Everything I might think about hurts to think about. It is better to just sit there and float, and try to avoid all the sharp edges.

Kerwin looks over his shoulder to Shepard. "He says he's not feeling well."

I am waiting to see what Shepard will say. I cannot avoid all my unpleasant thoughts, and there is the knowledge that I *should* be forcing myself out and about, dragging myself through the routine, and that makes it worse in some ways, but not enough to prod me out of bed. It all just feels like so much masochism…

I wait for a tongue-lashing from Shepard; I close my eyes in anticipation. But he doesn't say anything.

Interlude:
Southern California

It is March of 1967. I'm out in California with Ed White.

Apollo is off track. Ed and Gus Grissom and Roger Chaffee should have launched already on the first mission of the program. But during an unmanned pressurization test of the spacecraft, something happened: a spark, a fire. Sharp and short, but so intense it burnt everything and burst the pressure hull. The prime crew was in there days before, and the backup crew was supposed to be in there the next day. Nobody wants to think about what might've happened if it'd been a manned test.

So a few of us are at the North American plant in Downey, cleaning up the mess. The accident was a retrospectively obvious consequence of focusing too much on speed and taking quality for granted. And now the entire Block I iteration of the spacecraft, the initial version without many of the features we'll later need for lunar rendezvous, is being passed over; we're overseeing various redesigns of the Block II version to ensure it will be a truly spaceworthy craft.

To top it off, there's been bad blood in the press: sniping, anonymously sourced stories, talks of congressional inquiries. Somebody far higher than Deke is seriously pissed off. The upshot being that they've broken up Ed's crew.

It's patently unfair, and morale in the astronaut corps has been shot to hell, but I haven't heard Ed say anything about it. In fact, he's working his ass off to help get everything back on track. (Every West Pointer I've known has learned to operate at a level of activity that a normal person would probably describe as "manic." But Ed's one of the select few who can make it all seem effortless.) He asked for my help, so they've reassigned me, and we've flown out here together a few weeks in a row. We've spent many nights at the plant, observing tests, offering feedback on various arrangements of equipment. But we've just concluded a systems test that stretched on for over 26 hours. Despite a few catnaps in there, we're at a point of diminishing returns, productivity-wise, so they told us to head out early (which, by space program standards, means 5:30 p.m. or so rather than 9:00 or 10:00) and rest up.

And now we're eating burgers outside on the patio of some roadside joint. Night's falling; it's that time of day when the cars all start to look the same, dim metal and glass shapes barely visible behind headlights and taillights. Ed seems content to just sit there and take it all in. My mind, of course, is still back at work, foggy and cranky.

"Pretty aggravating, huh?" I ask.

"How do you mean?"

"The fire. The crew shuffle. None of it was your fault. Now...Schirra and Cunningham and Eisele get your turn."

"I guess we should've said more before the fire. Before all this stuff hit the papers," he says simply.

"What could you have done? Nobody wants to speak up in these situations. Gus was about as vocal as he could have been without losing the flight. And now he's lost it anyway."

He shrugs. "Buzz, there is nothing to complain about here."

"What do you mean, nothing to complain about? None of this is how it should be. If you had raised a stink, and stirred up all the shit that needed to be stirred up, they would have found someone else to tell them their shit doesn't stink."

"I've made my peace with it," he says. "In fact, I feel...blessed. That could've just as easily happened with us in there. Or in orbit. So to my mind, it was a pretty decent outcome. And it was a lesson I needed. You know how it is, all that Academy stuff. You're out in the halls, or up on the chalkboards, and everybody expects a flawless performance. And if you can't be perfect, you have to go behind closed doors and work your ass off until you are. And you do that until everything really is the way it's supposed to be. Well, I guess I needed a little deprogramming."

I give him a look.

"Buzz, look around," he says, waving a hand at the outdoor scene, a dark futuristic panorama of lights and silhouettes, traffic and palm trees and neon. "It's an absolutely perfect night. Gorgeous California weather. We're in the best country on the planet, doing the best job in the country, working towards a goal that has…transfixed humanity throughout recorded history. And it's in our grasp. We've got a night off, and we're outside eating cheeseburgers. What more could we possibly want?"

I shrug. Maybe he's right.

"Actually," he goes on, "I do want another burger."

"Jesus, where do you put it? I always feel like I'm having dinner with Paul Bunyan."

"High metabolism! I got in some pushups at the plant, and I'm gonna run tomorrow. Gotta stay moving, Buzz! That takes fuel."

"That's why you're out here, isn't it? Making sure they put enough food lockers in the spacecraft when they redesign it."

"You're on to me." He laughs. "This is important stuff, Buzz!" Then he gets up and grabs another burger. (Another man might seem like a pig eating so much, but not Ed White. He's always polite and neat about it, almost reverentially ravenous. And there's something entirely appropriate about his appetite; it's another way he's a touch ahead of everyone, a standout even in a crowd of overachievers, a Cadillac in a showroom full of Buicks.)

"Whaddaya think, go grab a beer somewhere?" I ask when he returns.

"Ehh, I'm beat. Let's just head on back, relax for a bit."

"Relax" isn't a word I've heard a lot lately, but I figure he's probably right, so before long, we're back at the motel. He flips through the TV Guide. "*Star Trek*'s coming on in a few."

"That'll work."

Ed turns on the TV and it's clouded in static. "All right. Let's see if our technical skills are equal to the common American television set." He turns the VHF dial and adjusts the rabbit ears. It still doesn't look all that great.

"Jesus, it's a good thing you're working on flight controls and not communications," I laugh. "Here, let me." I realign the antenna and the picture improves considerably.

The episode opens with Enterprise circling an alien planet.

The TV starship is being buffeted heavily by some unknown shockwaves, which turn out to be ripples of time displacement. Doctor McCoy arrives to tend to a wounded crewman; he accidentally falls on an injector and gives himself a massive dose of cortazine. In a flash, he goes stark raving mad; he flees the bridge on the ship's elevator, ranting about murderers and assassins. Cut to a cigarette commercial.

"Not a bad setup they've got," Ed says.

"I would kill to have that much room on a spaceship. You could fit every Gemini ever flown on the bridge alone."

"Come on, we're just getting started!" Ed laughs. "You can fit a lot of Wright Flyers in a C-141, too. Give it a couple centuries, Buzz."

"Why wait? You know, as long as we're out here working on a redesign..." (I look at my watch.) "...we could drive up to Hollywood, kidnap a couple set designers, take them back to North American. We'd have a roomier spaceship in no time."

Ed laughs.

The episode resumes. "The City on the Edge of Forever," it is called. Kirk makes a captain's log entry about the situation with McCoy. "In a strange wild frenzy he has fled the ship's bridge," he intones. "We have no way of knowing if the madness is permanent or temporary, or in what direction it will drive McCoy." The doctor, it turns out, is heading to the transporter room; he beams himself down to the planet, near the center of the time displacement.

In short order, Kirk and Spock and Uhura follow, along with a landing party: uniforms of gold and blue and red. They find themselves near a large arch: ancient ruins 10,000 centuries old, putting out waves of time displacement. The time portal awakens and starts talking; it announces that it is the Guardian of Forever.

Soon it's showing images from human history, like a television set that's somehow tuned in to signals from long ago. "Behold...a gateway to your own past," the Guardian says. The portal starts showing scenes from the twentieth century: howitzers firing, soldiers rushing across a cratered battlefield. "Strangely compelling," Kirk says. "To step through there, and lose oneself in another world..." And then McCoy appears from nowhere and jumps through the portal.

Uhura tries to communicate with the Enterprise, but she can't reach them. "Your vessel, your beginning. All that you knew is gone," the Guardian solemnly intones. To which Kirk says: "McCoy has somehow changed history. Earth's not there, at least not Earth as we know it. We're totally alone."

"Whoops," Ed adds as the commercials start to roll.

"My father's always been…obsessed with the past. I don't get it. You can't go back there. It's always getting further away. Why not look ahead instead?"

Ed shrugs. "We are in a profession that focuses on the future."

"He was, too, though! He was a…pioneer of aviation!"

Ed nods. "Yeah, I remember you talking about him." (We've known each other long enough that there's always that danger of having the same conversation two, three, four times. But Ed's never been the type of guy to make you feel like an ass for repeating yourself.) "That's another thing we've got in common: a legacy to live up to."

"Legacy." I snort. "I never wanted to follow in his footsteps. I love him, but…I've always needed to mark out my own path. And this is one way. Avoiding all this…fucking nostalgia. That's all he talks about, what he's already done. Driving around pointing out old history like it's…more real than reality. 'Here's the field where Goddard and I did this,' and 'Here's the restaurant where Jimmy Doolittle and I did that.' For a pilot in particular, it seems like you'd want to keep moving forward. I mean, that's how flight works…"

"So you're saying: time flies, it doesn't drive," Ed chuckles.

I laugh. "Yeah, something like that."

When the show comes back, Kirk and Spock have decided to travel through the portal themselves, to prevent McCoy from altering the past. They have to rewatch all of the imagery flickering past and judge their leap exactly. The portal is shrouded in smoke and fog; when the time seems right, they leap into the clouds.

They emerge on a city street with posters for a boxing match in Madison Square Garden. It's America in the 1930s.

"So it's a time travel story instead of a space travel story," I observe.

"Every story's a time travel story," Ed points out. Then to the TV: "Jeez, guys, go to a time I haven't seen, at least! They're stuck in our childhood."

I laugh.

Kirk and Spock explore their new surroundings, looking absurd and self-conscious in their Starfleet uniforms. Kirk spies some clothes hanging out to dry on a fire escape and says: "Well, we'll steal from the rich and give back to the poor later." They're stopped by a meat-and-potatoes Irish beat cop; Kirk stumbles through a comical lie attempting to explain Spock's alien ears. "My friend is actually Chinese…he caught his head in a mechanical rice picker."

"Honor code violation!" I holler, as Mr. Spock puts a Vulcan neck pinch on the cop and the two scamper off with their stolen clothes.

Ed laughs. "Lying *and* stealing. They never should've made it through Starfleet."

The men flee to a basement, where they get changed and discuss their predicament. It seems impossible that they'll randomly run into Dr. McCoy in the past. But Spock points out that they could somehow be drawn towards the same time and place. "There could be some logic to the belief that time is fluid like a river. Currents, eddies, backwash." he says, putting on a skullcap to hide his pointy ears. Kirk asks if this is true, to which Spock replies: "I didn't say it was true, Captain. I said we had no other hope."

Then a beautiful woman comes down the stairs and asks what they're doing there. Kirk admits that they've stolen clothes and fled from a cop.

"Oh, now he gets all honest!" I laugh. "Once there's a woman involved..."

"Charming and disarming," Ed chuckles.

The woman runs a charitable organization, the 21st Street Mission. Kirk and Spock go to work for her; soon they're eating soup and bread in the mission, listening to the woman preach to the other homeless men. "One day soon, man is going to be able to harness incredible energies, maybe even the atom," she says. She talks about voyaging to the stars "to give each man hope, and a common future." Her name, it turns out, is Edith Keeler.

Before long, Edith Keeler and Captain Kirk start falling for each other. She has a sense that he belongs in another time and place, that things are somehow disconnected and wrong. But soon they're going out on the town; Kirk charms her with stories of novels that don't exist, and planets yet to be discovered. Meanwhile, Spock builds an electrical contraption with a lot of metal and lightbulbs, like a microfiche reader that can read newspapers from the near future. He pulls up a headline with a picture of Edith Keeler that says: SOCIAL WORKER KILLED.

Kirk comes back and asks Spock what he's discovered. Spock finds another newspaper article from six years hence which discusses Edith Keeler meeting with President Roosevelt. Then the recording device short-circuits and catches on fire.

Kirk seems intrigued by the presidential meeting, but Spock offers up the other alternative: "Or, Captain. Edith Keeler will die this year. I saw her obituary. Some sort of traffic accident." Kirk muses: "She has two possible futures. And depending on whether she lives or dies, all history will be changed." To which Spock replies with cold logic: "Suppose we discover that, in order to set things straight again, Edith Keeler must die."

"Now it's getting interesting," Ed says as the commercials roll.

"You think that could make a difference?" I ask. "A traffic accident and a war?"

"Sure, why not? Everything makes a difference. Look at the fire. Look at the accidents we've seen in our careers. Small decisions, big consequences. Somebody replaces an engine, or waits to change an indicator light, or tries to stay under the clouds in bad weather..."

This summons painful memories: Charlie Bassett, the crash. "I try not to think about that stuff. I tend to get a bit...fatalistic."

"I think we all do. You have to. You do all the preflight checklists and tests, but if it's your turn..."

"Do you ever get the feeling that it's all...wrong somehow?" I ask. "Like we took a wrong turn somewhere back, and things aren't the way they're supposed to be?"

He gives me a strange look, uncomprehending. "Everything's the way it's supposed to be, Buzz."

"Yes, but who's to say, though?"

He thinks about it for a minute. "I guess, for me, it's just part of having faith. If you believe in God, you have to believe things are the way they should be. That all these supposedly random things happen the way they're supposed to."

The episode resumes. McCoy arrives in the past, still raving about assassins and murderers. He realizes he's on Earth in the twentieth century; he breaks down weeping about doctors who "sew people like garments." Meanwhile Kirk and Edith Keeler are spending more time together; she fantasizes that all the money spent on war and death could instead be spent on life: space travel and exploration. Kirk's clearly smitten.

When he goes back to his room, Spock's getting the memory circuit back up and running. Kirk watches anxiously. Spock reads more from the device, discussing news reports about a growing pacifist movement in the 1930s, led by Edith Keeler. It apparently delayed the U.S.'s entry into World War

II, giving Germany time to complete nuclear experiments. "She was right," Kirk says. "Peace was the way." To which Spock responds with chilling words: "She was right. But at the wrong time. With the A-bomb, and with the V2 rockets to carry them, Germany captured the world."

Kirk tells Spock he's in love with Edith Keeler. To which Spock responds with pure logic, like a glass of cold water to the face: "Jim. Edith Keeler must die."

Out in the hallway, the two bump into Edith. She stumbles; Kirk catches her and keeps her from falling down the stairs. She mentions offhandedly that she could have broken her neck, and thanks Kirk for saving her. But Spock pulls Kirk aside and points out that Keeler could have died then and there. He says: "If you save her and do as your heart tells you to do, then millions will die who did not die before."

Meanwhile, McCoy finds his way to the 21st Street Mission. Edith Keeler takes him in, and soon he's back to normal: gentle and emotional, and grateful for her care.

Soon, Edith Keeler's back out on the town with Kirk, getting ready to go to the movies. A normal peaceful night, until she mentions Dr. McCoy. This gets Kirk's attention: the object of their time travel is finally at hand. He jerks into full alertness as if coming out of a trance: no longer a starry-eyed romantic, but a man with a fateful mission. He runs across the street just as Dr. McCoy comes outside. Edith Keeler, confused by all of this, crosses the street herself to see what was going on...

Then: headlights, and a truck's dark silhouette. A crash.

We both sit there for a few moments as the chilling ending unfolds. Then, credits and the familiar theme music. At last we're staring blankly at the flickering commercials.

Finally, Ed reaches up and turns off the set. I get up and use the bathroom, and when I come back out, he's on the phone with his wife, talking about nothing.

•••

I fall asleep, then wake suddenly. Not much time has passed.

Ed sleeps soundly in the other bed, the peaceful sleep of the pure of heart. I try to lie still, but my mind is fully charged: circuits closed, capacitors full. I do not know why I'm so restless.

I glance over at the dead lamp, the vacant desk and chair, the dim edges of the room; I watch as the occasional pair of car headlights angles through the edge of the heavy curtains, sweeps the darkness from the corners for a few brief moments, then slices back out to leave us in gloom once more.

I think of poor Charlie Bassett, my old neighbor.

•••

It's February of 1966. Charlie and Elliot See are in a T-38, flying to St. Louis in bad weather alongside Tom Stafford and Gene Cernan. And in the deteriorating weather, both planes botch the runway approach and circle around to try again. Charlie's a great guy and a helluva pilot, near the top of everyone's list, and we all know he'll be a shoo-in for the big missions. But Charlie's in the back seat of the T-38. And when See makes the turn, he loses too much altitude. At some point, he realizes his mistake and hits the afterburners, but it's too late. Their plane hits the roof of the McDonnell Douglas plant, and both men die instantly.

In the weeks afterwards, everyone mourns them, but the whispers around the astronaut office are that See was a fair-weather pilot, too used to the sunny skies of Southern California, too unaccustomed to checking the instruments in bad weather. So the purest sympathy falls on poor Charlie, who was sitting in the back with his hands off the controls, and ended up victim to an accident he might have avoided if he'd been flying.

What's worse, in the shuffling of crews afterwards, Jim Lovell and I end up with the Gemini XII mission. I get my first flight into space, in no small part, because my neighbor and good friend died a horrible death.

•••

I attempt to sleep and fail miserably. I should be tired. At around 10:30, I slip out.

In the parking lot, I look around for a minute. It's clear there isn't really anywhere to go without the car. I get in, drive around for a while. Before I know it, I'm merging onto an expressway, swept up in the red taillight rivers of the electric Los Angeles night. (When you get on the freeway late at night in LA, it's still a traffic jam somehow, and you wonder, "Where the hell are all these people going?" But you don't know where you're going, either.)

I get back on the surface streets. I figure I'll stop and get a drink, at least.

The place I choose is a dive, a dark oasis in the neon sea.

Inside: a man behind the bar, and two on the other side. One's a neatly-trimmed but slightly overweight businessman in a three-piece suit; he sits there reading a book in a circle of light. The other's a dirty postman with acne scars so bad I can see them even though he's in the shadows.

I order up a Schlitz. For a moment I just sit there, relaxing, pleasantly anonymous.

The man in the suit pulls out a pen and underlines several lines in the slim paperback he's reading. Then he leans back with a satisfied air, returns the pen and retrieves a cigarillo, and asks me for a light.

I make a show of patting myself down for the matches I know aren't there. "Sorry. Stopped carrying them when I quit."

"Well, aren't you special," he says.

"I had to quit. I can't step out for a smoke break in my line of work."

"What do you do, friend?"

Do I want to go into all of it? The endless question: What's it like up there? No. So: "Oh, you know. Government work."

"Top secret, huh?"

"Not exactly." I eye him suspiciously. "Why, what do *you* do?"

"I'm a mathematician."

I chuckle. "I work with a lot of mathematicians, a lot of physicists. They say all physicists want to be mathematicians, and all mathematicians want to be God."

He laughs. "Probably true, having been a physicist as well. Given the absence of God, I guess I've made it as high as I can."

"Looking down from the ivory tower?"

"Academia? No, no, no, no. No, I do government work. Top secret." He smirks. "I put in my time at Princeton, but they're a bunch of...insular idiots, scrapping over...turf and tenure. They wouldn't recognize a good idea unless...some undergrad came up with it and they had a chance to steal it."

Finally the postman speaks: "You think the government is the place to get away from thieves and idiots?" His uniform is ratty and disheveled, and beside him, there's a sack that looks like undelivered mail.

The suited man hoists his sherry. "Who's the bigger idiot? The man in government who makes decisions that shape the world, or the lowly schmuck who has to live in that world?"

"Don't forget, I'm a government man myself," the postman replies. A woman materializes, from the bathroom, perhaps, an ugly woman with enormous breasts and barely enough clothing to hold them in; she sits next to the postman, and he places his hand on her thigh, far higher and more inward than would be acceptable in polite society. "And it does have its perks."

"Well that's charming," the mathematician smirks. "I'm not one to judge, but…"

"But what?"

"Are you supposed to be whoring around in uniform?"

"What are you saying, you fink?" the postman asks angrily. "Gloria here is a respectable housewife. I met her on my route."

"Delightful," the mathematician says, and lifts his glass again. "Here's to the seediness of the common man, ever mistaking craftiness for intelligence."

"Just what are you saying?" The postman rises as if to fight.

"Nothing. Nothing at all." The mathematician drains his drink.

"Just remember," the postman continues. "Whatever your big ideas, they depend on people like me to actually make them happen. I am the front line of the government, I am the representative, I am the one people actually see."

I turn to the mathematician. "So what is your big idea?" I ask.

He shakes his head at the postman and turns back my way. "Oh, I've done some work in game theory, nuclear strategy and all that, but my favorite work is still back in physics."

"Ahh. Lemme guess, you're one of these modern physics types? Collapsing functions, electrons orbiting in a probability cloud, the dual wave and particle nature of light depending on the observer..."

"There is no observer!" He pounds the bar so hard the ashtray rattles. "How can it all work, if there is an observer? A man is watching a double-slit experiment, he observes a photon behave a certain way. But what if there's another observer, observing that observer? Does he see the same thing? Yes. If Bohr is correct, if it is the observation that pins down that quantum event, for that moment, it is that observation that collapses the wave function, and all these other possibilities cease to exist. So how can he, this other observer, if they're observing independently, how can he see the same thing, all the time?"

"But everyone does see the same thing."

"Sometimes it seems that way," he says.

"No! Everyone sees the same thing." Now I'm the one getting testy: no longer the disinterested observer, but something uncomfortably more like a participant. "How do you explain that?"

"Multiple universes." He takes a satisfied puff on his cigarillo while the bartender replaces his drink.

"Multiple universes? How many? One for every person?"

"No. Infinity."

"That's preposterous."

"That's the only way to make sense of it all nowadays. At every decision point, there is another universe born. Or, not born, but...it splits, like an amoeba. Both parts are the same as the original, but they go on to different things. The same history, different futures, even though the source material is identical...it's a universal wave function, and it never collapses. What's a decision you made today?"

"I decided to come here."

"Instead of?"

"Instead of staying in the hotel room and calling it a night."

"So there. There is another universe where you DID stay in, where you are sleeping soundly right now."

"But that decision, it isn't all an either/or thing. I could have stayed in my hotel room asleep, I could have woken up my roommate, I could have left the room at 9:30, at 9:31, at 9:32, at 9:32 and 16 seconds, 17 seconds, 18 seconds...I could have gone for a drive, I could have ended up at a different bar, I could have gone and bought a gift for my wife, I could've driven my car off a cliff..."

"Yes. All decision points. That is what modern physics demands. There is a universe for all of these things, with you in all of them."

"That's insane. There would be so many universes from my decisions tonight alone. An infinite number just from me, tonight."

He laughs. "Do you understand how big infinity is?"

"Well..."

"Obviously you don't," he says. "You could drive a spaceship along an infinite line at the speed of light for the entirety of your life, and have your children and grandchildren do the same when you die, for a hundred thousand generations, and there would still be as much ahead as there was when you started. If there was an observer, which there isn't, they could see the before and after and they wouldn't think the spaceship had moved at all. And that's just one line, one direction, one dimension. There are infinities that are still subsets of other infinities. All the odd numbers, one, three, five, and on and on to infinity, and all the even numbers, and together they're another infinity, and that's still just integers, so they're still subsets of yet another infinity. 1.000000 and 1.000001 and 2.345498 and 2.3454981, and on and on. Pi itself goes on for infinity, and that's just one infinity in an infinite number of infinities, and that's just among real numbers..."

"Do you even believe what you're saying?"

He laughs, like it's all a big game. "All the precious modern physics, everything the hallowed Bohr worked for, that is the inevitable corollary, if you carry the ideas through."

"That's insane. How did you come up with this?"

He gives a nod down at the book. "Borges helped me a bit." Then he raises his snifter of sherry. "Along with copious amounts of alcohol."

"How does your consciousness not know all these other universes, then? Wouldn't these other versions of me still know they're me?"

"You are only conscious of the one that keeps you alive."

"So everyone that's dying in my universe, is living in their own?"

"Exactly," he says.

"Like...*Star Trek* or something," I mutter.

He snickers. "This is so much bigger than *Star Trek*."

"All right. So am I in your universe, or are you in mine?"

"You probably think I'm a bit player in yours," he says. "But you're playing a walk-on role in mine." He sips his sherry, self-satisfied.

"Jesus Christ, like life isn't...lonely enough already. No wonder you need to drink. So...everyone, really? The bartender? The postman?"

"I'm not a bit player in your universe," the postman interrupts.

"Oh, I'm sure you think you're not," the mathematician replies.

"I'm not!" The postman stands up. "Just because you...think you're the center of the universe doesn't mean you are. This beer is real. Why can't you just shut up and enjoy it?" He grabs the woman, moves toward us. "Gloria's tits are real. My fist is real. Your face is real."

With a start, I stand up, backing out from between them. "Look, is all this necessary?"

"He does this all the time," the bartender mutters. "Take it out back!" he says to the postman.

"Look, this is absurd," the mathematician replies. "You're too drunk to fight anyway."

"I'm drunk enough to feel no pain, which means I'm drunk enough to kick your ass," the postman responds, and stumble-lunges forward, falling against the barstool and the bar while grabbing at the other man.

In a flash the bartender's coming around the bar to separate them, yelling: "Take it out back, Chuck!"

"I will, if he's not afraid!"

"If this is your universe, you should win, right?" I tell the mathematician.

At this, he stands, removes his jacket and vest and his glasses, and lays them neatly on the bar.

I have the sense that no good could come of this, so I hang back as they head out back, the postman practically falling over, the mathematician with a barely perceptible wobble. Gloria shakes her head in disgust as they pass, and comes over to sit next to me. We drink. I steal a glance at the paperback the mathematician was reading: *The Garden of Forking Paths*.

The other two are out there for a while. We hear muffled grunts and a clattering of trash cans.

They come back in, arms around each other's shoulders, both disheveled now.

"Well, there will soon be an infinite number of other universes where I kicked your ass," the mathematician says.

"It's alright, I had you at a disadvantage," the postman replies. "I wasn't worried about taking a hit to my face. It couldn't possibly look any worse."

"You can say that again," the mathematician says.

To which the postman responds with a sucker punch.

The bartender comes around to pull them apart. "Come on, guys, knock it off!"

"Jesus, get me out of here, will you?" Gloria asks, and before I know what's happening, she has her hand on my thigh.

I jump like a scalded cat. "Oh, look at the time. I really should be going. I have to work tomorrow, in my universe."

But the postman's seen enough. He lunges. At her.

He shouts: "You ugly whore!"

I deflect him away, and he clatters to the floor between the stools and the bar, and I think I hear something like "...no-good stuck-up prick," and now at last he's trying to come up off the floor after me, but the bartender's holding him back as I back off, and it's clear there's no longer any value to being here, so when the bartender says: "You might wanna leave, buddy," I say "Yeah," and peel off a twenty and set it down and head out.

•••

The next day I ask Ed again: "Do you think everything's how it's supposed to be?"

We've spent the morning working with the quality assurance types, a bunch of serious-looking young go-getters in ties and short-sleeve-shirts, studying blueprints and using gauge blocks to compare tolerances to design specs. And now Ed and I have broken away for a quick lunch at the executive cafeteria, the so-called "golden trough." (We make it a point to eat there often, to talk about the issues we've seen with the people powerful enough to address them, all those executives living high on the hog.)

"It's getting to where it's supposed to be," he says. "These guys are sharp. And the test sounds like it's going…"

"No, in general. LBJ. Vietnam. Life. Everything."

"Compared to what?" he asks. "It's not like there's a…set of gauge blocks you can put together to check it all out. Make sure the world's manufactured according to spec…"

"If there was a portal, like in the show, would you go back and change something? Stop the fire, keep all this from getting off track?"

"Still thinking about that, huh?" He grins. "Well, there isn't, so it doesn't matter. Like you said, there's no point even trying to go backwards."

"Yeah." I survey the room anew. All the while, executives are trickling in, all these bright men, the brains of the body that's building the machine that will take us to the moon. "I guess you always have to assume there's a path forward from disaster."

Venus Mission

Part III: CME

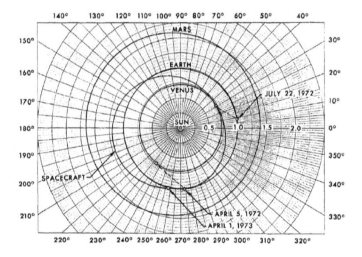

Disaster strikes a little over a month after the flyby.

Nobody feels it, not right away. I'm the first one to see it, but that's only because I'm the one on the telescope, staring at the sun. And I don't recognize it for what it is.

Disaster looks like opportunity at first.

"All right, there's a large spot in active region 107," I say for Houston's benefit, even though they're over six light-minutes away now. We're looking through x-ray filters; the sun's a violent maelstrom, and yet it's a strange refuge from all the craziness back home, the news reports about the massacre in Munich, and the airline hijacking in Detroit, and bombs in Belfast, and the fall of Saigon.

"Got something good?" Kerwin asks.

"Yeah. Think it might be a flare. Very high PMEC count here. I'm going to start the JOP."

"Careful on film," Shepard says from the other side of the deck.

"I've got a feeling this one'll be worth a few frames." I'm eager to finally capture the whole solar flare cycle. Or to recapture it, I should say.

"You said that about the last one, too." Shepard snips.

I want to get mad. But he's right. I have burned up frames on flares that fizzled out. And my thinking has been…fuzzy. My post-EVA funk only lasted a couple days; I'd spent most of the time down in the sleeping chambers, on sick call of sorts, until the morning I'd finally grown disgusted with my lethargy, at which point I'd floated upstairs to heat up the breakfast trays, gingerly stepping back into my routines as if nothing had happened. I waited to see what the others would say, but they said nothing.

Since then, I've been eager to make up for lost time, eager to make up for everything. But there's some vague uncertainty permeating my mind like a fog; I have been relying on the lists more and more, double- and triple-checking as I go.

"No…this might actually be the most intense event we've seen so far." I snap away happily: pictures across the visible spectrum, through the hydrogen-alpha filter, images from the x-ray telescope and the ultraviolet spectroheliograph. The spot gets bigger and bigger.

"Boy who cried wolf, here," Shepard doesn't even look at the monitors.

"Umm, the PMEC is over 800."

Kerwin floats over and glances at the small TV monitor in the console. "Wow. That does look like it's worth a few pics."

(He has, of course, already taken pictures of the full solar flare cycle, but those photos are still floating in space, along with the rest of our pre-flyby telescope film.)

"PMEC is still climbing," I say. "This is really intense."

"That's a loop building up, out of frame." Kerwin points to the tip of a jagged scar on the monitor near the edge of the flare. "Zoom out for a bit."

"I'm...uhh, I'm in the middle of the flare JOP. I want to make sure we're getting all of it."

"Buzz, zoom out," Shepard snaps, even though he's floating over by the DSKY and still hasn't looked over to see what we're talking about.

I snap one more flare pic and then dial down the telescope magnification so the sun's whole disk is in view. The scar we'd seen is part of something spectacular, a massive S-shaped slash across the sun.

"Is that a coronal mass ejection?" Kerwin asks, amazed.

"This is a lot bigger than any we've seen." We've seen looping prominences before, smaller ones, relatively speaking, although still large enough that you could roll the planet Earth underneath them. But this dark area stretches across the sun's entire diameter. "This is almost like those pictures from December."

"What happened in December?" Shepard asks.

"That thing they talked about in training," Kerwin explains.

"What satellite was that?" I ask. "OSO-7?"

"Yeah. They took a grainy picture on its coronograph. Looked like a flash. Huge. Really bright, so much so that they thought it was an error with the instruments at first. On the second image, they saw it had moved, like this huge mass had lifted off the sun. But they still had a hard time making sense of it."

"Well I guess now's our chance to get some better pictures."

I switch over to the coronograph so we can get a good look in visible light at the growing body of solar material. Over the next twenty minutes or so, we watch it swell visibly. It's hard to get a really good shot, because the slash is rising towards us edge-wise. This is when it occurs to me that I should be concerned.

I key the radio mike and speak into my headset, a voice into the void: "Houston, Explorer, we are going to put some imagery over the TV downlink. Hope you're monitoring it. This is...unlike anything we've seen up here." Then to Kerwin: "It does look like those...uhh...magnetic mechanisms are at work."

"Yeah. Almost like...rubber bands or something."

"Rubber bands?"

"Yeah. All the magnetic field lines. Like the sun's a ball of rubber bands, and because the middle's rotating faster, they're stretching, and eventually they snap, but since they're magnetic, they stick back together to others." Kerwin sounds a little off lately.

"Magnetic rubber bands?"

"I guess...I think. And they're throwing off material when they snap. You get the idea."

I'm dubious. "And the material they throw off still stays in a big loop."

"And there's radiation."

"Magnetic looping radioactive rubber bands." It does sound odd. I've been studying the sun for months, and I know what he's getting at, but it still sounds odd. "Too bad we don't have any regular magnetic rubber bands on board. Might make for a good educational film."

It occurs to me that I'm getting a little uncomfortable. My weak bladder's caused its share of hassle in my life; right now it's telling me to turn the console over to Joe and go take a leak. But I don't want to be robbed of this. Nobody's photographed anything of this sort, not with instruments as good as ours. Whatever I've done wrong so far, this is a chance to make up for it. I force myself to ignore myself, my body's sad limits; I lose myself in work, and time dissolves for a while more: Ten minutes? Twenty?

The headset voices come back: "Explorer, Houston, we are monitoring the large solar event on your downlink. Getting some concerning info from OSO-7. Be prepared to..." The transmission crackles, but it sounds to me like something-something command module.

"Command module?" I ask.

Shepard looks concerned and angry. "Houston, Explorer. We do not copy. Please repeat and explain your last about the command module.'"

I will myself to stay still. The entire area is lifting off, rising like a steam bubble in a pot of slow-simmering soup, only it's two-dimensional, more or less. And then at last, the bubble starts to burst, flinging material all over, much of it spaceward, towards us.

"Wow." I'm still photographing, but it's hard not to just stare in wonder.

"Gentlemen, I do believe that's a coronal mass ejection," Kerwin says.

"Did you get that, Buzz?" Shepard's floated over at last.

"I think so. We're still transmitting TV. Hopefully they caught all of it."

Shepard transmits: "Houston, Explorer, please tell us you caught that, over."

I remain transfixed. The x-ray images are spectacular: it's like watching a volcano in slo-mo. Parts of what erupted are falling back into the sun, but the mass that's lifted off is substantial, and it's clearly continuing on towards us, and as I do the math I realize it isn't slow at all, it's just so big that you forget it's also fast. I run the numbers again in my head. They sound impossible.

I need validation. "Wait, the sun's what…865,000 miles in diameter?"

"More or less," Kerwin says.

"And how long did that thing take to lift off? Under an hour, right?"

He sees where I'm going with this. "It had to be under an hour. And it's hard to tell looking edgewise, but the ends of the loop are more than a solar diameter away from the limb now. So that's well over a million miles an hour..."

"So it should reach us in a few days. That'll be interesting."

I see a flicker-flash, in a dark corner high against the ceiling. Then another down in the latrine hallway. I've never seen two in such quick succession.

Then Shepard says: "What was our last from them?" Meaning the last transmission. "Did they clarify about the command module?"

And it occurs to me we should have had our response by now. An awful icy hand grips my stomach. "Houston, Explorer, comm check, over."

Shepard speaks into his own headset. "Houston, Explorer, we've received no comms for several minutes. Please confirm..."

Again I see a flicker-flash. And another. "I swear, I'm seeing those flashes again."

Kerwin gets a look like he remembered something. He pulls out his dosimeter. "Uhh, gentlemen, what do your PRDs say?"

We carry the dosimeters in a pocket on our thighs; they're about the size of a pack of cigarettes. I fumble for mine, and when I see the numbers, all I can say is: "Oh."

Underneath the word RADS, there's a series of black and white rotary digits, like the odometer of a car. The device is incremented in units of .01, but the whole number seems completely off from what it was, improbably high now. And the last couple digits are moving visibly.

None of us has ever seen that, in all of our time up here.

"Jesus," Shepard says.

"They wanted us in the command module," Kerwin says, so cold and urgent that we forget he's the junior crewmember. "We need to get up there now."

All the exciting solar work now feels like nothing. I abandon the console and float into the hallway. As I pass the bathroom, my bladder twinges with regret: I should have gone while I had the chance. I head up the tunnel, with Kerwin and Shepard right after.

The command module is dark and depressing, unlit and chilly.

"Explorer, Houston," we hear at last in the headsets, crackly and far away. "We're recommending you drop what you're doing and get to the command module. There may be radiation associated with this event, and the shielding should be much better in there. Please acknowledge. Over."

To Shepard I ask: "How long do they want us in here?"

He gives a look of mild annoyance: of course he doesn't know any more than I do. "Houston, Explorer. We have moved to the command module. Please advise if you want us to turn it on, and how long we'll be up here. Over."

"That's, what 180, 190 rads more than it was?" Kerwin is looking again at his dosimeter. Then, to Earth: "Houston,

Explorer, sorry for the double transmission. We're seeing some heavy readings on the dosimeters. Science Pilot is now 53901 and climbing. Over."

"Gotta be a glitch." I turn. "Right?" The last word sabotages whatever certainty the rest of the statement held.

"Well I don't feel anything," Shepard says.

"That's not how it works with radiation," Kerwin replies. "At least at this dose. It's not one you could actually feel right away."

"But we will feel it?" I ask.

"We will."

•••

We start to settle in to the command module. I fold up the center couch, and there's a little more room.

"It's climbing a lot slower now," Kerwin says, taking yet another look at the dosimeter. "We're still getting some rads, though. They're probably not gonna let us back down there until this is over. And that might be a while."

"There we go," Shepard says. "Buzz, you want to turn it on now, or wait for confirmation?"

"I...uhh...gotta take care of some bladder business first. Guess I'll have to do it up here."

I dig through the lockers for all the pieces of the contraption, the condom with the tube and the urine bag, all the stuff we've avoided on this trip, except for the spacewalks. Now that I'm thinking about the fact that I have to go, I can barely think. When it's all assembled, it feels like it's just in time; instead of the overall awfulness of everything, my mind's narrowed to this bliss, this blessed release. But it's over soon enough.

The radio comes back on: "Explorer, Houston. It appears the charged particle activity is still increasing. Go ahead and power up the command module when you get a chance. We're going to have you stay up there until further notice. We copy the PRD dose. Please keep us informed of sym..." (Static.)

"Symptoms?" I ask.

Kerwin nods. "Symptoms."

•••

It takes time for Houston to tell us more; it takes so long I start wondering if something's happened to the comms.

While we wait, the loneliness feels magnified a hundredfold. Plus there is this overwhelming notion that something massive and irrevocable has happened, something we cannot understand, let alone stop. To keep my thoughts at bay I start turning on the command module, running through the checklist. That helps a bit.

At last we hear from Earth: "Explorer, Houston. The CME looked pretty bad from down here. You may see some symptoms in the next few hours. Glad you've got a doctor on board. We will work out a plan to keep things working if you can't work. Over."

"Houston, Explorer. We will keep an eye out for symptoms, over," Kerwin transmits.

"That's it?" I sputter. "Isn't there...something more we should be doing?"

"There isn't a lot they can do for us," Kerwin says. "This is high-energy radiation. Gamma ray and x-ray photons. And protons accelerated to near-light speed. If we were on Earth and this was a...nuclear plant accident or something, it would be more about keeping us from ingesting isotopes that were emitting alpha particles. Something like that, we could take iodine, at least, to keep our thyroids from picking up radioactive iodine from the atmosphere. But here..." He gives a weightless shrug. "Particles and shielding. The more mass between you and the source, the better. That's why these things don't affect people as much on Earth...they're not just protected by the magnetosphere, but the mass of the atmosphere."

"What kind of symptoms are we talking here, doc?" Shepard asks.

"In the next few hours? It's possible we'll get some nausea. Maybe some trouble on the other end of the digestive tract. You can also see some..."

I turn back to the checklist. The lights are on now, and everything's looking a little more comfortable, but I'm having a hard time focusing. Or harder. I read the checklist. I reread it. "Wait, we're not up on the comms here. Are we?"

Kerwin gives me a look. "...some of that."

"What?"

"That can be another sign of ours."

The sentence I've heard makes no sense. "Ours?"

"A.R.S. Acute Radiation Sickness, the thing we're talking about?"

"No, uhh...what's a sign?"

"Confusion."

I take a long pause. "Are you sure?" I smile.

"Very funny."

"What else?" Shepard asks.

"We covered this in training, didn't we?" Kerwin seems surprised at our ignorance.

"I don't know, did we?"

Shepard gives a little look, like: come on. "What else?"

"Hair loss. Fatigue. Basically it kills off a lot of the very active cells, like in your bone marrow, so your white and red blood cell counts go really low. But yeah, at higher doses, you get extreme confusion."

"You know, I don't think we did cover this in training. I think you're a little...uhh..." I give a look that says: mixed up.

"Hardy har har," he says. "'Physician, heal thyself,' right?"

He's quoting as snappily as ever, *Honeymooners* and Shakespeare, so I'm hoping we're going to be OK. But it feels like gallows humor.

"Well I don't feel any different," Shepard says.

"It takes a few hours at this dosage. It wreaks havoc on different molecules, and that starts to have effects at the cellular level. Like I said, depending on how it hits the bone marrow, we could really be wiped out for a few weeks."

My stomach twinges. I don't know if it's angst, or the tip of something bigger.

But I need to work. This part's my responsibility. I double- and triple-check the comms switches. At last I'm confident enough to transmit: "Houston, Explorer, we are up and running on the command module comms. Over."

I gather my thoughts, organize the objects floating about my personal space.

The next transmission arrives soon enough it's possible they haven't heard our last. "Explorer, Houston, we're..." The crackly voices in the headset sound more distant than ever. "...have you cease work on any non-flight tasks. We want to..." (Static.) "...ment. We'll run the numbers. Then if necessary, we'll take care of the..." (Crackle.) "...rection scheduled for 29 September. Over."

"Erection?" Shepard says, just to us.

"I'll let you handle that one solo." I laugh.

"I heard alignment and course correction." Kerwin says, then keys the mike. "Houston, Explorer. We copy alignment and course correction if necessary. We'll get started in a moment. Over." Then to us, again: "They get it. We might not be able to work for a while."

I get back to throwing switches. These are routine tasks, but there is an extra tension to it now, knowing it isn't part of the plan. If we are off course, we need to fire the engine and rectify it now, or we won't be able to, for who knows how long. But we hadn't planned on staying in the command module for an extended period, so we'll have to keep a close eye on the fuel cells...

Enough. Those decisions are days in the future. I force myself to concentrate on the here and now. "Moving on to alignment."

"We're going to run a Program 23, right?" Shepard asks. "Venus and three stars?"

"Yeah. Get a state vector and see if they want to do a PAD for a burn."

"All right."

The computer program requires us to measure the angles between the stars and a planet, to confirm our position in the Solar System. I float down to the lower equipment bay, to the telescope and sextant; I key the commands in to the computer so we can look back at Venus, the former object of our desire, already 16 million miles away now.

"Do you mind if I take a look, Buzz?" Shepard asks, with something like humility.

The telescope attached to the sextant is only one-power, so it's an odd request; we could observe it far better in the manned module, whenever we're allowed back down there. Then again, this way we can see it as it really is. "Be my guest, captain."

He floats on down to see for himself; he lingers at the eyepiece like a man looking at a picture of an old flame. "Hard to believe we were ever there."

I can't see Kerwin from where I'm at, but I hear a smile in his voice: "If we were ever there."

Shepard floats off. I take another look: Venus is bright and distant, not much more than another star. I plug the measurements into the computer to transmit them back to the ground.

Then Shepard taps me. I'm expecting an order for some other flight-type task, but it's: "We may as well get started on dinner."

"OK."

In the headset I hear: "Explorer, Houston. We copy your..." (Static.) "...mission. The state vectors are close. We will run everything..." (More static.) "...RTCC and see if we have a PAD for you."

"Houston, Explorer, we copy," Shepard replies. "Send us a PAD if you have one. Until then, my crew needs to be fed, so we're gonna eat while we can. Over."

"Is it just me, or are the comms worse up here?" I ask.

"Yeah," Kerwin says. "It's like it's dipping every so often."

"We'll take a look while we eat," Shepard says.

Kerwin gives a little look like: what is the point of dinner? But he doesn't say anything.

We have a few meal pouches up here: not the full dinner trays, but enough to tide us over. When I stop and think, though, I'm not quite as hungry as I probably should be; it feels like we're going through the motions, more from hopefulness and force of habit than anything. Routine feels awful until there's a chance that you won't be able to do it anymore. Then it becomes a refuge.

I dole out the food packets while the computers crunch through the numbers, 70 million miles away. We do still have hot water up here; we heat up the packets and crack them open.

"Football's coming up in a few weeks," Kerwin observes.

Shepard looks down at his pouch like he's wondering what he's doing. "What's there to be excited about? Oilers are gonna suck. Patriots are gonna suck. Miami and Dallas are gonna be tough to beat again. We're probably better off not seeing all the carnage."

"Are you more of a Patriots fan now that they're New England instead of Boston?"

"I'm just glad they rejected that...idiotic name change." Shepard talks, but I'm watching his food pouch. It hasn't moved. "Bay State Patriots. What Masshole thought of that?"

"I am looking forward to getting back to some games," I chime in. It feels good to be talking, rather than thinking about the fact that I suddenly don't want to eat.

"I'm looking forward to walking," Shepard says. "Getting some serious rounds of golf in, to make up for all the ones I've missed…"

"I think we've all earned the right to kick back a bit, after this," Kerwin observes. He's peeled open his pouch of meatballs but seems in no hurry to dig in. I focus on his spoon. It doesn't move.

"I do want to stay busy," Shepard replies. "Whatever I do. I don't know how much any of us is going to have to do at NASA after this. I'm sure we'll all end up moving on at some point. Some of the guys have talked about beer distributorships. I guess it's a good steady cash flow and a decent amount of work, but you can also kick back a bit, especially if you've got an established brand and a solid territory. But I think I'll stick with the bank stuff. As long as there's some challenge, some competition…"

Shepard still hasn't eaten anything; I'm sure he'll take a bite after this, but he doesn't.

"I don't know what else I want to do," I admit. "It would have been easy to get out after the moon. It would've been the easiest thing in the world. It was practically a job just sorting through all the job offers. But…I don't know."

"It's a different world when you don't have someone else telling you what to do," Shepard says.

"It is. You know, it's funny, all the opportunities I had…the thing I thought about most was just going back on active duty. It's nice being part of something bigger. You don't have to figure out what to do, just how and when. And I guess that's something we'll all have to..." I'm not sure what to say or how to say it. "...I guess you get so used to being a part of something. And this job in particular. You wonder who you are without it. Mike Collins, obviously he left, he's a diplomat now, and he seems to love it. But I don't know what I'd be if I wasn't an astronaut."

"Excuse me, gentlemen." Shepard wipes his face to clean off the food he never ate. Then he turns his head towards the bottom of the console, like he's heading for the tunnel and the manned module.

"You're going down there?" Kerwin asks.

"Couple minutes. It won't kill me to use the bathroom like a human being, will it?" Shepard asks, then floats down out of sight.

"You're not eating?" I ask Joe.

"I gotta admit, I'm not exactly hungry. You?"

In the thin atmosphere it's hard to tell, but I think I hear something from down in the direction of the bathroom, sounds of sickness. "No. Not exactly."

Shepard floats back up.

"You all right, Al?" Kerwin asks.

Our commander's looking a little downcast. Still, I'm expecting something incorrect and innocuous, like: fine, never better.

"I think I am...uh...having some symptoms," he says at last. "Definitely some nausea."

He doubles over, but before we can rush to his aid, the radio comes back on.

"Explorer, Houston…" (Static.) "…got a PAD for you for an SPS burn. Based on…" (More static.) "…pler shift, some discrepancy in your delta-v. We'll give you a minute to get yourselves collected, and we'll read you the numbers."

We still haven't figured out why their signal is cutting out every few seconds. I scan the instruments and see the strength dipping, and the pitch and yaw needles moving. We'll have to figure it out. "Make sure the DSE is recording," I tell Kerwin. Then to Earth: "Houston, Explorer, we copy PAD on the way. Standing by to receive. Mission commander experiencing some nausea, but we'll do what we have to. Over." Although of course it doesn't matter what we transmit right now; their next words are already on their way, and ours will cross paths with them somewhere in the void.

"DSE is recording," Kerwin says.

I need to get ready: I pat myself down for paper and pencil, but no luck. My stomach twists, with worry and more. Where is the pencil?

"Explorer, Houston. Here we go…"

Kerwin taps me on the shoulder and hands me what I need, not a second too soon.

"…orrection. SPS/G&N 87202 plus 0.72, minus 0.13." (Despite the distance I can recognize Paul Weitz's voice. He's reading very slowly and deliberately. I'm praying for a smooth transmission.) "HDT ignition 20:03:01.92, plus

271

0011.8, minus 0000.4, plus 0023.7." (I copy the numbers in the blanks on the PAD worksheet; Kerwin watches as I write.) "Roll 283..." (A splotch of static renders the next words unintelligible.) "...44 Block is N/A; Delta-v T 0022.2, 00:2, 0017.2; Sextant star 30..." (More static.) "...rest of the PAD is N/A. GDC align, Vega and Deneb. Roll align 003, 143, 373. No ullage."

I stare down at the missing number blanks, anxious: we can't fire the engine if the worksheet's incomplete. And I'm sure the recorder didn't pick up everything we missed.

Then the radio comes on again: "We will read through a second time in case you missed anything. SPS/G&N 87202..."

I'm relieved; I copy fervently. But when they get to the middle of the PAD, again there is static. We're still missing numbers.

Weitz continues, oblivious: "...Roll align 003, 143, 373. No ullage. We've built in time for a readback. Over."

They have given us time to confirm the parameters of the burn. But if there's nothing on the tape, it will take 12 minutes to fill in the missing blanks. And there's always a chance that transmission will be garbled. And Shepard's sick, and I don't know how much time we have. My stomach churns...

"You get those numbers?" I point to the empty spots. Kerwin shakes his head no.

I key the mic: "Houston, Explorer. We did not copy the numbers for roll and sextant star. The rest of the PAD is as follows…" I regurgitate the columns of numbers. "We will play back the DSE and see if we got anything. Over." At the end of the transmission, I check my watch: 19:40, Houston time. I force myself to breathe. Even if there's nothing on the DSE, we should still have time for them to retransmit the missing numbers.

"Reception's getting worse," Kerwin says.

"Yeah. Take a look at the S-Band, will you? We need to see why we're getting those gaps."

He studies the indicators for the radio and the high-gain. I float down to the Digital Storage Equipment and play back the last transmission from Earth, staring back at my worksheet. Sure enough, the recording's garbled. We need the next one to come through clearly.

"The needles are moving," he says. "It's like it's not tracking properly. I'm going to cycle the breakers and see if that does anything." The old standby: turn it off, and turn it back on.

In the meantime, it's time to take stock. Shepard is doubled over. Beads of sweat cling to his forehead. Our uneaten food packets float about the cabin.

"You all right, Al?"

He grumbles something like: Not a happy camper right now.

"We got this." I hope it's true.

Again I look at the time: 19:49.

I pluck the food packets out of the air and grab a few stray bits that are drifting towards the air vents; we'll have to put it in the airlock whenever we're allowed back downstairs. The smell of the uneaten food offends my nose and that, in turn, turns my stomach. I swallow hard.

19:51.

Do I have time to go to the bathroom? No, best not to risk it. I police up my workbook and pencil and float back to the console and wait. My insides are rumbling now, a volcano ready to blow. I imagine the citizens of Pompeii gazing up at the smoking mountain; 11-year-old me chuckles a little at the absurd analogy, and 42-year-old me shakes his head in judgment.

At last, the radio crackles on in our headsets: "Explorer, Houston, understand you did not copy part of the PAD. Your transmission was garbled…" (Static.) "…know what you missed. We are going to read through twice more so we can make the burn time we…" (Garbled.) "…ll give you a minute to prepare. Over."

"Jesus, we don't need all the numbers." My blood's now rising along with the bile. "It's ten minutes to the burn. We just need roll and sextant star."

And Kerwin says: "I think we're coming through garbled to them, too."

It chills me to realize he's right. Nausea grips me; bile rises and I choke it down. "All right. Get the DSE back recording."

"I think we need to switch the tracking to…"

He pushes his headset aside and vomits: ugly brownish acid-smelling globules that reverberate as they float towards the side of the command module.

I drop pencil and workbook and try to head off the mess before it hits the console.

"No...the PAD," Kerwin sputters. "I'll get it." He feebly moves his hands up to capture the foulness, and I retrieve my airborne writing implements, and he heaves and shakes again.

And the radio revives, and I place pencil to paper because Kerwin didn't get the recorder reset and I need to get it right this time, and all the numbers are coming, unstoppable: "Explorer, Houston. SPS/G&N 87202..."

I vomit, a long convulsion.

It happens fast, and I try to move my arms and my headset so most of it misses, and I try to pay attention to the radio, but what's happening is all-consuming. I vomit again and again and again and again, my insides feeling like they want to come out, bitter acid mouth taste everywhere, harsh against my teeth, and I've never been so disgusted and frustrated with my own body.

By the time it's over, I've missed the rest of the numbers.

•••

For the next few hours, we take turns getting sick in the tunnel and getting sick in the manned module hallway and getting sick in the bathroom. No one wants the extra radiation dose from being down there, but we also don't want to foul up the command module any more than it already is. In short order, the tunnel and the hallway are disgusting. And we're having other symptoms, too.

"Goddamn," I moan from the tunnel. "I wish we had a regular bathroom."

"Or even two of these bathrooms," Kerwin adds weakly as he pulls down the curtain.

"A bathtub," Shepard says from the hallway. "That was the..." He pauses and convulses: dry heaves now. "...oh, God. Sorry. I didn't think there was anything left."

"Me neither. My stomach just hasn't gotten the memo yet."

"The first thing I learned," Shepard continues wearily. "Back in my rookie drinking days. If you've...if you've got it coming out both ends, shit in the toilet, puke in the tub."

"Even a sink," Kerwin says. "Man, the things you take for granted." He looks down at the dosimeter. "We should really get back upstairs."

I frown. "You want to leave this kind of mess up there?"

"We don't have a choice. And we can put on the fecal containment garments, at least."

I make another face: astronaut diapers.

"That's not a terrible idea," Shepard admits.

I try to allow my mind to float back and analyze this objectively, as an engineering problem of sorts. With one end of the digestive tract covered, and the other running out of material to expel, things should be more manageable. I float back upstairs and retrieve the garments from the equipment bin.

"Didn't think I'd need these for another few years," Shepard says.

"Yeah. Shoulda been at least another…two or three, right, old man?"

He gives me a dirty look that breaks into a sickly smile.

We settle back in to the command module, our shelter from the radiation storm. We still feel awful, and there are periods of incapacitation, but during the interludes we can do a little work. So we clean as best we can, weary and reluctant, finding patches of foulness floating in air and clinging to the bare metal surfaces of the tunnel and seeping into junctions behind panels. We wipe it all down in slow and miserable fashion and throw the cloths and tissues into a jettison bag. Still the lingering smell triggers spasms of nausea.

"What else, doc?" Shepard asks.

"Well, we need to stay hydrated," Kerwin says.

"I don't know if that's an option right now," I point out.

"Let's see what we can do."

I choke down a little water. It comes right back up. The horrible watery blob quivers in front of me, mocking me as it drifts towards the bulkhead. I did not need another mess to clean. I want to cry from frustration. Instead I unscrew the top of the water bottle and corral it all back inside. I will sort it out later.

"I'll tell you," Shepard says, bone-tired. "I've been wiped out by a sunburn before, but this is ridiculous."

"It's not exactly a sunburn," Kerwin says, and Shepard gives him a look like: I know.

"Explorer, Houston. Copy your comms and health issues. Please stay in the command module tonight. We're going to..." (Crackle.) "...the course correction for at least another day..." (More crackle.) "...should be time to get it done once this round of symptoms passes. Over."

"And before the next round hits," Kerwin mutters.

Houston and the PRDs are both saying the same thing: the storm of charged particles hasn't abated, and we're best off staying in the command module indefinitely, to try and avoid the worst of the radiation. I eye the indicators for the hydrogen and oxygen tanks. These power the fuel cells, and so determine how long we can stay up here.

"We're going to be tight?" Shepard asks.

It is iffy, so I say what we all already know. "We can't stay up here forever."

•••

We settle in for the night, Kerwin and I on the side couches, Shepard curled up in the lower equipment bay.

Once all else is done, I write:

> *6 SEP 1972*
>
> *CME today. Dosimeters over 200 rads. No way to calc absorbed dose. Some comms*

> *difficulties. Could not perform course correction. Symptoms of ARS.*

My mind races: high-energy thoughts bouncing around all clear and crisp and sharply defined, ricocheting off one another and careening through the mind so violently that one imagines them doing damage to the soft tissue. I am eager for them to decay, to collide in new patterns that will cause them to destabilize, fragments of consciousness spinning off and disintegrating like particles in a cloud chamber.

•••

The radio comes on, the headset attached to the Velcro area on the side of the cabin.

Houston's telling us about another CME.

For some reason we are able to get the telescope operating in time to observe it. It's even larger than the first one.

We pull out the PRDs and stare in horror. They read: 99999.

•••

In the morning we get going wearily. We don't quite know what to do with ourselves. No one much wants to deal with the normal rigamarole of heating up food packets if we're going to end up not eating again.

"Explorer, Houston, we should let you know that news of your situation has broken..." (Crackle.) "...will arrange a comms window with your families as soon as..." (More crackle.) "...the meantime, just know that the whole world's praying for your safe return. It's not how you wanted to make the papers, I'm sure, but you've got a lot of..." (Static.) "...for you. Tentative plan for the day is to let you rest and recuperate, try and fix the comms, execute the course correction tomorrow, and power down the command module as soon as practical." (Static again.) "...take it day by day from there. Your health is our first priority. Give us your status when you can. Over."

To us, Shepard speaks: "We should be good with that, right?"

My head aches. Power down the command module as soon as practical...there is a fuzziness to the words, an imprecision at odds with the exacting specifications used to build the machinery. But we do have enough hydrogen and oxygen to power the fuel cells for a few more days. So it's not my preference, but it is doable. "I guess we have to be."

"OK. Joe, you want to give 'em a report?"

"Houston, Explorer," Kerwin transmits. "Appreciate your giving us a sick day. We're still a little under the weather. I guess we forgot there is still weather up here. Gastro-intestinal symptoms seem to be tapering off. Priority for the day is getting cleaned up and rehydrated. We should be a go to retry the course correction tomorrow. Over."

I'm pretty sure what I'm nursing is a dehydration headache, a hangover of sorts. Tentatively I put the water container straw to my lips. I take a sip and taste absolute foulness.

"Jesus fucking Christ." I shake my head, absolutely disgusted. I've forgotten about the mess from last night, the water I upchucked and then collected back up. The acid taste won't go away. My face puckers and squirms like a trapped animal trying to get away.

"What's wrong?" Kerwin asks.

"That...wasn't entirely water."

Shepard gives a tired little laugh. "Probably didn't age well either, did it?"

I have to laugh a little. "No. No, it did not."

Then it's time to vacuum out the offensive mess, to turn the valves that connect the hose to space so we can suck the foulness out into oblivion.

"Hey, the vacuum still works," I observe drily.

"How about that," Kerwin smiles.

I rinse my container, soap it up, then rinse it again. Then I rinse it again. And again, for good measure. And one more time. And another more time. And then once more. And again, just to be safe. And then once more. At last I fill it and drink some water. It sloshes around in my stomach like it's not a part of me, like coffee in a thermos, or propellant in a fuel tank. But this time it stays down.

We clean more thoroughly now, wetting rags and wiping everything.

For lunch, we nibble on packets of butter cookies, one of the few dry crumb-type foods we have up here. They sit well enough.

We do want to resolve the intermittent signal from Earth before we attempt the course correction again. From the indicator needles it looks like the antenna's slewing, and we can't tell why. So we experiment, switching amplifiers and beam widths, changing it from automatic to manual tracking; when the beam's on its widest setting and we've manually steered the antenna towards Earth, the signal gets better.

I allow myself to believe the crisis has passed.

•••

We're up in the command module for another night. The dosimeters are still slowly ticking upwards, but it seems the rate of change has tapered off.

> *7 SEP 1972*
>
> *Cleanup and recuperation. Quite a headache. Ready for the end of it.*

We have no way of knowing when it will be safe to reoccupy our home.

I sleep fitfully.

On Earth, one tosses and turns; here there is no heaviness to it, but the end result is the same: futile attempts to get comfortable, and an exaggerated sense of the pressure on one's bladder. I have to move far too frequently to empty it. I can see Kerwin stirring in the electric glow of the console, and here and there I hear a harrumph from Shepard, over in the dark recesses behind the launch couches.

I'm annoyed by the fact that they're annoyed by me. But I'm annoyed by me, too.

• • •

The next afternoon, we're still in the command module, ready at last to retry the course correction. My stomach has settled down, but I'm still tired and disgusted. Houston has walked us through the preliminaries for the alignment and course correction. They've built a tremendously fat amount of time into the leadup for the burn, in case we have the same comms issues.

"Houston, Explorer. Program 23 is complete and I have clear LOS to Venus. Will be taking sightings on Rigel, Arcturus and Deneb. Over." Methodically I work, measuring the shaft and trunnion angles and writing them down on the worksheet, then entering them into the guidance computer. When that's done, I grab a few tired sips of water. I'm waiting for acknowledgment. I check the time: 15:03.

Right then, the spacecraft jostles ever so slightly. All the instruments blink, a brief electric hiccup, like in prison movies when they're electrocuting someone and the lights cut in and out. And in that moment I see the flicker-flashes, a lot of them all at once.

"What was that?" Shepard asks.

"Looks like a power surge of some sort."

"Not sure why the spacecraft moved."

"Me neither." Eagerly I scan the panel; everything's a little off. "I have a fuel cell light on number 1, a fuel cell disconnect, AC BUS Overload 1, Main Bus A out."

"Shit."

"Let's reset the fuel cell."

Once I flip the switch, it seems everything is fine. I allow myself to pretend nothing happened.

15:09.

To the ground, I speak: "Houston, Explorer, the spacecraft...moved a bit and we had a slight power transient. Briefly lost the fuel cell. It looks like everything's back to normal. Let us know when you want us to send the state vector. Over."

15:10.

The radio comes on, too soon for them to have heard me. "Explorer, Houston. We're waiting for you to begin Program 23. When complete, send the stars and sightings. Over."

I check my watch. Eleven and a half minutes ago...they should be where I was then. And that was before I started Program 23. Wasn't it? I am not sure why I don't know. How many minutes does it normally take to forget what time it is?

Shepard's mood's growing more foul by the minute. Even Kerwin looks a little irritable.

"We'll sort this out," I tell them. Then: "Houston, Explorer, Program 23 is complete. Stars are...uh, Rigel, Arcturus and

Deneb. Shaft and trunnion angles as follows..." I rattle off the numbers. "We had a power issue after that, but we're back up. Ready to transmit the state vector whenever you are ready."

15:13.

The radio comes back. Again, too soon for them to have heard my most recent words. "Explorer, Houston. We copy clear LOS to Venus. Rigel, Arcturus, Deneb."

I sigh, exasperated. "Houston, Explorer, not sure if you copied my subsequent transmission. We had a power transient here, but we are ready to send the state vector. Over."

I wait.

15:14.

I count backwards from now, creating history from memory before it's too late. In a few minutes, we should hear them acknowledging the power issue, and our reassurance that everything's OK.

15:15.

The others are giving me looks, but I don't want to start talking to them and potentially miss Houston's response.

Then at last: "Explorer, Houston. Comm check, over." It is not a response.

"Houston, Explorer." I refuse to believe that this is an issue. "We are reading you three by four. We've completed P23 and the alignment and we are ready to transmit the state vector. Let us know how you're reading us. Over."

I make extra careful note of the time: 15:16. I look at all the switches on the panel. I know I haven't moved any of them, but I look and look again.

More waiting.

15:17.

"Explorer, Houston. Comm check, over."

I know we have the S-Band on the manned module as well. So even if there is a transmission issue, we have another transmitter, whenever we're able to go back down there. But I still need to respond. "Houston, Explorer. We are reading you three by four. Not sure if you're reading us."

Shepard looks like he wants an explanation.

Bracing for an interrogation, I figure I'll answer the questions before he asks: "Signal strength from them is the same as it's been. Nothing's changed with the setup. I haven't touched the panel."

The look on his face melts into something almost merciful. "I know you haven't, Buzz."

"We'll switch over to the manned module S-Band once we can go back down there."

"Yeah."

Kerwin is looking down at his dosimeter. "Gentlemen, can you take a look at your PRDs?" It's a normal professional request, reasoned and measured, but I get the undercurrent, the awful truth: he's scared.

I look, reluctant: 56020. "That jumped a lot, didn't it?"

"Was that another CME?" Shepard asks.

"I think it was part of the same one," Kerwin replies flatly. "The 'mass' part. Wednesday was the high-energy photons. Light's what...670 million miles per hour? So we got it as soon as we could see the event. And there were protons that were accelerated by that, probably like a bow shock. But you remember that whole massive arc of plasma lifting off the solar surface? That was still heading towards us, this whole time. And it wasn't dense enough to hit us hard, but obviously, plasma's a great electrical conductor..."

My heart sinks and hits my stomach, which starts rumbling again. "So that transient..."

"There could have been a discharge. Out through the antenna, via the amps. They were designed pretty robustly, but they weren't designed for this."

"Are you saying we actually passed through something?" Shepard can't believe it. (To be fair, neither can I.) "Even at this distance, with the inverse square law and all that?"

"The size of that event, it could've easily been a couple billion tons of material when it started," Kerwin says.

"Jesus." Shepard shakes his head. "All right, let's cycle all the breakers. Turn it all off and get it back going again, back to the last good configuration."

I get to work, despite my bad feeling.

"We still have the manned module high-gain," Kerwin feels compelled to remind everyone.

"Whenever it's safe to go back down there," Shepard says.

•••

I have a hard time believing all of this is happening. Given the redundancies in the comms systems, the multiple USB exciters and amplifiers and antennae, and all of the combinations with which they can be combined, it doesn't seem possible that we've lost voice communication with home. I find myself thinking, at last, of Joan and the kids: wondering if they still have the squawk box rigged up in the kitchen, imagining the conversations, concern and alarm and maybe even hysteria. Although then again, there's a chance someone cut them off, just to keep them from worrying...

Enough. I don't want to think about any of this.

"I need a break, quick," I tell the guys, and avail myself of the bathroom contraption.

If you are venting urine directly into the vacuum of space, there are engineering problems one doesn't run into on Earth, or even with the quasi-normal toilet in the manned module. Specifically, if you open the valves before you start urinating, the suction from the tubes that connect your urethra to outer space will leave your johnson in a pinch. But if you just start peeing without the valves being open, the condom fills with urine and bursts, and you're chasing down yellow goblin globules for the next half hour. The trick is to start your flow a split second before you open the valve;

everything sprays gloriously out into the universe, a yellow burst of evaporating droplets that's easily more interesting to look at than most of what you see in interplanetary space. I pay close attention and forget about everything else, and it all goes smoothly.

Then I look down at my dosimeter: 56021. I turn to the others, who are still cycling breakers and checking switches on the console. "Uhh, can you guys look at your PRDs?"

"Another spike? Jesus." Shepard says.

"No, no, it's...I think it's flattened out."

Shepard sees where I'm going: "Wonder what it's like down there."

"Let's do a little experiment," Kerwin suggests. "We'll write down all our dosimeter numbers, put one of them down there, wait an hour, and see if it's changed more than the ones up here."

"Sounds like a plan," Shepard says. He volunteers to deliver his dosimeter down to the main deck, and after we scribble down the number, he goes. It's a little gesture; after all we've absorbed, I'm not sure how much of a difference those couple minutes would realistically make. Still, I can't help but appreciate it.

The resetting of the comms is done. We're still getting no indication that Houston has heard us. But I am encouraged, a little, by the dosimeters.

Sure enough, when Shepard goes back to retrieve the PRD, it's only gone up 0.02 rads, virtually the same as the ones we're wearing.

"All right," he grins. "As commander of this mission, and in absence of guidance from Flight, I do believe we're safe to reoccupy the manned module."

As we float on down, ground breaks in, Weitz's voice weary in our headsets: "Explorer, Houston. Comm check, over." Hopefully we'll be able to answer soon enough.

It is refreshing to go back down, the topsy-turvy transition from tunnel to hallway and into the relative roominess of the main deck, the telescope console and the kitchen area, everything looking strange and familiar, like an old friend.

"Joe, get comms up and running, and let us know when we're patched in."

"All right," Kerwin starts flipping switches.

"Good to be back," Shepard says.

"It is," I concur.

"OK, we're up on the manned module comms," Kerwin says. "Going push-to-talk."

"OK." Shepard seems nonplussed, despite everything that's gone wrong in the past couple days. "Houston, Explorer, we've had a power transient. We've lost the command module comms, but we're back up on the manned module S-Band. How do you read? Over."

I take extra care to make sure my mic isn't transmitting back to the world. Then to Al: "I'm gonna hit the bathroom quick." He nods.

Once I'm alone in there, I strip down. I've had the fecal containment garment on for a while, and it is beyond time to clean up a little. There is foulness of a strange consistency.

I wipe up tiredly. We have a few spare containment garments, but not many. The bathroom itself smells awful. When we took turns down here, during the great sickness, we did not take enough time to clean. So I do a little.

Then I look again at the black spot on my neckline, the one I was worried about not so long ago. I almost have to laugh. The way things are going, if I have time to die of cancer, I'll be a lucky man.

The radio: "Explorer, Houston. Transmitting in the blind. We've received no comms and no telemetry for over an hour. Please acknowledge. Over."

Kerwin replies eagerly: "Houston, Explorer, we read you three by four. We've switched from CM coms to the manned module. Please acknowledge. Over."

16:48.

I float back out, and all of the sudden I feel all wrong. The clock has reset, but my mind's creating crazy scenarios.

I drift over to the console, just to be an extra set of eyes. Of course everything looks normal: signal strength, antenna pitch and yaw. Shepard and I trade a weary awful look. He looks haggard and old.

16:52.

From distant Earth: "Explorer, Houston. Transmitting in the blind. We've received no comms and no telemetry for over an hour. Please acknowledge. Over."

Just like upstairs, the S-Band system in the manned module has two amplifiers, and the antenna can be dialed to beam widths of 40.0^0, 11.3^0, and 4.4^0, with corresponding increases in signal strength as the beam narrows. And the S-Band has a backup mode that changes how voice is transmitted, clipping the signal and transmitting directly on the main carrier to gain an extra few decibels of signal strength.

Over the next few hours, we try every possible permutation and combination.

Nothing.

Everyone is impressively calm, steady and quiet, with none of the tension and pettiness that have cropped up at odd moments earlier in the mission. Or rather they seem calm, and whatever disturbance is within me stays down there, never reaches the surface, because I want to work smoothly, to work the problem and figure it out. And in those hours I feel a strange affection for my crewmates, some combination of Platonic and brotherly love, even towards Shepard, even in spite of everything: we seem to work best when the stakes are highest. And after we've tried everything, we do not despair; we simply reset all the comms circuit breakers again, and reconfigure everything again, and verify from the S-Band indicators that the antennae are pointed steadily back at Earth, and we try it all again, working from memory, the months and months of living and breathing these systems.

Still: nothing.

•••

22:30.

We dine in silence, a late tired dinner.

It is nice to be back home in the manned module. And the food is sitting well enough, but the comms outage isn't. None of us wants to think about what this means. We are all the type of people who will do anything to accomplish the mission. But we've done everything.

You have to assume it will all work out in the end. If you don't, why even start?

"We should power down the command module," I point out to Shepard as we tidy up. "We don't want to get tight on the margins for the fuel cells."

"Yeah," Shepard says. "It doesn't look like we'll be doing the course correction any time soon. You'll be OK on your own?"

"I can probably do it in my sleep at this point."

I am close enough to sleep that there's not much difference. I plod through the checklists. I am exhausted and ready for bed, but I take my time. Absent-mindedly, I click the Push-to-Talk button on my headset. I'm so bone-tired I don't really think about what I'm doing, but I do find myself slowly tapping out a familiar rhythm. Dot-dot-dot-dash-dash-dash-dot-dot-dot. S.O.S.

There is an inescapable sadness as I power down the spacecraft this time. I wonder when we'll power it up again.

Back in the manned module, they've turned down the radios for the night, so low they're barely audible. I don't blame them. It is too depressing to hear the regular comm checks, the resignation in Crippen's voice.

I float back down to the sleeping chambers with my journal, and write:

> *8 SEP 1972*
>
> *Hit by remnants of CME. Possible electrical damage to amplifiers. Houston is not receiving our communications. Could not perform course correction. Not sure when or if comms can be restored.*

I cannot believe any of this. I can't help but wonder if we can survive anything else going wrong. Or if we can survive this, even. I can't linger too long on these dark thoughts. But tonight, they do at least drag me down to sleep.

●●●

The plasma hits hard.

There is a slow roll moment at first, and then it builds and builds and builds.

Within a minute we are tumbling like a leaf in the wind. The solar panels are all on the manned module, so it's catching the brunt of it, and we can hear metal groaning, the spacecraft stack trying to break apart, the solar panels straining under the unexpected physical loads.

We hear a tearing of metal. It shouldn't be possible to hear anything outside the hull, but there it is, transmitted through the metal itself, a groaning and snapping.

Then: silence.

All the lights go out.

•••

In the morning, over breakfast, we discuss our plans for the day. We're eating tiredly, but we're eating. The radios are still down low and we can barely hear the voice that comes on every five minutes, like a super slow metronome. It's enough to make me miss even the worst news days.

"We should do the blood draws," Kerwin says.

"The blood draws?" Shepard's absolutely incredulous.

It does sound like a strange request. Every two weeks, we've been taking samples of blood and freezing them in an airlock on the cold side of the craft, so that when everything's all said and done, they can get a look at how our physiology responds to a year in deep space. Obviously now there's some question about the importance of all the old routines. Then again, there isn't a lot else to do right now.

"Might as well," I concede.

Shepard shakes his head tiredly. "Are you kidding me? This guy's way too eager to be doing this. I think he's part vampire."

"Dr. Acula, at your service," Kerwin smiles thinly.

We roll up our arms and get to it. Each of us is trained, and it goes smoothly enough, until Shepard stops. "Wait a second." He floats over to the radio console.

"Come on, Al, you can't get out of every medical..."

But Shepard turns the volume up, and that tells us to shut up. We catch the tail end of the message.

"...Morse S.O.S. late last evening. Please attempt another Morse transmission as soon as possible. Over."

Then, silence.

"Jesus. Did we test the Morse yesterday?" Shepard asks.

"We...no, I don't..." I sputter. "We were so fixated on voice and data." I have to laugh a little: we were so confident that we knew all the ins and outs of the radio that we never actually pulled out the checklists and followed them to the end, where the last-resort procedure is to use the push-to-talk button as a Morse key.

"I didn't think about it," Kerwin says. "I guess that's what we get for not following the checklist."

Shepard gives him an ugly look, but we're all excited enough about reestablishing comms that he can't stay mad for long. "I guess," he smiles a little. "Who sent an S.O.S., though?"

It takes me a second to even remember that I'm responsible for this. "I think I tapped something out on my headset. When I was shutting down up there. I was so tired, I didn't even stop and think about what I was doing. I…"

Again, the transmission: "Explorer, Houston. After reviewing comms from yesterday, we believe we received a Morse S.O.S. from you late last night. Please attempt another as soon as possible. Over."

The news is so good that we're all grinning now, even Shepard. "All right, who wants to go?" he asks.

"I think my Morse is pretty decent," Kerwin replies.

"Let's…all right. Message them: 'Houston, Explorer…'"

"I'm not sure we need that," I interject. "I know, radio discipline, you-this-is-me, but I think they're gonna know it's us…"

Shepard smiles a little wider, and continues. "'…Hit by remnant of coronal mass ejection. Possible electrical discharge and damage to high-gain amplifiers. Spacecraft otherwise running smoothly…crew health good…what else?"

"Crew health unchanged," Kerwin suggests. There's an uncomfortable undertone to the word choice: we may have more symptoms coming.

"…Crew health unchanged. Please advise. Over." Shepard writes it all down and hands it over, while I turn my headset to listen-only and set everything up so we can get the cleanest possible transmission.

"All right, here we go," Joe starts transmitting: Dot-dot-dot-dot and the slightest pause and then dash-dash-dash, and then all the rest of the message, and even though it's all just information, a long series of bleeps and blips, there's something in the transmission pattern that sounds eager and exciting and hopeful.

•••

We wait thirteen minutes. We fill the time with mindless tasks. Then: nothing.

"Jesus," Shepard shakes his head.

"They're translating," Kerwin says. "Nobody speaks Morse anymore."

And sure enough, at the fourteenth: "Explorer, Houston…" (Crackle.) "…part of your transmission. Copy possible electrical discharge…" (Static.) "…advise crew condition and spacecraft system status. Over."

"We're getting those dips on the signal strength," I observe. "Just like we had upstairs." Still, it's something.

"I should have sent it three times," Kerwin says. "Here, let's go again." And he re-transmits the sequence over and over and over, a steady and solid transmission.

We look over the radio once more. It sounds like we're having the same steerable antenna issues, but down here, the direction indicators are steady. It seems we've done all we can to catch their signal cleanly when it comes back. We try to go back to our normal business: trash in the airlock, personal hygiene. But it is hard to think about anything.

We clean.

We wait.

We check watches, and curse ourselves for doing so.

We check again, and it seems our watches are cursing us, telling us again that time does not move at our pace, but rather the other way around.

At last, a response: "Explorer, Houston. We copy electrical discharge…" (Static.) "…crew condition. Transmission breaking…" (Unintelligible words.)

"We're getting gaps," Shepard says.

"It's like what was happening upstairs." I add.

"Looks steady here, though," Kerwin says.

Shepard: "Yeah, but it sounds worse."

Something occurs to me, something large and obvious. "Can we actually look at the S-Band?"

"The indicators say it's steady," Kerwin says.

"Never trust the indicators," Shepard mutters.

Kerwin grimaces painfully. "I thought it was 'Always trust the indicators.'"

I float over to the window. Each steerable antenna has four parabolic dishes arranged in a quad, like two sets of Mickey Mouse ears. When the system's in AUTO mode, the transmitting and receiving work together: a signal comes in from Earth, and the system measures signal strength in each of the dishes and then turns the antenna structure so that the strength of the signal is more or less equal across all four of them, which ensures that the antenna is pointed squarely at Earth when we transmit. We can only see the very top of the manned module antenna by looking at an angle from the top of the main window.

I peer out. It stays rock steady for maybe eight seconds, then briefly dips out of sight, pitching up and down really fast, like Double Mickey is nodding yes, or falling asleep.

"It's moving. Every few seconds. Are you seeing anything on the pitch needle?"

"No," Kerwin says. "Steady. Signal strength is going in and out on that rhythm, though."

"So maybe that's it. Antenna failure and partial indicator failure. It's like it's losing the signal strength from the top dishes, and it steers itself all the way down to pick it up, and it bumps against the bottom and that wakes it up."

"All right. Let's try Track Mode from AUTO to MANUAL," Kerwin says.

It sounds like a good plan. He flips the switch.

Except when I look out the window, the antenna has dipped out of sight. "Probably should have had you flip it when it was pointed up," I say. "All right, let's steer it back up."

"I'm steering it."

"I'm still not seeing anything." I look over at the controls. "You're steering it down."

"Crap."

I look back out and the antenna's still not visible. "You can bring it back up."

"I'm steering it."

I look back and sure enough, he's doing the right thing now. But when I stare back out into the blackness: nothing. "Not responding." I check my watch: we have a few minutes before the next transmission's due back. "Let's cycle the breakers."

Again, the easy stupid hopeful solution. But no luck. The antenna remains stubbornly pointed down, away from Earth.

"OK, Track Mode back to AUTO," I suggest.

"AUTO," Kerwin confirms.

Still nothing. I am wondering if it's somehow stuck from running the controls the wrong way. If Shepard had done it, I would mention the possibility, but since it's Kerwin, I don't. He probably feels bad enough as it is.

"We must've burned out the motors." Shepard's kind enough to say "we," even though we all know it's a "you," and we all know who. "Running the controls the wrong way."

"Yeah," Kerwin swallows heavily.

The transmission comes in but it's a garbled series of words, completely unintelligible.

For as bad as things seemed last night, this feels worse: we can't even listen any more.

We don't even bother with a response.

"We're going to have to repoint the spacecraft," Shepard says. "Point the antenna that way."

The answer's so obviously correct that none of us bothers to discuss it.

"Maybe 120 degrees around the z-axis," Kerwin suggests.

"That sounds about right."

Kerwin plugs in the commands and the gyros go to work; the window has been pointing almost directly away from the sun, but once the maneuver's over, I see a scythe of light along one edge, and then a shaft stabbing into the cabin.

"All right," Shepard pats Kerwin on the shoulder. "Let's go again. 'Houston, Explorer. Repeat your last. Transmission garbled due to high-gain pointing failure. Spacecraft repointed to allow cleaner reception. Believe we have lost all S-Band amplifiers due to electrical discharge. Crew health unchanged."

Kerwin keys it all in, another series of dots and dashes; he transmits it again and again and again, not excitedly this time but not wearily, either, just solid and steady and even.

We take turns floating over to use the bathroom. We wait and wait. We try not to think.

And yet there is something...not comfortable, but satisfying: shared effort in the face of shared peril.

After another interminable delay, Houston's answer comes back, more crackly and muddled than we've heard before. But it sounds like they copied our transmission, at least.

"We could repoint the stack a little," Shepard says. "Fine-tune it based on the signal strength."

"A steerable spaceship, instead of a steerable antenna," Kerwin comments.

I like it. "We'll have to get them to talk a little longer first. Have one person watch the signal meter and another working the fine adjustment attitude controls."

"Better than nothing," Shepard says. "All right. 'Houston, Explorer. We...' What do we want to say?"

"'Houston, Explorer. Reception still garbled.'" I dictate. "'Attempting attitude adjustments to increase signal strength during reception. Please keep talking during next transmission to allow fine tuning. We...' I don't know...what else?" By now I'm feeling slightly warm. I'm wondering if this is the onset of new symptoms, or the fact that the sun's now hitting us differently, missing the sun shield and hitting the main window and heating us up a little. Another thought occurs to me, and I look over at the voltmeters from the solar panels. They are low, practically at zero.

"The buffer batteries should be picking up the slack," Kerwin observes, reading the concern on my face.

"Yeah." It's not the end of the world; we can run on batteries for several hours before we have to get the panels back perpendicular to the sun so we can recharge. But it's another thing we'll have to keep in mind.

"Let's go ahead and transmit," Shepard says. "'Please keep talking to allow fine tuning…' What else?"

"Give our love to our wives and children," Kerwin says. "Tell them we'll be home soon. Over."

We transmit again, and again, and again. I do feel warmer. I can hear the environmental system straining to keep up with the increased thermal load. I'm getting a little antsy about the power situation. I know they know it's an issue, but I want to make sure they know how much of an issue it is.

"Batteries are running down a little faster than they should be," I say at last.

"Maybe we can reduce our load for a bit," Shepard says. "Pull the cooling system offline."

We do so, and the warming increases. Soon the others are glistening; I feel beads of sweat moistening my own forehead as well. This is the first time on the entire trip that the spacecraft's felt uncomfortable, temperature-wise.

"We may need to power the command module back up just to talk to them," Shepard says. "Use the omnidirectional antenna."

He might be right. I don't like it, but he might be right. "We will really have to budget that out, if that's going to be the case. We can only draw so much power from the fuel cells."

"Can't we run power back from the manned module to the command module? Power the radios that way?"

"Not if the command module's powered down." Given the months still ahead of us, it may be the case that we have to talk to Earth only when absolutely necessary, rather than whenever we want.

We watch the voltmeters. The batteries are still draining faster than I'd hoped. The hot air seems to be activating unpleasant smells, all the filth we've not completely cleaned. I feel awful, not sick, but thick and irritable, somehow anxious and lethargic at the same time. I want to go somewhere. I want to do something. I am overwhelmingly conscious now of how miniscule our resources are, on the grand scale of everything. If we let the batteries run too low, we won't be able to use the gyros to get the solar panels pointed back at the sun. But the others aren't saying anything. I'm trying to keep my mouth shut, be a good crewmember.

"We're going to need to repoint soon," I say at last.

"Soon," Kerwin echoes.

"Another couple rounds and we'll go back," Shepard says.

I am not satisfied with this answer. "We are gonna eat into the margins on the batteries."

"We need to get a clear plan for the next 24 hours," Shepard says. "We're gonna need to try the course correction again."

"We can do that tomorrow."

"As long as symptoms hold off," Kerwin says. "We'll mention it next transmission. See what Houston has to say."

I am not happy with any of this. My body grows sticky. Even as I float, weightless, I can feel a heaviness settling in to my bones.

• • •

We retire early to the sleeping chambers. We have spent much of the day determining the length and width and breadth of our predicament. There is a tentative plan to power the command module back up and try the course correction tomorrow, and I am hopeful we can get back to some semblance of normal mission tasks soon. But for now it is time to take stock.

I am not sure if I am feeling quite normal. I do not say anything to the others. I am not sure if they're feeling normal. I do not ask.

I root around in my books, but I do not find anything new. "Got anything to read?" I ask Kerwin.

"I did just finish a little exploration story."

"Sounds fun."

"I don't know if 'fun' is the right word. It's about the British expedition to Antarctica, Scott's expedition."

"He died, right?"

Shepard's been eavesdropping, and now he chimes in. "Hey, don't spoil the ending! I might want to read it."

"Yeah," Kerwin says. "Reached the South Pole after Amundsen, and died on the way back, along with the whole rest of the polar party. The other members of their expedition eventually found them, and their journals. One of them wrote this. It was a big suffer-fest, for all concerned."

"Sounds delightful." It should keep things in perspective, at least.

He flips the book towards me; it tumbles, weightless, free.

I read the title: *The Worst Journey in the World.* "So much for English understatement, huh?" I open it up, and see something I want to share: "'Polar exploration is at once the cleanest and most isolated way of having a bad time which has been devised.' I have to say, I now have grounds to challenge that statement."

"We're not as clean as we used to be," Kerwin points out.

I settle in and read some more.

I make it a point to stay still. If I don't move, I don't have to think about the fact that moving doesn't feel normal.

•••

I wake up paralyzed.

On second thought, it only feels like paralysis because motion takes so much effort. I can move. I just really really really don't want to.

My mind's fogged with fatigue.

I don't understand it. This is not supposed to be happening. I am waiting for the others to come floating over to see what's wrong, just like after the flyby when that strange lethargy overcame me. I am waiting for judgment, condemnation, or even those puzzled looks that say: What the hell is wrong with you?

But this feels different.

At last it occurs to me that this is the onset of the later phase of symptoms, the crash in blood cell counts, the long second phase where you just have to wait for things to get back to normal. So the others aren't in any hurry to get out of bed, either. And there's a strange sense of relief in this. (As a cadet, you realize there is comfort and safety in group action. If you're the only person doing something, you're a lot more likely to get in trouble than if everyone else is doing exactly the same thing.)

I survey my sleeping quarters as if seeing it all for the first time: the small fluorescent light above my head (caged in metal to protect against accidental breakage), the burn-proof Beta cloth bag of books tied to the wall so it won't float away, the metal tube of the vertical bedframe, the brown sleeping bag, the loose straps binding us up to give some illusion of security and snugness while we're hanging there weightless. It is by no means roomy. But I don't particularly want to go anywhere.

Eventually some combination of bladder pressure and concern for my crewmates pushes me out of these cozy confines.

Shepard still sleeps, somehow serene in repose. Kerwin is up, at least, but still in his sleeping closet; he looks like a high school student shoved into a locker.

"Do you feel as awful as I do?" he asks.

"Yeah. This is it, huh?"

"This is it."

I float off to the bathroom, eager to use it and get back to motionlessness. Everything else (communication with Houston, course correction) will have to wait.

•••

We eat breakfast a little after lunch. Getting out the trays and heating them up feels like a Herculean task. At first, it's just Kerwin and I.

"We are going to have to transmit a message soon," I tell him, between small lethargic bites of sausage and dried fruit.

He looks over at the voltmeters. "Buffer batteries are still charging back up. We'll see what Shepard says."

"I thought we were going to have another day at least before all this kicked in." Meaning the symptoms.

"I thought so, too."

I take my time formulating a question. "What happened?"

"If I had to guess...the background radiation. We weren't starting at zero, dose-wise. We've been irradiated at a lower level for the past five months. We've probably been showing some of the other signs of that already."

"Like what?"

"Confusion."

"You never talked about that."

"Very funny."

I think back to some of the small errors of the past few weeks: Kerwin steering the steerable antenna the wrong way, me drinking from the container I'd thrown up in. What is the average error rate of a 42-year-old brain? What's my error rate, normally and now? How much of any recent increases might be due to the long-term effects of cosmic radiation, versus the short-term effects of solar radiation? Not easy questions to answer. The scientific process has its limits: you don't have a large enough sample set for every experiment. You don't get a control version and an experimental version of your own mind. Maybe in a parallel universe...

Shepard joins us, but doesn't say much.

"How long is this going to last?" I ask.

"Weeks?"

"Weak weeks." I am not looking forward to anything. Not for a long time. "What are we going to do?"

"Obviously not much."

After lunch, we do the least amount of cleaning that seems prudent.

Then we repoint the spacecraft stack, directing the stuck antenna earthward so we can tap out a quick message to Houston advising them of our status, and listen for their response. NASA has every right to be upset at how the mission's proceeding, and I'm curious to get some sense of their level of frustration with all this waste: the communications outages, the cancelled experiments, the lost telescope time, the massive decreases in our workload and productivity and output. In those long and silent minutes, I imagine all the responses to our failures that must be pouring forth: angry letters from taxpayers, newspaper editorials lambasting the program, maybe another furious song from that yahoo who wrote "Whitey on the Moon."

But after the delay, we get: "Explorer, Houston. Please take whatever rest you need to ensure a speedy recovery. Your wives and children send their love, and we will set up communications windows with them as soon as practical. A lot of people are pulling for you, and not just your work family and your NASA family. The American people, and all of us here on planet Earth, are eager for you to get back in good health and return home safely. Our thoughts and prayers are with you. Godspeed, and get well soon."

We tap out a thank-you, then go back to our normal attitude: sunshade back in position, solar panels flat, stealing power from the same angry sun that tried to kill us.

●●●

Throughout the day, we rest. It is difficult to imagine working. And yet the boredom is killing me.

We get the telescope console back up and running. It's not so much about refusing to take sick days, as it is about keeping an eye on our nemesis. The sun looks relatively placid, but it's safe to say none of us will look at it the same way again. There's a lack of trust that's settled in. So we keep everything on a low magnification, the sun's full disk in view, just so we can do something if another prominence starts rising our way.

Otherwise, we take it easy.

Early in the afternoon, I pull out my nighttime reading. The Brits in Antarctica were at the vanguard of exploration; only sixty years ago, that icy continent was the far limit of the human experience, so I can't help but feel a certain kinship across the decades with the author, a man with one of those unnecessarily pretentious English names: Apsley Cherry-Garrard. Soon, I'm underlining sentences here and there. *The really important thing is that nothing of what is gained should be lost.* And later:

> *Whilst we knew what we had suffered and risked better than anyone else, we also knew that science takes no account of such things; that a man is no better for having made the worst journey in the world; and that whether he returns alive or drops by the way will be all the same a hundred years hence if his records and specimens come safely to hand.*

There are pages about a group of them wintering on a place called Inexpressible Island, living in a small ice cave lit by blubber lamps, singing the *Te Deum* to cheer themselves up, watering down their hot cocoa to stretch out their meager supplies, killing seals to eat and cutting them open to find fish "not too far digested to still be eatable." Suddenly I don't mind the monotony of the meal trays.

Later that night, I write:

10 SEP 1972

Bone weary. Reading about the Brits in Antarctica. Determination to survive—and to leave full records in the event they didn't, so others would know what they went through, and profit from their knowledge. If someone learns something, all is not lost.

The thought flashes: a logbook of a doomed expedition. If we don't survive, this will be like Scott's diaries from the polar journey. The only record, something to be read after the fact by whoever's piecing it all together. But who? I imagine: the dead spacecraft approaching Earth, no course correction, passing by and slowing down but resisting capture, flung back into solar orbit. Or coming down in some godforsaken jungle in Borneo or Sumatra or somewhere, men with machetes hacking their way to a charred cone of metal that somehow landed very nearly in one piece. Or: somehow miraculously on the planned trajectory, but with nobody to jettison the manned module or the service module, the whole stack tumbling on reentry, and recovery ships waiting hopefully, no comms from us but still hopeful, until they see a smear of fire across the sky...

I don't want to indulge in negative fantasies. But it's hard to do otherwise now.

If this book can guide the future explorer by the light of the past, it will not have been written in vain.

•••

Over breakfast the next day, I bring this up, in an elliptical way.

"So how far off-course are we, still?" I tiredly sip my coffee, my feet anchored in the footrests. "I mean, do you think it's that bad?"

The others float, haggard and exhausted. "They do tend to be worrywarts," Shepard says.

"My sense," Kerwin adds, "is that it isn't that bad yet. My mind was elsewhere, but I don't think it was a long burn time on the PAD."

"So we're still on track to get back to Earth, even if nobody makes the course correction?"

Shepard gives me a look like: What's that supposed to mean?

"Look, we all know, they're essentially small-c conservative," Kerwin says. "The event happened, and the docs on the ground told them we might be out of work for a few weeks. They looked at the calendar for those few weeks, and the only mission-critical task was the alignment and course correction. So they figured it makes more sense to try and move it forward than back."

"Well, yeah, of course. It'll probably be a longer burn after," I comment. "But say it doesn't happen at all?"

"Why wouldn't it happen?" Shepard asks.

"Well, the dosage we got..."

"Are you saying, 'What if we don't pull through?'"

"Well, there is a non-zero possibility now, right?" I look at Kerwin, and he nods.

"You're as bad a worrywart as they are," Shepard says.

"I'm just saying, what kind of eventualities should we plan for? We should plan for the realistic. Nobody wants to say it out loud, but this is realistic now. So where's the spacecraft going to end up if we're not around to do the burn? Possibly in interplanetary space. But maybe it will reenter." I can see that they're seeing it now, these dark fantasies I had from last night. "All the logs, all the records, the micrometeorite package, the flyby film from the SIM bay. If there's any chance of it surviving without us, we should take that chance. We don't want it all to go to waste, right?"

"It is a valid point," Kerwin concedes. "I mean, the telescope film, the canister that's outside, I don't see us going back out there to get that any time soon. But other than that, we'd want to bring everything over to the command module early..."

"The command module isn't going to survive reentry if the other modules are still attached," Shepard says. "I mean, if the stack reenters whole and starts breaking up, the manned module would probably break off early, but then you'd have the CSM all together. On its own, the command module's stable enough to survive, but attached...it'll probably go nose first, burn up..."

"My point exactly." I'm weary and worn out, and I do not want to talk about this, but I feel like we have to.

"So, what...if two of us are out of action, the third one has to..." Shepard doesn't need to finish the sentence, because we know what he's talking about: the last remaining person will jettison the modules so the lonely little command module can continue its journey home, a space capsule and a time capsule, a little silvery relic of our last days. "Jesus, you are morbid."

"I…I mean, none of us wants to think about it. But we don't want to waste what we've done up here, either…"

"Obviously that would be an extreme last resort," Shepard says.

"Obviously."

Tiredly we complete our meals and clean. None of us says it out loud, but all we want is to go back downstairs and rest. I hope I am just being a worrywart.

I float off to the bathroom. When I'm cleaning up, a clump of hair comes off in my hand.

•••

"I'm not feeling entirely well," Shepard confides to me later downstairs, when Kerwin is upstairs taking his turn in the bathroom. His hair looks patchy; I wonder if he's lost any, too.

I do not ask. Instead it's: "You don't want to talk to the doctor?" with what I hope is an appropriately small grin. "He told me a while ago we don't have to worry about being grounded any time soon."

"Very funny."

"What's the problem?"

"I'm…uhh, I think I'm a little feverish."

I place the back of my hand on his forehead. He's surprisingly warm. "We need to talk to Joe."

"I never like admitting this stuff."

"You think I do?"

A reluctant sigh. "It's not just the normal pilot thing, it's...Louise, my family. God is the great doctor in the sky, all that Christian Science bullshit. They get you convinced the antidote to illness is happiness."

"Well I'm fucked, then," I deadpan.

He doesn't laugh. I don't know how much he's really listening to me at all now, so much as saying something that's been on his mind for a while. "When I had my ear thing, all those years I spent grounded, I tried it. I mean, I think I tried it. I was willing to try anything." He does sound tired and weak, a human being at last. "Maybe it was a catch-22 situation. I couldn't be healed unless I was happy, I couldn't be happy unless I was healed, and back on flight status. All I know for sure is: if thought could have cured me, I'd have been back up here in no time. But I had to cave in. I went to the doctors who knew what to do. And it worked! I made it back up here." He sighs, a long and lonely sigh. "I made it back up here. The moon and Venus. I guess you don't always know what's good for you."

It occurs to me, not for the first time, that he's six years older than me, and eight years older than Kerwin: already a grandfather. Maybe his age is making a difference, and not for the better. But I need to say something good, something with intention. "We'll...we'll get through this."

Now he is listening. "Since when did you become the voice of positivity?"

I chuckle. "Laughter's the best medicine. Maybe you can heal us."

Now his eyes are far away again. "I do want to talk to Louise again. That's the…" He pauses and convulses. "…that's the thing. Despite all the crazy religious stuff, she was a helluva woman. All the moving around, all the crazy behavior on my part, she stuck with me, through it all. I wasn't always a good husband, but man, she was a good wife."

"She *is* a good wife," I correct him. "Joan, too. And I…I cheated on her. I was having an affair when we left. She was glad I was going to be gone so long. She was afraid, too, she had a bad feeling about all of this. But home, all the arguments…I was hard on her, I was hard on all of them. I had so many expectations. But I was a bad husband myself, looking back."

"I do want to talk to Louise again." There is something in his tone that's disturbing: a resignation, a lack of hope. Again he convulses.

The curtain to the main deck is pulled back: Kerwin's head in the hatchway, a tone of deep concern in his voice. "Gentlemen, the telescope's showing solar activity. We need to get back up to the command module."

• • •

There is not time for much: I grab a Bible and the Antarctica book and my journal, and by the time I have everything, Shepard is already floating on up. I follow, and as I pass the telescope, I see on the monitors an x-ray image: another loop rising towards us.

Then, back through the tunnel. To save energy, I run an abbreviated powerup. We get the fuel cells going, and turn on the heaters, and that's it. We are in survival mode.

We float there in the new normal, an uneasy tenuous air of negative expectation. We're all thoroughly tired, ready to rest already. I open the Bible to Job and start reading the first chapter. There's talk of Job's opulence, and then the cruel discussion between God and Satan about whether Job will turn his back on God if things go wrong; then comes the absurdly awful chain of events that befalls Job, followed by his serenity in the face of calamity.

My hair is falling out in clumps now. The others, too. No one's trying to hide it anymore. Or maybe no one can. The Lord giveth and the Lord taketh away. Blessed be the Lord.

> *11 SEP 1972*
>
> *An unexpected return to the command module. Shepard is feverish. We're all going very prematurely bald. Naked I came into this world, and naked shall I leave.*

I sleep fitfully, thinking of the end, the three of us gone, the spacecraft reentering months from now, tumbling, burning up, a Viking funeral.

●●●

In the morning Shepard is practically incoherent. Our dosimeters haven't gone up much this time, less than 10 rads, but Shepard is obviously suffering from what came before.

Joe gives him antibiotics. We power up the radios and transmit a Morse status over the omnidirectional antenna. It takes a while to understand their response, but in the end there is not much. There's little they can do but acknowledge our predicament.

I am tired, and the symptoms have not gone away. If I move too fast, I get lightheaded. I stay in place in front of the console and read. Job and his dialogues, and when I get bored of that, the Brits in Antarctica, sledging across the sea ice between camps on the fringe of the continent, seeing their ponies stranded on ice floes, axing them to death lest they suffer.

But it is not all bad. *The warm glow of the sun with the keen invigorating cold of the air forms a combination which is inexpressibly health-giving and satisfying to me, whilst the golden light on this wonderful scene of mountain and ice satisfies every claim of scenic magnificence,* Cherry-Garrard writes. *No words of mine can convey the impressiveness of the wonderful panorama displayed to our eyes.*

I look to the windows: blackness. This is what we have left. Months and months of this.

•••

Another night in the command module. This CME doesn't seem as intense as the first one, but Kerwin wants to keep us safe in case there's a last spasm from the sun.

Every trip through the tunnel to the bathroom feels like an epic odyssey. It requires conscious thought and effort to move. I am weary beyond words. Shepard is beyond that, even. For him, we give up on the bathroom and wrestle him back into one of the fecal containment garments.

The last of my hair has fallen out, everywhere. Everything else is still all wrong. But this is the most visible symptom. We all look strange now. Not just bald, but eyebrowless.

Shepard's fever has not gone down.

"Al," Kerwin says wearily. "We need to give you another dose."

Shepard mumbles something.

"You're fighting an infection. The radiation killed bone marrow. Our white blood cell counts are low."

Again Shepard mumbles.

Kerwin gently places a pill in the other man's mouth. "Swallow, Al," he urges. He is kind and hopeful but also insistent. "Come on. Swallow."

I want this all to end.

●●●

In the night, I wake with a start.

Shepard is moaning, a soft anguished haunting moan. He's behind us, in the lower equipment bay; I pull myself between the couches to see. His eyes are closed. I put my weak hand to his forehead and I'm startled by the heat. He rolls away weightlessly under my soft touch, and his body convulses in a fever quiver.

"Al. Al." Whatever ill will I'd had for him has vanished with his sickness. "Al." Even during the worst of it, when we'd been butting heads, I wanted to get back on decent terms with him, but not like this. Anything but this. I want to emerge from this nightmare, to wake back into the ordinary routines that once seemed like such drudgery. I want him to get better, to snap back into character and be the same cantankerous asshole he's always been. I am shocked at how much I want it.

He shudders, unconscious, and moans.

I squeeze a blob of water from the drink bottle and gently cup it onto his forehead. It coats his skin like gelatin, then seeps past the bald ridge where his eyebrows should be. I gently try to wipe the stray water from his eyes. I want to help. I don't know if I'm doing any good. I don't know if I'm doing anything.

There's water clinging to my fingers. I'm too tired to go looking for a washcloth. I dab my hands on my coveralls. I look at Shepard and hope.

He falls silent.

●●●

In the morning, he is gone.

I wake and look: nothing. An empty space. And Kerwin still over on the far side, asleep.

I am still weak. Even weightless, it is all I can do to investigate. I pull myself under the console and up through the tunnel. Nothing.

I am trying to imagine what happened, if he woke up and tried to go to the bathroom, or if somehow in his fever he thought he'd be able to use the radio in the manned module. I am afraid to look over at the main deck. But it is empty.

Somehow I am perplexed and relieved, but only for a moment.

I pull myself over and look down into the sleeping chamber, and at last I see his lifeless legs.

•••

I don't know what to do. Not right away.

If I were my normal self, I could come up with some plan. This is not something we prepared for in any way. There are no body bags on board.

As a pilot, death is all around you. You are familiar with it, even if it's uncomfortable. (And in fact you shouldn't be comfortable with it, for that discomfort keeps you alert, keeps you sharp.) But even though you're familiar, it is invisible. It usually happens offstage. You see a splash of fire on some Korean hillside below, and afterwards an empty bunk, and you are sorting through someone's possessions, deciding what to throw out and what to send back home, but you have to remind yourself it's real, for it feels like playacting, bad fantasy, like at any moment they will walk through the door and ask what you're doing with their stuff.

Sometimes you do end up at a crash site, and that is tough. There's a sickly sweet smell you can't forget because you know what it is. And you may see the remains, and that is upsetting. But there is a disconnect between what you see and your memories; you know they are the person you knew, but there is still an unreality to it all. And it is someone else's problem to actually deal with it, to clean it all up. And then at the funeral you just see the closed casket, and it feels unreal yet again.

I want to turn back, to head back upstairs and close my eyes to all of this.

But it is indisputably real. And it is my problem.

Shepard is floating there, his feet almost at hatch level, legs slightly splayed, head and arms down at the far end. It's like I'm looking down into a barrel or a well at a man hanging by his feet.

All of the sudden I feel desperately alone.

I do not want to go down there. But I know if I do not go, I will know that I didn't go. And that will not make it easier to deal with any of this later on.

I try to nudge his feet, to move him off to the side so I can make it down there easily. As I'm pulling myself down there, his legs brush against me, and I shudder.

He is pale.

I want to turn back.

I do not know what to do.

He is pale and his eyes are closed, and his face is contorted in an unnatural way. I'm glad his eyes are closed, but the paleness and the facial expression keep me from pretending this is anything other than death.

His skin is cold.

I touch him just for a second, for the briefest flash of a second. I remember the heat of last night's fever, and it seems impossible that his fire's gone cold. It occurs to me that this is the first time I've touched a person that isn't alive.

I do not want to be here. I do not want to breathe. I breathe at last and realize the air is no worse than normal, not yet. I do not know what I expected.

I try to grab the loose cloth of his coveralls in a way that I will not feel the firm mass of the body beneath. I turn him, slowly, so his head is upright relative to the way we normally sleep. It requires some careful thought and effort to avoid bumping his head against the bulkhead, and here and there I feel his body, and I shudder, but I do not bump his head, and I find some pride and satisfaction in that.

I ease him into his hanging sleeping bag and zip it up to his neck. I do not know what else to do.

I am exhausted and I feel desperately alone. I do not know if Joe is awake yet, but I know I am going to wake him. I have never been so eager to wake someone up.

•••

I float slowly back through the tunnel, tired already from exertions both physical and emotional. Kerwin still sleeps. For a second I hesitate, hoping he'll wake on his own, but he doesn't, and seeing him there, eyes closed, I am all the more anxious to end this loneliness.

I nudge him. "Joe."

He doesn't wake up.

"Joe. Come on."

Nothing.

A black panic wells up in me. I tap him insistently on the shoulder with all the energy I can muster. "Come on! Joe!"

"What?" He wakes into a fog, a semicoherent morning stupor; he sounds uncharacteristically irritable.

"Shepard's gone."

"Wait." He weakly rubs his tired eyes. "Where did he go? How could he go anywhere?"

He doesn't get it yet, so I have to explain. "No, he's...gone."

The meaning sinks in. "Oh. Oh, no. This is..." His chest expands, a deep sorrowful breath. "Jesus, I didn't...I knew he was in bad shape, but I didn't..."

No words can cover the enormity of this.

"Yeah."

He glances back behind the couches. "Wait, he's...where did he go?"

"He's...I don't know how it happened. I don't know if he was fumbling in a blackout, if he tried to go to the bathroom in the middle of the night, or what. He's all the way down in the sleeping chambers. I put him in his sleeping bag. I didn't know what else to do."

"Yeah but...what's his condition?"

"Well...he's gone." Here I fumble for words, wondering if he gets it after all. "I put him in his sleeping bag for now, I...I don't know what..."

"No, was...was he pale?"

"Yeah."

"Cold?"

I nod.

"Was he stiff?"

"Well, I was trying not to move him around too much."

"Yeah, but...we need to know." He's alert now, at least, sharp and alert, and there's a relief in that, to be talking to a human that's firing on all cylinders, mentally, at least. "Pallor mortis, algor mortis, rigor mortis, livor mortis. Those are the stages." And yet he's still tired. Both of us are still thick in the sickness. Speaking and thinking still takes work. "Pallor first, but the others start to happen concurrently. Livor mortis, we probably won't have up here. The blood pools down at the bottom of the body. But rigor..."

"Yeah."

We both stop for a moment, tired again, maybe, or because the reality of what we're talking about continues to seep into the deep recesses of our minds. "We didn't prepare for this."

"No, we didn't. But we have to do something before that point. As bad a shape as we're in...that will be a serious health hazard. We'll have to wrap him up, seal him off, something."

I breathe, a heavy breath. I still cannot believe it has all come to this. "He is in the bag."

"I don't know if the sleeping bag is gonna...as that stuff happens, there's..." He doesn't have to sketch it all out. We have months left to go up here, months with a body. We both know what that entails.

"Maybe his suit..." I suggest.

"Yeah. We'll get him in there. We'll have to do that." Wearily he moves towards the gap in the couches, back to where the EVA suits are stowed.

"Wait, are you..." I am weary beyond words and I do not want to do anything else today. It feels like something we need to prepare for, mentally and emotionally, something to psyche ourselves up for and do first thing tomorrow.

"Buzz." His look snaps me out of my stupor. "We're in a race against the clock here. Nobody knows if this stuff happens slower up here, or faster. If we're going to do something, we either do it now, or we have to wait."

"How long?"

"Three, four days maybe. And by that time, all the other stuff will be setting in." He doesn't have to say it, but my mind fills in the words: putrefaction. Decomposition.

"Yeah, you're right." I sigh. "Let's get moving."

•••

Soon we are at work.

Kerwin's removed Shepard from the sleeping chambers and brought him up to the main deck so we'll have more room to maneuver. And I've retrieved all the EVA suit parts from the storage bays.

We're both most concerned about the main article, the Torso Limb Suit Assembly. It's a one-piece garment with a zipper that goes from crotch up the back to the shoulder, so even under normal circumstances, it takes some work getting into it. And even though we can dispense with certain preliminaries, like the liquid cooling undergarments, it certainly wasn't designed to put someone in there without their cooperation.

"How do you want to handle this?" Joe's tone makes me realize I'm in charge, as far as he's concerned.

"We could draw straws." It feels wrong to make even a weak joke, but it also feels necessary.

"Actually, if you're OK with it, you can hold the suit, and I'll try to work his feet in."

"OK." I realize he realizes how uncomfortable I still am, and I'm relieved. But I feel guilty to be avoiding the worst of it.

"I am a doctor," he gently reminds me. "This isn't my first time dealing with this stuff. We should probably undress him."

"Let's just try and get him in there first."

We work with a minimum of chatter. There is a silent reverence that sets in, in the presence of a body. Slowly and carefully we manipulate his legs down into the suit. His feet get stuck somewhere below the suit's knees. I tug and tug, to no avail.

"Let's...lemme move around here." Kerwin maneuvers to better help massage everything into position, and we try again. Still no luck.

"All right, you're right," I sigh. Even this meager work has thoroughly tired me out. "We need to get his clothes off."

"Yeah."

"I need a break first, though."

"We're tight on time here."

"I need it. I think you do, too."

"Yeah."

We take our bathroom break. Neither of us have completely recovered from the gastrointestinal symptoms; there is some blood and mucus and foulness, and the same weary cleaning afterwards.

Then, a snack. Our energy levels are very low, and we force ourselves to choke down some cookies as we plan our attack.

At last we get back to Shepard. The coveralls he's wearing are two-piece, and we wrestle his shoulders out of the top, then work the bottoms down from his hips and off of his feet. Exhausted, I rest for a moment, floating idly.

"How are we looking?"

"He's starting to stiffen up."

"All right. All right."

For the long underwear, we opt for scissors. Kerwin cuts and I float next to him with the vacuum hose to police up any stray bits of thread. Then at last, the fecal containment garment, another gross mess. All the clothing and scraps go in a Beta cloth bag.

At last Shepard floats naked, unnaturally white and ugly. His hips are slightly bent, and his arms are forward, like a drowned man on the surface of the sea.

"Here we go," Kerwin says.

Without the friction of the extra layers of cloth, his legs slip smoothly into the suit. We work the rest of it up to his shoulders. I worry that we've taken too long to get to this point; I can tell there's some stiffness now in Shepard's arms. Joe struggles, frustrated.

I swallow my pride and my bile, and move over to help. Together, we massage arms through sleeves and work the suit up over Shepard's tense cool shoulders. Then we work to flatten him out. When we're done with all that, I shudder and take a moment to collect myself.

"Thank God that's done."

"Yeah."

I grab the goldfish bowl.

Kerwin interrupts. "Let's do gloves first. I'm more worried about those. I don't want to break anything." Meaning fingers.

Again I feel the need to pull my weight, so I grab one hand while Kerwin does the other.

His fingers are a little stiff.

I have to massage them to get them into the gloves.

I fantasize about other things.

After some trial and error, we get the gloves all the way on and locked. Then at last, the glass helmet, round and pristine. Once it's on, it's a little easier to imagine he's asleep in there, that this is just some bizarre EVA rehearsal.

We float back for a second and contemplate our handiwork. Then I realize: "We're not done yet. We need to get him up there." I nod back towards the command module.

"You want to take him home with us?"

"Well I don't want to see him every day." A guilty little chuckle. "Or at night when I'm trying to fall asleep."

"We better get going, then."

Kerwin floats up into the tunnel, maneuvering backwards so he's upside-down relative to us. Relative to me. I ease Shepard up slowly, so Kerwin can keep his head and shoulders from bumping into anything. It occurs to me that

I'm still thinking of Shepard as Shepard, as himself, as present but unresponsive, even though he is not himself anymore. There is a body, and no one lives there anymore.

"All right." Kerwin's muffled and distant, blocked from view by the corpse. "Head's almost at the turn." Some more mumbled somethings.

"How's that?" I have to move it to one side to hear a little better.

"I said we need to slow it up."

This is the tricky part. We need to maneuver the body around the bend at the end of the tunnel, under the end of the control panel. There are plenty of edges and corners, and we don't want to crack the helmet. If we do, it'll defeat the whole purpose of getting him in the suit. The bowls are pretty thick, and we do have tape if there is a smallish crack, but neither of us wants to risk it. The suit's made to protect what's inside from the outside; now we need it to work the other way.

Kerwin mumbles something.

"What's that?" Apart from the macabre aspects, it feels like we're movers trying to bring a large couch up a tight and winding stairwell, yelling around the corners.

"I think we need to flip him." Joe's mostly under the panel now, contorted around. "Bend his hips again."

"I don't know if I have the leverage." I move up in the tunnel, close to Shepard's legs. I can't move them very far. "Try now."

I hear some muffled noise that sounds like: OK. I push Shepard forward and there is a little strange resistance and I hear: "Stop! Stop stop stop!" and something terrible that sounds like fabric tearing.

Joe never sounds this anxious, and when I hear it there is a deadness in me, an awful angst, and I wonder if we've just torn a hole in Shepard's suit.

I speak hesitantly but professionally. "Tell me I didn't do what I think I did." But inside it's: Why do I keep fucking up?

I see Joe maneuvering to see. "It's…uhh. Yeah. It's a tear."

Shit.

"His shoulder caught on the latch of the inner hatch. I shoulda moved the hatch." Like all good Catholics, Kerwin insists on taking the blame.

"How bad?"

"It…" I see him awkwardly reaching around and probing with fingers. "All right, that's a relief. I think it's just the Beta cloth."

I breathe, overwhelmed. The outermost suit layer's just there to protect against micrometeoroids and to reflect some of the sunlight and thermal radiation; the inner layers, the pressure suit layers, are still intact.

"Lemme move the hatch somewhere else."

"OK. Don't lose it." It feels good to chuckle a little.

"Yeah, we might need it later." He disappears.

A flood of weariness comes over me, the sickness still not past, and all I can think is: I hope so. My stomach's turning; I don't know if it's from the radiation, or the job.

We try again, but it doesn't get any easier.

We try turning him and maneuvering him at different angles. We try moving his hips. But we stay stuck. We're all the more skittish about violating the suit integrity now, and he's just stiff enough now that we can't quite pull it off.

"Maybe we should stop for today," Kerwin says at last.

"I still want him up there."

"I do too, but...we can..." His next words aren't quite audible.

"How's that?"

"Here. Back him down."

I draw Shepard down into the manned module hallway so Kerwin and I can speak face-to-face. He maneuvers down to talk to me. "I said we can try again in a couple days. He's in there." Meaning the suit. "We've done the important part."

"Yeah." I wish we'd done more. How do you know when you've done enough for the day? Does *enough* exist? "Yeah. All right. Well, let's put the EVA helmet on him at least."

"Yeah."

This will keep us from seeing whatever will be going on inside the suit, for however long we'll be looking at it. Kerwin floats up to retrieve it while I reposition Shepard.

At last, the outer helmet. Before I close the gold visor, I force myself to take a last long look. His head is angled forward, and the neck ring's right under his nose, like he's trying to reach something down inside the suit. I murmur a silent prayer. Then I flick the visor down. There is nothing more to see.

•••

Upstairs, we tap out a Morse message using the omnidirectional antenna: *Admiral Alan Shepard KIA. Succumbed to secondary infection related to acute radiation syndrome early in the morning of 13 September 1972. Body placed in EVA suit to isolate remaining crew from biological processes. Remainder of crew still dealing with radiation symptoms but otherwise healthy. Over.*

We await their reaction. Minutes and minutes and more empty minutes.

Then: "Explorer, Houston. We…uhh…copy your transmission. Your health and safety are foremost in our minds. Calculations indicate you will need to shut down the CM soon; you have approximately one day of operational margin remaining on fuel cells. Will set up windows for communication using manned module antenna. Please transmit first…" (White noise.) "…opportunity. I say again…" They rattle through the transmission once more, then close with: "Godspeed. Over."

"When can we talk again?" Kerwin asks.

"We'll say tomorrow. Noon. Repoint the manned module and transmit."

"Yeah."

I scribble it down: *Shutting down command module after this transmission. Please save responses for next comm window 1200 hours HDT 14 Sept. We will be in position to receive.* I read this, and look back at the message we transmitted and feel: coldness. We're sending what we needed to send, operationally, but something is missing.

"What did he say to you the other day?" Kerwin asks. "Before we came back up here?"

I write more: *Tell Louise her husband spoke lovingly of her in his last conversation, and longed to be with her again. Please offer our heartfelt condolences to her and the rest of the Shepard family. We did all we could.* There is more I need to say to Louise, so much more, but it will have to wait until we're home. *Over.*

Kerwin taps it all out, the warm beeps of the push-to-talk, and when that is done we shut everything down once more and float back downstairs, past the telescope console again.

I can't help but notice the sun has calmed down at last.

• • •

When my helmet clears the hatch at the start of the EVA, I look up and there it is, sculpted and carved and sharp, with nothing between me and it but my faceplate: Mars.

The surface is beautiful, all reds and oranges and browns, finely detailed and wind-blown, and there are mountains and valleys and plains, and we can see the edges of the ice caps, top and bottom.

In front of me and below the Red Planet, the wet workshop looms, the massive Saturn third stage, our home for the past several months. During launch there had been nothing in our living space but liquid hydrogen and the triangular metal grid of the floors. All our equipment, sleeping gear and provisions for the trip, was packed in the docking adapter area; we'd spent the first few days of the mission just setting everything up, taking it into the massive main area and assembling and unfolding it all in carefully choreographed sequence. There's enough volume in the craft that we have something no one else has had in the history of space exploration: serious room for gymnastics, for aerial flips and twists and somersaults. They supplied us with a projector and several movies; in our off time, we rigged up a Beta cloth projection screen and brushed up on the classics, *The Bridge on the River Kwai* and *Rear Window* and *Double Indemnity*. We've been busy as well with telescope observations and planetary probes; we've already flown by Venus, and will do so again before the mission is over. But now it is January of 1978, and we are at Mars.

"See any little green men?" Shepard's voice is warm in the headset.

"Even my eyesight's not that good," I reply. "It looks like a quite a place to explore, though."

"We'll get there."

There's a lot to be done: retrieval of equipment and film packages, photography, inspection of the thruster quads. But for a brief moment I relax and imagine people, our children or their children, exploring the new world below, driving through ravines and up massive mountains, gazing in wonder at the endless red desert.

•••

There's one last thing to be done.

We've left Shepard in the hallway by the bathroom; we can't get him all the way back to the lower equipment bay, but we can leave him in the tunnel, at least. So we ease his rigid body up there, taking extra care again with how we move him, both out of concern for the suit's integrity, and respect for the man who is no more.

Then: the tunnel cover hatch, valves open per normal procedure. He will be out of sight and at peace, at least.

Neither of us needs to say anything more, not right now. There is an unspoken tired agreement that we've done everything that needs to be done for the day.

We return to the sleeping chambers numb, shattered.

I go back to reading, the history of Antarctic expeditions somehow now warm and comforting. Cherry-Garrard is describing the great luxurious sleep they enjoyed in the long polar nights. *Perhaps it is true of others as is certainly the case with me, that the more horrible the conditions in which we sleep, the more soothing and wonderful are the dreams which visit us,* he writes. And later: *And if the worst, or best, happens, and Death comes for you in the snow, he comes disguised as Sleep, and you greet him rather as a welcome friend than as a gruesome foe.*

It occurs to me that we will have to move Shepard if something happens to one of us and we have to implement the plan we discussed, the last-ditch plan for the preservation of records and scientific knowledge.

I realize I feel odd. I place the back of my hand to my forehead: it's warm.

●●●

Gus Grissom and I are descending towards the surface of the moon.

It is February of 1969, and we are set to achieve Kennedy's edict with months to spare, but we aren't thinking of that; we aren't thinking of anything but the present, the sharpness of reality, the intensity of the tasks at hand.

We fly with windows rotated down at first, to measure the landmarks passing by and make sure we're on track. Then we rotate upwards so the landing radar can get a lock, flying feet first and face-up like mixed-up superheroes. The trajectory is good but program alarms are flashing, yellow lights on the computer, and the radio chatter going back and forth, terse GOs after seconds of excruciating delay.

And then pitchover, the spacecraft rotating so we can see the landing site at last. The computer is flying us towards a field of boulders.

Gus takes over and starts aiming us further downrange, while I put my eyes back on the fuel gauges and the altimeter. I barely look out at all. Watching the moon is Gus's job, watching the gauges is mine. And I keep calling out the numbers, and soon Houston is barely responding; everyone is holding their breath except Gus.

I risk a glance a few hundred feet up and see the shadow of the lunar module: our shadow on the moon.

"Thirty seconds." Charlie Duke calls out our fuel level. We have never been that low and landed in the sims.

"Forty feet," I call.

"We're picking up some dust," Gus says, and I get goosebumps, because this is the first thing we've never said in the simulators. This is the first real thing.

"Bingo," Charlie calls, and this means we are about to go dry, we should abort.

"Ten feet," I call.

"Engine stop," Gus says, and we fall the last few feet and hit the moon hard.

We hit hard, and everything in the lander rattles, and we bounce, an excruciatingly slow bounce, like a cartoon where physics don't quite work right, and it feels like a couple seconds before we come down again, at an angle now, and I feel like we're going to topple over.

But then we tip back to something like vertical. Frantically we survey the gauges and everything is within reason, everything is OK, and there is no need for the post-touchdown abort. We are on the moon and it is real. My mother, the moon.

I clap Gus's shoulder and shake his hand. "Lord, what a ride," I say, "Houston, Traquility Base. It was a rough touchdown, but the Eagle has landed," and after the pause Charlie Duke says, "Eagle, Houston. I guess we can start breathing again," and over the airwaves I can hear cheers from the control room, but it doesn't matter, on our end it is back to procedures and checklists, making sure nothing is damaged, safing the spacecraft.

I think: we hit so hard, surely we've sprung a leak. But the air pressure gauges are steady.

Then Houston gives us a STAY. And here we are, on the moon and in no rush to leave, so at last we can take off our helmets and gloves and relax a little. Outside it is remorselessly, relentlessly flat and empty, like a dirty gray beach that stretches out to the horizon. It looks warm and sunny and inviting, even though the sky of course is black.

I take communion on the moon. Most people don't know it, but I'm a church elder, and I've packed communion and a tiny chalice and a little vial of communion wine in my personal preference kit. I've cleared it with Deke beforehand, and per his suggestions, I keep my on-air comments general in nature, bland and inoffensive enough to provoke harmony, rather than lawsuits. When I pour the wine, it swirls around for a long time, slow and graceful in the low gravity. I murmur a quick Bible verse from a printed card: "I am the vine, and you are the branches. If you remain in me and I in you, you will bear much fruit, for apart from me you can do nothing." And in silence I eat the wafer and drink the wine.

The tentative plan calls for a rest period, as if it were a relatively normal workday, as if you can just land on the moon for the first time in human history and then go to sleep at the end of the day. Obviously that's somewhat unrealistic.

So we talk it over with Houston and decide to push ahead, to go outside on the moon.

The checklists are long and elaborate, and it all takes longer than it did in training. But then it is done and we are suited and depressurizing. Peeling back the front hatch, almost, a rush of particles into the void.

Gus goes first, of course, just like we'd practiced so many times, shimmying backwards on hands and knees through the open hatch, then climbing down into the history books. (He's always been a man of few words; there was a famous incident where he was called on to make a speech at a factory, to the workers making the Atlas rocket, and all he said was "Do good work." And now it's simply: "We made it.") I stay behind for a few minutes to snap pictures and power down the lander and send the camera out on the clothesline-like conveyor.

And at last here I am, crawling backwards myself. It is not difficult, but I have to concentrate. My heart is beating fast, not with fear but adrenaline, excitement and sharpness, that knowledge that nothing I have ever done is as momentous as this.

Then: down the ladder. It is not flimsy, but it is sleek and slim, aluminum, perfectly designed and machined like everything else on the lander to have no more mass than necessary, slender and insignificant compared to what we've done.

Once I step off the lander and look around, it is apparent how much nothing there is. "Magnificent desolation," I say. There's something strangely compelling about so much emptiness.

Around then I look around again and realize I can notice things a little better. When you look towards the sun there are deep shadows, lots of gray and black, and in the other direction it is all tan and washed out, like a beach. And yet it is truly alien, unlike anything I've seen, for obviously there is nothing that has been shaped by wind or water, no evidence of anything but cosmic bombardment. The surface of the moon is like an object lesson in probability: big craters fewer and farther between, and the distance between them directly proportionate to their size, and smaller and smaller ones in between, but all distributed unevenly, with random clusters here and there. And we can see larger features, like the boulders we've flown over, and with no atmosphere everything looks so incredibly close, all the way to the horizon, which we know is a mile or so out, but which still looks near enough to touch.

But of course we have to go on about our tasks: moving the TV camera away from the lunar lander, collecting samples of soil and rock, planting the flag. We have practiced it all, but of course everything is slightly different in reality. The cable for the camera is soon covered in moon dust, which makes it hard to see, and we nearly trip over it several times. The flag has a folding arm along the top so it won't just droop lifelessly, but we can't get it all fully extended. There is a seismometer and a laser reflector to deploy, and we have to keep everything level and not cover it with moon dust in the process of setting it up. And in general, there is too much to do to really figure out how we feel about being there.

I am in the middle of this when Houston patches us through to the president.

"Good evening, Buzz and Gus," Johnson says, that Texas drawl still familiar after transmission across the void.

"Good evening, sir," Gus says.

We wait for the normal transmission delay. Then: "For as long as man's looked to the skies, he's seen the moon. It's the destination we've all longed for, more visible to us than any far-off mountain range or swath of jungle, and yet further from our grasp. It is my great pleasure to congratulate you two for making real what we've all dreamed about. And it is a tremendous honor to be your president while you planted the flag of our great nation upon this alien world."

"Thank you, sir," Gus says.

"Yes, thank you, Mr. President," I echo.

A delay. And at last: "For whatever divisions our nation and our planet have suffered these past years, we are united in our praise for your great triumph, our hope for your safe return, and our eagerness for greater journeys yet to come."

"It is our great pleasure to be here, Mr. President," I say. "And we all know we wouldn't be here without your leadership."

"Thank you," President Johnson says. "I have a lot more questions for you! But I suppose they'll have to wait until I see you on the *Hornet*."

"We look forward to it, Mr. President."

And with that, it's back to work.

Gus has a plaque to place on the lander. It says: *Here men from Earth first set foot on the moon. We come in peace for all mankind.* It is engraved with pictures of Earth, and signatures: Gus, me, Mike, President Johnson.

We don't get all that far from the LM in those short few hours outside, probably only 100 or 150 feet. The point is just to be there. It's an operational exercise; there are scientific goals, but by and large it is a test flight, to prove it can be done.

And I'm fine with that. When at last it is time to head back inside, I do so without rancor or regret. It is clear that this is a strange and hostile place, not at all the type of environment where you can just kick back with a glass of whiskey. (Until we set up a base, and maybe some sort of dome, it will never be home, never anything but a place of spacesuits and tightly controlled environments and uneasy vigilance about checklists and procedures.) So I go up the ladder without hesitation. We haul two boxes of moon rocks up on the conveyor line, and then Gus comes up, and that is that.

We have to do an initial repressurization so we can remove our outer helmets and backpacks and connect our hoses directly to the lander. Gone is the silence, the strange cocoon of sound surrounded by soundlessness; we can again hear the noise of the lander's pumps fading in slowly with the air. But once those tasks are done, we have to depressurize again, to kick the backpacks out the front hatch and leave them on the moon so the lander's ascent stage engine won't have to haul them back into orbit. This is a key part of the plan to ensure a safe liftoff: relentlessly throwing away every bit of excess weight.

Then we close all the valves again and start the second repressurization, the final one. As the air comes back I start to hear, again, sounds outside my helmet, the breathing of the machine, whirring of air through filters like a long exhalation, a sigh of relief.

•••

In the morning I'm in a fog.

Joe looks tired and worried. I am worried for him. I am ashamed of my infirmity, and yet I don't envy him the lonely months ahead if something happens to me.

At the appointed hour, we repoint the spacecraft so the stuck antenna set is facing Earth. Houston sends us some flight information, then Joan comes on, calm and warm and reassuring, and then Shirley comes on to talk to Joe.

I'm grateful, tremendously grateful, but exhausted as well.

By the time that's done, all I can think of is getting back to bed. Consciousness is difficult to bear, but there is a pleasant space on the edge of it: dreams and visions of the past, of alternate pasts, of impossible futures, forking and splitting, or just hazy and warm.

•••

We land hard on the moon.

The spacecraft bounces and almost topples over, and there is a great rattle of equipment. We are in our goldfish bowl helmets, suited up and isolated from our spacecraft, which in turn is isolated from the lunar environment by its thin metal skin. Houston issues a STAY, but shortly afterwards I realize the noises outside are dimming, all the pumps and motors in the lunar lander, and sure enough, the pressure gauges are dropping, dropping, dropping. And the sounds of the machine fade away until there is nothing but my anxious breathing.

We cannot isolate the source of the leak. We spend less than two hours on the surface of the moon, suited up and inside the spacecraft all the while. We take a few reluctant pictures, then lift off to catch the command module on the next orbit.

•••

I wake again and do not know if it is a new day.

Joe is placing a pill in my mouth and imploring me to swallow.

He has every reason to be alarmed by all of this, and yet I can see he's most worried about me.

"Don't want to lose your last patient, huh?" A weak dark joke.

He smiles thinly. "Sense of humor: not improved."

•••

We're flying above the surface of the moon, Ed White and I, and there are more and more program alarms, and initially they are telling us we're a GO, but then the landing site is uneven, full of boulders and craters, and we are flying horizontally for what seems like forever, intermittently dipping down but still seeing nothing, and I know the plot of our flight path is making it look like we're cautiously taking short steps down a long flat staircase.

And then at last Charlie Duke calls out "Bingo" and we are still 200 feet up, and his words are two seconds old and the engine is already starting to sputter.

"Abort, abort, abort," I call, and Ed hits the button with no perceptible hesitation, and all the pyrotechnic charges and guillotines fire in sequence to separate us from the now-useless descent stage, and the ascent engine lights and there we are, suddenly accelerating upward and away from the dead gray moon, that once-distant goal that we came so close to touching.

Deke has promised that, if we can't land safely, we should abort without hesitation, and we'll be first in line for the next flight. But as we speed back towards the heavens, I can't help thinking Deke will be overruled.

Everyone has that one thing that they do better than anyone they know, and for me, it's rendezvous, the mathematical calculation of angles and speeds that will bring two orbiting spacecraft together. There's a lot that's counterintuitive about it; you have to fire your engines against your direction of travel and drop into a lower orbit if you want to catch someone that's above and ahead of you, for instance. But I wrote my dissertation on it, and I worked hard during Gemini to help us perfect the techniques, and now I feel completely in my element. Dr. Rendezvous, they've been calling me behind my back, for it's one of my favorite topics, one of the few things I feel comfortable talking about at cocktail parties. And now that's what we're back to, rehashing old things rather than experiencing new ones, and I'm in my element.

It all goes well, far more smoothly than any simulator, every bit as stress-free as the descent had been stressful. The rendezvous radar works perfectly, and soon we're in visual range of Columbia, gleaming bright and metallic above the dull moon. And after some quick photography and dispirited radio chatter, there is the last gentle movement of our two spacecraft together, and then the metallic rippling of the docking latches, the confident metallic sound of one thing going right, at least.

There is not much to do on the way home. I read Psalms, sneaking in a little faith, at last: *When I considered the heavens, the work of Thy fingers, the moon and the stars which thou hast ordained, what is man, that thou art mindful of him?*

And now Earth looms large in our windows. Against the black of space, she looks very welcoming, cool and blue and forgiving of our absence.

And soon we are looking through the hatch window as the first bright hot wisps of plasma whip past, curling and trailing off into the distance

We are plunging into the atmosphere at 25,000 mph. We'd started in a massive rocket, so big it rivalled most buildings, and now all that remains is tucked away in a space smaller than some tents, a little metal shell buffeting through its fiery passage back home, windows filled with an orange and pink glow.

And at last that fades and we're in the familiar thick blue atmosphere. The drogue chute fires and pulls out the three main parachutes, and there they are above us, orange and white and full and round and beautiful.

Down we float. I move my hand to the circuit breaker that will let Mike cut the chutes once we hit the water. And I brace for impact, but we catch a swell and land gently and there we are, upright in the stable 1 position, sky filling the windows, not quite safe on *terra firma*, but *mare sorta-firma*.

Before I know it, we hear the helicopter, and there is a frogman outside, and we're signaling that we're OK. And it occurs to me that it's over, my job as a crewmember, and now we are individuals again.

•••

I wake, weak still.

There is a smell wafting through the manned module, an awful smell, ugly and foul. Death. I do not understand it. We've taken every precaution.

I can't help but wonder: Why?

"The vents," Kerwin says. "The vents on the EVA suit. The outlet valves. We should have thought of this before. There's always going to be an outflow if there's overpressure. And with the chemical processes that are happening, there's going to be overpressure."

"What can we do about it?" I want to leave my bed and help. I don't know if I can.

"I'd say close the vents on the inner hatch cover."

"We don't want the command module all fouled up when we do have to go back up there."

"No, you're right." Kerwin floats in front of me, his head haloed by the light from his chamber, an uncertain angel. "I'll take care of it. Tape the vents shut on the suit, maybe."

"I want to help."

"No. Absolutely not. Not in your condition." He gives me a look. "You don't have to do work to be valuable, Buzz. Stay down here. Get some rest. Doctor's orders."

He floats back to the main deck, in the direction we keep saying is up. He is gone for a good while. I know he is working, but I do not hear anything.

I read some Job. There's a section where Elihu's responding to Job's complaints that strikes me:

> ...for God is greater than man.
>
> Why, then, do you make complaint against him that he gives no account of his doings?

*For God does speak, perhaps once, or even
twice, though one perceive it not.*

*In a dream, in a vision of the night, [when
deep sleep falls upon men] as they slumber
in their beds,*

*It is then that he opens the ears of men and
as a warning to them, terrifies them;*

*By turning man from evil and keeping pride
away from him,*

*He withholds his soul from the pit and his
life from passing to the grave.*

*Or a man is chastened on his bed by pain
and unceasing suffering within his frame,*

*So that to his appetite food becomes
repulsive, and his senses reject the choicest
nourishment.*

*His flesh is wasted so that it cannot be
seen, and his bones, once visible, appear;*

*His soul draws near to the pit, his life to the
place of the dead.*

I am eager for Joe to come back, but it does not feel like it
will be enough. There is a heavy sadness that overtakes me
with ease when I am not moving. It feels so easy to slip into
sleep or death.

●●●

All through the run-up to man's first moon landing, nearly hidden amidst all the positivity and good feeling, there's been a virulent strain of paranoia periodically springing forth, from naysayers in hysterics about hypothetical moon germs causing catastrophic pandemics. To allay their fevered fears, NASA keeps us in quarantine for two weeks after we get back. It's been planned for some time, but now that I've been up there walking around, it seems all the more absurd. The lunar surface is an open-air solar furnace, a wasteland of dust and rock that's blasted for 14 days at a stretch by the undiluted sun, and constantly irradiated by cosmic background radiation; if anything, it's an environment tailor-made to sterilize.

But eventually we emerge from our aluminum cocoon, and the dry days of isolation give way to torrential publicity.

We're jetted from one end of the country to the other, feted by ticker tape parades in New York and Chicago and formal dinners with mayors and governors; we're presented with plaques, medals, commendations, framed photographs, custom-made track suits, engraved sterling-silver punchbowls, keys to cities.

And we're invited out to the Texas Hill Country for a couple days at the LBJ ranch.

We arrive by helicopter in the early afternoon: the three of us and our public affairs man all dressed sensibly in suits and ties, plus wives and children in their Sunday best, which has become everyday attire. When we touch down at the ranch's dusty airstrip, three cars are waiting to drive us over to the main house; LBJ himself is leaning against the first one, wearing jeans and a red collared shirt. A photographer flits about, snapping pictures of it all.

"Pleasure to see you fellas again," he says, looking over our clothing as he vigorously shakes our hands. "Glad we don't have to worry about moon germs this time. Y'all are a little overdressed, though!"

"Sorry, Mr. President." The PA man apologizes on our behalf. "There was some uncertainty about the schedule and activities."

"Oh, we're not gonna do anything formal," LBJ says. "These boys need a break! A chance to relax after all that hard work."

Somehow I sense the uncertainty originated up top, that LBJ was waiting for us to show up dressed up so he could tell us to kick back. Still, I'm not complaining. I've spent the bulk of twenty years under routines and schedules: not only seeing the day's time all planned out and measured every morning, but also every uniform and suit and change of clothing. And it's always refreshing to be told (officially ordered, it must be said, for the man is still our boss, when you follow all the organization charts) to throw on some blue jeans and get comfortable.

We drive the short ways back to the big beautiful house, which all of us have visited at one point or another during Gemini. There are Secret Service agents on hand, but the president makes it a point to help us carry our bags upstairs.

When he's gone, I turn to Mike: "Well, he was certainly eager to see us again."

"He's been eager this whole time," Mike says. "I had a dream on the way back from the moon that we'd splashed down, and we were climbing out into the recovery raft, and the frogman took his mask off, and it was President Johnson."

We change and head back downstairs ahead of our wives. LBJ laughs when he sees us. "You boys somehow always manage to look a little uptight. Even with jeans on."

"I think Buzz starches his," Mike says.

"Iron only, no starch," I reply.

"Well, let's see what else we can do to loosen up a bit." We follow him into the kitchen, where he produces several Styrofoam cups, which he fills with water and ice and a prodigious pour of Cutty Sark. "Better?"

"Better," I smile.

"I got a gift for each of you." He hands out cowboy hats, fresh Stetsons for each of us, every one a perfect fit. I only think for a brief moment about the work it takes to make things seem so easy, the discreet phone calls to NASA for bodily measurements, the careful instructions to department store managers, the scheduling of deliveries and the payment of bills... "Now, what say we go for a drive? Take a break from the womenfolk and get some fresh air."

We pile outside and into his big Lincoln Continental. The top's down, open to the spring Texas sun and the blue sky, which once again looks limitless. LBJ pulls out down a dusty ranch road. A pair of Secret Service men follows in another automobile at a respectful distance. Our car slowly pitches and rolls over the bumps and dips like a ship on a lazy sea.

"Glad to be done with everything?" LBJ asks.

"It is nice, Mr. President," Ed allows.

"It's nice to be in a convertible without...a city of people screaming and cheering," I say from the back. "I kinda wish we'd trained for the publicity. After Gemini was one thing, but now...there's this...hunger in everyone you meet. Like they want a physical piece of you."

"Nice to be popular, huh?" LBJ says over his shoulder.

"It's something," I allow. "I don't know if it's nice."

"If you think it's hard being popular, you should see what it's like when it's gone." The president takes a drink and wheels the car around a bend.

"I try not to talk politics too much, being an officer and all," Ed says. "But it seems you're as popular as you need to be these days, Mr. President."

"Ha. Whatever popularity I have nowadays, I probably owe to you boys."

"Or Frank Borman, at least," I chuckle. When that famous picture of the earth from the moon came out smack dab in the middle of the election, many took it as a sign that the country was still on the right track; in a way, it was a campaign ad every bit as effective as the anti-Goldwater flower child had been four years before. Whereas our landing was more of a post-inauguration valediction, confirmation after the fact that the country had been wise in granting him one more term. Still, his poll numbers are up from the pre-election lows, and there's hope that something good will happen in Vietnam, at last.

"So are you glad to be done with everything, Mr. President?" Mike asks.

He laughs. "Done with campaigning, at least. That is mighty nice," he allows, and allows himself another long sip of his drink. "Although I will admit, whenever I get back here, I think I should have retired when I had the chance!" Abruptly he stops, holds his cup out of the car, and taps it on the side. The Secret Service agent gets out of the trailing car, comes up with a bottle, and fills it back up.

Then to us: "How 'bout a fillup, boys?"

I offer up my empty cup. "Don't mind if I do."

By the time we roll back to the ranch, the cooks are preparing for a barbecue, setting out a massive cast-iron cauldron of baked beans, spinning a hog carcass on a spit over an open fire. Soon we're sitting down outside at picnic tables covered with red-and-white checkered tablecloths, our plates piled with pig parts. There's very little talk of the presidency, or the moon; mostly it's LBJ hamming it up for the womenfolk.

We end the night standing around the fire pit, drinking. Our wives have left, to contend alone with sullen children, bedtimes, etc. And Lady Bird's disappeared to Lord knows where. So there we are, alone again with LBJ, standing and swaying drunkenly, with the glow of the fire flickering on the mesquite trees.

"Those were wonderful words you had about President Kennedy, sir," Mike Collins says. "Back on the ship."

"Kennedy," Johnson snorts. "Kennedy was a nice boy. Typical rich kid. Oh, I mean no disrespect, he faced some hardships with his back, did great things in the war, and all that. But Kennedy couldn't have gotten us up there. His daddy did too much for him, for him to be really strong. He never would have been a senator without his daddy."

We say nothing. Sparks fly into the warm Texas night. The moon looks a little thicker than it did when we launched, a fat waxing gibbous, ripe for the picking.

"My daddy never amounted to much. A politician who can't get anything done is just about the most useless creature on God's green Earth. They say you can't pick your parents. Well, I wanted to pick another father, other than the one I got. I used to feel sorry for myself just thinking about him." Johnson does not look at us but sort of stares off into the dark distance, slowly swirling his whiskey. "Maybe it was a good thing, I don't know. I eventually figured I could learn some lessons from him all the same. Learn to be strong where he was weak. And later I figured, who's to say you can't pick? You can adopt a child, why not adopt a parent? So I made it a point to unlearn all the lessons my daddy taught me, and learn from the men who could get things done. Study them like a book. It's better to study people than books, you know. Roosevelt, Rayburn, Russell, my 3 Rs. And that's what I've done. And here we are."

We sit in silence, sipping our drinks.

"I've got no sons. At least, not that I know about." (The president gives a sly grin. He's obviously drunk. Not that I'm one to judge.) "My daughters are wonderful girls. The light of my life. And with great daughters, you get great son-in-laws, grandchildren. But still...you boys have sons, don't you? Namesakes."

Mike doesn't say anything. I'm just drunk enough that it takes a moment to form a coherent reply. "Well, I gotta admit, Mr. President. I never much liked being a 'Junior.' And I never liked my name. I never wanted to...inflict it on my sons. And having a father like mine who got a few things done in his life...well, you love him, of course, but you do want to...avoid the glare, sometimes."

We all drink, and think, or give a look like we're doing so, anyway.

"I do feel sorry for your kids, in a way," LBJ says, with a nod up to the sky. "The first men to leave Earth and go somewhere else and walk around. How can any kid live up to that?"

"Well, there's a lot more to be done up there, sir," Ed says.

"Yeah, I suppose so."

We stand there silent in the flickering firelight. When at last LBJ speaks again, it's a question he could have posed to Ed, but he stares straight at me instead. "So. Really, no bullshit. What did it feel like?"

It's the question I hate, but I'm drunk enough to give an honest answer, at least. "Honestly, Mr. President, I didn't pay attention to what it felt like." I grin. "I had a lot of work to do. I was too busy just trying not to fuck it all up."

This gets a big hearty laugh.

He leans in closer, closer than any man would ever do in polite company, closer than I get to my wife some weeks, and he speaks only to me: "Thank you for putting my name on the moon."

• • •

I feel a little better. But the smell has gotten worse.

I do not understand it. I know Joe; I'm sure he did a thorough job.

"The smell...it's worse," I tell him.

"I did everything I could," he said. "It seemed like it was getting worse before I closed the hatch, even. I think just moving him around was enough to..."

He doesn't need to say any more; we don't want to think about this, much less talk about it. But we are going to have to do something.

"We can't go on like this. We're going to have to do something."

Joe takes my temperature. That's back to normal, at least.

We have to do something.

• • •

Ed's funeral.

West Point in February is a relentlessly dreary place. Other times of year, there's a contrast with the rest of the world: splashes of color on Storm King and the Crow's Nest, and the hills across the river. The eternal cadet joke is that West Point is the place where fun goes to die; in spring and summer and fall, the rest of the world looks alive, at least, and one can dream of escape, either to the glorious hills, or onboard silvery commuter trains to electric white New York, only an hour away. But in winter it feels like the Gothic architecture has somehow sucked the color from the rest of the planet, like death has contaminated the land.

We've driven through Thayer Gate, a forbidding portal of gray stone. Across the river is a mansion that, according to cadet lore, was used to film *The Wizard of Oz*. Coming here feels like Oz in reverse, like the trip back to Kansas, or worse. We roll past the Hotel Thayer and on down Thayer Road, big beautiful houses above us on the left, the icy river below us on the right, and through the tangle of barracks and academic buildings, and then into openness at last. There has been much construction since my cadet days, and much more is going on now, but here it feels the same, the open expanse of the snowy Plain, the barracks like arms reaching towards it. And of course all of it, past and future, built of stark gray granite.

We are not stopping here, of course; we are proceeding around to Washington Road and down to the Old Cadet Chapel and the cemetery.

It does not seem possible that we are here for this. The best among us always seem impossibly alive, in constant motion, immune somehow to the stillness, not only now, but in perpetuity. And Ed most of all.

Pat is in the car with me. Pat, and the kids. Beautiful Pat, eyes full of an impossible sorrow whose depths know no bounds. We have spoken of practicalities and arrangements. It is difficult to know what else to say, difficult to look at her, even.

"Lots of memories, I'm sure," she says to me.

"Yeah." I think of Ed: friendships, conversations, adventures, all over now, forever. He has done great things; he has marked the earth with his presence, at least, but that must be cold comfort to her now. I don't know what else to say, but I know I must say something else. "It's hard to believe it was home. But it does still feel like home."

"I'm glad we're here, at least," she says. There had been talk of Arlington instead, talk and pressure, but she'd held firm, and we'd held firm with her. "He would have wanted this, at least."

We arrive at the cemetery and disembark into the cold, a caravan of reluctant passengers facing the impossible. The same old scene: a panorama of cold stone and dead trees, a Hudson Gothic scene that Washington Irving would love. Now it has new meaning, awful meaning; now there will be new memories I could not have imagined two decades ago, new and bleak memories.

I see new gravestones. Some of these plots are under pristine snow, but there's one with dirt and snow mingled, and tracks leading up to it. Vietnam, other tragedies, lives cut even shorter than Ed's. Sons come home, young men sleeping in the cold. There is a sense of perspective in this, but there is also something deeper and darker, an infinite sorrow, the thought of other parents losing their only sons, their only children. Lives unremembered, except by them.

A contingent of cadets in long overcoats: young faces flush with cold. Chairs by the gravesite, and a caisson and a coffin and a flag. Everything has been perfectly prepared and arranged: a smooth and perfect machine whose entire existence feels like blasphemy.

We are all in place. An officer with a walkie-talkie gives a nod; the cadet at the head of the formation yells "Preeeee-sent Arms!" Rifles snap to vertical.

The T-38s arrive overhead, white against the gray sky, flying low: the missing man formation. Their engines howl, hollow and low, a sound that scrapes the soul.

This feels impossibly wrong.

•••

We have to do something.

The smell that permeates the manned module is impossible to bear; even if we could somehow contain everything, keep it all from getting worse, everything is already bad enough. It is difficult to eat. Difficult to think.

All I know is: we have to do something. And that thought alone stirs me into action. There is a brightness now, at the thought of doing something. My fever has gone and I feel that strange buoyant energy of the newly healthy. I still look bald and strange, but I feel well.

"We have to get him out," I tell Joe.

"Out?"

"Out. All the way."

"That's...that'll take some doing."

"Yeah." Another EVA, a depressurization with very little feedback from Houston...obviously something that wasn't on anyone's mission plan.

"Are you up for it?"

"I am. Anyway, we have to do it. This is...disgusting in here. We can't survive like this for months."

"No, we can't."

We talk through the plan: moving him all the way up into the command module, getting our suits on, turning the command module back on finally (as late as possible in the process, since we've already asked so much of it), plugging in to the environmental control system, depressurizing, opening the hatch, then easing him on out and casting him off into space.

"You're forgetting one thing. We still need to do the course correction."

"After," I say. "That has to come after this. After we get him out. It'll be a separation maneuver, too, like any time we jettison something."

Physics being what it is, once Shepard is out there, he'll be following along with us on the same trajectory for the next several months. It could even conceivably cause problems during reentry, if he somehow drifts ahead of us. Unless, of course, we change our trajectory afterwards, which we already need to do anyway.

"We're not jettisoning him." There is a tone of disappointment in Joe's voice at my word choice. "It's a burial."

This summons images of all those World War II documentaries, kamikaze attacks off Okinawa and such, burned and battered ships, canvas-shrouded sailors being slid offboard, commended to the eternal deep.

"Yeah, you're right." I can't help but think Shepard himself would approve. "A burial at sea."

● ● ●

We spend the rest of the day preparing.

I am anxious that I do well, that I do this, that I set things right.

"Are you up for it?" Joe asks over lunch.

"I have to be." The awful smell is everywhere, still. In weightlessness it can be hard to smell; the face gets puffy and the sinuses don't drain. But this is so bad it's all I can do to choke down anything. I grab my nose so I can take a few odor-free breaths between bites; it makes me feel like I'm choking on my food, though. "I'm the one with the full suit, the water connectors. Why do you ask?"

"A few days ago, you were...on your deathbed, it seemed like."

I look away, then back. "We're not going to have another chance to do an EVA, are we?"

"On this mission?" Kerwin looks at me, incredulous. "We'll barely have enough O2 in the service module to repressurize after this one."

"We should have a good forty minutes out there, right?"

"Why do you ask?"

"I'm thinking I should take care of a couple things outside."

"Like what?"

"Well, get down to the manned module high-gain antenna...point it back up so we can listen to Houston down there without repointing the spacecraft."

"That..." He stops and thinks. "That does sound like it's worth doing, actually. What else?"

"Oh, you know. Get a look around, see if anything else needs to be taken care of."

He looks a little skeptical, not that I blame him. "Are you up for all that? I can take the EVA, if you want. Just attach the O2/N2 connector hose from the umbilical..."

It occurs to me that this is the logical decision. He hasn't been out there yet, and I *was* pretty sick. And yet...no. There are a few things I need to do. "There isn't going to be much to see out there," I point out. "Sun and blackness. And you should be able to come out the hatch a little, head and shoulders. You'll get a little look around, you'll see. There isn't much to see."

"It's not that...I mean, I have been a little healthier through this whole thing..."

"I've been out there already," I point out. "I'm fresher with this stuff. I've seen all the handholds and guiderails recently. It's all fresh in my mind. I know what's out there, where I need to go. Practice is everything in this business."

He gives a little smile and shakes his head, just a little. "As long as you're feeling better..."

"I am."

We clean up our trays, dispose of our trash, get back to work.

I believe I am feeling better.

Here and there I do feel flashes of...what? Lingering sickness? Ordinary pre-work jitters? I cannot say.

I pride myself on being honest, on telling the truth at all times, at all costs. That was drilled into me as a cadet, and before. And yet you're also always told to put on a mask, to acknowledge orders and complete tasks and not let your voice betray your feelings.

It occurs to me, too, that there have been times where I've lied to myself, and it's propagated outwards from there. Conversations with Joan in particular.

I've told Joe I'm feeling better. I hope I'm being honest.

•••

Nighttime. Or space night, at least.

We retire to the sleeping chambers. I read more from Job, God's response: *Where were you when I founded the earth? Tell me, if you have understanding. Who determined its size; do you know? Who stretched out the measuring line for it?* And then: *Have you fitted a curb to the Pleiades, or loosened the bonds of Orion?* And: *Do you know the ordinances of the heavens; can you put into effect their plan on the earth?* God lays out everything, all the things God has done; God puts Job in his place, and at the end of this epic enumeration, Job says: *I have dealt with great things that I do not understand; things too wonderful for me, which I cannot know.* And Job repents, and God restores him to health and prosperity, and despite the epic suffering, everything's fine in the end.

I put the Bible back in the Beta cloth bag and try to go to sleep.

I float there for a good twenty minutes before it's clear that my mind has no interest in letting my body get some rest. Every thrum of a pump or whir of a fan seems like it has been tailor-made to keep me awake. I try to stay still and let sleep creep up. But my bladder betrays me: pressure, impossibly often, sends me back upstairs to the lavatory, and makes my mind move once more.

I cannot help but think this is the make-or-break point for the entire mission: if we pull it off, everything will be made good. But if we can't get Shepard out there, and can't get the manned module antenna pointed back away from the spacecraft, and pull it all off without instructions from Houston...

Finally I am digging out good old Cherry-Garrard for some late-night reading, a distraction to shut down the mind-machine. He tells of a side expedition before Scott's ill-fated trip to the Pole; he and two other men set out through the Antarctic night on a multi-week sledge journey, an impossibly miserable ordeal to an Emperor Penguin rookery. They endure cold so awful that the author fears his whole-body shivering will break his back; the night blizzard winds are ferocious; their tent is blown away. They despair of returning to their main camp alive; at several points, the author finds himself hoping for death. They do finally procure five penguin eggs and head back to their home base, and the author breaks two of the eggs on the way. Eventually, of course, they do make it back to their camp, where the specimens are to be pickled in alcohol for transport back to England. Three penguin eggs: a slender reward for the immense risk to three human lives. Is it worth it? What does it mean?

Nothing will mean anything if we don't survive tomorrow.

I read on: on the author's return to the main camp, a warm dry sleeping bag feels like paradise; he and his companions sleep "ten thousand thousand years."

I am grateful that our mission isn't ending in sickness and infirmity for me, at least. I am not going out quietly in my sleep. We have a chance to do something.

I read on, onto the start of the polar journey itself. There is a quotation from Tennyson's *Ulysses* at the start of Chapter IX. Kerwin has made very few notes in the book, but this passage is heavily underlined, and the page is dog-eared;

there are smudges of finger-grease on the pages so as to suggest that he has come back to read this often:

> *Come, my friends,*
> *'Tis not too late to seek a newer world.*
> *Push off, and sitting well in order smite*
> *The sounding furrows; for my purpose holds*
> *To sail beyond the sunset, and the baths*
> *Of all the western stars, until I die.*
> *It may be that the gulfs will wash us down:*
> *It may be we shall touch the Happy Isles,*
> *And see the great Achilles, whom we knew.*
> *Tho' much is taken, much abides; and tho'*
> *We are not now that strength which in old days*
> *Moved earth and heaven; that which we are, we are;*
> *One equal temper of heroic hearts,*
> *Made weak by time and fate, but strong in will*
> *To strive, to seek, to find, and not to yield.*

•••

And now it is the day.

19 September 1972, a day that had meant nothing whatsoever on our initial mission plan, means everything now. So we are here, and we are doing what we need to do, and there is great comfort in that.

We have finally been able to get Shepard up into the command module. I do not want to go into the details, but it was an unpleasant experience, a variety of awful sensations. And we have turned off the environmental controls in the manned module so it won't try to maintain pressure once we open the hatch, won't keep pumping air out into nothingness.

And now we are back in the command module, helmets on, Kerwin on the environmental control system hoses, and me connected to the umbilical, and as the oxygen/nitrogen mix begins to flow, it pushes the foul air out of our suits, and everything starts to feel clean and fresh and new.

"Suit pressure steady. GO for depress." Kerwin says.

"GO for depress." I am in the center, and I reach up for the dump valve, and soon we see the pressure dropping, dropping, dropping, and now again all of our clean bright surroundings are deadly; there is no life for us for now except in our suits, these small cocoons of cloth and rubber and metal and glass.

I feel a moment of weakness. Sickness? I do not know. It is too late to do anything differently, too late to do anything but *do*.

The hatch swings open easily and I pull myself out into the great bright blackness. When the spacecraft is sunlit and the visor is down, one can't see nearly as many stars as you see in, say, a night in Wyoming back on Earth, and there is some faint sadness in that. We are in the universe but cannot see it. But of course I cannot dwell on these things.

Through the suit I feel the gentle tug of Kerwin's hands on the umbilical, keeping it coiled and in the cabin, close against the edge of the door so we don't get Shepard tangled up in it when we are sending him out.

"Give me a little more play on the umbilical," I say.

Kerwin obliges and I reposition myself, body against the side of the command module, head and arms at the side of the hatch, ready to help.

"In position?" Kerwin asks.

"In position."

"OK, I'm going to send him out."

This is one of the parts I'm worried about, one of the things nobody's done, or practiced, even.

The back of Shepard's helmeted head appears in the hatchway and comes out, and then his shoulders. Joe is moving him out slowly and I am holding on to the handrail with one hand and minding the umbilical with the other, keeping it safe where it feeds through the corner of the hatch, making sure it doesn't get pinched or crushed. His body moves strangely, floats towards me, snags on the hatch; I have to push it away, and switch my grip on the handrail. But then at last: legs, feet.

"OK, he's clear," I say at last, and let loose a tremendous sigh of relief.

There's a lanyard attached to each of his boots; we tied them both on during the prep work. Kerwin's holding one still, and now I stop minding my umbilical and grab the other one.

"I've got him."

"OK. Letting go. I'll come out a bit and grab you."

Now Kerwin appears, head and arms and shoulders, about as far out as he can get without straining his short O2/N2 hose. I pull myself forward a bit and he grabs me gently, hands on my torso, and he moves me up and pushes my weightless body so I am more or less vertical now relative to the hatch, and all the while I am holding on to the lanyard and Shepard is floating more or less perpendicularly to me, and I can see the back of his legs and torso, his body floating unresponsive, and I can't help but wonder if this is what I looked like to him when he pulled me in after my last spacewalk.

And now I pull him in a little so I can get a grip on his torso, and Kerwin is holding on to my legs, and I fumble for a second and Shepard almost slips from my grasp, but then that's it, I have him, and everything is still going according to plan.

"OK, I've got him and I am in position."

"All set?"

"All set. I should say something, at least."

"Something?"

"A prayer, maybe."

"Go for it."

I take a second and compose my thoughts, and ask God for the words. Then: "Lord, here we are in the heavens with your servant Alan Shepard. A place of endless night, and endless light. We commend him to your care, that he may rest now in your presence, and rise again with you." Something about this feels wrong; I don't know that Shepard truly believed, and he certainly never acted like anyone's servant. But the words are out there now, and maybe they mean something.

With a gentle push, I cast him off, in what I believe to be a retrograde direction. Slowly, almost imperceptibly, his body gets smaller. And it does all seem so surreal: I used to belong to you.

"All right. Getting tight on time here," Kerwin says. "Back to the antenna."

"Back to the antenna."

We only have so much oxygen left in the service module to feed our spacewalk; we've done some calculations, and at the end of the mission we will now have to cast off the manned module as late as possible so we can ride out the last hours on the reentry bottle in the command module. So there is a tight timeframe to do everything left.

I feel weak all of the sudden. I don't know if it is lingering sickness. There is a touch of lightheadedness, and I would love a sip of water, but after everything that happened before, I do not have a drink bag in my suit.

"You OK?" Joe asks.

"I'm OK." I have to be. I cannot rest, cannot relax, cannot take any relief. I need to keep going.

I pull myself over to the handrails going up to the manned module. I head back up to that bright place, the scene of my failure. It is time to make things right.

"How are we on O2?"

"Tight. Maybe 20 more minutes until we won't be able to do a full repress."

"Guess we gotta stop talking."

There is a familiar tickle of water down near my neck.

I stop and take a breath. I think back to my spacewalk, the water in the helmet, and realize: it wasn't the drink bag at all; it must've been a leak in the cooling garment.

I don't say anything. I just turn off the water flow on my connector hose.

The high-gain antenna is down at the far end and around to the side. I work my way down the handrails slowly and deliberately. And now it is in front of me, the big round dish assembly pointed uselessly down.

New territory: I wasn't over here during the last walk. There aren't any footrests in position to work, and it's far from the nearest handrail. I reach up with one hand; I can't quite reach the truss on the back. I am anxious about losing my grip, anxious about the small blob of water I feel down by my neck. If I float off, away from the ship, Joe will have to reel me back in, and we'll have lost valuable time, time we may not have. And if the water blob gets in my eyes…

I have to let go.

I push myself over to the stem of the antenna. My fingers fumble for a second and I'm worried I'm going to bounce off. At last I get a good grip, and breathe.

I pull myself up a little, up the stem on the side away from the receiver horns. The water blob's clinging to my skin, but with the water flow to my cooling garment turned off, the suit feels like a sauna. Sweat stings my eyes. It occurs to me that the hair loss means my eyebrows can't wick away any sweat, can't keep it out of my eyes. I don't want to be up here blind again. I blink hard.

I clasp the antenna stem with my feet and work with both hands; I turn the truss up towards the heavens, in position to receive.

"Antenna repointed," I say. "Heading back to the handrail."

I pull myself over and my fingers fumble.

I bounce off the side of the spacecraft.

I am moving away, off into space, at the mercy of the umbilical, and I grab blindly, and somehow get a grip.

I pull myself over to the telescope housing. The camera film is in there, the second batch that I was supposed to install, the batch that Shepard did in fact install.

I know I can retrieve it. I know we can save it. We can get it into the command module now and have something to show for that telescope time, the photography of the flare and the CME on the day that nearly killed us. I can set things right.

I'm reaching up for the film latches when Kerwin's voice stops me. "We're outgassing faster than expected. I don't know if it's a valve in one of our suits, or…"

"How much time?" Even as I talk, I work. I am trying to slide the latches and they are not moving. I'm sweating harder. I blink and blink and blink again.

"We need you back in. Now."

I take one last long look at the film. I want to be the hero and bring it in, the Lone Ranger saving the day.

"It is really dropping," Joe says.

His voice reminds me that I am not alone. It occurs to me that this is not about me.

"Coming back inside," I say, flat and calm. Reluctantly I turn back for the main hatch and pull myself back down past the solar panels. I am not coming back in with the film, but I am coming back in, under my own power this time. Surely that counts for something.

And now I am back at the end of the manned module, coming back head-first, and I pull myself over the edge and I can see the command module hatch now, and Joe's voice freezes me.

"We aren't going to be able to do a full repress. Unless we use the reentry bottle."

"We can't do that."

An awful dilemma: use our reentry oxygen now, buy ourselves a few months, and maybe run out on the way in, minutes from safety, once we've cast off the manned module. Or suffocate now because we don't use it. A catch-22. For a second I think: this cannot be the end.

My eyes are stinging. I breathe hard: "There's enough in the manned module, right?" For a second I envision the next few minutes (and possibly the last) of my life: a partial repressurization to who knows what, then trying to take the hoses off and close the valves and get down there fast, still with air in the suit, but CO_2 building up, wanting to pass out...

Joe's reluctant sigh. "I can't get down there with my hoses."

A dead awful silence.

Then I look down at my umbilical. "I can."

"Wait, what?"

"I'm on the umbilical, I can get down there through the tunnel. It's long enough."

I hear the hesitation in his voice, the doctor's skepticism of a man who was on his deathbed a few short days ago. "An internal spacewalk," he says. "That might work."

"It has to."

I am at the hatch now and looking in, the old familiar scene new and exciting again, looking normal except of course we know what it all means, there is nothing outside the helmet, no air and no sound, and nothing inside but our voices and our breathing and our heartbeats.

I flip up the gold external visor. "All right, let's go."

Coming in, I see Joe's head in the clear glass of the goldfish bowl, watching the gauges intently; he looks at me and smiles, just for a moment.

And I am easing myself on down past the console, all the electric lights of the gauges and buttons, and now past the notch in the bottom, and around the bend slowly, slowly, slowly, carefully, and I want to not get tangled up and keep moving free, but now there is a reluctant tug.

"Watch it. Here, lemme get the umbilical," Joe says. "There. Free to keep moving."

And now I pull myself down, see the hatch cover stowed, the latch that tore a hole in the outer layer of Shepard's suit, and if we had thought of this yesterday, we would have moved everything out of the way, we would have done a reconnaissance of our route with this in mind, looking out for sharp edges, anything that could threaten the suit's integrity, and we'd have moved what we could and taped up what we couldn't, but of course we did not do that, and there is no time for regrets.

"Umbilical is clear and hatch is closed," Joe says, and it warms my heart: he is not anxious; he is not panicking; he is doing his part.

I pull myself down slowly, carefully. I keep waiting to feel a tug, but: nothing.

And now I am in the tunnel, the bright round familiar tunnel, and my face is really sweating now, and my vision feels a little dim, not lack of oxygen, but exertion, after so many days of weakness and sickness.

Joe's distant voice. "All valves closed. Waiting on you."

I stop. I take a few breaths. I press on.

And now back through the hatch into the manned module, the metal hallway of our temporary home, harsh and airless now. I catch the glint of broken glass: a shattered gauge somewhere.

"Almost home."

I start to pivot back upright. I am feet from the environmental control system now, feet from success. To strive, to seek, to find, and not to yield...

Something stops me: a tug on the suit, down by my legs.

I review my mental imagery, trying to remember what's there: the curtain from the toilet? I move as gently and slowly as possible, but then I kick a little and feel something: a tear?

"Hold on a sec," Joe says. Then: "Go."

I look down at my pressure gauge and see the needle start to dip.

I do not have much time.

But I am free and clear and I float the last little way forward into the main deck, and of course there is silence here, too, all the pumps and motors that were keeping me up last night now voiceless, nothing but my breathing, except I hear a whisper down by my feet...an airy hiss...

And now I am at the controls, and the sweat salt stings my eyes, and I am almost blind, but I start with the large beautiful white dials, and my breathing's getting harder, or maybe it's the strain, and my vision's getting dimmer, but I keep turning, and soon I have turned the last dial, and the whisper sound is slowing down, and now I'm hearing Joe sending Morse on the omni, dots and dashes, telling them we're ready for the course correction, and now beautiful sounds outside my helmet, all those wonderful machine sounds that sounded so obnoxious last night now fading back in, wonderful and bright...

Interlude:
Moscow to Houston

It is December of 1973. Richard Nixon is president. We're in Moscow, heading to Star City, the seat of the Soviet space program; we'll be the first Americans to see it.

I'm not sure what I'm doing here, or in general.

For years now, I've been thinking about leaving NASA and returning to active duty. It's been on my mind ever since I almost became the second man to walk on the moon; I'm starting to wonder if I'll ever get back up there. But there's hope in this trip. And it has been interesting, at least: flying behind the Iron Curtain; disembarking at the drab airport; being driven through the dreary winter city streets with their paucity of cars.

Dave Scott's with me. The Soviets seem most interested in him, of course, because he's not only walked on the moon, but driven a car on it. He's always been a cool customer, though, a man to keep his feelings behind concrete walls and barbed wire, guarded even more closely than mine.

Our Zil limousine is by far the largest car we've seen here; it looks vaguely American, like an old Packard. There's a translator sandwiched between us in the fair-sized back seat, a young American kid from the embassy. There's a cosmonaut in the front: Pavel Belayev. Our driver, I can only assume, is KGB. And even if he's not, we're working under the assumption that the car's bugged. Still, Dave and I chatter a little as the city flashes by.

"This place makes West Point look colorful," I say.

Dave gives a wry little half-grin. "I guess it's paradise if you don't like traffic."

The driver doesn't flinch. I'm sure he speaks English, but he's got a good poker face. Belayev turns to the translator and says something that, in my limited Russian, sounds like: What did they say? And the translator says something I don't understand.

Then, to us: "I told him you like the clean empty streets."

At last I see an ever-so-slight reaction from the driver; his cheek lifts in what might be a tight little smile.

We stop in the center of the city for a brief ceremony, to lay a wreath for Gagarin. I'm more than a little jet-lagged, but it's fascinating just to be here and see all of this: Lenin's red granite tomb, the onion-domed cathedral, the massive brick fortress walls with their square towers, all these targets we once dreamed of bombing.

After that, it is a good hour's drive up to Star City.

I try to stay awake, to pay attention; it is a strange trip down forested country roads, far from anything resembling civilization. I think of executions and secret prisons and gulags. There is nothing, then there is a gate in the snowy woods, and on the other side, buildings and cars and street lights, the Soviet version of the future.

•••

After we deposit our bags, there's a mellow reception at a dingy banquet hall, with vodka and caviar, and more vodka, and more vodka.

Dave has a hard time keeping up; I start feeling more and more at home. At one point, I wander over to him and place a heavy hand on his shoulder. "I'm starting to like the Soviets." It's meant to be a discreet whisper, but it comes out somewhat more loudly, so much so that a few cosmonauts and KGB types turn their heads.

"The vodka's flowing like water," he says.

"Not exactly."

He gives a look like: how do you mean?

I laugh. "There are places in the world where water is a scarce resource."

•••

"A joint mission to the moon?" Belayev's translator says tiredly the next morning.

We nod, although nodding hurts. Morning hurts. Life hurts.

The translator listens to more from Belayev, then speaks: "I'm assuming we would do some sort of orbital rendezvous. Launch separately and go together." He sounds pained and reluctant. I'm comforted by the fact that the Soviets are hurting, too, but it is a cold comfort.

"We already have a proven system to get to the moon," Dave Scott says. "There's no need to make things too complicated and try something else."

Again, hushed discussions between Belayev and the translator, and another man by Belayev's side. Then, from the other side: "So this would be an American mission, on an American rocket, with one Soviet crewmember?"

"Yes." Dave speaks. "Buzz here's already made the voyage, with Gus Grissom. He did everything but get out and walk around. He could command, and your cosmonaut would be in the role Buzz had before, of Lunar Module Pilot."

Again, hushed discussions, although with the frowning faces, I know the answer before I even hear a *nyet*, much less a translation. Then, at last: "We need a mission we can do together, equally. A mission that will make us both look good."

The day dissolves into an ugly blur of headaches and negotiations. Technical discussions of rendezvous missions in low Earth orbit, and training visits and atmospheric mixtures and docking collar specifications.

•••

There is more drinking at dinner, toasts to everyone's health, to the success of our venture; that gets me feeling better, at least.

Afterwards, there is another event planned, a film screening in a small auditorium. There is still drinking, of course, but it's somewhat more mellow; we serve ourselves from a small table in the back and take our seats. Belayev makes a brief announcement; the translator explains that this is a science fiction movie called *Solaris*, and it's basically their equivalent of *2001*.

The movie unfolds at a languid, dreamlike pace. I'm struck by the earthly imagery: crystal waters with long aquatic grass gently undulating beneath; a middle-aged man in a fog-shrouded meadow; a beautiful cabin, its reflection mirrored in a pond's tranquil surface. There is dialogue, helpfully subtitled in English. The middle-aged man, whose name is Kris, is lost in thought, haunted; he stands outside, and a rainstorm comes; it ruins his tea and soaks his clothes, and he doesn't seem to care.

Next, we see Kris reviewing a piece of film with another man. They watch black and white footage of scientists explaining recent events on a space station orbiting the planet Solaris. A pilot had gone missing on an exploratory flight over the planet's ocean, and they'd sent helicopters out to search for him. One of the rescue pilots, a man named Burton, returned traumatized. The scientist explains: "He was in a state of shock, which was highly unusual for a man with 11 years' experience in spaceflight."

I shift uncomfortably in my seat; I get up and go back to the drink table; I mix myself another in the dim flickering projector light.

Onscreen, Burton gives his report. He describes being lost in a fog over the ocean of Solaris, a thick fog, colloidal and viscous; he couldn't see the sun, only a red smudge. The ocean started seething and boiling. "I was being drawn into the fog, so I had to struggle against this for some time," he explains. "When I looked down, I saw a form of garden." The scientists review a film of the flight: black and white, with sun on the ocean, and ice fields. There are seething clouds, or maybe it's the ocean again; it looks brainlike. "But we don't understand. You filmed clouds," one of the scientists asks Burton. "Why did you film clouds?"

Burton launches into a monologue. His eyes are troubled; he's seen things he cannot explain. Most of the scientists say he's suffering from a hallucinatory complex, and symptoms of depression. But one man says they're morally obligated to continue the exploration of the alien planet. Solaris represents disjointed facts that strain credibility, he says. Then: "We're talking about the limits of human knowledge. By limiting movement forwards, we facilitate movement backwards."

I take my seat next to Dave; I can't help but notice the KGB man is sitting behind us now, close enough to eavesdrop, if he wants to.

The movie moves slowly, through discussions about the morality of science. Shots of Burton, older now, driving fast through a black-and-white city. It looks a little familiar; I catch glimpses of Japanese characters on the road signs: they are in Tokyo. Burton speeds through tunnels and under overpasses; the film switches between color and black-and-white; we see expressway lights, red and white, rivers of traffic forking and splitting.

I lean over to make a crack to Dave: "Tokyo must look like the future to the Soviets." He chuckles.

Onscreen, we see Kris burning pictures of a woman. Then: Cut to stars. He is in space, flying to the Solaris station.

We see Kris disembark at what looks like a landing pad inside the station. Nobody's around. Kris explores: the stark metal corridors are in some disarray, full of debris and sparking electrical wires. It occurs to me that Kris didn't arrive in a spacesuit—he's wearing normal clothes, and a leather jacket.

"The latest in Soviet space technology," I mutter, perhaps a little loudly; Dave grins a little, and there is some shifting in the seats ahead of us.

I have to admit: despite the cheesy sets, the movie's unsettling. Kris wanders the corridors until he finds one of the station's few remaining residents, who tells him one of the other occupants, Dr. Gibarian, is dead—a suicide. "He was almost always in a state of deep depression ever since these disturbances began," the psychiatrist explains to Kris, then adds: "If you see something out of the ordinary, try not to lose your head."

We see Kris in a rounded white room; it reminds me of what the future looked like five years ago. Then he goes to the dead doctor's quarters. It's in complete disarray: paper ticker tape everywhere, rugs draped over furniture and up on the walls. There's a note for the psychiatrist...a suicide note? And a silver pistol on his desk. Kris plays a video message from the dead doctor. "By now you are at the station and you know what happened to me." Doctor

Gibarian says. "I wouldn't want it to happen to others. I'm of sound mind. I'm telling you this so if it does happen to you, you will know it's not madness." The message ends.

I get up and fix another drink. I'm not quite comfortable with all of this.

I try to pay a little less attention to the movie. I don't feel like I can leave, not quite yet, so I sit there in the dark and try to avoid the images, and my thoughts.

Shots flicker by: Kris talking about a proposal to bombard Solaris's ocean with radiation, Kris staring out into the darkness. We glimpse unexplained characters, people who don't correspond with any of the station's inhabitants: a midget, then a beautiful woman. We see creepy camera pullbacks in the darkened corridors, and the woman's face in a frosted window, and the body of the dead doctor—the suicide.

I look over to Dave, looking for reassurance, perhaps.

Onward rolls the film: talk of ignoring advice, and insanity. Kris watches the suicide doctor's message again. The dead doctor says: "They won't understand." There is an unexplained child on the film with him. The doctor says, ominously: "I am my own judge." The end of his message sends chills through my body: "It has something to do with conscience," the doctor says to Kris. "I really wanted you to get here in time." He turns off the screen; the suicide's implied.

I look at my drink: I'm sucking on dregs, on the air between slowly melting ice cubes, on nothing. I shouldn't get another, not yet.

Onscreen, Kris sleeps, and dreams of a beautiful woman. It's the woman from the picture he was burning before; she's a brunette with an incredibly striking face. He wakes, and she is there watching him.

"Not a bad looker," Dave murmurs. "I guess they've got that, at least."

But my mind is on the movie now. The woman is almost impossibly beautiful; I feel a pang of sadness, knowing I'll never know her. She kisses Kris and lays next to him; I have the sense that she's his wife, or that she was. The suicide pistol is at her feet.

Kris starts to undress her. There is a needle-mark on her arm. He looks truly disturbed.

With that, Part I ends; I stretch and wander off to the bathroom and fix myself another drink as an organ interlude plays.

"Odd movie," Dave says.

"Yes. Odd."

When the movie starts back up, Kris is sending his wife away on a rocket. He puts her through the hatch and steps away to a crude launch console that's far, far too close for anything resembling safety. The rocket rises away ridiculously slowly, spewing fire. Kris is still barely ten feet from it, so close his clothing's singed by the flames. It's impossibly absurd; I catch myself laughing aloud.

More heads turn up front. For the sake of our hosts, I know I should settle down, but I whisper to Dave: "That's one way to get rid of your wife, huh?" And then: "They do seem to be falling behind us in the special effects race." He gives a grim grimace.

Onscreen, Kris explains to another scientist that his wife had, in fact, died ten years before. The scientist explains that what he'd seen was a "materialization of a concept," the physical embodiment of his ideas of her. These apparitions had been visiting the crew for some time, ever since they'd started radiation experiments, bombarding Solaris's ocean with strong x-rays. The other scientist, Dr. Snaut, explains that the ocean "probed our minds and extracted something like islands of memory." Somehow the planet Solaris was creating walking and talking people, physical beings, based on the crew's dark thoughts of the past.

At night, Hari, Kris's wife, comes back. She starts undressing and climbs into bed.

In the morning, he sees her clothes and knows it was no dream. He leaves and goes out into the hallway; she starts pounding on the metal door like some horror movie monster, and bursts through it, cut and bloodied and crazy.

Dr. Snaut can see her too, it turns out. He gives some ridiculous explanation for her physical existence; she's composed of neutrinos, he says, stabilized by Solaris's force field. He stares out the circular windows at the ocean below and explains that she's immortal. He wants to dissect her.

I watch all this and feel a deep sadness coming over me, a bleak heaviness I cannot comprehend. I start falling asleep; in between, I catch snippets of film: a waking dream, or a nightmare.

Snaut explains that the regeneration is slowing down; the ocean derives their guests while the scientists sleep, but they're going to transmit their waking thoughts and see what happens. Hari knows she is not Hari; she knows the real Hari poisoned herself. "The longer this fog lasts, the worse it will be for you in the end," she tells Kris.

There is a skip in time...more sleep? I'm vaguely aware I'm being rude, but this is a long movie, and I don't entirely care.

Onscreen, Kris and Hari go to the station's central library. It is, absurdly, no different from one on Earth: there are green-painted walls and black leather chairs and a large round wooden table; there are marble statues and globes and old books and candles and chandeliers. Snaut shows up and starts reading a book. "'They come at night, but one must sleep sometimes,'" he reads to Kris, then goes on: "That's the problem. Mankind has lost the ability to sleep." He gives Kris the book. Kris reads: "When I sleep, I know no fear. No hope, no trouble, no bliss. Blessings on him who invented sleep. The common coin that purchases all things. The balance that levels shepherd and king, fool and wise man. There is only one bad thing about sound sleep. They say it closely resembles death."

A shudder passes through me. I look around the auditorium at the assembled guests, heads silhouetted in the projector light. No one seems to react.

In the movie, the other station inhabitant, Dr. Sartorious, toasts Dr. Snaut. "We don't know what to do with other worlds," he says. "We don't need other worlds, we need a mirror."

I don't know what to make of this. I look at the guests for their reaction: nothing.

In their strange onscreen library, Dr. Sartorious is prattling on about the "foolish human predicament of striving for a goal he fears, that he has no need for. Man needs man." Then Snaut toasts Gibarian, the suicide doctor. "He died of hopelessness," Snaut says. "He thought all this was happening only to him."

Flickers of film, and consciousness: time starts skipping again, into blackness, and dreams, and in between, more scenes. Kris remembers winter on Earth. The Solaris ocean stirs and seethes. Kris hears a crash. He sees Hari, covered in ice; she drank liquid oxygen to kill herself. "Don't turn a scientific problem into a common love story," Snaut tells Kris. Then, horribly, Hari jerks awake, convulsing on the floor but finally coming to life. "I can never get used to all these resurrections," Snaut says.

I am tired and exhausted and heavy, fading in and out. I see scenes and quotes. "Love is a feeling we can experience but never explain" and "Maybe we're here to experience people as a reason to love." Kris is sick; there are fevered dreams and kisses, and scenes with Hari again.

Then she is gone.

"When man is happy, the meaning of life and other things will no longer interest him," Snaut tells Kris. He responds: "To ask is always the desire to know. Yet the preservation of simple human truths requires mystery. The mysteries of happiness, death and love." Then: "In any event, my mission is finished. But what next? Return to Earth? Little by little, everything will return to normal. I'll even find new interests and acquaintances. But I won't be able to give myself to them fully. Never."

Clouds over the ocean. Kris is hoping for his wife's return. I sleep and wake; I see shots that echo the beginning of the film: long-bladed grasses underwater. Kris is back at the cabin, but it is winter now.

I jerk awake to the end credits rolling. People are looking at me strangely.

"You were talking in your sleep," Dave explains.

I mix another drink, pound it, stumble up to my room, and collapse.

Somewhere in the night I wake from a blackout opening the door to a room that isn't mine. Angry Russian voices: I turn and run like a frightened deer. Darkness overtakes me again.

• • •

In the morning I'm confronted by the unexplained: gaps in my memory, bruises, looks of disappointment from Dave.

After another day of meetings, we fly back to Houston, from ice and cold and darkness to warmth and light. But something feels wrong.

My first day back, Deke pulls me in and tells me I'm being taken off the project. It's unclear whether I'll get another assignment. It's a week before Christmas.

I don't know what to tell my wife, don't know what to tell my kids, don't know what to tell myself.

I don't say anything, not that night. I cannot sleep, though; I'm restless and irritable, and I toss and turn; I want to shut off my thoughts.

•••

The next night, I stop off at the bar on the way home from work. I have one, then another, then another. I call Joan; she is angry. I stop at the liquor store, buy a bottle. I head home but decide I'm not quite ready. I head to another bar.

My night dissolves into darkness and splintered scenes: rain-slicked asphalt, slow-changing traffic lights, country roads, city roads.

Then: headlights. An oncoming car that swerves the same wrong way I do, like a sick funhouse mirror.

A brief look of horror on the driver and his wife.

A final crash into blackness.

Venus Mission

Part IV: The Voyage Home

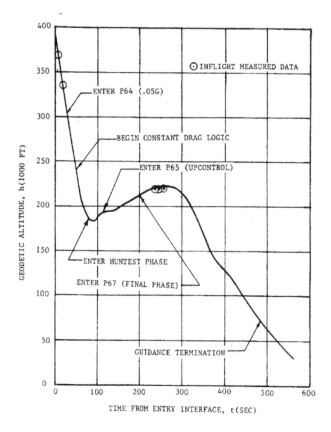

GEODETIC ALTITUDE, h(1000 FT)

TIME FROM ENTRY INTERFACE, t(SEC)

⊙ INFLIGHT MEASURED DATA

ENTER P64 (.05G)

BEGIN CONSTANT DRAG LOGIC

ENTER P65 (UPCONTROL)

ENTER HUNTEST PHASE

ENTER P67 (FINAL PHASE)

GUIDANCE TERMINATION

There is a library composed entirely of hexagonal galleries stretching out into infinity. On the shelves of the galleries are every book known to man, every possible book, all the combinations of letters one can imagine. There are books identical to one another except for a single letter; there are nonsensical books; there are stories that start out as narrative but dissolve into gibberish, and others that stay coherent. I am thinking that, if I look at enough books, I might find my story.

This library exists in the pages of another book, a slim volume of stories by an author named Borges, something from Kerwin's collection. Yet it's described so compellingly that I imagine it completely; the real world has fallen away; the cruel confines of the sleeping chamber where I have spent so much of the past year have vanished, forgotten for a few blessed moments in an infinite elsewhere.

The last few months, and indeed the entire latter half of the mission, have been strangely uneventful. Which is not to say it has been anything like we envisioned during the planning: it's just the two of us now, of course, Kerwin and myself. And we're still tapping out our messages home via Morse. It took weeks after Shepard's burial before everything started settling down, before we got used to our new normal. We've been plumbing the depths of the universe, using the x-ray telescope to peer out of the Solar System and into deep space, looking at the structure of the universe and sketching it out in great detail. We're observing galaxies arranged in clusters and superclusters, and the background radiation left over from the Big Bang; we're assembling copious notes, and transmitting reports on our findings.

And between all that, we've formed a book club of sorts. We've long ago exhausted our stores of conversational material; we know all there is to know about one another. So we're trying to read and discuss everything we have onboard. The Borges book is weird, but memorable: stories about made-up languages, and an author trying to recreate *Don Quixote*, and a man trying to dream a man into reality. Some of the ideas seem rather outlandish, but as Kerwin says, nothing ever becomes real without first becoming an idea. It's called *Garden of Forking Paths*. I'm quite sure I've never seen it before.

I take a break and float on upstairs to the bathroom. I'm still thinking about the story I just read: if there are infinite books in the library, there are infinite versions of my story: versions where we never flew to Venus, versions where Shepard's still alive.

I find myself looking at myself in the mirror. These are not the same eyes that were looking back at me a year ago; beyond the wrinkles at the edges, there is the weariness of having seen so much, and spent so much time so far from home. These are not the same eyes, but they wouldn't have been the same if I'd stayed home, either, so it's just as well that I've gone.

After floating back downstairs, I pour myself into the book once more. The title story, the final one, is about a Chinese spy in Britain during the First World War, on a mission the reader doesn't understand. He ends up visiting a professor, a Sinologist, no less, and they have a strange existential conversation about a bizarre Chinese manuscript written by the spy's ancestor, a book in which all possible outcomes occur because time itself forks and splits. The Sinologist tells his visitor: "…your ancestor did not believe in a uniform and absolute time; he believed in an infinite series of times, a growing, dizzying web of divergent, convergent and parallel times. That fabric of times that approach one another, fork, are snipped off, or are simply unknown for centuries, contains *all* possibilities. In most of these times, we do not exist; in some, you exist, but I do not; in others, I do and you do not; in others still, we both do. In this one, which the favouring hand of chance has dealt me, you have come to my home; in another, when you come through my garden you find me dead; in another, I say these same words, but I am an error, a ghost."

The story ends with a horrible twist, one that reverberates through me and lives on: thoughts and possibilities echoing inside my mind.

Our story's close also draws near. We have only one full day left up here, roughly 37 hours to Earth. Everything I see, all the aluminum walls and triangular floor grids that have come to seem so impossibly permanent, will soon be hurtling through the atmosphere, a fireball of molten metal.

•••

The last day is a day of collection and recollection.

We are preserving what we need, what we can; we are moving our records and journals up into the command module at last, and the film from the automated flyby cameras and our Hasselblads. And Shepard's belongings, too: we want to keep as much as we can, so as to have something to give his family.

As always when dealing with artifacts, there is a tendency to look at them and remember the past to which they belonged; if you don't keep moving forward, it's easy to end up mired in the molasses of memory. Of course our time here is finite, much more so than most times are for most people, but as the mission clock counts down, through 20 and 19 and 18 hours remaining, we still spend some of it in that strange slowness of nostalgia. But there is still work to do, reviewing the reentry procedures and heating up the meal trays and such, and I am grateful for that.

"How'd you like the book?" Kerwin asks over our last dinner.

"Odd read. Very bizarre. But it sticks with you."

We're both eating Salisbury steak, perhaps our favorite meal. There is a large stack of trays remaining, a full sixth of the food we brought on the mission, all the breakfasts and lunches and dinners Shepard never got the chance to eat; we've had some liberty to take what we like and ignore the rest. It is strange to remember that I once worried about running out of food.

"I thought it was a good one to finish with," he says, bobbing lightly in the zero-g. "Another way to explore the same things we're exploring."

"Do you think that's realistic? An infinite series of times? Parallel universes?"

He takes a bite, chews, thinks. "Hard to imagine, I'll admit."

"Impossible. I don't know what it is about some authors; they love these flights of fantasy. What's wrong with simple scientific truths? The known and the provable? The real world's strange enough."

"Every story's fantasy, in a way," he says. "Even history. You're recreating something that doesn't exist anymore; the only place to do that is in the mind of the reader. So they're filling in the blanks with images from their own past, faces they've seen, places they've been. If you saw the real thing, it would be different."

"But this one...time forking and splitting..."

He shrugs. "Maybe it happens at night, when you sleep. Maybe that's why you don't remember things correctly, or you find things in places you're sure you already looked. You've been cycled into a new universe, a new set of possibilities."

I take a bite of mashed potatoes and give him a funny look.

"Why not?" he asks. "If you believe in God, I'd say you have to believe God knows all the possibilities, everything that is and ever was, everything that could have been. Maybe it's all equally real in God's mind, and we are only conscious of one."

"Which one?"

"I don't know...the one where we're learning whatever lessons we need to learn."

"None of this is science. You couldn't prove any of this."

"Why would God be provable?" he asks. "Why would God take away the fact that you have a choice whether or not to believe?"

"Parallel universes...I just can't see it."

"You can't see the world when you're in the womb, either," he says. "Is it hard to believe there are things that will forever remain beyond our understanding?"

"We should go with the simplest explanations, though, right? If someone's making outlandish claims, it's on them to back them up."

"The modern physics explanations sounded outlandish to everyone who only believed in Newtonian physics. Still, it could be..." He cocks his head like he's trying to readjust his thoughts. "When you think about the Big Bang, the moment of creation, and then this...this theory that it'll all collapse back together, it could be that it's one universe, with fixed endpoints, and all these possibilities in between, and yet the certainty that it will all come back together in the end."

"But now isn't possibility. Now is real."

"Maybe it's like a guitar string," he says. "The ends are set in place. You pluck it and you see it in this hazy shape, this vibration; you can't be sure exactly where it is right at the moment you're observing. You put your finger on it, and it's fixed into place there, where you are. Like that present moment, living and observing, is what condenses the cloud, is what collapses the probability matrix and turns all the hazy possibilities into reality. But still it's vibrating before and after. The future's this…hazy mess of possibilities, but the past is, too; all of the possibilities that got you to where you are could have been real."

"You think?"

"Who knows? If we knew what God knew, we'd be God. Is it possible to fit all that up here?" He taps a finger on his temple.

I smile a little. "I keep thinking of what you said about these structures of the universe. The galaxies, how they're in clusters and superclusters, and there are these massive voids, and you said it looks like the neurons in the human brain. What if it is?"

"Are you saying we're in a giant mind?" He chuckles. "What, are we in our own minds? Whose mind is it? Mine or yours?"

"I hope for your sake it's not mine," I laugh. "As you know, it's a little twisted up there." I have been eating the rest of my tray, saving the meat for last, delaying gratification. I've also avoided this particular meal tray for the last few weeks of the mission, so I'd enjoy it more when it got here. It does taste good, but there isn't quite enough somehow.

Something's missing. I take the last bite, and wish I had more, and find myself thinking: Now what?

"Maybe it's God's mind," he says.

I can't help but smirk. "God would have to be pretty tall."

I look up. The mission clock is counting down. We are eager to be home, eager to see it all new, but it occurs to me that we will miss this, too.

•••

In the morning, we leave the sleeping chambers for the last time.

I double-check the storage areas and make sure to secure the Beta cloth book bag; I look one last time at the smooth metal walls. It feels like checking out of a hotel room, going back to front, inspecting the bathroom, the vanity, the bedroom, then looking under beds and opening every drawer, and finally standing in the door and looking it over once more. (Except here, of course, there's no point just looking "under" anything...if you left something behind, it's probably floating.)

"Don't forget to make your bed," Kerwin jokes.

"Yeah, right? Talk about your unnecessary tasks." Still, the sleeping bag looks sloppy just hanging there; I pull the drawstring tight and flatten it out.

Then I float over to Shepard's area one last time and see, tucked beside the frame, something I'd missed: a note of some sort, paper sealed in an envelope with LOUISE on the front. I can't help but wonder what's in it, and why I hadn't seen it before.

Upstairs we use the control moment gyros for one last attitude change; we swivel the spacecraft stack again and look at Earth, big and blue and bright and colorful, all the mottled brown and green landforms, the impossible complexity. My heart swells. We're both speechless.

Before leaving the main deck, we look around again at the galley area and the telescope console, at everything we will never see again.

•••

And now we're up in the command module.

I'm in the left couch, the commander's seat, and Kerwin is in the rightmost spot; we wanted to preserve the spacecraft's rotational symmetry and flight characteristics during reentry, but the result of course is a sad ugly gap in the middle, like a missing front tooth.

But we are powered up, and everything's working correctly, and the command module batteries are charged, and the voyage is coming to a close at last.

"We might be close enough for voice on the VHF now," Kerwin says.

"Let's give it a shot." I flip the switches. "Houston, Explorer. Comm check, over."

I wait. Nothing.

"Houston, Explorer. Do you read, over?"

Then: "Explorer, Houston. We are picking you up via ARIA. Good to hear your voice, Buzz."

This catches me short: I choke down the feeling welling in my chest, and blink away what might be tears. We have work to do. "Houston, Explorer. I believe you have a PAD for us."

"Explorer, Houston. That we do. MIDPAC, 000, 153, 000..." They rattle off the numbers, all the wonderful numbers that tell us how we'll be aligned when we hit entry interface, and the latitude and longitude of our splashdown point, and the distance and time we'll be travelling through the atmosphere, and the starting point for the entry monitoring system scroll, and the time we can expect to see our parachutes.

●●●

We delay casting off our modules for as long as possible, right up to the entry interface, almost.

The service module goes first. This was not in the original plan, but it is basically depleted now. Then, at last, manned module jettison: a quick final jolt. It is strange to see it changing size in the windows, part of our past now, a home we can never revisit.

"Gravity should be interesting," Kerwin says.

"Yeah." Obviously nobody's been up here this long, and there has been some speculation about how we'll hold up, whether we'll be able to handle our reentry tasks. Given the health aftereffects of the CME, there's all the more cause for concern. The most alarmist of the doctors said we'll be squished like grapes, that our brains or hearts will fail once we hit the high gs.

"Gotta admit, I'm curious how we'll hold up," he adds.

"Before we went to the moon, they said the dust would ignite when we got it in the spacecraft," I tell him. "They thought it would literally catch on fire, like one of those...electrostatic dust explosions in grain silos. If I was the type of person to listen to the naysayers, I'd never have taken this job." It occurs to me that I've told him this before.

But he's a good enough guy not to remind me. "Me neither." There is a long pause, then: "Let's keep talking, though."

"Yeah."

Entry interface is an arbitrary point 400,000 feet up; we pass through it, and the clocks start. "FDAI at 153 degrees," I call out. "Looking good."

Through the window I can see the service module and the manned module chasing us, and I know they should start tumbling and falling behind, but there is always some concern. I am looking as well for a third something, much smaller, probably miles behind us now.

"Coming up on .05 g." Our bodies are settling into the couches for the last time, and from the clocks and instruments I can see we're right on target, 29 seconds after entry interface.

Outside the window, I can see plasma now, wisps of plasma whipping past, and the colors getting thicker, orange-red but bits of yellow and even a little green and blue and purple here and there. I can see the manned module starting to tumble now, starting to heat up and tumble, and the service module is behind it now.

"Quite a sight," Kerwin says. "Like you're in a neon tube."

"Yeah, I always like it." I scan the EMS display. There is a cellophane graph that has started to roll, and our trajectory's being inscribed on it, these thousand-plus miles of fiery passage. "EMS is working fine. 0.3 g and...whoa!"

Outside, there's a terrific cataclysm, an explosion of plasma and sparks off in the slipstream, with some bits hurtling onwards and others fluttering off.

"What the hell was that?"

Out there now I see a myriad of fiery meteors chasing us, and slowly falling behind. I look again for something that probably isn't there, something apart from all of it, a man-sized streak. No luck.

"Service module must've hit the manned module," I tell Kerwin. We are sinking deeper in the couches now, pressed heavier and heavier. "Wow, that really feels like more than it is."

"Yeah. 1.5 gs. 2 gs. P64 is working fine."

I'm being squeezed now, uncomfortable; our bodies are flat in the couches and everything's operating on pre-programmed parameters, so there's not the same danger of blackout as there is in a fighter, where your torso's upright and the blood gets pulled from your head but you must keep actively flying. Still it is strange and harsh. And now outside it is all color, no glimpse of space or Earth, and the pressure is building, building, building.

"5.4 gs...5.8...6.1...6.2..."

"Man," Kerwin gasps. "Feels like...12."

And then it abates, just a bit; the reentry program is designed to bring it back down to 4 gs and hold it for a few more seconds, and it's still intense but we are in the atmosphere now, dug in deep and slowing like we need to be, slowing down so there is no risk of us skipping out of the atmosphere and ending up in orbit, and everything is going according to plan but it is difficult to pay attention to that, difficult to think of anything beyond the squeeze.

"OK, P65," I call out, and we can feel the craft rotating, right on time; because the command module is weighted, it has a slight lift vector, and now we're pointing that back upwards to ascend out of the atmosphere briefly, although we're slow enough now that we'll be falling back to Earth shortly one way or another.

We fly on for a couple minutes like this, the glow lessened now, the EMS cellophane showing that we have ascended a bit, and then P67 takes over and we start heading back down, and the g-forces start building again and I can tell from the EMS trace that we are slowing, slowing, slowing, and soon falling more or less straight down.

"P67 terminated," I say. "SCS in effect."

We keep watching the instruments, watching, watching, watching. Outside there is the strange full brightness now of daytime sky, harsh and unfamiliar. And there is the keen awareness that all of everything still hinges on these next few minutes, on the drogue mortars firing those parachutes out on schedule, and the drogues cutting away, and the mains firing, all of it packed and prepared and installed over a year and many millions of miles ago.

"Apex cover jettisoned," I say. "Waiting on 9:32 for the drogues." According to the PAD they gave us, the first parachutes should start deploying soon, so there is some concern when that doesn't happen.

"9:35."

Angst.

"9:40."

And then at last, there is the *whump*, and they are firing off and de-reefing.

"Drogues are deployed! Cabin relief valve is open."

"Wonderful news," we hear in the headset.

And with the valves open we are breathing Earth's air at last, fresh and real, and though the ocean is still miles below, I swear I can smell the salt.

The drogues cut away at last, and the main parachutes deploy, orange and white and glorious in the sunlight, and they are full and round and beautiful, and unless you've been hanging under a full parachute, life suspended, you cannot appreciate what a spectacular sight it is, and even through the singed windows, I swear I can see every detail, every beautiful stitch of fabric.

We are falling through clouds, glorious silver clouds, not thick but scattered, shiny and bright. Of course now we are at normal gravity, but it still feels like so much more.

"We have visual," the air boss calls in our headsets. "Looking good. Swells maybe two feet. Nice gentle seas."

When at last we hit, we hit hard, a violent splash that doesn't feel real, but it is real. We are home at last.

Somehow we end up in Stable I position, upright. Everything feels impossibly heavy.

There are post-landing tasks; Kerwin has to cut the chutes like I did three years ago, and we have to safe the spacecraft and power it down, we have little tidbits of work to do, but over and above all else, in the big empty spaces between those moments, there is that unreal feeling that this is now real again, life on planet Earth, and the dark year of travel now past will soon start to fade, with some sharp details still remaining but so much of it becoming just a hazy memory.

Outside, the helicopters chop the sky, circling like sharks. Our spacecraft bobs gently on the ocean swells. The seascape outside feels far too bright. We both feel weak, lightheaded. Our hearts are pounding.

"Swimmers in the water," the air boss says. "We'll have the recovery collar attached shortly."

When I see the frogman at the hatch, it occurs to me that this is the first new face I've seen in a year.

"Recovery team has arrived," I announce. "Post-landing tasks complete. Explorer is signing off."

And with that, we're done.

•••

Given our long stay in space, they're recovering us differently than they did after the moon, bringing us directly on to the ship rather than cracking the hatch while we're still afloat. The *Ticonderoga* steams over to us and soon looms above, a massive gray overhanging cliff outside the windows. And soon they are hauling us up via crane, the entire capsule, with us still inside.

We're still lying on the couches. Joe looks ill.

"Hey, you're not supposed to get seasick."

"Very funny." He does not laugh. He truly looks miserable.

I am eager to get out of the spacecraft, to climb out under my own power. They set us down on the aircraft elevator, which has been lowered to the hangar deck level, and there is a period of a few minutes while they make preparations outside, and I get out of the couch and nearly fall down, I feel so impossibly heavy.

I've unlocked the hatch, and now it swings open, and there is a platform and a red carpet leading off into the cavernous hangar deck, and it occurs to me that Joe should go first, so I help him out of his couch and he gets sick all over me, all over the floor, and I nearly slip helping him up and out, and they are reaching out for him, other Navy doctors placing hands under his arms and guiding him down the steps to the carpet, past the dignitaries and the clicking shutters of the cameras.

And then I clamber out. I slip and stumble and nearly bust my face on the hatch; I cannot believe how strange it feels. And I want to walk down on my own, but my head is spinning, and there are corpsmen beside me now, and I stumble again getting out.

"You didn't tell me you turned the gravity up to four," I say, and allow them to help me down the stairs.

Ahead, the hangar is a shadowy cave. Although my head is spinning, I can't help but take a look over my shoulder at the great Pacific. The sea and the sky and the clouds all seem so impossibly vast now, this great amazing ocean expanse, all bright and clean and infinite again.

•••

We spend the next few hours being poked and prodded and measured and gauged: a blur of needles and lights and mirrors and scales and EKG pads. It's a battery of medical tests every bit as invasive as the ones we took to become astronauts, a bookend to go with the one I got up front. They have to make sure you're healthy enough to go up there, and afterwards they have to make sure you're healthy enough for normal life.

There are questions about me and about Shepard. They question Joe and me separately. I am vaguely uncomfortable about this. But eventually it is over.

Mid-afternoon, the ship's radiotelephone patches a call through to Houston so I can talk to Joan.

"It is good to hear your voice, Buzz," she says.

"It's good to hear your voice, too." I'm not sure what else to say. This is all so strange and new.

"I wasn't sure you were going to make it back."

"Neither was I."

"The kids are really eager to talk to you."

"I'm eager to talk to the kids."

"I'll put them on in a sec. I'm just…" There is a pause and I hear a sniff, and I realize she is crying. "When that thing with the sun happened, and they lost communication, they came to the door, and…later on, the thing with Alan, I was trying to hold it together, but…I didn't know what to tell them. I…" Her voice dissolves now into sobs.

"We're OK," I say. "It's gonna be OK, all of it is…"

"…and then the thing with your father, it's just…"

"What happened with my father?"

The sobs soften, turn to confusion. "Wait, they didn't tell you?"

"Tell me what?"

She tells me. I am numb.

•••

By early evening, we are walking unassisted for longer stretches, although it still feels strange. The ship's barely moving; one has to deal with the normal naval architecture issues, bulkheads with oval hatches rather than plain

420

doorways, and so on, but even in the short flat hallways I feel odd, like I have to relearn locomotion.

There is a memorial service for Shepard on the fantail deck. It's solemn and tasteful and moving; I'm surprised when I cry.

We dine on steak and ice cream, with the captain and the head of the support contingent. There is a professionalism and reluctance to bother us, but curiosity does eventually get the better of them, and they ask all the usual questions: "What was it like up there?" and "How does it feel to be home," all those questions I don't know how to answer. I don't entirely mind, because the food's amazing, the most magnificent meal I've ever tasted.

Afterwards we get to stroll up on the flight deck. The carrier's suspended all normal operations for us; there are curious enlisted men gawking over by the island, but officers keeping them at bay, so we have it to ourselves, the whole massive expanse of black steel under endless sky.

I wake in the middle of the night and need to go to the bathroom. I know where I am but I am groggy; I see the dim shapes of the bunk, and the wedge of light from the hatchway, and I push myself off the bulkhead like I can just float over there, like I'm still weightless and can cross the room with a push of the fingers.

I spill out of the bed in a tumble of sheets and blanket, and fall to the deck's cold gray steel.

•••

Two days later, we have to fly to Santa Barbara to meet President Reagan.

We get an early breakfast in the wardroom, waffles piled high with strawberries and cream, strip after strip of greasy but delicious bacon, coffee so hot it must've been brewed directly from a steam pipe.

"We never got to meet President Humphrey," I say as we eat. "Poor guy. What did he get? 180 days?"

"Second shortest presidency in history," Kerwin says. "Almost half of it as a lame duck. Although Garfield's wasn't much longer, and he spent a lot of his dying." He chuckles. "It's weird to think we've got the star of *Bedtime for Bonzo* as president."

The helicopter ride is uneventful, but it is great to see land, a thin hazy band on the horizon at first, gradually acquiring color and definition, growing into beautiful chapparal-covered mountains.

We're flying to Vandenberg Air Force Base. As we set down, I notice a little clot of people in bright civilian clothes on the tarmac, and no press to be seen. I peer closer: Joan and Shirley and the kids.

The helicopter doors open and the crew chief gives us a grinning OK, and for a blissful moment, all tension and troubles and past arguments are forgotten; we rush to our families, and are lost in a blur of hugs and kisses.

This has all been scripted and planned without our knowledge; it's a little disorienting, but I can't complain. Once things have settled down, a suited civilian, someone I hadn't noticed before, claps me on the back and speaks in my ear. "The president wanted to make sure you had a chance to see your families first."

"Give the president our thanks," I tell him.

The man chuckles. "You'll see him soon enough."

•••

We spend the next few hours catching up over lunch at the officer's club, which has been cleared out for us. There's still no press, and no president. Joan chatters on and on, filling us in on the details of the deception, the benevolent plotting that went in to making all these arrangements, the packing of suitcases for us back home, the planning for a couple days of vacation for us and the wives, with the kids packed back off to Houston.

There is a last battery of tests at the medical clinic. I generally feel normal, but once, when walking down a long hallway, I find myself unconsciously drifting rightwards towards the wall.

We change from our flight overalls into civilian clothes; they're mine, but the fit is strange and loose. Then we're whisked into a caravan of cars. There's a smattering of press outside the gates of the base, but no stopping to acknowledge them.

•••

The ride takes an hour, takes us up, up, up into the Santa Ynez mountains, and again outside the gates of the president's ranch there are a few newsmen and cameras, but we do not stop.

The president's property is beautiful, rolling grassy pastures and trees, and then a cute little adobe ranch house and stable, like a scene out of Steinbeck. The president and Nancy greet us under the awning out front.

"Welcome to Rancho del Cielo," he says with a warm movie-star smile and handshake.

"Heavenly Ranch?" Kerwin says.

"Or 'Ranch of the Skies.' Although I guess you two have seen more of the heavens than most of us ever will in this life."

"It feels like heaven to me," Nancy says. "When we realized we were going to be spending some time out east, we knew we'd need a little place to get back to. We'd had our eyes on this property for a little while, and we just had to get it."

"A California White House, huh?" Kerwin says. "Just like the Texas White House?"

"There's only one White House," the president says, warmly but firmly. "That one's the people's house. This one's our house."

"Well, it's a pleasure to be here," I say. It is really a gorgeous little place; for as much as I've been looking forward to getting back home, I have to admit it's nice to have a little diversion, a little distraction, another little place to explore.

"How are you feeling?" the president asks, and it does sound like he really wants to know.

"Mostly back to normal," I say, and Joe nods.

"Well, if you're up for it, we can go up and watch the sunset."

We pile back into the cars and drive up, up, up some more, and then where the road gets rough we get out and walk a bit. Gravity feels more or less normal now, but we do stop for a couple breaks.

"Hope you don't mind the little walk," the president says the second time we stop.

"Not at all, Mr. President."

"I'd have saddled up the horses, but I wasn't sure you'd be up for that."

"It is nice to stretch the legs a bit." I force a smile, although the words are true. "And I've been on my share of hikes, back in the West Point days."

"West Point." He smiles warmly. "I played a West Pointer once."

"I remember. *Santa Fe Trail*. You were...George Custer."

"Hopefully not an omen," Nancy says.

"I was a kid when that came out...but that woman. Your love interest, whoever that was. Beautiful."

Joan gives me a look.

"Olivia de Havilland," Reagan says. "It was a fun shoot, most of the time. We had a graduation scene. The costume department put us in that grey coat with all the buttons.

Worst costume I ever had! I tell you, I've gotta give you credit just for wearing that thing more than once. Those were some uncomfortable uniforms."

I chuckle. "That they were, Mr. President."

"Beautiful place, though, that school."

"I haven't seen any place prettier," I tell him. "Although this is up there."

And at last we are at the summit of one of the peaks, looking around in wonder at the magnificent views, and I am catching my breath, and it does feel good, amazingly good, to be out and about.

"I always think of Psalm 121 when I'm up here," the president says. "I look to the hills, from whence cometh my strength. My help cometh from the Lord, the maker of heaven and earth."

It is a lovely sentiment, but I can't help thinking there's something more, a line he's waiting to deliver. But it's too beautiful now to think about the future; the sun is dipping low, down the mountain range to the west, casting long and exquisite shadows across the low points of the rumpled and beautiful California terrain, all golden and green and gorgeous, and there are just enough clouds over there that you can look straight at the sun now; it looks like it does in one of those Japanese prints, far different than I've seen it in quite some time, and different than it is: large and fat and orange, warm and mellow and forgiving.

● ● ●

In the morning we wake and head out to the terrace.

Yesterday's clear air is gone, replaced now by morning California mountain haze; it obscures the distant vistas and softens and flattens the trees; it lingers in the folds of pasture and wafts across the mirrored surface of the pond out back.

Joe and I sit drinking coffee while we wait for the president. It is difficult to believe we were in space for a year, difficult to believe it's over, difficult to believe everything.

"I'm still upset I couldn't get the film back inside," I tell him.

"When you almost drowned?"

"No. Shepard's canister, the one from after the flyby. I tried to get it in on that last EVA."

Joe shakes his head a little. "I didn't know you were gonna try."

"I didn't tell you. I knew you'd say no."

"You know..." (He smiles.) "...it might not have mattered. The amount of high-energy radiation we got, the film would've been degraded. I'm sure there were some images still, but very cloudy."

"Hmm...so the other stuff, the stuff that we took with the Hasselblad?"

"Might be the same," he says. "Those rolls were with us in the manned module, right? They got all the radiation we got. These may end up being the most disappointing set of vacation photos ever taken."

I'm disjointed, disbelieving; I do want to find an excuse to hope. "Those ones might've been more protected...we had some stowed away..."

He shrugs and smiles. "I guess we'll find out, huh?"

The president comes out of the house, coffee mug in hand. Joe and I stand and offer our good mornings. He gives a little gesture like he appreciates the courtesy but doesn't need it, and we all settle back down.

"Well, I have to tell you, there's a little bit of business I wanted to discuss here," he says. "And I guess I should get right to it. We're cancelling the Apollo program."

Joe and I sit there, slack-jawed.

"It's been a tremendous set of missions, and a great honor to the country. You've raised all of our sights as to what man can accomplish. But it's also been a big government expense, a costly set of missions. We've done what we needed to do with it, so it'd be a waste to spend more on it. It's time to focus on making space exploration safer and more cost-effective."

"This is...quite a surprise, Mr. President," I say at last.

"Short of Alan Shepard, I know you two have sacrificed the most for this program. I know you want that to mean something. And it does." He pauses to let us know this is real. "But it's time for a new beginning. There's plans for a space shuttle, a reusable vehicle that won't have to be thrown away after every mission. They tell me it'll be able to launch commercial payloads and bring down the cost of space exploration. And we'll have greater capabilities for military missions. We can launch from here, from Vandenberg, overfly the Soviet Union, and be home in ninety minutes."

It is difficult to believe that I'm hearing what I'm hearing, but I am, in fact, hearing it. I glance over at the adobe wall. There's a bronze plaque which reads: ON THIS SPOT IN 1776, ABSOLUTELY NOTHING HAPPENED.

"The Apollo program is...there's a lot that hasn't been done yet, Mr. President," Joe says. "Mars flybys, the space station..."

"It's time for a new beginning," the president says. "The rockets we have, the multiple stages, it's like...throwing away a limousine and buying a new one every time you go to the store. We need to be more cost-effective. Anyway, I wanted to tell you two before we make the announcement."

I am not sure what else to say. The decision has been made. The man is, after all, our boss.

• • •

We spend the rest of the day exploring the ranch. Joan and I go for a couple walks, looking at the stable house, the placid little pond, the strands of trees. We talk about my father, and our future. My mind is elsewhere.

In the afternoon, we are packing up, back into the cars for the ride down the mountain.

This time, there is a press conference at Vandenberg, out on the tarmac, a podium and flags and a roped-off set of photographers. The sun is dropping towards the Pacific. I look for Venus but I cannot see her; I remember at last that she's ahead of us now, orbitally, no longer the evening star.

There is a speech. The president goes on about sunsets and sunrises, and new mornings to come. My mind is elsewhere.

•••

We fly back to Houston, an excruciatingly long flight across the darkening country.

By midnight I am back at home, and nothing feels real. There is that sense when seeing the familiar after a long interval, that feeling of: has it always looked this way? Then comes the depositing of bags, the slobbering greetings from deliriously excited dogs, the touring of rooms to see new posters of new rock stars. And once that's done, I slip out back.

Alone in the backyard, I look above the trees at the distant stars, at the waning crescent moon, and a reddish spot: Mars.

•••

We spend a week in debriefings, separately and together, going over the mission in rigorous detail, setting down facts and opinions and recollections, getting it all down before memory fades and time takes its toll on our minds. It is important that nothing should be lost.

I'm expected to write a full report as well. I get started on it in between meetings; I try to work on it at the end of the workday. I don't feel like I have the right to go home without making some progress on it, and I miss several dinners as a result, much to Joan's consternation. But I do not make much progress. I make several false starts and spend many minutes staring at the blank paper curled over the typewriter rollers. I do not know what to say.

There is talk of this new program, this space shuttle, and a few people are enthusiastic about it, but the overwhelming sense is one of despair; there are no flights on the schedule any more, no moon landings or Mars flybys. Someone mentions to me that I'm lucky, that I at least made it somewhere else, and this mission which had seemed like a dead end was, in fact, the best thing anybody's going to get for a while.

I do not feel lucky.

•••

One night I do not go home, but instead drive to the Shepards' place, which I still think of as the Shepards' place, even though it is now just Louise's.

There is a ceremony scheduled for the end of the week, a small private ceremony for the NASA community, but I want to talk to her before that. They don't (or rather, she doesn't) live with us, in the nice low ranch houses under the live oaks; Shepard had picked up a place in a high-rise downtown, an expansive place with sweeping views of the city.

On the way, I stop at the bar for a drink or two. I know I need to talk to her; I know I need to face this. I do not want to do it alone.

Then at last: the final drive, the parking lot, the doorman, the call upstairs, the interminable wait for the elevator, the final walk down the hallway, the knock on the door.

She looks awful; she looks like she's aged a decade, at least. She welcomes me in, and we sit and have a drink.

"We did all we could," I say. "He and I had a few arguments, here and there, but at the end of the day, we were all in it together, and we all did everything we could. He spoke of you often. The last conversation I had with him, you were on his mind. He said…" I do not know what to say; I do not think I should recollect it all, or paraphrase his thoughts. "He said a lot."

She does not say anything to this but just nods, grimly and appreciatively.

"When we were cleaning up his effects, right before reentry, I found this." I hand her the envelope, slightly crumpled but still sealed, with LOUISE on the outside in his unmistakable handwriting; I realize now it was the last thing he ever wrote.

She accepts the envelope and thanks me, but does not open it. I finish my drink and leave.

●●●

There are publicity tours and speeches again. Life dissolves into takeoffs and landings, car convoys to hotels, hurried changing into evening wear, dinners with mayors and presidents, and an audience with the pope. And, with Joan, drinking and arguments and ultimatums.

• • •

On our first trip back to Acapulco, we fight late into the night. We've been married over twenty years, but I don't know if I can make it another month. I am thinking about a woman, a woman I met a year before the mission. I am still wondering if I made a mistake, if she is behind me or ahead of me now.

I am scheduled to dive the next morning, a little charter boat with a couple tourists. We chat a little; it seems they're all from the high Great Plains, from Saskatchewan and Winnipeg and Calgary, down here to bake in the Mexican sun until the Canadian cold is no longer even a memory. I don't tell them who I am; I turn back to the bright sun on the blue waters, and swallow aspirin until my stomach hurts as much as my head.

Still I am thinking of conversations, with Joan and the other woman, replaying them in my mind, what I said and what they said and what I should have said. There is some distraction in the inspection of equipment, aluminum tanks and glass gauges and black rubber tubing, but soon enough, that is done and we are sitting on the back of the boat and again I am thinking, thinking, thinking.

Only the water brings relief; we push off the back of the boat, and there is the blessedly strange and familiar sensation of floating, all the once-heavy equipment now moving loosely. And then at last, pressing the button for the buoyancy compensator, the beautiful hiss of air in those seconds before your ears go underwater, and then a new world, water and bubbles and silence.

I cannot stay down there forever.

•••

Back home, there are days when I don't get out of bed and I don't know why.

There are trips to the hospital, reluctant consultations with doctors and psychiatrists, pills and shocks, bright fearful days wandering sterilized hallways. I talk about many things with the doctors; I talk about Joan and the other women I've loved, and Earth, and Venus; I talk about my father and my mother and the sun and the moon.

I do not talk about the drinking.

•••

We move to Los Angeles. Our new house is out in the mountains; there is more space here, space for explorations and wanderings and still more animals.

I write, I think, I work. I try selling myself; I try many things.

It doesn't make a difference. The house is larger than we can afford. There is never enough money. I find myself thinking about Shepard and all his dealings, about the oil wells, how he would have made out like a bandit in late '73 when the embargo hit. I do not know why the simple things that are so easy for others are so hard for me: marriage, money.

These things proceed on their inevitable trajectory. I just don't know what to do with myself.

On my first night alone in the house, I am afraid of being asleep, afraid of being alone. I wander outside and stare at the stars and think and think and think. It is colder than I expected up here in the hills this time of year. I do not know what I am doing; I do not know if I want to avoid sleep, or just delay it until it hits like a hammer and I don't have to lay there in bed and think. I start up the coffee pot and brew a full urn; I drink Irish coffee late into the night, a sad confused mixture that offers temporary warmth.

• • •

I am in a meeting. These people are here because they want to stop drinking, or because they have stopped and want to help others stop.

I am not sure if I want to be here, or if I just don't know where else to go. I have been experimenting with different career paths: serving on corporate boards, doing endorsements, writing books, and somehow now I am selling cars at a dealership on La Cienga. I've remarried and re-divorced. And through it all, there's been drinking.

Someone told me that this may, in fact, have something to do with my other problems. I'm doubtful. But I just don't know what to do with myself, so here I am.

The room is somehow both decrepit and clean: floorboards that have been worn down and waxed and worn down and waxed again, rickety metal folding chairs, Chairman Mao-sized posters of the two founders, lists of steps and traditions in red and black lettering, an ancient Bunn-O-Matic coffee machine that smells like it's burned so many pots it should have a kill tally on the side. The sugar's clumped up in a glass-and-metal shaker; the creamer's in a cardboard canister, which means of course that it is that powdered crap. But if it's this, or no coffee, I'll take this.

I make my cup and take my seat and wait to be noticed. Nobody seems to pay me much mind. There is a listless man behind a desk reading from a binder full of instructions: greetings and readings and such. When he asks if anyone's at their first meeting, I raise my hand and say my name. Everyone claps. It's been a while since anyone's applauded anything I've done, and I'm surprised how good it feels.

After all the introductory stuff, a man named Chuck starts talking, an old man who seems strangely and bizarrely happy, so much so that it's difficult to believe he ever had a drinking problem. "I didn't come in here with any notion of having a good or happy life," he says. "I just wanted to rub out some of the record. I was a failure as a husband and a father and an employee. I was a failure as a human being. And I just wanted to erase some of that." He talks about powerlessness over alcohol, about drinking to be happy and ending up sad, about drinking to make friends and making enemies instead, about drinking to feel like part of the crowd and ending up feeling alone. He says some people are drinking because they want to die but are too afraid to commit suicide; he says others keep drinking because they don't think it will kill them, but then it does.

"It's because we have this thirst that can never be satisfied," Chuck says. "It can never be satisfied by physical things, because it's a spiritual thirst. It's a thirst for peace of mind. That's our problem. We're restless, irritable and discontented *without* alcohol. That's our problem."

He goes on: "I didn't realize that at the time, of course. I thought I had a lot of problems when I was out there, and I thought I had to drink to take my mind off those problems. I thought I had lots of problems, but I just had one problem. I believe it's the same problem all of you have, although you'll have to decide that for yourself," he says. "That problem is ego. What is ego? Well, I define it as 'conscious sense of separation from.' Separation from what? From others around us. From God. From good. From life. The ego tells me I can be happy, just as long as I pile up enough. Enough of whatever I think I need, whether it is booze or women or money. But the thing is, the ego can never be satisfied. Never! So if I'm running my life based on ego, I will just try to pile up more and more, and the more I get, the more miserable I'll be. But just as there is one problem, there is one solution. And for me, that is 'conscious sense of union with.' Union with what? Again: God. Good. Life. For me, those are all the same thing.

"So recovery from alcoholism doesn't just mean staying dry, putting the plug in the jug. That has to happen first, but beyond that, I have to start living in a way that drinking feels unnecessary. Or else I'll go back. The opposite of alcoholism is connection, to all of these things, real connection, not based on ego. Not based on dominating, or being dominated, but based on real relationship. Which means I have to listen as much as I talk. I can't tell other people what they see. I can tell them what I see, but I have to listen to them when they tell me what they see, because no two humans see all the same things. Nobody.

"And I have to work to change." He smiles. "I used to think I had to drink because of the way the world was. I had to, because I couldn't change the world. Well, I learned in these rooms, it isn't the outside world that makes me drink, it's when things are broken and twisted inside of me! When I work on my insides, everything that's outside starts to feel OK. And I'm going to tell you this: heaven and hell are the same place. Because before I got sober, I sat in my living room chair and drank, and made everyone else miserable, and made myself miserable, and it was hell. But now, I've still got that same living room chair! And I sit in it now, and I have pleasant conversations, and I listen to others, really listen, and it's heaven. But I have to change me. I have to work these steps and work on what's inside of me, to turn hell into heaven. So I'll leave you with a great quote from Carl Jung, who was a great friend of this fellowship. He said, 'He who looks outward, dreams. He who looks inward, awakens.'"

There is applause. There are comments and sharing. I do not say anything.

Instead, I get up and head back to the coffee machine. I pour a little heap of creamer into the bottom of my too-small Styrofoam cup, then a bit of sugar, then pour the coffee on top: better mixing through engineering. There are sad little bubbles as the coffee penetrates the creamer below; I mash the plastic stirrer in there and mix up the clumps.

After all of it is over, people are crowding and milling about, asking for my phone number and telling me theirs. I take a few phone numbers, but it's all a bit overwhelming; I get out of there as soon as I can.

•••

A young couple's strolled onto the car lot.

I watch them from the air-conditioned showroom; I linger there on the cool side of the glass, stroking my newly-grown beard and sipping hot coffee from a Styrofoam cup. The thermostat's low enough that I'm not sure whether I'm drinking for caffeination or warmth.

I know I should go out there, but I watch.

Their faces and arms are glistening and slightly golden, highlit by the morning sun. They're holding hands as they compare sticker prices. She looks uncomfortable; I keep waiting for her to take her hand back and wipe off her sweaty palm, but she doesn't. But I can tell he's the one who started it. And somehow this makes me feel like I know the guy, for I feel the same thing, this desire for physical affection in spite of physical discomfort. My second wife said something similar on our first date.

"You want to take 'em, Buzz?" The sales manager's sidled up behind me.

"Might as well." I try to voice what I think is optimism.

"You got this." He claps me on the shoulder, a buddy clap, hard enough to slosh my coffee.

How did I get here? From the moon to this mundane world of quotas and commissions and 12.9% APR financing? I wipe coffee from my fingers and the cup, and wonder.

"I'll watch from here," the manager continues, oblivious.

I walk to the door, hesitate. The lot's festooned with sale flags and streamers hanging listlessly in the dead morning air, shining harshly in the California sun; now that I'm here choking down panic, it seems even stranger that they make these places look so festive, every last one like an absurd parody of a party.

No guts, no glory. Well, no glory either way, but I might as well do something. I open the door at last to a blast of summer heat, the cold showroom air billowing out with me and then dissipating; I sip my coffee as I walk out there under the canopy of tinsel. It occurs to me too late that I should've left it inside.

I've spouted plebe knowledge back to angry upperclassmen. I've talked to kings and presidents. I can do this. "Morning, folks. How can I help you?"

"We're just getting a look," he says. "Figured we'd check out the 1978 models while they're still around."

"Well, I'll be glad to help you out. I'm Buzz." I've talked to kings and presidents. And now I'm doing this.

"Joe. And this is Amy."

Handshakes all around: firm, confident. I'm good at that part, at least.

"So, tell me, Buzz..." He's a young guy, 23 maybe: young and anonymous, with a beautiful wife. And for a second I think: what I wouldn't give. Then: "Wait. Buzz." His eyes dart around the lot like it's *Candid Camera* and he's trying to spot the film crew. "Wasn't that...wait. You *are* the moon guy!"

"Yeah, that's me. I look a little different these days. Grew a beard." I wince inwardly at the unspoken question that always comes next, the one written on their face when they hear this: What are you doing here selling cars?

"What are you doing here selling cars?"

Then again, sometimes it's spoken. "Well, I've...lived and worked around machines all my life." I sputter. I'm absurdly aware of the coffee cup in my hand, and kicking myself for not leaving it inside, and half-wishing I'd put something in it to loosen up. But I know I've got to keep talking. "And I...well, I know a reliable ride when I see one. Take this Cadillac here..."

"I don't know if we're in the market for a Cadillac," the woman finally speaks; she pats her belly, which, now that I'm looking that low, is showing signs of early pregnancy. "Maybe something a little more economical."

"He can tell us about the Caddie," the man says.

"Well, as you can see, it's a beautiful car. A really nice sturdy machine. I'll tell you, when we rode the lunar lander down to the moon, it was a pretty flimsy thing. They had to engineer it to be so thin that, when it was pressurized, the door actually bulged outward a little. But not these doors!" I open the door and slam it. "See? Nice solid reliable doors. And getting out? In the lunar lander, you had to crawl on your hands and knees, backwards. You had to angle your body just right so you could scoot out without getting hung up on the hatch. But there will be no problems getting in and out of this baby. Even with a baby!" I grin expectantly.

She frowns. "I'm not pregnant."

I am destroyed. "Well, I...uh..."

"We are thinking about starting a family. If we can learn to be a little responsible." She looks down at the sticker in the window. "Gas mileage isn't that good, huh?"

I cannot tell a lie. "No, it probably isn't the best car for that. I have to say…"

She starts walking towards the cheaper cars.

He doesn't move. "What was it like on the moon?"

"Well, it was a pretty amazing place, really." I deflate a little. And yet I'm oddly relieved. These are comfortable familiar stories now, if a little annoying to repeat. "You'd kick up dust, and it would just go up in a little arc and come right back down. And of course, no clouds. Just…stark, very stark and clear. Everything was exactly what it appeared to be. It was bright, really bright, like you were on a beach, but so much sharper, all the lights and shadows. It was really easy to move around and work…"

"But what did it feel like?

The question I hate. "I…I don't know. We had a lot of jobs we had to do, we'd trained for years to do those jobs. I didn't really stop and think about what I felt like. We didn't have time. We were too busy trying to get everything done…"

His eyes wander a little, off down the line of cars; I can tell I'm losing him. What do people expect to hear? An amazing, transformative experience, maybe: something that will let them know all of this means something. But how can you explain that if someone doesn't already believe it? You could talk forever and it wouldn't be enough. Al Shepard always answered the same way, his stock asshole two-second three-word answer: Super! Loved it.

"…I…people seem surprised when they hear this, but…I had a big important job, and a lot of people were watching, and I was just trying not to fuck it up."

He chuckles a little.

"Which, speaking of jobs…" I look back down at the car.

"I have always kinda wanted a Caddie. Good, solid, American-made. What were you saying about the mileage?"

"Well, the mileage isn't all that great, to be honest. I don't know your financial situation, but if that's something you're worried about…"

"What seems to be the problem, gentlemen?" The sales manager's at my elbow now, sounding jumpy and excitable.

"No problem," I say.

"Buzz here was just telling me about his time on the moon."

"You know, we drove cars on the moon," the manager says, rapidfire. "And short of driving a car on the moon, I think this is the coolest ride out there. Sometimes women get a little skittish about getting a car this big, but I think a guy like you shouldn't settle for anything less. This is a car that tells the world you're important. If you want wealth and power to come your way, you've got to attract it. And these days a car like this is the only way to do it. Just the other day, I…"

He's talking fast and loose enough that it seems unnatural. I fade back a little, and he doesn't seem to notice.

I wander inside and go to the bathroom, and when I come out, they're inside, the guy filling out paperwork on the sales manager's desk, his wife standing above them, arms folded with displeasure.

I want to forget all of this.

I retreat to my office and pick up the phone. I pull out one of the numbers from the meeting, a guy I'd talked to for a little bit before I'd left, a guy named Clancy.

"Hello?"

"Hey, it's…Buzz. I met you the other day. At that thing."

"What's going on, Buzz?"

"I want a drink."

There's an emptiness on the line, but only for a second. "What am I supposed to tell you? No? It's not my job to tell you not to drink. If you want to drink, go drink. It's your business. I'm not here to stop you. I'm here to tell you how to stay sober, if you want to stay sober. That's my business."

"I don't want to drink."

"OK, then. There's meetings today, if you want to meet up. We can get started on the…"

"I'm still at work."

A longer pause than before. "Wait, where is it you're working again?"

"A car dealership." I look through the glass partition at the rest of the showroom and reassure myself: no one's paying attention to the fact that I'm in here.

"Buzz, is that really what you want to be doing with yourself?"

"No."

"Well, why are you there, then? Have you sold any cars?"

"No, not yet." Out on the showroom floor, the sales manager walks the young couple to the door, opens it for them, shakes hands with the man.

"Well, I don't know you that well, but it sounds to me like you're not a car salesman. It sounds like they're just using you to make themselves look big. Are you actually being useful, to yourself or them?"

"I want to sell a car."

"Is that humility talking, or your ego?"

"I want to sell a car."

The sales manager walks past, sees me alone in the office, gives me a look. I hang up the phone, hoping he'll keep walking.

No luck.

He sticks his head in. "Buzz, you got a minute?"

"Sure thing."

"That guy, why didn't you close the sale?"

"Well, his wife was…"

"His wife wasn't the customer! He wanted a Caddie, you should have sold him a Caddie."

"Financially, I didn't think he was…"

"It's not your job to make their financial decisions for them, Buzz." He sighs. "Look. This is America. Everyone stretches themselves somewhere, in some area of their life. A house that's too big. A boat they don't need. If they don't do it with us, they'll do it somewhere else."

"Yeah."

"And besides, we've got inventory we've got to move. We've got to get the best price we can for it. When the new models come in, people aren't interested in the old ones any more."

"Yeah."

"Look, it's a tough business. But you're a tough guy. Hell, you had to be, to do all you've done. But you gotta get comfortable around the customer." He leans forward; I can see a little of what looks like blood at the base of his nostril. "You're asking them to do something that may be hard for them. The only way to do that is to be comfortable. Whatever you gotta do to make that happen, make it happen."

●●●

It is later that same night and I am drunk, horribly awfully drunk yet again, and things have gone horribly awfully wrong yet again, and while they've gone wrong before (arguments, accidents, adultery, etc.), now they have gone wrong in an unfathomable way, for I am at the local police precinct, under arrest, it seems.

Me, arrest. Another A, worse than the scarlet one, like a varsity letter you're competing not to get.

We won't go into all the details.

But I am under arrest, and it didn't even occur to me right away that things had gone so very wrong, for when the officer arrested me, he'd been extremely polite about it, like "Sir, I'm going to ask you to take a little ride with me," with a hopeful little uplift at the end of the sentence, almost as if he was asking for a favor, like he was seeking my daughter's hand in marriage, or he wanted the pleasure of my company on a pleasant automobile excursion. Hell, he never even used the word "arrest." And I could tell he was practically a kid; he looked twelve or maybe fifteen, tops, and using my logical brain (which I haven't done all that much tonight), it seemed like he was about the same age as my son. And with all this talk about kids not respecting their elders these days, when one calls you "Sir" and asks for a favor, that's behavior you want to encourage, right?

And he wasn't putting me in handcuffs or anything, he was sort of shepherding me from behind, so somehow it didn't occur to me until we got over to the squad car that I'd be sitting in the back, regardless of my preferences on the matter, or whether or not I'd asked to ride shotgun. And sure enough, it was just like all the mindless cop shows, no locks on the doors, windows that didn't roll down, etc., and suddenly my level of drunkenness wasn't nearly enough to match the awfulness of it all.

And now we're in front of the booking officer, an older guy with a lumpy Irish potato of a face. And my hopefulness is coming back, for I've formulated an escape plan of sorts: some remnant of me is sure it'll all be funny to them, maybe, like once we get to know one another, they'll see how silly this all is, just a simple comedy of errors.

"Last name?"

I smile stupidly and give it.

He writes it neatly in the blotter without looking up. "First name?"

"Buzz."

After the last letter, he pauses, and looks up with something I don't imagine you see much on a thick Irish police veteran: confusion.

"Tell the sergeant your real first name," the kid says.

"It's Buzz! BZZZZZZZZ. Buzz. Like what I've got now." In my drunkenness, this is hilarious. "It was Edwin. I had it legally changed."

The kid: "He says he walked on the moon."

"Very funny, wiseguy," Mr. Potatohead says. "What's your real name?"

"That's my name!" I lean forward on the desk and grin stupidly, like I'm actually going to impress him, but it occurs to me my appearance has changed, and maybe that's why they're not getting the joke. "I have a beard. I didn't used to have a beard. But it's me."

"Hands off the desk, mister." But he looks down and sees my class ring, my crass mass of brass and glass, my bold mold of rolled gold. "Wait, you are..." And just like the guy in the car lot, he looks around like it's *Candid Camera*, like Allen Funt's going to pop out at any moment and tell him it's all a silly sham, which at this point I kinda still feel like it is.

"Yep! And you know what my mom's maiden name is? It's MOON. M. O. O. N. Moon, moon, moon, moon, moon."

"Shhhh!" He shushes me, which I don't expect, but when I look around there are other officers curiously eavesdropping on the proceedings. "Good Lord. This is..." He looks up at the kid. "What are we booking him for?"

The kid comes over behind the desk and whispers something in his ear.

"Uh-huh," the sergeant says. Then to me: "Finish what you were telling me. Quietly."

"My mother's maiden name is Moon," I whisper.

"Not that quietly."

"Moon. Isn't that funny? Moon. How's that for being born under a bad sign? Except I guess it's not, it's a...good...heavenly body. But I can't go back there anymore! I've lost access to this heavenly body."

And now he just shakes his head a little, and if this were one of those corny cop shows, it'd probably be the point where he says: Now I really have seen it all. Instead he goes: "Well I would say it's a pleasure to meet you..."

Another glimmer of hope. "You want an autograph?"

"Well, I..."

"It's OK. I don't mind. We can take care of this right here! Take some pictures together. This doesn't have to be a big deal, does it?" I'm babbling. I don't know what I'm saying. I just want this all to go away, to dissolve into handshakes and backslaps and good feelings.

He leans back. "Look. Colonel..."

"Buzz! I insist." I continue, oblivious, fumbling around on my person for a pen.

"Look. Buzz. If I may call you that. I'd say it's a pleasure to meet you..."

I don't have a pen in my pockets, but there's one on the desk there, and I lunge for it. "Sometimes I charge, but I guess for this, I..."

"Stop!" He snatches the pen away. "Look. I'd say it's a pleasure to meet you, but it's never a pleasure to meet anyone under these circumstances. Especially someone who should know better."

This at last snaps me back.

He continues, looking straight at me, relentlessly. "So I don't want your autograph. My kids, they look up to you guys. We all look up to you. We followed every mission, we were all watching together when you landed, I let 'em stay up to watch all the coverage. And now...I don't want to get your autograph and have to explain how I got it. Besides, it'd be unprofessional. In fact, if you are offering to give me something valuable, a favor in exchange for a favor, well, that could be construed as bribery."

These words smack me. And now there is a sadness welling up in me, moon-shaped pools of tears welling at the bottom of my eyes, and all I can think is: pathetic. Pathetic. Pathetic. Whatever else I've done in my life, this is me here now, a drunk under arrest.

"But we could play this a few different ways. In fact, I..." He looks down at my last name already written indelibly in the blotter. "Let's just sit down and have a little chat. Hansen..."

The youngster perks up: "Yeah, Sarge?"

"Get a chair here. And get us some coffee, would you. One for me and one for...Buzz, here. Cream and sugar?"

"Uhh...that's fine."

Hansen parks a chair besides me and disappears. I sit.

"I take it this is the first time you've been arrested."

"Yeah."

"Bad night?"

"Well, I've...to be honest, I have...this is...this has been a problem. The drinking stuff. I totaled a car a while back, I've made an ass out of myself on many occasions, I..." Again I break down, all the sorrow and the shame. "...I've been trying to quit, I just..."

At this, a little impish glimmer of a smile appears on his face. "So, yeah, the thing of it is, there's people who have no business drinking. I'm one of those people. I told myself it was the stress of the job, everything I'd seen and done. And I thought, 'Oh, I don't do it every day. Work hard, play hard,' and all that. But regardless, I've got no business drinking. When I drink, I...well, let's just say, when I drink, I'm no better than anybody I arrest."

I nod dumbly.

"I was always judging people harshly, too. That was the thing of it. And that added to my level of stress. I threw the book at people, even knowing that I just as easy coulda been in the book. But I've learned to be...fair. The thing is, as a cop, the less serious the crime, the more latitude you have in how to deal with it. You understand? Some people just need to make some changes, and once they do that, they don't end up coming back to places like this."

"I've been trying to change. It just hasn't worked."

"Trying? Like how?"

"Well, I've been meeting people, trying to get sober. This guy Clancy was telling me today..."

"You know Clancy?" He smirks. "Well I'll be a sonofabitch. So maybe we know some of the same people. Which is funny."

"Oh, yeah!" And here I make the mistake of smiling.

"Well, you know those people, but you're still here." He frowns, leans back. "So you really really should know better. And I'm talking to you while you're still drunk, so it might be a waste of breath."

I deflate.

"I will say, some people don't get it right away. They still think they can figure it out on their own. You don't know if you're doing them a favor if you let 'em off easy. They need bad things to happen to them before they're willing to change. If you prevent that, you might just…" Hansen comes back with the coffee. I take mine. The sergeant just sits his on the desk and continues. "…you might just be helping them think they can get away with it. You might be aiding in their destruction. You understand?"

I don't know what to say, so I go back to the dumb nod.

"Maybe you do, maybe you don't. Sometimes reporters come by here. Reporters from the *Times*, on the police beat. And we don't always like them, but they are members of the public, and the public has a right to know what we do as cops, because they are paying our salaries. Sometimes they do get to look at the blotter, see if there's any names they recognize." He stares again at me. "And some people, well, frankly, they need that level of shame and humiliation to actually make some changes in their life. Lotta cops, they do the wrong thing, their friends keep 'em out of trouble, and it does 'em no good. They get drunk at home one night and they eat their service revolver. You understand?"

I'm not sure I do, but I nod.

"OK. So I don't entirely know what to do here. Do you?"

"No."

"Fair enough." He gestures with his hands and knocks the Styrofoam cup over, right on the blotter, spilling it all over the new page with my name on it. "Oops! Son of a bitch.

Looks like I ruined a page." He tears it out and crumples it up. "You know what this means?"

I look at him stupidly until I see that he does, in fact, want an answer. "What does it mean?"

"I don't know. That's up to you." He stares deep into me. "I mean, obviously, there was some sloppiness on my part that led to a clerical error. But you can read into it whatever you want. Maybe a professional courtesy. Maybe a wake-up call. I don't know if it's good or bad or what. If this is what it takes for you to do what you need to do, it'll be the best thing that ever happened to you. But if you go out, get behind the wheel drunk, and kill someone..."

I take a deep breath. Such things are certainly not outside the realm of possibility.

"All I know is, for now, you're free to go." He gestures behind me to the lobby, to the three steps leading down to the glass doors out front, and the dark uncertainty of the Los Angeles night.

•••

Eventually, I quit drinking. I have to. Or else I die, and in the meantime, live in a way that dying seems like the better option.

It takes work to stay sober and find happiness. It takes a lot of work, actually, writing in massive notebooks, following new and unfamiliar procedures to take stock of things, dealing in the unfamiliar territory of feelings and emotions, of places inside of me I've never seen; and after that work, it takes still more, bringing someone else along for the ride, talking for hours over coffee about all of my relationships, waking up to everything I've done, and everything I'm capable of doing.

Still I find myself staring up at the sky and dreaming.

I find myself buying notebooks and slide rules and calculators, trying to get ideas out of my head and down on paper, sketching out drawings of possibilities, crunching numbers to make them real. I imagine a new way to design a spacecraft, walls filled with water to absorb cosmic and solar radiation, and perhaps a massive loop of wire that could be cast out into space and charged with current to create an artificial magnetosphere. I calculate planetary orbits and resonances between them, and imagine spacecraft cycling between the planets regularly, like ships on the great trade routes.

In the meantime, I do what I can to enjoy my days here on Earth, to truly enjoy them and live in the moment, to ski and scuba dive and have fun, not to get away from anything or anyone, but to live more fully.

I know I will never leave the planet again, but I do not want to end my days staring at pictures of myself and reliving the high points. (There are those in the service who assemble all their plaques and trophies on a living room wall so they're all in one place: an I-love-me wall, a barricade against bad feelings, a shrine to the ego. There are those among my former coworkers who glory in their uniqueness, who take pride in having done things no one else has done. I cannot live that way. I want others to have these experiences, too; I no longer want to be alone.)

I try to stay busy, but I catch myself thinking sometimes about parallel universes, these strange possibilities. Sometimes it feels like a waste of time: if these visions can't be made real, does it do any good to think about them? Still, I wonder. Maybe there are an infinite number of universes, and we're only conscious of the one where we've made the right decisions to learn whatever we need to learn. Or maybe there's only one universe, vibrating like a guitar string, a cloud of possibility, a wave function with fixed endpoints; maybe time collapses all those possibilities into the firmness and reality of the here and now, and then at the end it cycles backward, erasing history and mistake and memory until we're back at the Big Bang and all is new again, and like a wave crashing into a seawall it reverberates, turns forward once more, and when each of us returns we get to redo it all, with no knowledge of what we did before, and the chance to run through it again, and make it all slightly different.

Would I make all the same decisions if I could do it over again? Who can say? I know when I see the stars that there are so many places I can never go. I know I've learned to love this life here on Earth, and not just the adventures; I've learned to wake up and pour a cup of coffee and spill in the creamer and watch it swirl; when I'm in the right frame of mind, it's as beautiful and intricate as any planet or nebula.

But waking and dreaming are both part of life. So I still go out at night and look at the stars and the planets, the places I'll never go, and the places I've been. And often I pick one bright spot out of the night sky, one spot redder than all, and brighter than most: Mars. Maybe in some other universe, I've already been there. Perhaps in another, you'll be there soon.

ACKNOWLEDGMENTS

I love space stories not just because they give me the opportunity to be an astronaut without dealing with training and rejection, but also because of the built-in structure: a mission with a clear beginning, middle, and end. One doesn't necessarily need to come up with the bones of the story; one can simply unearth ones that were buried decades ago. I first heard about the preliminary studies for a manned Venus flyby while browsing Wikipedia; David Portree's articles on the topic for *Wired* were an excellent extra resource to flesh out my understanding. What's more, when I contacted him, he was gracious enough to provide copies of the original preliminary studies, the primary source materials he'd read to understand the various mission profiles and probe packages.

- NASA Technical Memorandum X-53434, "Analysis of an Interplanetary Trajectory Targeting Technique with Application to a 1975 Venus Flyby Mission," Bobby Ellison, April 12, 1966
- Bellcomm, Inc. Document TR-67-600-1-1, "Manned Venus Flyby," M.S. Feldman et. al., February 1, 1967
- NASA MSC Internal Note No. 67-FM-25, "Preliminary Mission Study of a Single-launch Manned Venus Flyby with Extended Apollo Hardware," Jack Funk and James Taylor, February 13, 1967
- Bellcomm, Inc. Document TR-67-730-1, "Preliminary Considerations of Venus Exploration via Manned Flyby," D.E. Cassidy et. al., November 30, 1967

While there were several different proposals, the Funk and Taylor document provided much of the basis for my narrative, and I can't thank David enough for sending me a copy.

One does get somewhat paranoid about technical accuracy while writing such things; while the documents gave me a good idea of mission timeframes and timelines, I wanted to know accurate spacecraft speeds and communications delay times for each day of the mission. Towards that end, Daniel Adamo was an invaluable resource. He designed a trajectory which aped the Funk and Taylor document, which provided me the essential details to feel confident in my narrative; he also plotted everything out in Celestia so I could see what Venus would look like at various points during the mission. He truly went above and beyond the call of duty, and far beyond what the average person might do to help a stranger from the internet. (He also made several very astute edits to my first manuscript draft.)

I owe Benjamin Honey a tremendous debt of thanks for supporting my previous books, and for getting me in touch with Dan. Ben does great work for NASA; in his spare time, he runs an excellent blog at "Rockets From Cassiopeia." (He also tweets at @spaceguy87.)

Dr. James Logan of the Space Enterprise Institute was gracious enough to give detailed answers to several of my emailed questions about radiation in space, and the potential effects of a large coronal mass ejection (and cosmic background radiation) on astronauts in deep space. He also passed along some very interesting papers: "Space Radiation: The Elephant in the Room Trumpets," a commentary he wrote in February of 2016, and "The Day the Earth (Almost) Stood Still," a piece on coronal mass ejections that he published in September of 2014.

David Hitt's *Homesteading Space* was an invaluable resource for learning about the program of solar observation carried out during the Skylab missions in 1973-74. I adapted these programs for my fictional crew so they'd have something useful to do on the long voyage. David was also a great help in discussing the personalities of some of the astronauts he knew, particularly Joe Kerwin.

I used NASA Document SP-402, "A New Sun: The Solar Results From Skylab" to sharpen my own understanding of the sun, and as fodder for Kerwin's dialogue on the topic in my manuscript. It's a delightfully well-written document, and well worth a quick Google search.

I modeled my fictionalized protagonist on details of Buzz Aldrin's life as recorded in his books *Return to Earth* and *Magnificent Desolation.* They're both very worthwhile reads. (On a personal note, I particularly admire Buzz for his candor and willingness to discuss the lows of his life as well as the highs; these discussions give courage to all of us who have dealt with similar issues.)

Neal Thompson's *Light this Candle* is absolutely essential reading for anyone interested in Alan Shepard, or the early space program, or anyone who just wants to read a cool biography; it's lively, engaging, and thoroughly researched, and it was a tremendous aid in my efforts to capture a version of this complicated and fascinating man on the page.

I read a good deal of mission transcripts to try and fill in the blanks at various stages in the mission with (hopefully) convincing dialogue. Of particular value were the transcripts for Apollo 11, 14, 15 and 16, and for the first, second and third manned Skylab missions, which are of course confusingly numbered as Skylab 2, 3 and 4.

Details from the descent of the Venus probes were inspired by passages in *Rockets and People,* Boris Chertok's excellent memoir of the Soviet space program.

Jay Gallentine's *Infinity Beckoned: Adventuring Through the Inner Solar System, 1969-1989* is an enjoyable and highly readable guide to early robotic space exploration, and the science and technology behind our earliest real searches for life on other planets.

Dragonfly: NASA and the Crisis Aboard Mir by Bryan Burrough is a compelling book about the human stresses and strains that can manifest themselves during long-duration spaceflight. (This book's about one of the forgotten near-tragedies of human space exploration, but if you'd like a break from space, Burrough's *Public Enemies* is one of the most gripping pieces of nonfiction I've ever read.)

Fallen Astronauts: Heroes Who Died Reaching for the Moon (by Colin Burgess, Kate Doolan and Burt Vis) is an interesting look at astronauts and cosmonauts who perished before their time, and sometimes before they'd even flown. The book was a great help learning more about Ed White, Gus Grissom, Elliot See, and Charlie Bassett.

My friend Victor Gonzalez was gracious enough to house me during my visit to Spacefest VII; he and his wife also talked to me at length about radiological sickness, and the symptoms thereof. On top of that, he recommended the Apsley Cherry-Garrard book *The Worst Journey in the World*, from which I've quoted extensively.

Francis French has been a tremendously great source of online support, knowledgeable reading, typo spotting, and friendship throughout the publication of the Altered Space series. I had the privilege of finally meeting him in person this year at Spacefest VII, and he's every bit as funny and engaging and decent in person as he is on the internet.

I'm tremendously grateful to Emily Carney for her enthusiasm and support for this series, and for helping moderate the *Space Hipsters* group on Facebook, which is an absolutely wonderful place to geek out with like-minded space fans.

W. David Woods's *How Apollo Flew to the Moon* was a great resource on the technical details of the Apollo spacecraft, and was particularly useful in researching failure modes for the high-gain antennae. I somehow hadn't read it when I wrote my previous Apollo-inspired story, *Zero Phase*, but I'm wondering now how I got by without it. He was also gracious enough to speak with me a bit at Spacefest, and to provide some contacts with others who could help me with some of my technical questions.

Hugh Everett III, the scientist behind the "many worlds" hypothesis of quantum mechanics, only appears briefly in the manuscript (alongside *Post Office*-era Charles Bukowski, no less), but his ideas loom large in the book's themes. Anyone interested would do well to read Peter Byrne's excellent biography *The Many Worlds of Hugh Everett III: Multiple Universes, Mutual Assured Destruction and the Meltdown of a Nuclear Family*.

Jorge Luis Borges's work was, in turn, an influence on Everett, and myself; his *Collected Fictions* (trans. Andrew Hurley) is a must-read for anyone with a serious interest in literature; this is one of those books that reminds us why we read.

The drinking escapades in the Holiday Inn scene were inspired, in part, by anecdotes told by one of my uncles. (Not that I don't have crazy drinking stories, but his are better.)

"The City on the Edge of Forever" is, of course, one of the absolute classic episodes of the original *Star Trek* series; I happened to be rewatching it on Netflix when I was getting started on this manuscript, and I was fortunate to get to this episode when I did.

John Hersey's *Hiroshima* and Svetlana Alexeivich's *Voices from Chernobyl* were both incredible books, and great sources of inspiration for the radiation-related scenes.

Andrei Tarkovsky's *Solaris* is a strange and compelling and haunting movie, well worth watching.

The speech in the recovery meeting is inspired by *A New Pair of Glasses* by Chuck C., a contemporaneous speaker from the Los Angeles area.

I owe a debt of gratitude to everyone involved in Chicago's independent publishing scene, and an even bigger debt to everyone involved in this crazy shared dream that is Tortoise Books. I love all of you tremendously.

I'm particularly grateful to Logan Ryan Smith, a very talented author who's been incredibly supportive of this series, and who was gracious enough to read and comment on an advance copy of this manuscript.

I'm also tremendously thankful for Giano Cromley, who's an amazing author and a stalwart member of the Tortoise Books team. He caught a great many errors in the manuscript.

While I hope I've done a decent job of depicting the technologies and personalities that might have been involved in an early-70s Venus flyby, I'm sure I stretched some of them a little for the sake of what I hope is a good story. Any errors or distortions are mine alone.

ABOUT THE AUTHOR

Mr. Brennan earned a B.S. in European History from the United States Military Academy at West Point and an M.S. in Journalism from Columbia University in New York. His writing has appeared in the *Chicago Tribune*, *The Good Men Project*, and *Innerview Magazine*; he's also been a frequent contributor and co-editor at Back to Print and <u>The Deadline.</u> He resides in Chicago.

Follow him on Twitter @jerry_brennan.

ABOUT TORTOISE BOOKS

Slow and steady wins in the end, even in publishing. Tortoise Books is dedicated to finding and promoting quality authors who haven't yet found a niche in the marketplace—writers producing memorable and engaging works that will stand the test of time.

Learn more at www.tortoisebooks.com, or follow us on Twitter @TortoiseBooks.

Printed in the USA
CPSIA information can be obtained
at www.ICGtesting.com
JSHW022202140824
68134JS00018B/821